D0349895

KAREN SANDLER

awakening

a tankborn novel

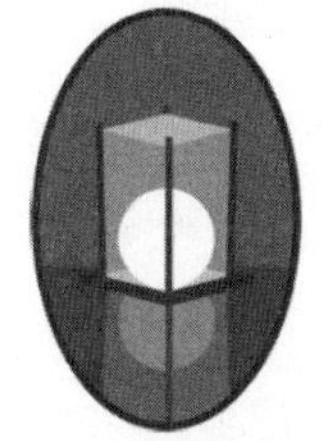

Tu Books
an imprint of Lee & Low Books, Inc.
New York

TU BOOKS, an imprint of LEE & LOW BOOKS Inc.,
95 Madison Avenue, New York, NY 10016
leeandlow.com

Manufactured in the United States of America by
Worzalla Publishing Company,
March 2013

Book design by Einav Aviram
Book production by The Kids at Our House
The text is set in Adobe Caslon Pro

10 9 8 7 6 5 4 3 2 1
First Edition

Library of Congress Cataloging-in-Publication Data
Sandler, Karen.
Awakening / Karen Sandler. — First edition.
pages cm. — ([Tankborn ; volume 2])
Summary: Fifteen-year-old Kayla's life has changed completely, but now she must save her fellow GENs from a deadly virus before she can focus on freeing them from slavery.
ISBN 978-1-60060-982-4 (hardcover : alk. paper) —
ISBN 978-1-60060-983-1 (e-book)
[1. Genetic engineering—Fiction. 2. Virus diseases—Fiction.
3. Slavery—Fiction. 4. Science fiction.] I. Title.
PZ7.S2173Aw 2013
[Fic]—dc23
2012048626

To Gary, always at my side through meltdowns and happy dances.

And to my dad, Sam.

THE CONTINENT OF
SVARGA
NORTHWEST .... 22 SECTORS
NORTHEAST .... 20 SECTORS
EASTERN .... 19 SECTORS
SOUTHWEST .... 18 SECTORS
CENTRAL WESTERN ... 27 SECTORS
N
NORTHWEST TERRITORY
NORTHEAST TERRITORY
CENTRAL WESTERN TERRITORY
EASTERN TERRITORY
SOUTHWEST TERRITORY
BADLANDS
UNINHABITED
THE WALL
THE SOURCE
SHEYSA RIVER
PLATOR RIVER
CHADI RIVER
FAR NORTH TB
JUPA TB
CATI GEN
TINGA GEN
CRETH TB/LB
PED GEN
ESA TB/LB
DAKI GEN
SKYLOFT TB/LB
RET GEN
ADHIKAR
SAREDA TB
MAF TB
AMIK TB/LB
TAQ GEN
NAFI GEN
SHAFTI TB
NITHA TB
FEN GEN
QAF GEN
BEQAL GEN
TEF TB
PATHI TB
OIKA TB/LB
FALT GEN
PLATOR TB/LB
MENDIN GEN
LEISA TB
DAIZA TB
CAYIT TB/LB
PLAKIT GEN
MUT GEN
TWO RIVERS TB
CHADI GEN
SHEYSA TB/LB
FORESTHILL TB
HAK TB/LB
JASSA GEN
TELLIK TB
BELK GEN
GIAQI GEN
SONA TB
TB - SECTORS FOR HIGH-STATUS & DEMI-STATUS TRUEBORNS ONLY
TB/LB - SECTORS FOR MINOR-STATUS TRUEBORNS & LOWBORNS
GEN - GENETICALLY ENGINEERED NON-HUMANS ONLY

PROLOGUE

Everything hurt. The long red-black welts on her arms. The needle-like feel of the cold rain on her feverish skin. The way her head pounded as if it would literally explode.

Wrong, so wrong. The words spun in Raashida's muddled mind. She was a GEN and GENs weren't supposed to ever get sick. Yet she swayed on unsteady feet, her strength all but sapped. Her body boiled with such heat, she was surprised the rain didn't sizzle into steam.

The autumn deluge had swept in like a demon and soaked through her inadequate GEN-issue shift in an instant, filled her sturdy synth-leather shoes. She'd slipped in the thick yellow Lokan mud so often, her legs were covered to the knees with the nasty ochre stuff.

She should be home by now. Her nurture father, Qang, would be worried. But no matter how hard she squinted into the wet darkness, she couldn't see the street that led to Qang's flat.

She stopped, struggling to clear her thoughts. Why would

she be going to Qang's? She wasn't an under-fifteen anymore, still living with her nurture father in Mut sector. She'd been Assigned already, hadn't she? Sent off by the trueborns how long ago? She couldn't remember, couldn't remember Qang's face. Wasn't even sure what her own face looked like.

Raashida skidded again in the slick mud and groped frantically in the darkness for something solid to break her fall. Instead she slammed to all fours, pain shooting up her left leg as her knee hit a rock. She managed to struggle to her feet again, but she couldn't put more than a gram of weight on her leg without gasping with the pain.

What if her knee was broken? Trueborns expected GENs' self-healing to properly knit their wounds. If an injury were bad enough to cripple her, gene-splicers would drop her in a gen-tank, reset her, and maybe even re-jigger her DNA to make a new GEN.

"Infinite, save me," she whispered, the prayer drowned by the roar of the rain. Would He even acknowledge her plea? After her third beating by her trueborn patron, she'd turned her heart against Him. She wasn't even sure where her prayer mirror was.

What was that glow? Was it real? Or just a fever dream? Or could it be the Infinite was coming for her, his brilliant light cutting through the darkness?

As she stumbled toward that faint gleam, biting back a scream of agony with every other step, the light grew brighter. She could make out the lines of a shack. The deafening fall of rain grew even louder as it hit the plasscine roofs of the shack and the near-invisible neighbor to it just beyond.

Lowborn shacks, no doubt, and a GEN like her unwelcome,

storm or no storm. She would have walked on, but her good leg gave way, her body too weak to keep her on her feet. As she lay there, rain pelting her, she despaired that the Infinite would let her die in the dark.

Then she heard a faint cry from within the shack. Her heart clutched inside her. She knew that voice. It was her nurture brother, Fabi. She'd left him behind on Assignment day, hadn't seen him since.

No way to stand and walk. She dragged herself to the door, nudged it open wide enough to pull herself inside. In the yellow light of a flame—she could smell the acrid tang of drom dung—she made out the pallets on the floor. There lay fourth-year Fabi bundled in rough blankets, a woman stretched out close beside him. Fabi's hair had changed from curly brown to wispy blond, and she couldn't see his GEN tattoo on his cheek, but she knew him anyway. The changes she saw were just a fever dream.

Her teeth chattering from the rain, Raashida dragged herself across the shack to the pallet. With the last of her energy spent, she fit herself alongside Fabi, opposite the strange woman. The woman's eyes fluttered half-open, then closed as she dropped into sleep again.

Fabi whined and shifted under his blankets, his sleep no doubt disturbed by the wet chill Raashida had brought in with her. She started shuddering, her teeth chattering, and she feared she'd disturb Fabi even more. With the last of her energy, she tapped into her GEN circuitry to warm herself, then wiped the mud and wet from her hand. She set her palm on his cheek, and reveled in the look of his face.

A new heat seemed to explode from the center of her, different than the warmth her circuitry generated. It moved across her chest, along her arm, out her hand, into Fabi's cheek. Her nurture brother squawked in complaint, briefly rousing the woman again, but to Raashida's relief, neither woke.

That flood of heat from her to Fabi seemed to have stolen the breath from Raashida's chest. She had to fight to fill her lungs again. Her heart, a rasping beat in her ears, slowed and stuttered, slowed and stuttered. Her circuitry jolted her heart again and again, but her heart continued to fail. She couldn't keep her eyes open, couldn't move even to take her hand away from Fabi.

The flicker of light through her eyelids dimmed, the stench of drom dung faded. The cold and wet became meaningless. The drum of the rain softened to silence.

One moment there was a last breath and a heartbeat. The next there was nothingness.

Shona woke with a start, the glare of sunlight in her eyes, the brightness bleeding in through the partly open door of her roughly built bhaile. What did it matter if she hadn't shut the door properly, or if rain now soaked the edges of her one good rug? She couldn't bring herself to care when her dying son lay beside her.

Or maybe he was dead already. She couldn't tell if the weight against her back was warm or cold in the chill air. She'd wrapped him as tight as she could after lancing the pus from his infected foot last night until poor Wen screamed with the pain. Then she'd squeezed the last of the vac-seal of medicine into the slender crook of Wen's arm.

AWAKENING

The anti-germ in the vac-seal had been a single adult dose, all Shona could afford to buy with her few dhans. The minor-status trueborn who sold it to her said to give Wen a light squeeze each day for ten days. But it had been hard to do it right, and surely some days she'd dosed too much and some days too little.

Then last night she'd been so exhausted by days of grief and worry, she'd been all but dead to the world as she slept. She remembered Wen crying out once, and had tried to struggle awake. But then he'd quieted. She'd been so fearful that cry had been his last, and she was too much a coward to face that truth in the middle of the dark night, so she let sleep take her again until morning.

Her heart ached, heavy as a stone in her chest. Wen had been her last chance to send a part of herself into the next generation. With the boy's father dead and she a year into the change that stopped her monthly bleeding, she would never bear another child. She was an old woman now. Her wrists and hips already throbbed with the joint-ache.

Time to turn and look at Wen, Shona told herself. See if her son had been taken up by Iyenkas, the twin brother gods become one. Truly, death and eternal life with Iyenkas would be better than the agonizing pain poor Wen had suffered through.

Shona tossed aside her blanket and creakily elbowed herself up. Tugging down her night shirt against the chill, she took a breath to fight her tears.

"Mama?"

She froze. She forced herself to turn, sure she'd gone mad and had imagined Wen's sweet voice.

He was sitting up in his blankets. Grinning at her with his bright mischief.

And a woman lay beside him. Not a woman, a GEN female. Even if her skin hadn't been too black to be anything but a non-human, the tattoo on her left cheek would have given it away. Her myriad long braids lay scattered around her shoulders.

"I'm hungry, Mama," Wen said.

Shona snatched Wen up into her lap. She had nothing against GENs, but she wasn't sure she wanted one touching her son. Although it looked as if the female had done exactly that. Her hand still rested on the dent in the pillow where Wen's head certainly had been.

Wen patted Shona's hand with a certain urgency. "Hungry, Mama."

Shona felt the coolness of her boy's touch, the strength in his wiry body. With shaking hands, she unknotted the dressing around his foot. It had been clean when she'd wrapped it on last night, now it was soaked through with blood and pus.

But when she pulled the last of it free, the oozing wound was gone. She laid the complaining Wen on her pallet to bring the foot closer to her view. Even opened the door wider for more light, despite the autumn chill.

No more festering gore in the arch of Wen's foot. Not even a scab. Only some dried blood that gave way when she spit on her thumb and scrubbed while Wen giggled and writhed in ticklishness.

Her gaze slid to the GEN lying motionless beside Wen's pallet. In that moment, she realized just how still the female lay.

"Want a sugarfruit, Wen?" Shona said, her voice trembling.

"Yes, yes, yes, yes!" he shouted, jumping up and down with each word.

Usually Shona hoarded sugarfruit. She gladly handed a whole one to Wen, only taking a moment to cut away a bruise in the juicy red fruit. Then she threw a blanket around Wen's shoulders and set him on a stool by the door.

She went back to the GEN female. Shona wasn't like the trueborns who refused to touch a GEN skin to skin. Lowborns like her didn't believe in that superstition, and it didn't bother her a bit to press her fingertips to the back of the GEN's hand. The female's skin looked even darker contrasted with Shona's pale flesh. Even as she registered the cold lifelessness of the GEN's hand, heat tingled up Shona's arm, across her shoulders, and down her body with a syrupy warmth.

Shona glanced at the female's chest, waiting for a breath to lift it. None did. Shona shifted her fingers to the GEN's wrist, but no pulse beat. The GEN was dead, had died right here in Shona's bhaile.

But not before she'd touched Wen. And now Wen was whole, his foot completely healed, his life saved.

She had to go outside, send a prayer up to the brother suns, Iyenku and Kas. Give her thanks to the dual god.

She leapt to her feet, tearing off the nightshirt, throwing on a blouse and skirt just as quickly. She was shoving her feet into shoes, plaiting her gray-dulled red hair when it hit her.

No pain. Not in her wrists. Nor her hips or knees. She bent each joint in turn; they moved freely. As if the joint-ache had been wiped from her body.

With a smothered cry, she scooped up Wen, still sticky from the overripe sugarfruit, and hurried outside. Along the way to the headman's bhaile, she flung her prayer up to Iyenkas. She could swear that Kas, the younger, lazy brother-sun, burned brighter in the sky in response.

"Aed!" she shouted. "Aed, come quick!" Every eye turned toward her—the women washing at the Chadi River, the sleepy children calling out their counting lesson, the old man repairing a boot in the sunshine.

The headman emerged from his bhaile, his hair still rumpled from his bed. Shona grabbed his arm and dragged the long-legged headman along, whispering to him what had happened. She carried the evidence on her hip, a laughing Wen who tangled strong, sticky fingers in her hair.

Aed had to crouch a little to get through her door. He knelt on Wen's pallet and did as Shona had, checking for pulse and breath.

"Dead," Aed confirmed. "And based on those welts"—he gestured at the long streaks of raised flesh—"from Scratch."

Shona clutched Wen closer. "Has she given it to him, then? Will he catch the Scratch?"

"It's a GEN disease, not a lowborn one," Aed said. "Wen is safe. But the enforcers will want her body."

Shona felt a little sick at the thought of a Brigade enforcer taking the GEN. "Gene-splicers will break her apart. Make new GENs of her."

"It's trueborn law. They want the body."

"She saved Wen's life. Took away my joint-ache."

Aed sat back on his heels and looked up at Shona. "What would you have me do?"

Shona considered. Throwing the GEN into the Chadi would do no good. Someone would fish her out eventually and the end would be the same. They couldn't burn her—an enforcer might notice the smell and smoke and see it was a GEN and not a lowborn they were sending up to the fiery embrace of Iyenkas, two-gods-become-one.

"Bury her," Shona said. "Dig the hole tonight after dark."

She could see from the pinched look around Aed's mouth that he disapproved of the primitive sacrilege of a burial. The lowborn believers of the Lord Creator buried their dead, but those who followed the true path of Iyenkas purified their dead with fire.

Still, Aed nodded, no doubt seeing the necessity of a burial. "The body will have to stay hidden in your bhaile until then."

At least the day would be cool enough to hold off decay. She threw Wen's blanket over the GEN to conceal it. She'd burn the death shroud later.

She and Aed stepped from her bhaile. Wen wriggled from her arms and dashed off to play with one of his friends.

Before Aed could walk away, she tugged his sleeve. "Did you feel anything? When you touched the GEN?"

Aed shook his head. "Just cold flesh."

Then that fire was gone with the GEN female's spirit, if a non-human had such a thing. Only she and Wen had received Iyenkas's miracle.

Shona stayed clear of her bhaile for the day, finding plenty of chores to keep her busy—her own washing, organizing the communal food stores, helping to prepare the evening meal that the village would share. That was another way Iyenkas's true believers differed from the lowborns who followed the Lord Creator. The others went their separate ways in their larger villages. Iyenkans united in fellowship with nearly every activity.

Aed had waited until the primary sun, Iyenku, had set and the brother-sun, Kas, lingered on the horizon before he told the other men. They didn't question the need, just picked up their shovels, paced out a kilometer downstream of the village and started to dig.

Shona whispered to a few of the women that she needed their help, asked them to bring whatever rags they could spare. She explained along the way about the GEN. They'd all seen Wen dashing along the riverbank with his friends and didn't question Shona's account.

They reached Shona's bhaile, arms laden with torn, stained cloths. Shona opened the door and went first.

She screamed and stumbled backward into the others.

The GEN was sitting up in her death bed. Most certainly, emphatically, alive.

1

One moment Kayla was deep in a dream, trueborn Devak Manel reaching for her with a smile on his dark, beautiful face. The next she was jolted awake, tossed half off the seat of Risa Mandoza's lorry as it hit a pothole. As Kayla tried to right herself, the lorry jounced again and she whacked her elbow and bit her tongue. The sudden pain drove the last forbidden image of Devak from her mind. Just as well—a GEN girl like her had no business mooning over trueborns.

Still muzzy from sleep, Kayla looked out the lorry's windscreen. Were they in Falt sector? No, it was Qaf. She recognized the grubby warehouses along Abur Street, the main thoroughfare of Qaf's central ward. Through her half-open window she could smell the rank Plator River just beyond the warehouses to their right. She could hear the river's roar too, as fat as it was with the recent heavy rains.

"What happened to our stop in Plator sector?" Kayla asked.

She'd been looking forward to a visit with Mishalla, her life-long friend. Mishalla, unlike Kayla, was no longer a GEN, her circuitry dissolved by the Kinship's treatment. Mishalla lived as a lowborn now.

"Zul called," Risa said. "Had to cut the Plator stop. Qaf warehouse pickup got moved earlier."

Resentment pricked inside Kayla. "I haven't seen Mishalla since her wedding a month ago. Nearly that since we've been to Chadi sector." Kayla's nurture mother and brother lived in Chadi and she missed them terribly.

"Next trip south," Risa said. "I promise."

Except Risa couldn't promise since it was the Kinship that pulled their strings. When Zul had set Kayla on her mission with Risa, he'd assured her that her new-found freedom would allow her frequent visits to her family and Mishalla. But Kinship business had taken precedence over Kayla's personal wishes, and visits home had been far and few between.

Kayla checked her internal clock. Nearly noon, but you'd never know it the way the twin suns hid behind thick clouds. She'd never lived through such a wet autumn in all her fifteen years.

The foodstores warehouse where they'd make their first delivery was just ahead, and Risa slowed the wide, boxy lorry to a crawl. A lorry as big as Risa's was ideal considering how much time they spent on the road. It was essentially a portable flat for the two of them, with its broad bench seat in front and sleeper bed and tiny washroom at the back. There was plenty of storage beneath and above the bed for clothing, medical supplies, food stores, and sundries.

But narrow GEN sector roadways, like Qaf's main street, barely accommodated the fifteen-meter long lev-truck and its big cab. The alley alongside the warehouse would take some tricky driving. But Risa squeaked into the alley with practiced care.

The lowborn woman couldn't avoid another tooth-rattling pothole that shook the lorry. "Gonna break a denking control relay," she muttered. "Chutting GEN streets."

The lowborn woman glanced Kayla's way, sending a silent apology for her language. An improvement over how she and Risa had started out four months ago. Back then, *GEN* would have been *jik* or *tat-face*, the epithets spewing from Risa's mouth as frequently as the juice from the devil leaf the lowborn woman chewed. The tension was made worse by the fact that they lived together in such close quarters.

Then two weeks into their too-close-for-comfort partnership, one foul word too many broke Kayla's patience. A shouting match followed, Kayla demanding that Risa stop, all the while shaking with fear that the lowborn woman would have Kayla ejected from the Kinship and maybe reset to boot. Instead, Risa respected Kayla for standing up for herself and her people. After that night Risa did her best to watch her tongue.

As Risa negotiated the small apron behind the warehouse, Kayla caught a glimpse of graffiti scrawled across the big plassteel door, dark blue words written diagonally from corner to corner.

Risa scrutinized the jaggedly written words in the lorry's console vid screen. "What's it say? Not any script I've ever seen."

Kayla grinned. "That's GENscrib. Compares the local Grid supervisor to the back end of a drom."

"Not the whole back end." Risa creaked her rusty laugh. "I'da been more specific."

One eye on the vid screen, Risa got the big lev-truck backed up to the loading dock and killed the suspension engine. Kayla shut her window and grabbed her rain hat in deference to the glowering sky, then slid from the cab. She scanned for signs of enforcers along the row of warehouses backing up to the Plator River. "The graffiti must be fresh or the Brigade would've had it painted over by now. Can't risk GENs passing messages that way."

Risa smirked at that. Thanks to the Kinship, messages were flying from GEN to GEN and it wasn't through words scribbled on warehouse walls.

Kayla pulled herself up on the loading dock using the gene-splicer-augmented strength of her arms. Risa took the long way around to use the steps.

A few more words were drawn on the door's lower right corner. The jagged script was so small Kayla had to crouch and just about press her nose to the door to have any hope of reading it. It was GENscrib, but a variation she'd never seen before. It reminded her of the hand-written script in a decades-old journal she'd once found. It had been written by Zul, the elderly trueborn who'd helped start the Kinship. Zul called that kind of script *longhand.*

"What's that?" Risa asked, using the toe of her boot to tap the corner.

Kayla had learned to read longhand pretty well, so she studied the GENscrib with that style of writing in mind. "Free—" Kayla cut off her answer as she scanned all three words and their meaning sank in.

FREEDOM. HUMANITY. EQUALITY.

Great Infinite, who would be reckless enough to write

that where it could be seen by anyone? If an enforcer spotted her even reading the message, she could be reset for potential sedition. The Kinship might be fighting for those very things for GENs, but no one spoke that mission out loud, let alone wrote the words in public view.

GENs weren't free. They weren't human, at least according to trueborn law, let alone equal to anyone higher status than a rat-snake.

She backed away from the dangerous words just as the door rattled then rose with the grind of gears. Relief washed over her when the message rolled out of view.

"What?" Risa asked.

Kayla forced a laugh. "Something about free rat-snake meat. All you can eat."

Risa made a face, diverted by Kayla's lie. She could have told the lowborn woman—she trusted Risa with her life, why not the truth? But Zul and the rest of the Kinship were always telling them that the less any one of them knew, the less they could reveal at the Brigade's hands. Better to keep that message from Risa.

And what did it mean, anyway? No one from the Kinship would have dared write something so inflammatory in a GEN sector. It was probably nothing more than words written on a dare by some under-fifteen GEN.

Two brawny GEN boys, maybe a couple years older than Kayla, stepped out onto the loading dock. She considered asking them if they'd read the graffiti on the door, all of it. But likely they'd been genned the same as most dock workers. Stronger than average—though nowhere near her extraordinary strength—and with little imagination, better to keep them from balking at the dull work. She doubted they'd even noticed those dangerous words.

Risa's seycat, Nishi, streaked out of the lorry's cargo bay the moment the doors were open, hissing and snarling at the GEN boys, who scrambled out of Nishi's way. A flash of red-gray, she dashed into the brush along the riverbank, running as quickly on five legs as another seycat might on the usual six.

The GEN boys hung back, eyes wide. "Are there any more in there?" one of them asked.

"Just the one," Kayla told them. She laughed. "You're not afraid of that little thing?"

Kayla wasn't being fair. Seycats like Nishi might be barely knee-high to the tall GEN boys, but they could slash even a full grown man to ribbons with those claws and teeth.

To show it was safe, Kayla stepped into the bay. She piled two sacks of kel-grain on top of two stacked crates of synth-protein, and started toward the warehouse door. She cast a look over her shoulder and sure enough, the boys were trying to shift as much as she was, but couldn't budge a load that size. Risa knew better than to try to compete with Kayla's strength—she took only one crate. The boys finally gave in and settled for one bag and one crate each.

It started to drizzle with their first trip across the plasscrete dock, the force of the rain increasing with each load. Before long, the rain soaked right through Kayla's cheap duraplass hat. Risa's hat as well from the looks of it—the lowborn woman's dark, gray-speckled hair hung lank, and water soaked the back of her sturdy drom-wool shirt. Kayla's brown-beigey braid, which usually kept her long, tangle-prone hair under control, had unraveled in the dampness, curls and tendrils poking every which way. Risa's usually-pale skin looked even more pasty white in the cold. Even Kayla's hands had taken on a blue tinge despite her GEN circuitry kicking in to warm her.

Working doggedly in the downpour, Kayla trudged from lorry to warehouse and back until only a dozen crates and a half-dozen sacks of kel-grain were left. Her arms and shoulders felt like mush from the wet work. The two GEN boys had run out of steam too, carrying only one sack or crate each per trip.

Kayla toted the last three crates, following Risa, who had the final kel-grain sack slung over her shoulder. Risa slung the sack on top of the pile, then nudged Kayla, gesturing toward the front of the warehouse where a GEN woman waited.

Risa tossed over her sekai, which Kayla caught one-handed. Kayla started down the line of stacked crates and kel-grain sacks toward the GEN woman. The woman led Kayla to an alcove carved out of the warehouse space and sat behind a battered desk.

"I have the invoice here, Teki," Kayla said, setting the palm-sized reader on the woman's desk.

"Let me take a look." Teki picked up the sekai. Her other hand cupped over something on the desk and slid it toward Kayla.

Teki lifted her hand just enough for Kayla to see the edge of a thumbnail-sized thinsteel packet underneath. Teki's closed fingers concealed the packet from view of the netcam focused on her makeshift office.

"Twenty sacks of kel-grain?" Teki said. "I only saw nineteen."

"You might have missed that last one Risa brought in," Kayla said, leaning on the desk, her hand next to Teki's.

A sweep of Teki's hand toward Kayla's and the packet was safely in Kayla's grasp. "You're right," Teki said. "I didn't see it."

Her back to the netcam, Kayla tucked the black packet into a hidden pocket in her leggings. Teki held the sekai to her left cheek, and the device scanned the unique pattern of Teki's tattoo. Kayla took the sekai and did the same, although her tattoo was on her right cheek. The kel-grain and synth-protein delivery acknowledged by them both, Kayla made her way back to the loading dock. With another DNA packet to deliver to the Kinship.

She found Risa on the plasscrete dock, rain dripping from the wide brim of the lowborn's hat as she stared up the narrow alley to Qaf's main street. "An enforcer on Abur Street. Might just be a scheduled patrol."

"He didn't go to the seventeenth warren, did he?" The neighboring warehouse blocked their view of Abur. They could only see the top three floors of the warren.

"Don't know. Didn't dare go down the alley to look."

Kayla handed back Risa's sekai. "Maybe he's a GEN enforcer, not a trueborn."

GEN enforcers handled minor issues in the sector—mediating disputes between GENs, delivering Assignment tack to fifteenth-years a day or two before they were Assigned. So if the enforcer was a GEN, they might be okay.

"Walked like a trueborn," Risa said. "Like he owned the world."

"We could skip the drop," Kayla said.

"Long way to the next one," Risa said.

"But it's *my* jik skin that's at risk." Kayla faced down Risa. "Unless *you* want to be the one to take it in."

Risa squirmed a little. "Not how it works."

Kayla didn't like it, but Risa was right. The enforcer would see Kayla in the lorry and wonder why the lowborn driver was making the delivery and not the GEN Assigned to her.

"Well?" Risa asked, leaving the choice to her.

Kayla weighed the risk of keeping the packet against the hazards of confronting the enforcer. "Let's do it."

Risa whistled for Nishi and the seycat trotted from the brush. Nishi's irregular gait was unbalanced even more by the rat-snake dangling from her jaws. The seycat jogged up the stairs, across the dock and into the cargo bay.

Risa swung shut the doors and slammed home the latch. While the lowborn woman took the stairs to descend from the dock, Kayla jumped the meter and a half. Water from a puddle gushed up around her, soaking her synth-leather shoes. As she squished up to the cab, she patted her hip where she'd tucked away the packet.

Risa circled the lorry around the apron and back to the alley. They both stared right as they came even with Abur Street, peering through the rain at the seventeenth warren.

The enforcer was there, standing under the overhang that sheltered the front door. Risa eased back onto the street, turning right. Three warrens down, the lowborn woman stopped the lorry in front of the seventeenth.

The enforcer stared through the wet at them. He wasn't a GEN. Even through the rain-blurred glass of the lorry window, Kayla could see no tattoo on his cheek. The enforcer's light brown skin and the blue bali earring in his right ear confirmed he was a minor-status trueborn.

Even worse, the trueborn was a Brigade captain, not a grunt.

Just seeing him, a knee-jerk fear gripped Kayla, closing off her throat. The moment the captain spotted her, he zeroed in on the tattoo on her right cheek. Kayla figured he was wondering why her tattoo was on the wrong side, wondering what that might mean about her. She started to tremble, the gut reaction threatening the hard-won courage she'd built these last four months as part of the Kinship.

Keeping the lorry between her and the captain, Kayla headed for the bay to retrieve the last crate. Thank the Infinite their delivery was nothing illegal, for either a GEN or a lowborn to transport.

Nishi growled as Kayla stepped into the bay, setting a protective paw on her half-eaten rat-snake. The seycat had already bitten off the venomous head and its eight spidery legs.

Before Kayla picked up the crate, she knelt to stroke Nishi's damp head, to calm both the feline and herself. Nishi preened and purred a moment before sinking her teeth into the rat-snake's long tail again.

Carrying the crate, Kayla followed Risa from the lorry to the warren. She kept her mouth shut and her gaze on the muddy ground as they reached the front door.

The captain blocked their way. "You can't go in."

"I have business here," Risa said. She brought up the certification document on her sekai and held the device out to him.

He ignored it. "What's in the crate?"

He pushed past Risa and ripped the seal, jostling the crate as he yanked open the flaps. He might have knocked it from Kayla's hands if not for her extraordinary strength.

Knowing Risa's temper, Kayla locked her gaze with the lowborn woman's, narrowing her eyes in a silent warning. Risa glared back, but Kayla could see her swallow the sharp words she surely wanted to say.

"It's just what it looks like," Risa said. "Synth-protein. All spelled out in the cert doc. Trading it for sewer-toad venom."

"Toad venom." The captain snorted a laugh as he pawed through the half-kilo packets of protein. "Chutting worthless crap."

"Distilled venom makes a good painkiller," Risa said.

"For lowborns and tat-faces, maybe." The captain plucked out two vac-seals of the synth-protein, stuffing them out of sight into the carrysak strapped to his back.

He gave Kayla an evil look. "How'd you get yourself a jik, anyway, lowborn? Did you find yourself a runaway and think nobody would notice?"

"She's legal," Risa said. "I'm not sanaki enough to let a GEN runaway hitch a ride in my employer's lorry."

That was honest truth. Scratch victims were one thing—their lives were short and they deserved dignity in death. But a runaway was just too dangerous for Risa to transport. The Grid Monitoring System tracked the location of every GEN at every moment. It could take anywhere from five to zero days to figure out if a GEN had strayed from his or her legal radius—a specified distance surrounding the GEN's Assignment area.

Once the Grid knew a GEN had gone missing, it was no longer a question of *if* the GEN would be found, only *when*. So unless the GEN was established Kinship or could prove an imminent risk of reset, Risa had to turn the GEN away.

Risa held out the sekai again. "Cert doc verifies the GEN girl too."

Finally the captain snatched the sekai from Risa and bent his head to read it. Kayla tucked the remaining synth-protein away and closed the crate flaps, keeping one surreptitious eye on the captain. She dared a quick glance at his nametag. Harg was written in red on a black background. She tucked it away in her bare brain.

Harg stared hard at the sekai display, flipping impatiently through the cert doc, no doubt looking for a reason to deny Risa and Kayla passage. But the Kinship was well practiced at forging documents. The captain could cross-check all he wanted, click through every link in the text of the cert doc. Even contact the Northwest Territory Judicial Council. He wouldn't find a flaw.

In their four months of traveling, Kayla and Risa had successfully routed dozens of datapods and packets to the Kinship. They'd been lucky, but careful as well. Other lowborn-GEN teams, through mistakes like allowing runaway hitchhikers or letting slip incautious words, had met bad ends at the hands of the Brigade. Those lowborns had been imprisoned, some tortured and executed, and the GENs were reset, their souls wiped away.

Finally Harg thrust the device back at Risa and stepped aside. As Kayla passed him, she kept out of arm's reach, as a precaution.

The warren door opened into a small lobby. A narrow hallway off the lobby stretched to the back of the first floor. The sweet-acrid stink of scorched kel-grain hung in the air, competing with the funk of too many bodies crammed into too small a space.

Risa leaned to peer out the dingy window that looked out on the street. "I'll wait here. Keep an eye on him."

Pushing off her hat and letting it hang around her neck by its string, Kayla headed down the hallway, counting doors on the left. Some of them were decorated, small murals praising the Infinite or carvings scraped out of the plasscine of the door. More than one had a prayer mirror inset into the jamb to cast a blessing on everyone reflected in it. She wondered what happened when trueborns passed a prayer mirror, if the Infinite just ignored their image when it was transmitted up to him.

The seventh door on the left was unmarked, with only a thumb-sized mirror affixed to the jamb. Kayla shifted the crate to her hip and knocked.

A GEN woman opened the door, the tattoo on her left cheek a glittering silver against her light-brown skin. She glanced at Kayla's tattoo, her dark gaze narrowing like Harg's had. Kayla could see the woman's unease and suspicion, could almost hear her wondering if Kayla was genuine.

Kayla couldn't blame her. Two months ago, the safe house in neighboring Fen sector had been discovered by the Brigade. Despite using the secret exits, a dozen GENs had been spotted escaping. They'd all either been reset or had their DNA redistributed.

The Kinship needed close to a year to excavate and equip a safe house. Until two weeks ago, when the Kinship finished this one under Qaf's seventeenth warren, Kayla and Risa had had to cross over to the Northeast Territory to deliver packets.

Kayla accessed her annexed brain for the Qaf safe house code phrase. "Have you seen my prayer mirror?" she asked. "I lost it during the Festival of the Prophets."

"I haven't, but I have a spare I can lend you," the woman answered. She gave Kayla a small, tense smile. "I'm Bala."

"Kayla."

After another moment's hesitation, Bala stepped aside and let Kayla in. This was a single person's flat, much smaller than the one her nurture mother, Tala, lived in. Just one room, with a bed in the corner and the kitchen stuffed into an alcove smaller than Teki's office. No washroom, of course, since GENs had to make do with a communal setup.

Bala led the way to the kitchen alcove. "I leave for my warehouse shift in an hour. I can't be late."

"This won't take long," Kayla said. "Just a quick delivery."

Worry still pinched Bala's face, but she motioned to the counter where Kayla could set the crate. The synth-protein inside would be distributed in the warren.

Bala put her hand in the pocket of her full skirt, to grip her prayer mirror, Kayla guessed. Bala's lips moved as she muttered a silent prayer.

Done with her entreaty, Bala pressed a section of floor beside the radiant stove. A square of plasscine popped up. Bala lifted it out of the way to reveal a dark hole barely a meter wide.

Kayla had contended with worse. She was slender and short in stature, so it wasn't much trouble to lower herself into the hole and descend the ladder. Once she was low enough, she heard the thump of the piece of floor replaced, snuffing all light. She didn't mind that either. She could make her way to the safe house just feeling her way along the tunnel below.

She reached the bottom and had just started to turn when a hand dropped on her shoulder.

She swallowed back a shriek, terror ripping through her

that this had been a trap, that she'd been directed here just to be arrested by the Brigade. She had nowhere to escape. The tunnel was blocked by whoever had touched her and certainly there would be more enforcers waiting at the top of the ladder.

A flare of light blinded her. Spots swam in front of her eyes as she squinted to try to make out who'd accosted her. She could see a tall, broad-shouldered silhouette standing slightly stooped under the tunnel's low roof.

Then he held the illuminator between them, aimed up so they were both lit. And now she saw the straight dark hair, a little longer than she remembered, the high cheekbones, the perfect line of his jaw. He was everything a high-status trueborn should be, from his regal bearing to the perfect kelfa-brown of his skin.

"Devak," she whispered.

2

Kayla." The soft way he spoke her name made her heart ache. She remembered staring into those deep, dark eyes when she'd been Assigned to his family, how she'd been riveted by their intensity. She remembered kissing that mouth.

She forced herself to look away, focusing just past his shoulder. She was too flustered to even berate him for touching her in the dark and frightening her so. "How have you been?"

His jaw worked a little, his mouth compressed, and she realized the cruelty of the question. His father's arrest and his mother's abandonment might have happened four months ago, but Devak's life was still torn apart.

The way he was dressed told her everything. The fabric of his forest green korta was nearly as coarse as what the lowborns wore, the collar and sleeves unembroidered. Instead of the silver-infused spider-silk chains he used to favor, he wore a simple black cord around his neck, the Manel name written in trueborn script on an enameled pendant.

He'd never been one to flaunt the extravagant wealth the

Manels had once possessed. But not only were his clothes plainer, the diamond set in his bali was a near invisible chip. His bali used to hold a much larger diamond, a traditional fifteenth-year gift from his parents. Were Zul and Devak living so close to the edge that they'd had to sell the more extravagant stone?

"I'm fine," he said. "It's good to see you."

She heard nothing but rote courtesy in the words. "I thought I'd see you at the Two Rivers meetings sometimes. But you stopped going there."

His gaze slid away. "Pitamah doesn't want us all gathering in one place."

The Kinship spread the meetings out, parceling information here and there. Kayla attended a secret gathering in Two Rivers sector with Zul—Pitamah to Devak. Risa and Devak went to another in Leisa. When necessary, Kayla shared what she'd learned with Risa and vice versa. Other times, they would keep what they knew from the other to limit what any one person would be able to reveal.

But sometimes the need for secrecy chafed. *It's best this way*, Zul would say. But she'd get so twisted up inside worrying over what she was allowed to say to Risa and what she wasn't. Why couldn't she use her own judgment, reveal what she thought best to reveal rather than be constrained by Zul's dictates? Despite the lip service the Kinship paid to GENs being on equal footing with trueborns, it seemed they didn't give her much credit for thinking for herself without their constant guidance.

"But Zul said he would have switched with you," Kayla said. "He'd go to the Leisa gathering with Risa, and you could come to Two Rivers with me. You chose Leisa."

He didn't speak, his silence beating at her ears in the dark tunnel. She wanted so much not to care. Wished she could be angry instead of feeling an ache in the pit of her stomach.

Much as she wanted to confront him, she had to think of Bala, pacing with anxiety, placing herself at risk while Kayla wasted time with Devak. "Why are you here?"

His dark gaze pierced her. She felt pinned in place and didn't like it. "Same as you, I guess. To collect GEN IDs for new safe house candidates."

Before taking a GEN to a safe house or bringing them into the Kinship, they had to be erased from the Monitoring Grid, and before a GEN could be erased, Devak or another hacker needed the GEN's ID.

That was another reason Kayla was here: to pick up IDs of GENs waiting to be taken off the Grid and brought into a safe house. She and Risa would pass the datapod and packet on to the next lowborn or trueborn in the chain. It would eventually make its way to someone like Devak.

"All the trouble Risa and I go to, the care we take in passing on the datapods to keep trueborns like you safe, and you put yourself at risk by coming here to collect the IDs yourself."

Irritation flashed across his face at her criticism. Better that annoyance than the longing that cut so deep.

Devak let the illuminator drop to his side, casting his face into near darkness, obscuring any other reaction. He edged a little closer, straightening in the vertical tunnel access.

"They told me someone was coming for the pickup. I came out to save them the trip. I didn't know it would be you."

The words came out before she could stop them. "Would you have come if you'd known?"

He looked away again, casting his face even more into shadow. "Why wouldn't I?"

She wasn't sure she wanted to know the answer to that. She lifted her shirt and fished in her hidden pocket for the small packet Teki had given her, then held it out to him. He lifted the illuminator again so he could see to take it.

The light brush of his fingertips across her palm made her shiver. To distract herself, she asked, "How many Scratch victims are in the safe house?"

His expression grew grim. "Nine or ten in the sick room."

"Every week Risa and I are transporting more infected ones." They might refuse transport to runaways, but GENs knew Risa would keep the Scratch-afflicted out of trueborn hands. "Six were brought to us in Mendin sector alone."

Kayla hadn't believed the reports when they first came in. GENs so sick they were bed-bound, GENs *dying* of the mysterious illness. The gene-splicers built tankborns to fight off disease, to resist infections. GENs could heal faster than non-tankborns. Yet Scratch was fatal, and the Kinship medics had no idea what caused it.

"You got them all to safe houses?" he asked.

"One died on the way. Another"—her stomach knotted at the memory—"the Brigade confiscated. Took some persuading for Risa to convince the enforcers she'd been on her way to turn the GEN over to them."

"Most of the ones I saw were bad," Devak said. "A few still able to walk and talk, but most bedridden. Two were in the last stages. Nothing but red welts from head to toe."

Thank the Infinite the Kinship had figured out that Scratch wasn't communicable from GEN to GEN. Nor had any lowborn or trueborn been infected. But if GENs weren't catching it from other GENs, what was causing it? The Kinship medics had a half-dozen theories, but no answers.

She realized Devak was looking down at her baggy, ill-fitting shirt. "Risa doesn't dress you any better than Senia did."

Mean-tempered Senia had been the Manels' lowborn house manager. "The plainer I dress, the less attention I attract. Risa and I prefer it that way."

"But you can't hide that face." He brushed her cheek again, then tucked a strand of unruly hair behind her ear.

She could barely breathe. "I should go. Bala's waiting for me. Thank you for taking the packet." She turned to the ladder and started up it.

"Kayla," Devak said.

He reached up for her as she ascended, his palm grazing her from hip to calf. The contact seemed to burn her, even through the still damp leggings. She shivered at the slight pressure and paused her upward climb.

Hooking an arm around a rung, she turned to face him. His expression was still more mystery than meaning. "I don't know what you want from me," she said.

"I thought we were friends."

Friends. Her heart compressed, heavy as a stone. Once, she'd thought they could be more. When they stood together in Sheysa sector four months ago, she'd thought her chance at the restoration treatment would come soon. In that moment she would have turned her back on being a GEN without hesitation. Because she wanted a future for her and Devak, a happy ending like her friend, Mishalla, and her husband, Eoghan.

But after the restoration treatment, GENs like her and Mishalla would only be able to pass as lowborns. That was fine for Mishalla—the boy she loved was a lowborn too. But for her and Devak, the expanse between GENs and high-status trueborns was as wide as it had ever been. Even restored, becoming a lowborn, Kayla couldn't, shouldn't hope for anything but friendship with Devak. A trueborn-lowborn friendship wouldn't get her reset, but she couldn't flaunt it either.

"If we're *friends*," she said, "why have you ignored me all these months? Why have you refused to even talk to me?"

She waited for his defense, but he didn't offer one up. Then a sudden, painful thought occurred to Kayla. In the time she and Devak had been separated, he might have found another girl. An appropriate girl. A lovely, high-status trueborn girl.

It would explain his reluctance to talk to her on the wristlink. His coolness when he *had* spoken, the way he discussed only Kinship business. How could she blame him? With Kinship medics and gene-splicers focusing on a Scratch cure, there was no way of knowing how long it would be until the restoration treatment would be available to her. Even before Scratch had decimated the GEN community, the treatment serum had been scarce. And she'd put it off more than once because she knew how valuable she was to the Kinship as a GEN.

She continued up the ladder, letting the dream die. A last scrap of hope persisted—that he was following her, taking the rungs at double speed to catch up, right into Bala's flat. But if that impossible fantasy were true, it would be horribly risky for the Kinship, for Bala, if someone saw Devak. The fewer connections enforcers made between Kinship members, the better, especially when one of them was a high-status trueborn.

Still, when Kayla reached the top, she looked down. Gave herself just an instant to imagine that Devak was still at the bottom looking up at her. But of course he wasn't there. She saw only the dimmest illumination, and it faded as Devak continued back down the tunnel to the safe house. He would use a different exit.

She tapped at the bottom of the trap door, waiting for the all clear from Bala. The GEN woman lifted it away and gave Kayla a hand up. The instant Kayla was clear, Bala replaced the floor piece.

"I thought you would be gone longer," Bala said, suspicion in her tone.

"I didn't have to go the whole way," Kayla said. "Someone met me in the tunnel." Kayla didn't say who and Bala didn't ask.

Kayla had to get out, as far away from Devak as she could. She headed for the door, tossing "Thank you for your service," over her shoulder as she went.

"Wait!" Bala said. "You have to take this."

Kayla turned to see Bala holding out a small package bundled in plasswrap. Kayla stared at it stupidly for several seconds before remembering what it was. The sewer-toad venom.

It would have been a disaster if Kayla had emerged from the flat without it if the Brigade captain was still here. Kayla took the package, muttered another thanks, then hurried out.

Down the long hall, Kayla could see Risa waiting in the lobby, watching for her instead of at her post by the window. Alarm prickled up Kayla's spine.

As soon as Kayla got close enough, Risa said, "There are more of them."

Kayla didn't have to ask. More enforcers.

Kayla edged toward the grimy window. "How many?"

"Four more. Two have gone around to the back door. The other two and the captain are out front, plotting something."

"You think they know about the seycat den?" Kayla asked, using their code for *safe house*.

"Don't know. I got off a warning." Risa held up the wristlink on her arm.

"I saw Devak," Kayla said.

Speculation glittered in Risa's eyes, but she didn't pry. "He'd be the first to leave after a warning."

If he didn't do something stupidly brave like stay to get everyone organized, or to help carry the sick.

Kayla risked getting closer to the window so she could see better outside. It had stopped raining, and the primary sun, Iyenku, was punching a hole in the clouds. The sunbeam lit a Brigade Jahaja parked in front of the warren, blocking Risa's lorry from moving forward. There was no mistaking the familiar emblem emblazoned on the side in red and black. It was a larger, stylized version of the badge the enforcers wore on their uniforms, Loka's meter-high bhimkay spider, its fangs dripping blood.

Kayla gulped, her throat dry. "A multi-lev that big could carry at least twenty people. More if they pack them in."

"They wouldn't know how many seycats were in the den. Wouldn't they have brought a second Jahaja?"

"Maybe they figure some are too sick to escape," Kayla said. "They could come back for them later." Assuming they were even here for the safe house. There was still hope it was something else.

"We can't wait here forever," Risa said. "They'll start to wonder and sweep us up, too."

That same helpless fear she'd felt before seemed to set Kayla's skin on fire. She hated, hated, hated being afraid.

They stepped outside, and three pairs of eyes immediately fixed on her. Harg issued a sharp order to the other two and they marched into the front door of the seventeenth warren.

Harg went straight for Kayla. "On your knees, jik."

Seething inside, Kayla nevertheless dropped to the mud without argument. The thick yellow-brown muck immediately soaked into her already wet white leggings, ruining them. Harg wrenched the package out of her hands, glowering down at her as he ripped off the plasswrap. The bottles of sewer-toad venom scattered in the mud at his feet.

Harg picked one up and opened it, dabbing a bit on his tongue. He grimaced at the taste and spat, the spittle landing on Kayla's shirt.

Bristling, Risa stepped in close to Harg. "What'ya want with my GEN? That's good product you're ruining."

Harg narrowed his eyes at Risa. "Since I got here, only one jik has gone in or out of that warren. Yours. Hive of jiks like that ought to be busy. But I haven't seen as much as a sow and her kit."

Risa gave Kayla a sidelong glance, then focused back on Harg. "Not my problem GENs want to stay inside. You saw us go in, knew our business."

Harg tipped his head toward the lorry. "Even so, you'd do well to get clear."

"I don't leave without the GEN," Risa said.

"What do you care about a jik?" Harg asked.

"Don't give a rat-snake's ass for her." Risa spat too, although it landed nowhere near Kayla. "Trueborn patron paid good money for her Assignment, even more for my permit to transport her to do his business. Not going to do the toting myself, am I?"

Harg pushed Kayla's head backward with his black-gloved hand. "I don't like that this jik is here today. I don't like those kinds of coincidences."

Did that mean they *were* here for the safe house? *Oh, dear Infinite, don't let them have found it!*

Then Harg was unclipping his datapod from his belt. Kayla's gaze flew to Risa.

"Denking hell, don't need to download her," Risa said, wedging herself between Harg and Kayla. "Just ask me you want to know."

Harg's gaze slid over the lowborn woman. "Why shouldn't I download? What are you hiding?"

"Nothing," Risa said, a little too quickly.

But the true answer was *everything*. Kayla's annexed brain contained any number of Kinship secrets—like the code phrases for every safe house in the northern territories and the exact formula for the GEN restoration process. Then there were Kinship member lists, only partial, but enough to endanger a lot of people.

In any case, Harg would never get any Kinship data. A failsafe in Kayla's programming would detect the datapod and trigger her annexed brain to erase itself. At the same time parts of her bare brain would fry so that even under torture she couldn't reveal what she knew.

First rule for Kinship GENs: Never get downloaded.

Harg tried to elbow Risa aside, but the lowborn woman stood her ground. "Got all the GEN's specs right here." She fumbled out her datapod from a pocket. "You can denking well read this as well as her. My employer won't appreciate you digging around his private business and whatnot stored in her head."

Harg considered the datapod Risa offered, almost looked ready to accept it. Then he shook his head. "I'll see for myself." He gave Risa a hard shove and the lowborn woman stumbled aside.

As the mud soaked her knees, rage burst white-hot inside Kayla, burning away her fear. Trueborns never ordered Risa to prostrate herself in the muck. The lowborn woman never risked oblivion at trueborn hands. Torture, yes, but even that would be short-lived since the Kinship's machinations could rescue Risa fairly quickly. But by that time, Kayla's mind, her *self,* would already be destroyed.

Kayla gave Harg a slanting look. One quick wrench with her powerful hands and Kayla could snap Harg's neck. Probably take the other enforcers too when they returned. It would ruin her for Kinship work. She'd be the one living in a safe house—if the Kinship was still willing to protect her after she'd slaughtered trueborns.

Risa must have caught Kayla's murderous look because she said hastily, "Denk it, she's just back from being reset. Black market reprogramming. Gene-splicer said it takes time to settle in. Download now might wipe everything away. And putting my employer out like that would mean bad things for you," Risa finished meaningfully.

Kayla held her breath, struggling to get her temper under control as Harg absorbed Risa's lie. He asked, "What's her sket?"

"Strength," Risa said. "In her arms."

Harg shoved up Kayla's sleeves. "What's wrong with her skin?"

Her anger warred with shame. While her flesh everywhere else was an even brown-beige, on her arms were blotches of dark brown, light brown, black, every shade of human skin, even pale as Risa's.

"Skin disease," Risa lied, and the captain snatched his hands back. If the situation weren't so serious, Kayla would have laughed.

Harg swiped his gloved hands on his pants. "Not my fault your patron did his reset on the cheap. Jik'll be just as strong when I'm done with her." He reached for Kayla's right cheek again.

Reflexively, Kayla shrank back, crying out in her mind for the Infinite. With the datapod millimeters from her tattoo, the warren door slammed open and Harg turned away from Kayla. The two enforcers who had gone inside were dragging out a GEN man between them. They dumped him in the mud beside Kayla.

The other enforcers who had gone around to the back were returning to watch the fun. Which meant they likely hadn't found the safe house after all. This GEN was their only prey.

And now Kayla was as well.

The pale-skinned GEN man scrambled to his knees. "Please, no," he begged Harg, "please, please, no."

"You should be thanking me for resetting you, Axi," Harg said. "Taking you out of your jik misery."

The GEN man slapped his hands over his left cheek, covering his tattoo. "I needed the extra kel-grain for my nurture daughter. I would have put it back from the next ration."

"Should have thought of that before you stole it," Harg said, reaching out with his datapod. The other two enforcers grabbed Axi's wrists and yanked his hands to either side.

"NO!" the man screamed as Harg bent, datapod pinched in his fingers.

As Harg pressed the datapod to Axi's tattoo, Kayla had to swallow back a whimper. Axi jolted as Harg activated the datapod, then sagged. When the enforcers let him go, he flopped to the mud, as flaccid as a dead man.

He might as well be dead. He'd been reset, his personality wiped away. He'd be realigned now to become a different GEN, his Self replaced with another.

Harg retrieved his datapod from the GEN's cheek, wiped a bit of mud and blood from it. Claws of anger and horror ripped at Kayla's stomach as the captain fiddled with the datapod until the red light flashed green.

She glanced over at Risa, and her heart sank at the lowborn woman's helpless expression. A flash of movement up Abur Street pulled Kayla's gaze from Risa, but it was only workers filing from the foodstores warehouse—Teki, the two brawny GEN boys, and a couple of others.

"Don't move," Harg said to Kayla. "I might accidentally reset you instead of just download you." He laughed, the other enforcers joining in.

She could swear Teki was looking her way. Dangerous, since the enforcers wouldn't like the GEN woman's sudden interest.

Then Kayla felt the coolness of the metal datapod against her cheek and the bite of the extendibles into her skin. She forgot about Teki as she waited for the moment the Kinship failsafe would wipe away her annexed brain and turn her bare brain into a hodgepodge of disconnected memories.

Then the datapod yanked free of her cheek. Harg collapsed at her feet, blood oozing from his head. She slowly processed the ringing in her ears, the rubble still raining down around her.

Someone had blown up the foodstores warehouse.

3

As Devak stepped from the access tunnel, the controlled panic of the safe house evacuation mirrored his own explosive emotions at having seen Kayla again. Two lowborn men who had been watching for him relayed Risa's warning about the arrival of the Brigade, then pulled shut the heavy plassteel door to seal the access from the warren. The door's purpose was to slow down the Brigade, but to Devak it seemed symbolic of the way he'd cut himself off from Kayla.

Lowborns and GENs ran every which way, some shouting orders to others, some stacking supplies by one of the four escape tunnels. The plasscine tables and benches used for meals had been shoved to one side, the cupboards in the kitchen alcove had been stripped of supplies. Shadows cast by the overhead illuminators crisscrossed the plasscine floor and voices echoed off the rock walls that the Kinship had carved out of the bedrock.

Devak checked the alcove used as a sick room and spotted his best friend, Junjie, taking a tissue sample from one of the

Scratch victims. That had been his mission here, collecting samples. When he spied Devak, he packed away his gear and emerged from the sick room.

"Can we help?" Junjie called out to the lowborn safe house manager hurrying past. "Maybe get the Scratch patients out?"

The lowborn man turned toward them, walking backward. "We won't move them until we're sure the warren entrance has been breached. You can help best by getting out with what you came for."

While the plassteel doors had been pulled shut on two of the escape tunnels, two were still accessible. The ambulatory residents were using one to pack out supplies, the other was the one Devak and Junjie had entered through two hours before. He and Junjie hurried into that one, Devak switching on his illuminator just in time as the closing of the heavy plassteel safety door obliterated all light.

From behind him, Junjie asked, "You got the packet?"

"Yes."

Devak caught himself just in time before revealing to Junjie that it had been Kayla who'd brought it. Junjie knew how Devak used to feel about Kayla and for a while kept coming up with wild ideas about how the two of them could be together. Devak could pretend to be a GEN, and they could live up in isolated Daki sector. Or Kayla would be restored and Devak would become a lowborn like her, and they could travel with the nomadic allabain lowborns.

Devak finally told him to leave off, that he was over Kayla, had his eye on a trueborn girl instead. Lies, and Junjie knew it, but he was a good enough friend to stop sharing his schemes.

The tunnel climbed, which meant they were about at the

halfway point. As he stared into the ill-lit darkness, Devak remembered the surprise of seeing Kayla, the way his stomach had roiled with exhilaration and hopelessness. All his work at forgetting what he felt for Kayla had been torn away in those few minutes in the tunnel. He'd been transported back to four months ago in Sheysa, when he'd last spoken to her, when he'd thought there could be a future between them.

Even with her hair in that crazy tangle, her clothes baggy and damp from the weather, it had taken everything in him not to pull her into his arms. He was so grateful to see her untouched by Scratch despite the time she spent in GEN sectors, where Kinship medics suspected the infection originated. Something in the soil, maybe, or the water. Thank the Lord Creator it wasn't infectious GEN-to-GEN. And thanks to Him that as dangerous as her and Risa's work could be, Kayla had kept herself safe.

The tunnel ended at a ladder like the one Kayla had descended. Devak went first, carefully lifting the plasscrete trap door. He dodged the dirt sifting down into the hole.

"Clear," Devak said, throwing the trap door aside.

He climbed out into a narrow passageway between two warrens. Junjie quickly followed and they replaced the trap door, tamping the dirt back on top of it.

Just beyond the back of the warrens, a narrow footbridge crossed the Plator River from Qaf to Falt, another GEN sector. They hurried across, then slipped through the screen of sticker bushes that hid his great-grandfather's AirCloud lev-car.

Devak sighed with relief once he and Junjie were both inside the AirCloud. Beside him, Junjie squirmed in his seat.

"We should go before the Brigade notices us," Junjie said.

"No enforcer's going to question me." It sounded arrogant, but even the tiny diamond bali he wore would make a minor-status enforcer hesitate to confront him.

"Even so," Junjie said, peering through the sticker bushes at Qaf, "I have to get back to the lab. Guru Ling will want the samples I collected."

Guru Ling, Junjie's boss at the gen lab where he worked, wasn't Kinship. But she was so obsessed with finding a cure for Scratch, she didn't question where Junjie's samples came from.

Devak started up the AirCloud's engine and crept away from the river. He had to move slowly along the bumpy plasscrete berm that provided flood control here.

Junjie glanced at the chrono on his wristlink. "I lost track of time. I shouldn't have stayed so long."

"Guru Ling shouldn't be that upset over an extra hour or two," Devak said.

"I don't have the freedom you have," Junjie said. "Not anymore."

Devak could have kicked himself for forgetting the obvious. Junjie was minor-status now, no longer even the demi he'd been a few months ago. His family had lost a rank when his mother died. Since the only adhikar his mother had owned had come to her through the death of Junjie's father, that adhikar went to her cousin by marriage. Junjie had to live with his mother's sister now in a mixed trueborn-lowborn sector.

The Tsais had always been on the lower edge of demi-status. Their skin color was a shade or two too pale and tinged with gold. Their eyelids didn't have a fold, and their faces were too round.

Devak felt a little ashamed that he'd taken such note of the Tsai family's facial features and how it affected their status. "Rank doesn't matter in the Kinship," Devak said, to soothe his own guilt.

Junjie laughed. "Then why do trueborns all stick to their own at Kinship meetings? The lowborns and GEN teams sit with each other, but it's like there are big fat lines separating the trueborn ranks that they never step over."

Devak didn't like it, but what Junjie said was true. He'd seen even Pitamah sit only with his old cronies at the few Kinship meetings Devak had attended with his great-grandfather.

Turning away from the river, he reached Falt sector's pothole-pocked main street and upped his speed a fraction. Junjie sat silent beside him, maybe thinking about the samples he would deliver to Guru Ling, or wrestling with some knotty gene-bending problem he'd been given.

Junjie adored the technical puzzles of chemistry and genetics. He would have wished for exactly that kind of work if he'd had the choice. But it didn't seem fair that being a minor-status, Junjie could never hope for anything higher than a tech position.

As a high-status trueborn, Devak could some day take a position as a director in an office, or possibly even make his way up the ranks in government to become a member of Congress. But Junjie was boxed into the tech fields, for no reason other than his family now owned less adhikar land than they once had.

Wasn't that exactly what the Kinship was trying to change? And if Devak could be friends with a minor-status like Junjie, why not be friends with a GEN like Kayla?

Because it's different. The thought fell like bitter poison in his stomach.

It had all seemed so clear in Sheysa when he and Kayla had held each other one last time. His feelings for her had been good and bright and powerful. They would have to be patient. It would be difficult navigating even the trueborn-lowborn divide when the treatment removed her GEN circuitry. But someday she would be restored and they would find a way.

But then his life got torn apart when his father went to prison. His mother left him and Pitamah to fend for themselves. She'd taken with her the adhikar she'd brought into her marriage and managed to claim most of Pitamah's since he'd given it over to Devak's father, Ved, some years ago.

She'd even appropriated three-quarters of Devak's adhikar, declaring she'd be acting as his regent since he was two years away from his majority. Never mind she'd never sent so much as a dhan Devak's way since then. If not for the strings pulled by Pitamah's friends, Zul and Devak might have ended up minor-status like the Tsais.

The hope he and Kayla had shared in Sheysa had vanished with his adhikar. He came to understand that each step down in status degraded others' opinions. It did not pass the notice of other trueborns that he and Pitamah clung to their high status by their fingernails. Bring Kayla into the picture and trueborn scorn would bury them all, with Kayla getting the worst of it. How could they change anything for the better then, when no one would listen to them anymore?

They would be safe only within the cocoon of the Kinship, at meetings or in Zul's Two Rivers home. But wouldn't that be worse, if he could only show his feelings for her in those closed meetings, away from the outside world's eyes? Wouldn't that hurt her more?

He'd closed her out of his life, thinking it was best for her. But based on what he saw today, she hadn't seen it that way at all. He'd hurt her when he'd never meant to.

He supposed his great-grandfather was right. Devak had had long conversations with Pitamah about Kayla. Devak would go on and on about all the reasons it wouldn't work between a trueborn and GEN. Pitamah's only response had been that Devak had to clear the air with Kayla. It wasn't fair of him to change the rules between them without telling her.

He brought his attention back to the pockmarked local road of Falt's central ward. He had just transitioned to the properly maintained cross-sector road when a muted *boom* echoed across the Plator River.

"What was that?" Devak asked, pulling over. He tried to see behind him past the row of warrens.

"Don't know," Junjie said. "Hang on."

Junjie jumped from the lev-car and ran back to the nearest alley between the warrens. As he trotted back to the AirCloud, a cloud of dust or smoke drifted up above the roofs.

"I bet it's a demolition," Junjie said as he swung back into the lev-car. "Explains why the Brigade was there. Likely rousting everyone from the building Social Benevolence ordered destroyed."

"It wasn't the warren above the safe house?" Horror washed over Devak at the thought.

"No, it looked like the warehouse opposite. We should get out of here. Don't want to attract attention."

Devak pulled back onto the cross-sector road, picking up

speed on the smoother roadway. He gnawed over the strangeness of the Social Benevolence demolition. SB demolished warrens all the time, because they were falling down from shoddy construction or to build them bigger to house more GENs.

But the warehouses were simpler construction and SB generally did a better job building them. And they rarely reached full capacity since the trueborn managers of GEN goods always shorted the deliveries, skimming off the top whenever they could. So why would SB destroy one warehouse to build a bigger one?

A sudden realization stabbed him in the gut. Kayla would surely have been out on the street when the explosives took down the warehouse.

"What about—" Devak stopped himself before revealing that he'd seen Kayla. "The Brigade would have made sure to get any GENs off the street too, right?"

"Oh, yeah. The enforcers would have cleared everyone out before a demolition. Probably why they went into the warren, to warn them. That debris can fly pretty far."

Devak had to be satisfied with that. He'd find out next time Kayla or Risa called Pitamah. Or maybe after dropping Junjie off he'd call Risa on his wristlink.

He turned from the north-south highway onto the east-west exchange that led to the mixed sector, Plator. Once they crossed over the border out of Falt, he merged onto the skyway. Below them, housing blocks and green spaces whipped by.

"Are you and Guru Ling getting anywhere on curing Scratch?" Devak asked. "Or finding a vaccine?"

Junjie made a face. "Since it's only the two of us really focusing on it, we haven't made much progress. There seem to always be much more important trueborn illnesses to be cured." His voice took on a sarcastic edge. "Like nose warts and toe rashes."

"At least the Kinship medics and gene-splicers are working on it too," Devak said.

"Which means no one is making restoration serum anymore. Hundreds of Kinship GENs could be free by now if it wasn't for the Scratch epidemic."

GENs like Kayla. Four months ago, she could have had the circuitry in her body dissolved by the restoration serum. But there had been only one dose left, and Kayla let her friend Mishalla have it. Devak wasn't sure he could have made that sacrifice himself.

Kayla had had other chances for the treatment since then, but had continued to refuse it in favor of other GENs. Now her transformation was put off indefinitely because of Scratch.

Why had she kept saying no, letting others go first? He understood her choice in favor of Mishalla. The two of them were close as sisters. Kayla knew Mishalla wanted to be with Eoghan. With Mishalla's circuitry gone, there were no status problems to keep them apart.

Devak wondered if it had anything to do with him. It wouldn't be as easy for him and Kayla to be together as it was for Mishalla and Eoghan. But surely by now he didn't matter that much to Kayla. He would think she'd want to be free of being a GEN anyway. No longer under the control of trueborns and always at risk of a Brigade reset.

Almost as if he'd read Devak's mind, Junjie asked, "Would you feel differently about Kayla if she did it? If she became a lowborn and wasn't a GEN anymore?"

"I would be glad for her to be restored," Devak said.

"You're not really answering my question," Junjie said.

"I told you before—"

"Yeah, yeah, nothing between you and her." Junjie leaned toward him. "You lie badly."

Devak sighed into the stretching silence. "Even if there was something between us, how could we ever be together?"

Junjie fixed him with his dark, steady gaze. "You would have to give up a lot."

Maybe everything. Could he?

They were nearing southern Plator and the lab where Junjie worked. Plator was filled with minor-status like the Tsais living alongside lowborns, mostly the more affluent who ran their own businesses. Moving from a trueborn sector to a mixed one would have been the greatest shame for most trueborns, but Junjie said he liked living so close to the lab.

Could I live in a mixed sector? If Kayla were restored right now like Junjie had suggested, no trueborn sector would accept them. They wouldn't even be allowed in the minor-status trueborn neighborhoods of a mixed sector. Their only choice would be one of the lowborn neighborhoods. Could he live with lowborns?

Could I give up everything?

"Junjie, I don't know."

Junjie nodded. "At least now you're telling the truth."

"I *do* want what's best for her. But I'm so mixed up about what that is."

"Maybe you're not the one who's supposed to figure that out."

Devak took the next exit and dropped off the skyway.

They wound their way through south Plator's local streets in silence.

Devak pulled up to the low-slung building that housed the lab. This was headquarters of the Genetic Augmentation and Manipulation Agency, but the building was as boxy and plain as a GEN warren, with only a small sign beside the door inscribed with the GAMA initials. But as simple as it was, GAMA headquarters was better built than any tankborn warren, with plassteel beams and high-grade plasscrete walls. After all, trueborns had to work there, and even minor-status deserved someplace safe.

But not those they created, the GENs. Devak didn't miss the irony.

He put aside his gloomy thoughts and turned to Junjie. "That experimental stuff you've been giving to Scratch victims—has it been helping?"

Junjie sighed. "No. It's made to give a little jolt right away, then help the symptoms over time. But none of the GENs we've tried it on showed any improvement at all."

"How many GENs have you tested it on so far?" Devak asked. "Maybe it only works with some."

"Hundreds," Junjie said, gathering up the carrysak at his feet. "We're allowed to use all our treatments on the ones . . ."

As Junjie's voice trailed off, it took Devak a few moments to figure out what his friend meant. "The ones the Brigade brings to you."

Junjie nodded. "All the Scratch victims the enforcers *confiscate*."

Confiscate, experiment on, and then destroy. Rat-snakes writhed in Devak's belly again. What if Kayla were Scratch-infected and carried off by the Brigade before the Kinship could take her to a safe house?

The mere thought cut his heart to shreds.

Junjie climbed from the AirCloud and waved goodbye. Devak drove away, his thoughts in a tangle.

Admit it, to yourself at least. You still care for her.

But he couldn't make the world change. Couldn't take the burden of trueborn judgment off Kayla's shoulders. Wouldn't she be freer without him? Maybe giving her up was the better sacrifice to make.

4

Dodging falling debris, two enforcers pelted off in the direction of the warehouse. Another dropped to his knees in the mud to check Harg. The enforcer—Pena, according to his nametag—screamed into his wristlink for a medic, for Brigade backup.

The last enforcer lay crumpled in the mud. But while Harg still breathed, the other enforcer lay still, the side of his head bashed in.

Kayla brought a hand up to her left cheek, then stared numbly at the blood on her fingers. Her cheek stung with pain. She hadn't even felt the gash until she'd seen the blood. Now she registered other aches—her left shoulder and hip, her left knee—where pieces of debris had struck her.

She scanned wildly for Risa and saw her slumped against the lorry. The lowborn woman shook dust from her hair as she hurried to Kayla.

"Blast threw me against the lorry," Risa said. "Saved me from worse hurt."

She rubbed at her forehead, where something had scratched her.

Kayla puffed out a sigh of relief that Risa was okay. Teki and the other GENs were long gone from the ruined warehouse. Their timely departure had to mean they knew in advance it would be destroyed. And they'd just delivered all that food.

The front wall had collapsed onto Abur Street. Flames shot into the air triple the height of the warehouse, fed by the oil-rich sacks of kel-grain stored inside. So much food gone to waste. Trueborns wouldn't be in any hurry to replace it, which meant empty stomachs in Qaf.

Risa shifted, planting her foot in the mud right up next to Harg's hand. "I got pick-ups to do," she said to the frantic enforcer tending Harg. "Can't stay here all day."

Pena glared up at her, fear, desperation, and arrogance in his eyes. "You don't go anywhere, lowborn. Or your jik sow."

Kayla realized with the other two across the street, Pena was the only able-bodied enforcer left. A quick punch of her fist and Pena would be lying there in the mud beside Harg. She'd need only a half-strength blow to kill him, to dent in his skull like the dead enforcer. So easy. Kayla gripped the folds of her shirt, keeping her hands anchored.

"Look," Risa said. "We got nothing to do with that." She gestured toward the wreckage of the warehouse.

"Harg told me you were over there before you came here," Pena said. "You could have set the bomb while you were there."

"Then why'd we come over here?" Risa asked. "Why not jet our way to the next sector over? Look at the way that chutting crap dented my lorry. Employer won't be happy."

Pena stared at Risa. Right up front, no trueborn ever

trusted a lowborn, not after the riots. But he was rattled by the explosion and Harg couldn't tell him what to do.

He fussed with his bali, smearing the small blue stone in his right earlobe with a little mud. His mind seem to grind as slowly as the Chadi River at the end of summer.

"Give me your employer's name," he said finally. "He checks out, you can go."

"Vagish Mohapatra," Risa said, and Pena's eyes went wide at the high-status family name. "Of Leisa sector," she added unnecessarily. The enforcer would know what sector the Mohapatras hailed from.

"Looks like this one has more sense than the other one," Risa quipped as Pena called the Northwest Territory Brigade headquarters and passed on the information. Kayla knew what would happen next—someone within the Brigade would call the office of Judicial Councilor Mohapatra, and the councilor would acknowledge that he employed Risa, that Kayla was Assigned to him. What the councilor wouldn't mention was that he was part of the Kinship.

"Go," Pena finally said as the medic's lev-car pulled up.

Risa couldn't help Kayla to her feet, not with the enforcer watching. So Kayla levered herself out of the mud on her own. The gash on her cheek beat with pain in rhythm to the throb of her other bruises. As she was swiping mud off her hands onto her blouse, Risa fumbled her tin of devil leaf and dropped it.

"Pick it up, jik," Risa said.

Kayla reached for the tin, searching the mud for whatever Risa intended for her to find. She spied what the lowborn woman had dropped the tin next to, just out of reach of Harg's fingers. The captain's datapod, pressed into the mud by Risa's boot print.

Kayla palmed it the way she had the packet from Teki, then straightened, both tin and datapod in one hand. She gave the tin to Risa, datapod hidden underneath. They'd turn it over to Zul, see if they could glean anything valuable from it. If nothing else, it was one more datapod to ferry information.

As they walked to the lorry, four more enforcers arrived in a Dagger lev-car. Flying plasscrete had shattered the windshield of the Jahaja parked in front of the warren. The lorry was battered and the passenger side-mirror sheared off, but otherwise undamaged.

Kayla didn't breathe easy until they'd backed away from the warren—after a tense negotiation to persuade the newly arrived Brigade Dagger to give them room—and into a nearby alley to turn around. They had to wait for the passage of yet another Brigade Dagger, then Risa pulled onto Abur Street, traveling back the way they'd come.

There was no racing away from the scene, not on the pockmarked local road. It would draw attention to them anyway. They could hear the sirens of more Brigade lev-cars arriving.

Kayla checked the console vid screen for a rear view, saw two more Daggers blocking Abur Street. "All those enforcers here can't be good for the safe house."

"Nothing we can do about it," Risa said. "Sent off another message. They'll hunker down."

"Who would have blown up the foodstores warehouse?" Kayla asked. "Not the Kinship, surely."

"Not their style. And wouldn't have done, that close to a safe house, for denking sure."

Kayla remembered what had been scrawled on the warehouse door. FREEDOM. HUMANITY. EQUALITY. Could that have anything to do with the bomb?

"Could it be lowborns?" Kayla asked.

Risa tossed her a narrow-eyed glare. "T'isn't the GENs lowborns hold grudge against." Then she shrugged. "Wouldn't gain the lowborns nothing blowing up a GEN warehouse."

"Wouldn't gain anybody," Kayla said.

A few moments of silence, then Risa slanted her a look. "You okay?"

A beat, then Kayla said, "Why wouldn't I be?"

"Enforcer almost wiped you away," Risa said.

White-hot anger spurted up at the reminder of the close call. She shrugged as if it didn't matter. "Can't let them get the safe house codes, membership lists."

Risa stared across the cab at Kayla. "Wouldn't have really killed that enforcer, yeah?"

Of their own accord, Kayla's hands tightened into fists. She imagined the thud of contact against Pena's skull.

"Should get that cut on your face cleaned up," Risa said, pulling Kayla from her thoughts of revenge.

She'd almost forgotten it, but now it throbbed. "I'm a mess. I'll get mud on the sleeper bed."

"Strip here," Risa said with a smirk. "I won't look."

Even if she weren't an old woman—nearly thirty years past Kayla's fifteen—Risa only had eyes for her wife, Kiyomi. Risa wasn't quite nurture mother to Kayla—no one could replace Tala in that role. But maybe an auntie, if GENs had such a thing.

Kayla shimmied out of her muddy leggings and shirt,

wadding them up before pushing aside the curtain that concealed the sleeper behind the cab. Kayla washed the yellow muck from her hands and face and knees, then used sani-wipes from the washroom cupboard to cleanse the gash in her left cheek. The moist cloth stung the wound.

She propped up her prayer mirror on an eye-level shelf to check the damage. The cut was a good four centimeters long, but not deep, thank the Infinite. And it was in her left cheek, not her right where her tattoo was.

GENs healed rapidly, maybe twice the rate of a trueborn or lowborn. But it always took a little extra time for a GEN's programmed nervous system to re-wire the tattoo after an injury there. Since it was her bare left cheek, nothing would be left in a week's time but a bit of redness.

After pulling on a clean shirt and set of leggings, she took the muddy clothes into the washroom next to the sleeper.

The shirt and leggings got a half-hearted rinse in the tiny sink. They had a good-sized water tank on board the lorry, but not enough for the luxury of daily laundry. That had to wait until they reached their next destination.

Her hair needed a re-braid, but she just didn't have the patience for it. She did what she could to smooth it and tuck some of the escaped curls back in the braid.

By the time she'd settled back in her seat, Iyenku and his brother sun, Kas, had surrendered to the rain again, both sulking behind the thickening clouds. Only late afternoon, but with the drenching rain, it was dark as dusk.

They pulled clear of Qaf's main street and continued along a canyon of warrens that gave way to thickets of sticker bushes and yellow scrub flowers. The packed-gravel track was narrow and where it meandered too close to the Plator River, the shoulder was muddy and treacherous. But Risa continued grimly on.

They reached the north-south cross-sector road that was blessedly well paved and properly maintained. Risa slowed to make the turn to head north, then gunned the suspension engine to pick up speed.

All at once, a girl staggered from the sticker bushes and into the roadway. Kayla shouted, "Stop!"

Risa didn't react. With only meters before impact, Kayla grabbed the wheel to yank the big lorry clear. The ponderous vehicle fishtailed, while Risa fought to get control. The lorry threatened to tip, screaming as the suspension engine sputtered and the undercarriage sank to scrape the pavement.

Finally the lorry came to a stop, half on, half off the pavement, pointing nearly south. Risa turned to her, blazing with anger. "What the chutting hell was that all about?"

"I couldn't let you hit the girl!" Kayla said.

"What girl?" Risa snarled back.

Kayla pointed back down the roadway. The girl still stood there, swaying in the downpour.

"Oh, sweet brother suns." Risa clutched her throat. "Didn't even see her."

"Better get the lorry clear. I'll go get her."

Kayla jumped from the cab, running back down the road into the storm. The girl—a GEN—didn't move, her short dark hair pasted to her head, her skin an unhealthy white.

But when Kayla got nearer, she realized that what she'd taken as strands of dark hair stuck to the girl's face were actually dark welts. Two on her right cheek, one on her left, cutting through her GEN tattoo.

The marks of Scratch. No wonder the girl seemed so disoriented.

Kayla took the girl's hand. "How about we get out of the rain?"

The girl didn't move. As Kayla tugged at the girl's hand, heat seemed to sizzle up Kayla's left arm and briefly throb in the gash on her cheek.

Kayla led the girl to the lorry that Risa had managed to get back onto the roadway and facing north again. Kayla motioned for the lowborn woman to come around back to the bay.

Kayla opened the bay doors carefully, worried that Nishi might bolt out. In the light of the bay illuminators that Risa had switched on, Kayla spotted the seycat curled up in the corner on a pile of empty kel-grain sacks. With her stomach full of rat-snake, Nishi apparently had enough sense to stay put in the storm.

After the three of them had climbed inside, Risa closed the door. In the half-light of the bay's illuminators, Kayla got a better look at the girl. Where her tunic and leggings were ripped, no doubt by sticker bushes, more lines of Scratch were visible—on her arms, her belly, her thighs.

"How long have you been sick?" Kayla asked.

"I'm not sick," the girl said.

Kayla pushed up the unresisting girl's sleeve. And saw what she'd never seen before. "Risa, they're healing."

"What do you mean?" Risa said, coming in for a closer look.

"The scratches are all scabbed over." Kayla struggled to wrap her mind around the impossible. "And here—those marks are pale, not even red. And the skin there is smooth. No welts."

"No one recovers from Scratch," Risa said.

"Maybe some do." Hope blossomed faintly inside Kayla.

"Get her to a safe house?" Risa suggested.

"Call Zul at the least and get her off the Grid. What's your name and ID?" Kayla asked.

"I . . ." The girl's brow furrowed. "It's . . ."

"You don't remember?" Kayla turned to Risa. "Could the Scratch have damaged her bare brain?"

The girl shook her head. "Do remember. Except . . . my name is Gemma 4727. And my name is Gabrielle 6181."

Kayla glanced over at Risa. "There were a few GENs in Chadi sector that went by two names. But not two IDs. Even if she were reset, that should have wiped out the original ID."

"You remember anything else, GEN?" Risa asked.

The girl didn't answer. Her pale skin grew even paler and she started shivering so violently, Kayla feared the girl would hurt herself.

"Gemma!" Kayla shouted, but the girl didn't respond. "Gabrielle, use your circuitry to warm yourself."

The glassy-eyed GEN girl just kept shivering. The clamminess of her skin told Kayla she wasn't in any state to use her circuitry.

"Shock, I think," Kayla said. "We'd better get her into the sleeper."

There was no way they could take her back out into the downpour, which meant they'd have to use the access hatch between the lorry's bay and the sleeper compartment. But getting her up to the hatch required the GEN girl to climb a ladder from the lower bay to the higher level of the sleeper and cab. The girl looked ready to collapse, not at all fit to use a ladder.

"I'll pull her up," Kayla said.

She hurried up the ladder, slid aside the hatch cover. Easy enough for Kayla to squirm through the half-meter square opening, small as she was. The tall, slender girl would be more of a challenge, especially since she would be near dead weight.

Not just near, but total, Kayla realized as the GEN girl passed out and slumped in Risa's arms. "Hey!" Risa shook her, tapping her cheek with an open hand. "Wake up, you!"

"Gabrielle!" Kayla shouted through the hatch. No reaction. "Gemma!"

The girl's eyes fluttered open. She tried to focus on Kayla.

Kayla reached down through the hatch. "More Gemma than Gabrielle. Let's assume that's her name."

Risa propped Gemma against the ladder, stretching first one limp arm then the other in reach of Kayla's grip. Kayla lifted the GEN girl slowly, taking care not to bump her head as she angled her through the hatch.

Once Kayla got Gemma settled on the sleeper bed, she stripped the girl, dropping the soaked tunic, leggings, and underthings back through the hatch to Risa. She quickly dressed Gemma in one of Risa's shirts and a pair of the lowborn's leggings. The girl was too tall to wear Kayla's things.

Kayla piled blankets on top of the ice-cold girl and slipped under the covers with her. Holding the girl close, Kayla used her circuitry to crank up her own body heat. As her warmth soaked into Gemma, the girl's shivering eased.

Kayla called out to Risa, "The clothes help identify her at all? House GEN? Factory GEN?"

Risa's voice drifted up through the hatch. "Drom-wool tunic fit for a demi-status trueborn's house, but the skivs and leggings are factory-issue. A plain metal prayer mirror."

"I don't suppose she has any secret pockets." Not likely Gemma was Kinship, but worth asking.

"Naw. Nothing."

A moment later, Kayla heard the *whomp* of the small incinerator in the bay as the energy core destroyed Gemma's ruined clothes. Even though the garb revealed no clues to Risa and Kayla, they might to someone else. The enforcers searched the lorry on a regular basis. Always better to avoid questions.

Kayla pulled her legs out of the way as Risa squeezed through the hatch. The lowborn woman set Gemma's prayer mirror on a shelf just above Kayla's own.

"How's she doing?" Risa asked. "Looks better."

Gemma's shallow breathing had deepened and some of the color had returned to her cheeks. As Kayla had hoped, Gemma seemed to be generating her own body heat now. Safe enough to leave her by herself under the blankets.

Kayla slipped from under the covers, then snugged them more tightly around the GEN girl's neck. She dropped out of the sleeper area to the cab. Risa followed, pulling shut the curtains between the cab and the sleeper.

Risa slid into the driver's seat. After starting the lorry's lev-engine, she unstrapped the wristlink from her arm. "Contact Zul?"

Kayla accepted the wristlink and took her own seat. The lorry swayed as Risa got all six suspension drives onto the pavement. With practiced jabs of her thumbs, Kayla entered Zul's contact number, then the security code that would put her call through.

Her stomach clenched as she waited for Zul to answer.

Sometimes Devak picked up for his great-grandfather. Could he have gotten all the way down to Two Rivers by now? All the unresolved questions between her and Devak tumbled inside her.

But it was Zul's tired voice that drifted from the wristlink. Likely she'd woken the old man. Except when Zul was hyped up with crysophora, Devak's great-grandfather spent far more hours sleeping than awake. Even in the wristlink's small display, he looked twice his hundred-and-three years.

No use asking how he was. Zul's body had been breaking down for years, his nervous system debilitated by an experimental precursor to the circuitry in Kayla's own body. In a way, Zul had been the first GEN, never mind he was a high-status trueborn.

She quickly told him about the explosion at the warehouse across from the safe house. "The GEN workers all left before the bomb went off," Kayla said. "They had to have been warned."

Zul's sharp gaze fixed on Kayla through the display. "Did you see anyone around the warehouse besides Teki and the two boys?"

"No."

"No other clues to what happened?"

"No." But then she remembered. FREEDOM, HUMANITY, EQUALITY, written on the warehouse door.

Of course she should tell Zul. He would want to know. But she held the words back.

Because telling Zul meant turning the problem over to him as she did every other troublesome Kinship issue. He'd tell her, *We'll take care of it*, and she'd never hear how the problem turned out.

Zul kept her in the dark nowadays just as much as he did when she was first Assigned to him. Back then he kept more secrets than he revealed. It made sense at first—he didn't know if she could be trusted with knowledge of the inner workings of the Kinship. But hadn't she proved herself trustworthy a hundred times over? Especially when every day she put her very identity, her Self, on the line, risking a reset at the Brigade's hands.

If she kept the information to herself, she could try to learn more on her own. Keep her eyes open, try to find out who was behind the Freedom, Humanity, Equality inscription. It might very well have nothing to do with the warehouse explosion.

"I really didn't see anything," she said finally.

Despite Zul's sharp gaze that seemed to read her mind, she went on to the discovery of Gemma and the GEN girl's twin identities. Zul must have been even more tired than he looked because he didn't question the change of subject. In fact he waved her off when she said she'd send him the IDs.

His image disappeared as he handed off the wristlink. Kayla's stomach tightened again in expectation of speaking to Devak, but then a different, familiar voice came from the wristlink—Jemali, a medic who'd been a friend of Zul's for decades.

Jemali smiled kindly from the small wristlink display. "I'll take the IDs and send them on."

Kayla called out Gemma's twin GEN IDs and her second name. Jemali repeated them back. He promised that someone in the Kinship would let them know when Gemma had been removed from the Grid so they could take her to a safe house.

She signed off and handed the wristlink back to Risa. The

lowborn woman must have seen the disappointment in Kayla's eyes, despite the dimness of the lorry's cab.

"Yer climbing up the wrong junk tree, GEN girl," Risa said, although there was empathy in the lowborn woman's voice.

"It doesn't matter," Kayla said.

Risa looked like she wanted to call Kayla out on her lie, but she held her tongue, turning her full attention to operating the lorry. Full dark had fallen, the downpour lit by the lorry's front illuminators. Behind them in the sleeper, Gemma sighed, then her deep steady breathing resumed.

"Climb up there with her," Risa said. "Take a rest."

"I'll just curl up here." Kayla drew up her legs and sat sideways on the seat. She tapped into her circuitry to increase her body heat. Warm now despite her damp tunic and leggings, she fell into a half-doze.

Images flew in and out of her mind. Devak's touch in the safe house tunnel. The Brigade Captain Harg, his datapod hovering over her cheek. The warehouse exploding, the dead enforcer. Gemma stumbling into the road.

The squeal of the lorry's brakes snapped Kayla awake. "Is there another one?" she asked, half-expecting to see another GEN girl staggering from the sticker bushes. But then she saw the lights of Fen sector's central ward, its warrens and warehouses lit in the dark.

"We're in Fen," Risa said. "Going to find a place to settle for the night."

Kayla pushed herself upright and rubbed her eyes. Her left cheek, where the rubble had struck her, itched abominably. She rubbed it carefully, not wanting to disturb the scab.

Risa sucked in a breath as she stared across the cab at Kayla. "It's gone."

"What?" Kayla asked.

Risa splashed some water from her jug onto her sleeve. Without so much as a warning, she started scrubbing at Kayla's wounded cheek.

"Hey!" Kayla protested. "That—"

That hurts, was what she meant to say, an automatic response to Risa's vigorous rubbing. But then Kayla realized it didn't hurt.

"It's gone," Risa said again. "Your cheek is healed."

5

"You've seen me heal fast before," Kayla said. "It's just the GEN programming."

"Seen you heal in a couple days what takes lowborn or trueborn a week," Risa said. "Never saw it happen in hours. Without so much as a mark."

"It's just too dark to see." Kayla twitched aside the privacy curtain and retrieved her prayer mirror from the washroom, taking care not to disturb the still-sleeping Gemma. As she settled back in the cab, Risa turned the cab illuminators on full.

Kayla aimed her palm-sized prayer mirror to her left cheek. And stared at the reflected image.

Other than a bit of blood by her ear that Risa had missed, no sign remained that Kayla had been injured. No scab. No puffy flesh indicating the wound was still healing. Just smooth, light brown skin.

"Am I broken?" Kayla asked. At Risa's confused look, Kayla said, "My circuitry is supposed to work a certain way. Supposed to repair my body at a certain pace. Faster than you, but not like this. If it's hyper-healing me, something might be wrong inside."

Now Risa looked concerned. "Should ask Zul."

"Not tonight," Kayla said. "Not as tired as he was." Not to mention Devak would surely be there by now. She wasn't sure what would be worse—talking to Devak, or having him refuse to speak to her. "I'll run a self-check."

The self-check was crude and limited since trueborns didn't want GENs having too much control over themselves. But it could report a few error codes.

While Kayla initiated the self-check, Risa killed the cab illuminators and continued down Fen sector's main street. As Risa nosed into a dark alley between a Doctrine school play yard and an adjacent rubble-filled lot, Kayla's circuitry displayed the self-check results in her annexed brain.

Kayla read the codes, then told Risa, "Everything is operating correctly."

"Need to talk to Zul," Risa said. "Get you a Kinship medic."

Kayla shook her head. "I need a tech for the circuitry. Medics only handle the meat."

Risa flinched at Kayla's use of the word meat. But she of all people knew that was what trueborns thought of a GEN's body. Not to mention what the Brigade said when it came to handling "renegade" GENs—kill the jik, save the meat. Meaning, save the DNA for the creation of future GENs.

Kayla and Risa took turns in the minuscule washroom. Once they'd both finished their nightly routine, Risa regarded Gemma sprawled across the bed that Risa and Kayla usually shared.

"Wake her?" Risa asked. "Or maybe we draw for the cab seat. Other one can sleep in the bay."

"I'll take the bay," Kayla said.

The rain had stopped, so Kayla slipped outside rather than use the hatch and risk disturbing Gemma. The clouds had cleared enough to reveal a swath of black night sky. The stars scattered across that patch of heaven burned bright with all three moons muted by the clouds. The biting autumn chill seeped through Kayla's damp clothes.

Without thinking, Kayla activated her internal warming system. Tugging open the bay door, she stood aside as Nishi dashed to freedom and disappeared into the darkness of the alley. She'd have to leave the door open so Nishi could return with her night's prey.

Just as she stepped up into the bay, Avish, the second of the trinity moons, peeked through the clouds and sent a beam of light to the rubble beside the alley. Her gaze caught a bit of GENscrib scrawled on a broken piece of plasscrete.

Hopping back down to the ground, Kayla picked her way through the plasscrete rubble. From the broken furniture, kitchen oddments, and scraps of clothing scattered throughout, this must have been a warren. Chaff heads, scrub flowers, and even a few sticker bush seedlings had taken root, which meant it had been demolished weeks or even months ago.

As usual, Social Benevolence was taking their own sweet time getting the warren built again. Meanwhile, GENs would be jammed into what housing remained here in Fen or uprooted to another sector.

Kayla reached the roughly meter-square chunk she'd spied, likely part of an exterior wall. Moving the fifty-plus kilogram piece to better read the GENscrib, she waited for Avish's light to pierce the clouds again.

When it did, her heart nearly stopped in her chest.

FREEDOM. HUMANITY. EQUALITY. The same three words written in that nearly unreadable longhand GENscrib in Qaf.

She looked out at the ruined warren. The structure had to have been destroyed by Social Benevolence's order. Yet . . . wasn't that charring on some of the plasscrete pieces? Could the warren have burned first, then been razed?

Surely if this warren had been blown up like the warehouse had, Kayla or Risa would have heard of it. But the trueborns could so easily control information. If they wanted everyone to believe this had been a routine demolition, they had the means to do it. Any GEN witnesses could easily be reset. The Brigade that had to deal with the aftermath would know better than to talk.

Freedom. Humanity. Equality.

They were words nearly all GENs harbored unspoken in their hearts. Yet if the source were a GEN, why destroy a warren and make GEN lives more miserable?

Kayla returned to the lorry bay and nestled in a pile of scratchy plasscine blankets she and Risa used to protect fragile items. Her mind raced in a dozen different directions.

Who wrote the words? Were they a warning for the GENs in the warren to leave? Could they possibly be a vile joke of some Brigade members who'd learned a little GENscrib? Or did they mean nothing, written on a risky dare by some under-fifteen GEN before a routine demolition?

Kayla fell into a restless doze. Sometime during the night, Nishi returned. After the seycat finished crunching the bones of whatever unlucky rat-snake or sewer toad had crossed her path, she curled up next to Kayla. With Nishi's purring warmth, Kayla finally dropped into dreamless sleep.

Considering how upside-down everything had been the day before, Kayla was barely surprised when a Kinship tech called in the morning to tell her and Risa that Gemma couldn't be found in the GEN database. To double-check, the tech wanted Risa to download Gemma's twenty-digit passkey that identified the GEN girl's unique DNA sequence. Most GENs didn't even know there was a passkey stored inside their annexed brains, nor did they realize that the passkey was also used to reset GENs.

But when Gemma woke, Kayla and Risa discovered the girl *did* know the hidden purpose of the passkey. It therefore took some persuasion for the GEN girl to allow Risa to download the passkey using her datapod. But when Risa then uploaded the twenty-digit string to the wristlink and the tech checked it, there was no record of the passkey in the GEN creation database either.

After signing off, Kayla unearthed a last few redfruit and their store of nutras and handed them out to Gemma, Risa, and herself. The compressed, vac-sealed kel-grain bars were barely palatable, but they would keep stomachs from growling until they could restock the lorry's pantry.

Leaving Gemma with a nutra, a juicy redfruit, and a jug of cold kelfa drink, she and Risa went around to the back of the lorry. "What now?" Kayla asked.

"Girl's not on the Grid, can go to a safe house," Risa said. "Maybe over in Nafi sector. Out of Northwest Territory."

"You'll have to call Councilor Mohapatra again and have him change your delivery schedule," Kayla said around a mouthful of redfruit.

"Don't like bothering the councilor twice in two days," Risa said.

"We can't just jet up there on our own judgment," Kayla said, pointing out the obvious. Irritation pricked at her. "Although I don't see why not. If we think it's the right thing to do, why are we always having to ask permission?"

Risa shrugged. "Kinship rules. No way we can drop her at Qaf safe house, never mind it's closest."

"I'll go on ahead to the warehouse," Kayla suggested. "Let them know we're on our way."

GENs weren't allowed wristlinks, so the only way to communicate with them was to hike over there through the central ward. But Kayla didn't mind the trip, since it would give her a chance to search for any other cryptic graffiti that might be scrawled on Fen walls. She unearthed a last hidden redfruit and her prayer mirror, tucking the mirror into the pocket in the waist of her leggings.

Nibbling around the bruises on the redfruit, Kayla wound her way through Fen's alleys and rutted roadways toward the warehouse district. The recent rain had soaked the hard-packed gray-brown dirt and the resulting mud sucked at her feet. Her synth-leather shoes were sturdy enough, but moisture seeped through their seams and her socks grew damper with each step.

GENs crowded the local streets that intersected the alleys. Under-tens and under-fifteens flooded past her on their way to the Doctrine school where Risa had parked the lorry. Nurture parents, many with a baby or toddler in tow, accompanied the youngest ones. Non-nurturer adults, those GENs lucky enough to be Assigned right there in Fen, threaded through the crowd as well, headed for their Assignments on warehouse loading docks or in Doctrine school classrooms.

Some of the adult GENs, recognizing her as a newcomer to Fen, stopped to say hello, and lingered a little while in hope of news from other sectors. One woman, after discovering Kayla was widely traveled, motioned her to the entry of her flat where three second- and third-years clung to her skirt.

"Do you travel to Chadi sector?" the woman asked. "My nurture daughter, Lis, was Assigned there."

"I'm from Chadi." Kayla suppressed a twinge of longing for her own nurture mother, Tala, and nurture brother, Jal. "I'll look for Lis next time I visit. Send your good wishes."

The grateful nurture mother escorted her charges back inside and Kayla continued on. Who knew how long it would be before she could keep her promise to the woman, or for Kayla to see her own family?

She forged through the swarm of bodies, pausing to exchange friendly greetings, keeping a sharp eye out for any GENscrib scrawls, in that peculiar longhand or otherwise. She didn't see any scribbles, but she saw fresh swaths of paint on walls here and there. A crew must have been through Fen recently, wiping away any GEN graffiti.

For the most part the crew had left the artwork—she spotted abstract depictions of the Infinite's face, or ornate inscriptions from the liturgy on warren walls. But in the still-glum overcast, she couldn't make out anything that might have once been GENscrib under the dull beige paint.

She dove into a less-crowded alley between two warrens. Murals lined both sides of the alley—on the left, the Infinite placing the twin suns in Loka's sky; on the right, representations of the prophets, Pouli, Cohn, and Gupta. In spite of herself, Kayla's hand went to her waist, reaching for her prayer mirror.

She dropped her hand again without pulling it out, but could barely resist the urge to send a mental prayer to the prophets. Even though she now knew the truth about the three—that Pouli and Cohn were complete frauds and Gupta killed himself as repentance for his part in creating the GENs. Even worse, the liturgy of the Infinite was Pouli and Cohn's creation to keep GENs oppressed.

Still, her heart couldn't deny the existence of the Infinite. She'd come to realize that the deep knowing within her of that great Divinity hadn't really come from the false liturgy. What Pouli and Cohn had created had nothing to do with the way the Infinite had placed His hand on her heart throughout her life, when she'd most needed His love.

Morning sunlight punched through the surly clouds, illuminating the lower left corner of the mural of the prophets. The angle of the sunlight revealed the edges of what had been painted over just below the mural. She crouched to see if she could make it out.

Yes, there was GENscrib there, but what had been scrawled was another insult, this one comparing the hairiness of a certain member of the Judicial Council to a bhimkay's ass. No secret, mysterious messages.

She'd taken so long meandering through Fen's streets and alleys that by the time she reached the warehouse, Risa had already arrived. When Kayla would have climbed up on the loading dock to help ferry crates of processed plass-fiber to the lorry, Risa pulled her aside.

"Where you been?" she asked.

"The crowds were thick," Kayla said. "Everyone was hungry for gossip." Not strictly true, but close enough. "Did the councilor agree to change your routing?"

Risa shook her head. "Too risky, he says. Going to send a trueborn to pick up the GEN girl, like she was a reset to be realigned."

The weight of apprehension settled in Kayla's stomach. "They wouldn't actually reset her, though, right?"

Risa looked shocked. "Course not. Taking her to Nafi safe house, not a gene-splicer lab."

Of course. Kayla was just so edgy about the GENscrib messages, her imagination created peril where there was none.

"When?" Kayla asked.

"Evening. After dark," Risa said. "Less notice that way."

"So we can't head for Beqal sector until they've taken her."

Risa's mouth pinched with displeasure. "Leaves us idle after we unload."

They set to work, carrying out the crates and loading them in the lorry. They could have stretched the job out since they had nowhere to go after. But it wasn't in either one of them to shirk. They worked as quickly, carried as heavy a load with each trip as if they were late for their next delivery. At least it was dry work, the skies clear and sunny.

Partway through the job, Gat, the GEN warehouse manager, pulled Kayla aside. He gave her another DNA packet and uploaded new programming for the Grid into her annexed brain.

What he stored inside Kayla was only a fragment of the newest changes to the Grid programming. Not all the pieces were stored inside GENs, either. Lowborns would carry parts of the puzzle on datapods, and trueborn techs would hack into the Grid, steal fragments, and store them on their computers. Eventually all the pieces would be put together so the Kinship could continue to mask the true locations of hundreds of Kinship GENs.

The morning was gone by the time they finished loading. Both of them were ravenous after nothing but nutras, so they visited a food stand on Karpa Street for watered-down fruit melds and stuffed bread rolls. Risa pretended she didn't know it was ground rat-snake meat filling the bread rolls. They went back to the lorry to eat, bringing extra to share with Gemma.

As they were just finishing their meal, a lowborn woman a few shades browner and about a decade younger than Risa's forty-seven years approached the lorry with a smile and a wave. Risa caught sight of the woman—her wife, Kiyomi—and tossed aside the last bite of her bread roll as she scrambled from the cab. She took off running toward the woman and they jumped into one another's arms.

Their kisses were passionate enough that Kayla looked away. When she glanced up again, Risa and her wife were walking toward the lorry, arm in arm. Kayla slipped from the cab to meet them.

Risa grinned in uncharacteristic joy. "Didn't know Yomi would be visiting her sick auntie over in Amik."

Tall Kiyomi smiled down at Risa. "I wanted to surprise you," she said, her voice low and musical. "And I couldn't wait another week for you to return to Cayit."

Risa turned to Kayla. "Don't mind if I go back to Amik with Yomi? Spend the afternoon there?"

"I can go down to the warehouses," Kayla said. "Look for some work to keep me busy, maybe earn a half-dhan or two. You enjoy your time together."

The two of them walked off, their love for each other surrounding them like an aura. Watching them, Kayla's heart ached with hopeless longing. She would never be able to walk openly with Devak like that, even if she was restored. She and Devak could never be together the way Risa and Kiyomi were, the way Mishalla and Eoghan were, unless the Infinite cast aside the natural order and magically turned Kayla back into the trueborn she'd once been.

She shrugged off the pain and focused instead on finding work. There were plenty of GEN warehouse managers glad for an extra pair of hands, who were more than willing to pay a little cash for her labor. With the arrival of fall, lightweight summer tunics and leggings had to be toted to the cache warehouses, and replaced by warmer winter clothes. Even though a GEN could use her circuitry to regulate her body temperature, that effort still took energy, additional calories the trueborns didn't want to supply. Better and cheaper to give the tankborns warmer clothes.

Toting crates full of summer wear to the cache warehouse and returning with crates packed with heavier weight winter gear should have been a mindless exercise. But with each trip, Kayla wrestled with the ever-present ache in her heart that had been triggered by seeing Risa and Kiyomi's happiness. *Devak, Devak, Devak* rang in Kayla's ears with each footstep.

Even worse, it seemed around every corner she'd glimpse

some dark-headed GEN boy—a warehouse worker or a tech or even a nurture father. The boys were like shadows of Devak, never quite as tall as him, their skin never the right kelfa color. But they were close enough that her imagination filled in those details.

She forced mental blinkers on to close out those passersby and doubled her attention on the drudgery of her work. After all, this was what she'd been made for, a beast of burden built to carry and tote for trueborns.

6

By the time Kayla returned to the lorry, four half-dhan coins safely tucked away in her hidden pocket, Kas, the lesser brother sun, had nearly sunk below the horizon. Risa must have been keeping a lookout for Kayla because the lowborn woman made a beeline for her the moment she spotted her. Risa's cheeks were fat with devil leaf, and she chewed at a frantic pace.

"Brigade's been by here twice just since I got back from Amik," Risa said as they walked toward the lorry. "Want to know what we're doing, parked here all afternoon."

"What'd you tell them?" Kayla asked.

"The truth," Risa said. "Waiting on a GEN pickup."

"That's okay, then," Kayla said.

They reached the lorry and climbed into the cab. The curtain that concealed the sleeper had been pulled open and tied back. Gemma sat on the bed, her short dark hair neatly combed, her gaze solemn. The Scratch marks had faded completely from her face, leaving only smooth, pale skin and an unmarred tattoo on her left cheek.

"Lock the door," Risa mumbled, then spit out the devil leaf into a nearly full bucket.

Risa swiped at her mouth with the back of her hand, smearing a little devil leaf juice across her face. "First enforcer was satisfied, second ordered me to off-load entire cargo so he could inspect it."

Kayla's jaw dropped. "But you didn't."

Risa's gaze narrowed on her. "How could I, you gone and all? Had to call the councilor. Again."

"At the Council house?" Kayla asked. Someone would surely notice that Councilor Mohapatra received three calls from his lowborn employee.

"He was home. Had me put the enforcer on the wristlink. Threatened to send him to Belk sector." Risa sniggered at that.

"Did you ask when the trueborn would be here to fetch Gemma?"

Risa gave her another sharp look. "Me, chut away at a judicial councilor for taking too long?" She shook her head. "Some kind of sanaki GEN you are."

Kayla brushed off the insult. She'd heard Risa call plenty of people crazy. For Risa, it was almost a term of endearment.

So they waited while Kas withdrew all of his indolent light. The now-deserted warehouse district plunged into darkness.

Risa didn't turn on the interior illuminators. She probably didn't want to draw any more notice than they already had.

"Strange thing I heard in the lowborn village," Risa said softly after a long stretch of silence. "GEN girl came through there two days ago."

"Came through, like passed the village on her way to her Assignment?" Kayla recalled passing a lowborn village in

Foresthill as she'd headed for her first Assignment. "Plenty of GENs do that."

"Came through, like brought there by an allabain lowborn woman," Risa said.

The allabain were a lowborn sect that traveled from place to place, settling for a few weeks or months on the outskirts of mixed or even GEN sectors. They'd pick up a few dhans doing day labor, then move on.

"GEN girl stayed two days in the headwoman's house. Villagers spoke about her like she was Lord Creator Himself, or his only daughter, anyways."

"A GEN girl, the Lord Creator's daughter?" Kayla asked in disbelief.

Risa nodded. "In some other village, she brought a dead lowborn boy back to life. So they said."

Kayla vaguely remembered a myth she and Mishalla had read about a man who could raise the dead. But since they knew only the Infinite could control who lived or died, Kayla and Mishalla hadn't given much credence to the fairy story.

"The boy probably wasn't really dead," Kayla said. "He just got better on his own from whatever sickness he had."

"Likely," Risa said. "Ought to tell Zul, nevertheless."

Finally, Kayla spotted the lights of a lev-car bumping its way along Karpa Street toward them. Risa briefly turned on the lorry's front illuminators and Kayla was relieved to see the lev-car was an ancient WindSpear and not a Brigade Dagger.

Kayla allowed herself an instant of longing that it would somehow be Devak here for Gemma. Then the lev-car's door opened, and the interior light shone on the trueborn woman inside.

The woman, who said her name was Coria, climbed up into the lorry's cab, seeming not the least uneasy about sitting beside Kayla. Soft-voiced and kind-faced, Coria's light-brown skin and hair, along with the emerald bali in her left ear, identified her as a demi-status.

Most demis that Kayla met were mean and quick to offend, squeezed between wounded pride that they weren't good enough to be high-status and fear that they might someday slide into minor-status. But Coria seemed comfortable and confident in her rank, friendly both to lowborn Risa and the fragile GEN girl, Gemma.

The trueborn woman slipped a datapod from her pocket and put it up to Gemma's cheek. Gemma jolted a little at the prick of the extendibles, then her eyes went blank as Coria's datapod downloaded Gemma's annexed brain. Gemma's eyes came to life again as the datapod dropped from her cheek.

Coria fitted the datapod into her wristlink, then after a few moments, studied the display. Her brow furrowed.

Gemma leaned forward, trying to see the wristlink. "Does it tell you anything about me?"

"Only what we already knew," Coria said. "That parts of two identities have been programmed into your annexed brain, and neither match the GEN or Grid databases. But I've sent the full download to a Kinship personality engineer."

Now Coria turned to Kayla, holding out the datapod. "I have an upload for you. May I?" the trueborn woman asked.

"Why didn't you ask Gemma before you downloaded her?" Kayla asked.

Coria seemed flustered. "Because . . . I didn't . . . I don't . . ."

"Never mind," Kayla said. She knew why. A lot of Kinship

trueborns saw Kinship GENs as special, different than ordinary GENs. They would treat Kayla with unfailing respect, then turn and order a house GEN to clean the kitchen or weed the garden.

Kayla held out her hand for the datapod. "I'll do it myself." Coria hesitated only a moment before dropping the datapod into Kayla's palm.

"What's the upload?" Kayla asked, and she saw surprise flicker in Coria's eyes that Kayla would have the impudence to question her. So even a Kinship GEN like her hadn't yet risen to full respect in the trueborn woman's eyes.

But Coria recovered quickly, smiling at Kayla. "It's new code phrases for the safe houses. And membership changes."

Risa exchanged a glance with Kayla. *Changes* often meant they'd lost members. Lowborns killed, trueborns arrested, GENs reset.

Neither Kayla nor Risa knew the full Kinship roster. They were made aware of only those they might have need of, whose paths they might cross. Coria, for instance, had been stored in Kayla's annexed brain sometime back, in expectation for the demi-status woman's use as a courier. Occasionally they would be notified of alterations to the roster.

Best to get any bad news over with. Kayla applied the thumb-sized device to her cheek and felt the bite of the extendibles. She braced herself.

It wasn't good—three GENs reset, their personalities wiped away, a fourth GEN destroyed by a shockgun blast when she tried to escape. The names matched entries in Kayla's annexed brain, but there was no match in her bare brain, which meant she didn't know these GENs personally.

At the mention of one new member, Kayla's breath caught—Mishalla. How could she have joined the Kinship? Mishalla and Eoghan were supposed to be raising a growing brood of fostered children in Plator.

Kayla had begged Mishalla to stay out of the Kinship. Her friend was safe as a lowborn only as long as she stayed hidden.

But if she moved more into public view working for the Kinship, someone could recognize her, remember she'd been a GEN. She would be arrested. Gene-splicers would try to re-install Mishalla's neural circuitry in a gen-tank. Except as old as Mishalla was, her body would reject the circuitry and the installation attempt would kill her.

While Kayla mulled over Mishalla joining the Kinship, a last bit of programming shivered along her circuitry into her annexed brain. Distracted by that late bit of code, she followed its path to where it had stored itself and was surprised when she reached a mental dead end. There was no new programming in that location.

She'd sensed little internal hiccups along her neural system before, echoes of the upload. Generally it was junk data that her annexed brain rejected, which must be what this was since she couldn't find a trace of it.

The datapod finished and dropped from Kayla's cheek. She handed it back to Coria.

Coria smiled. "Everything upload okay?"

Kayla took a breath, about to mention that hiccup, the phantom code that apparently didn't exist. But instead she forced a smile back at the trueborn woman. "Sure. All okay."

Coria left with Gemma, tucking the girl into the back of

her ancient WindSpear. After they sputtered off, Risa turned to Kayla.

"Could stay here for the night, but it'd be risky, with the enforcers prowling."

"Let's just go," Kayla said. "We've lost a day anyway, when we should have been on our way to drop this load."

"Trade driving?" Risa asked. "Me first, then you?"

"As long as we're outside town when I take the wheel," Kayla said. "On the empty roads."

Which went without saying, since GENs were forbidden to pilot lev-cars. But few enforcers stirred from the central ward of the sector they patrolled.

But even if they could avoid enforcer attention, the thought of driving in the denser central wards terrified Kayla. She'd never operated a lev-car before meeting Risa, let alone something as big and awkward as the lorry. She'd just as soon drive the massive rig on wide, untrafficked highways.

So Risa took the first shift while Kayla crawled into the sleeper. As Kayla settled in, she heard Nishi's yowl, the high-pitched sound the seycat made when she went after prey. Rat-snakes sometimes squirmed their way into the lorry in search of spilled kel-grain. This rat-snake would be doubly disappointed—nothing but plassfiber and a seycat ready to hunt it down and eat it.

Kayla opened the hatch to see if Nishi would leave off her pursuit and curl up in bed beside her. But Nishi, nearly at eye level through the hatch where she perched on a tall column of crates, just glared at Kayla. The feline refused to budge, no matter how sweetly Kayla called.

One of those nights when Nishi was rethinking her close

association with humans and GENs, Kayla supposed. She shut the hatch to close off the chill from the bay, then curled up in the covers. She fell asleep almost instantly.

Kayla woke refreshed and swapped with Risa behind the lorry's wheel. Nishi climbed from the bay for Risa, her purring interspersed with growls as she curled up in the bed beside the lowborn woman.

Twenty kilometers into her stint, Kayla spotted a roadside sign. The marker was the only indication they'd crossed from Northwest Territory into Northeast and had left Fen sector and entered Beqal.

You wouldn't know it from the landscape. The same boulders littered the rolling plain, the same scrap grass lay flat by the recent storm's rage. Here and there a junk tree thrust up from the unforgiving dirt, sharp skeletal branches dull gray, the red fractals of the symbiotic host that lived along its bark invisible in the dark.

The lorry's front illuminators picked out a pair of giant bhimkay skittering through the mashed-down scrap grass. A shiver zipped up and down Kayla's spine as the spiders merged into the darkness. As big as they were, those two were young ones, barely hip-height on her, Kayla guessed. It was alarming to see them here in a populated GEN sector like Beqal. The bhimkay usually stuck to the more remote adhikar land in the center of each territory.

But trueborns didn't like the bhimkay on their adhikar tracts, never mind that was the safer place for the big spiders since so few people lived there. For the trueborns, it was all a matter of profit. The bhimkay sometimes foiled the electrified fences that protected the trueborn drom herds roaming their adhikar. A big enough colony of bhimkay could put a dent in a trueborn's wealth by killing their more vulnerable juvenile droms.

Even worse, she'd heard of a trueborn killed recently on his own family's adhikar. The youngest son of a powerful high-status Nitha sector family had been attacked by a bhimkay while surveying drom herds or kel-grain fields or a plassfiber mine. She couldn't remember the details. But the spider caught him and sucked him dry.

So the trueborns ordered their lowborn managers to drive off the bhimkay from their adhikar. The giant spiders had to go somewhere. It looked like at least a few had made it all the way from the adhikar reserve in the center of Northeast Territory to Beqal. If the bhimkay got brave enough to make their way into the central ward, it would be GENs and not droms killed. Which was shortsighted of the trueborns since a GEN was worth at least what a drom was—more if the GEN had a tech sket.

As she continued on through the night, she didn't spot any more bhimkay, thank the Infinite. She drove until Iyenku crept enough above the distant horizon that she could make out the silhouettes of Beqal sector's warehouses and warrens. Then she pulled over and nudged Risa awake. Risa took the wheel.

As early as it was, their destination, the plasscine extrusion factory, was still dark. Risa drove around to the loading dock in back and killed the engine.

"Go over to the safe house," Risa suggested. "Drop off the packet, get yourself some grub. I'll wait here, catch a few more winks."

Kayla left as Risa crawled back up into the sleeper. As

she threaded her way through Beqal's rows of warehouses and factories, the damp chill bit her skin. Her internal warming system couldn't quite keep up, so she alternated between cold and warm as she walked, her internal map guiding her steps.

This early in the morning, few GENs were abroad yet. She passed a nurture mother with an infant cradled in each arm, a couple fifth-years trailing behind. On their way to Doctrine School, no doubt. A few fifteenth-year boys, newly Assigned from the look of their wide-eyed uncertainty, crossed her path as they emerged from an alley. An older boy, maybe a seventeenth-year, smiled back at her as he came up behind and passed her, his teeth white in his red-brown face.

Most of the Kinship safe houses were excavated under warrens, but in some sectors like Beqal, the warehouse district was a safer location. In Beqal, the soil beside the Plator River was barely stable enough to construct the warrens on, let alone to dig beneath for a safe house. Under the warehouses, a natural cavern gave the Kinship a starting point.

The enforcer patrolling the warehouse district, too busy trying to stay warm in the morning chill, barely gave Kayla a second look. She walked briskly to make it clear she had a legitimate destination.

She turned into the alley between the foodstores and household goods warehouses. A GEN boy, as dark-skinned as Kayla's nurture brother, Jal, loitered near the warehouse door. He clutched something in his hand and inhaled from it. Some homebrewed rawseed zing, maybe, to get him through his upcoming shift.

Except the moment he spotted Kayla, he tossed aside whatever had been in his hand and approached her. His eyes were clear, his cheeks unmarked except for his silvery tattoo. Zing use mottled even the darkest skin with an ugly purple.

He made a swift scan up and down the alley, then said, "I've just been Assigned to Tellik sector."

This was one of the new code phrases Coria had uploaded. "The Infinite shines his face in every sector."

He'd started to turn toward the door as Kayla began speaking, then he froze at her final words. He stared at her, uncertainty clear in his dark eyes.

Kayla's cheeks flushed with heat as she realized her mistake. "The Infinite shines his face in *all* sectors."

Now the boy smiled. "This way." He opened the warehouse door for her and let her enter first.

As they zigzagged through the tall stacks of crates and full-to-capacity plasscine sacks of kel-grain, worry nagged Kayla. How could she have gotten the code phrase wrong? If it had been in her bare brain, she could have easily mixed up the wording; that part of her brain wasn't wired for exact retrieval.

But her annexed brain—the circuitry there was designed and installed to work with machine-like precision. Yet altered wording had spilled from her mouth. And what about that upload hiccup, when she'd been sure some new programming had been stored, then there had been nothing there?

First the hyper-fast healing and now a problem with her annexed brain. And what about how difficult it had been to keep her temperature regulated on her way here?

Maybe it all meant nothing. Or maybe it did mean something.

Maybe she really was broken.

7

As the tunnel leading to the safe house jogged sharply right, a murmur of noise reached Kayla's ears. As she continued toward the increasing light spilling into the tunnel from the safe house, the sound grew louder, separating itself into shouting voices, as if everyone in the safe house was calling out all at once.

Her first panicked thought was that an enforcer raid was imminent or even in progress, that the Brigade had breached one of the other access points. But the plassteel door at the end of the tunnel hadn't been slid shut. In any case, she refused to run to save her own skin if her help might be needed.

She stepped from the tunnel and nearly collided with a fourteenth-year GEN boy. The shouting was deafening in the cavernous space, voices echoing off the limestone walls and ceiling. With so much noise, Kayla worried they could be heard aboveground.

Then she saw the joyful, awestruck smiles on nearly every face. Everyone except the dozen or so Scratch-infected GENs dying in their cots surged in one direction—toward a tall high-status trueborn in the center of the room.

Zul Manel was here. Devak's great-grandfather, the leader and founder of the Kinship. He towered over nearly everyone here, both physically and with his presence, his high-status rank as obvious as the rising of the twin suns. His booming voice cut through the noise. An old tattoo marked his left cheek, a vestige of his first experimentation with GEN technology decades ago.

Everyone near him, everyone he spoke to, looked ready to kneel at his feet—GENs, lowborns, and trueborns alike. A pair of minor-status trueborn medics were giddy at his presence. The lowborns who managed the safe house and the GEN caretakers who did most of the hands-on work with the sick looked as worshipful as if they'd seen the Infinite Himself. Even the silent, dying GENs smiled wistfully as if wishing for one more moment of life to be with him.

Kayla couldn't stop herself from searching for Devak in the cavernous thirty- by forty-meter oblong room. Devak had the same Manel height as his great-grandfather. She should be able to see him easily even in this crowd.

Zul spotted her, then extricated himself from the crowd. He cut a path toward her, looking vigorous and strong, with none of the weakness she'd seen in him two nights ago. If he'd brought his lev-chair, she couldn't see it. Had he risked a dose of crysophora to be here? The powerful stimulant had nearly killed him more than once.

With a nod, Zul urged her to walk with him around the perimeter of the safe house main room. The cacophony of voices quieted as GENs and lowborns returned to the tasks Zul's arrival had interrupted.

A half-dozen workers streamed back into the small kitchen alcove. Opposite the kitchen in the sick room alcove, a pair of medics tended the Scratch victims. Other men and women busied themselves stitching torn clothing or minding the GEN and lowborn children, or sweeping the limestone dust that continually settled. A pair of oldsters, one GEN, one lowborn, whiled away the time by painting a mural on one wall, what looked like representations of the Infinite and the Lord Creator smiling, side by side.

Kayla couldn't help taking one last look around the room for Devak. Seemingly reading her mind as he often did, Zul said, "Devak's not here."

She squelched her disappointment. "No reason he would be, I guess."

Zul nudged her aside as a pair of rambunctious fourth-years dashed past them. "We can't always do what we want to do, Kayla."

Irritation flared up inside Kayla. "I don't even know what that means. Are you saying he'd be here if he could?"

"I asked him to come along." Zul smiled at a GEN woman who handed them each a cup of steaming kelfa drink. "He declined."

"Because he had something else more important?" Kayla took a sip of kelfa, steeling herself. "Or because he knew I'd be here?"

Zul swirled the hot spicy drink in his cup. "I told him I was coming here partly to meet with you."

She sucked in a breath as Zul's honesty cut deep. But she couldn't let the old man know how much Devak's avoidance of her hurt, especially if there was a chance he would pass that on to his great-grandson. Instead she shrugged and swallowed back her pain with another mouthful of kelfa.

They'd reached the sick room. Seeing the Scratch patients lying there ill and suffering, Kayla put aside her pain at Devak's apparent abandonment. They stepped inside the alcove, Zul ducking to clear the low doorway.

Those of the Scratch-afflicted who were awake stared avidly at Zul. He went from bed to bed, offering water, asking one of the medics for an analgesic for two who writhed in pain. Kayla did what she could, carefully lifting and repositioning one woman off an open sore on her hip. But it was Zul they wanted to see, Zul who gave them hope.

As they left the sick room to continue around the safe house, Kayla said, "You're walking around. You seem healthy. But it doesn't look like crysophora."

"This is something different," Zul said. "A special injection series. I feel as if I have ten times the strength I did with the crysophora."

Kayla handed off the two empty cups to a passing mess boy. "But just two days ago you were so tired you couldn't speak to me."

"My debilitation is so severe, that the injection sequence took longer to take effect in me than it does in others," Zul said. "I needed a few days of recovery time."

The safe house manager approached with a sekai and held it out to Zul. Zul scrolled through the display, then acknowledged what he'd read with a thumbprint. He and Kayla moved on, the busy crowd parting for them.

"What's this injection you're getting?" Kayla asked. "Another drug?"

"Not exactly." His evasive tone made Kayla uneasy. "More a treatment personally derived for me."

"Derived by who?" she prodded.

He pulled her into a private corner, near the tunnel where she'd entered. "Akhilesh Garud. The head of GAMA."

At the mention of GAMA, nausea crawled up Kayla's throat. The Genetic Augmentation and Manipulation Agency was responsible for designing and creating GENs. To her mind, GAMA, more than any other trueborn institution, was the source of GEN enslavement. They were the ones who tinkered with tankborn genes, contorting and twisting them to suit trueborn wishes.

"He can't be Kinship. Or is he?" Had the Kinship pulled a high-ranking GAMA official into its ranks?

"No," Zul said. "But he's doing some landmark work. He's a key figure in the search for a Scratch cure as well."

"But how can you trust him if he's not Kinship?"

Zul gripped Kayla's shoulder and gave her a little shake. "There are some good people who aren't Kinship. Akhilesh. Guru Ling, who Junjie works for. I wouldn't reveal Kinship work to them, but it would be stupid not to take advantage of their skills."

Kayla looked away, realizing she felt ashamed for questioning him. Then she got angry with herself, with her habitual response of always considering a high-status trueborn right and herself wrong.

She glanced up at Zul again, and saw his gaze had softened. "I'm sorry," he said, as always astounding her with his trueborn apologies. "I thought you might be happy with my improvement."

"I'm glad the injections are working for you," Kayla said, pushing aside her reluctance at saying the words. *I just don't trust it as much since it came from a non-Kinship gene-splicer.*

They started off again in another circuit of the safe house. The sharp scent of fried patagobi root spiced with a hint of curry drifted across the room from the kitchen alcove. GEN and lowborn young people were setting up trestle tables and benches in the center of the room.

"There are a couple of issues I wanted to speak with you about," Zul said. "One critical."

"What?"

They were passing the sick room again. Within the alcove, the pair of medics were pouring some kind of dark brown broth into cups. They passed the cups to the Scratch patients who could sit up. The prone they supported and encouraged to take a sip or two.

Zul cut through the main room to take a seat at one of the trestle tables. Kayla sat opposite him.

"First, the GEN restoration treatment," Zul said. "I'd asked the Kinship research team to fast-track the production of a dose for you. I was hoping we'd have it within the next week or two."

Doubt jabbed at her at the thought of restoration happening soon. She should have been rejoicing at the possibility. Why would she hesitate even an instant at the chance to no longer be enslaved to the trueborns?

Because her only path to freedom was to become a lowborn. To become someone else. She'd still have her thoughts and memories. But the treatment would change who she was. She wouldn't be a GEN anymore. She might have started life as a trueborn, but she'd only been a fourth-year when she became a GEN. It felt like she'd always been one.

And what about her nurture mother Tala and nurture brother Jal? How could Kayla become a lowborn without them? She couldn't free herself without freeing them.

Zul patted her hand to offer comfort she wasn't sure she wanted. "They told me they're just too caught up in the hunt for a Scratch cure. Production of the various experimental Scratch inoculations has been too time-consuming. And since GENs are dying from Scratch, that cure takes priority."

She held back a smile of relief. "That's okay. I can wait. What else?"

"Then the rather worse news." Zul leaned toward her, his long arms resting on the table. "Devak's father has vanished from prison."

Her stomach knotted, and the kelfa she'd drunk threatened to come up. "He escaped?"

His dark eyes sharp with anger, Zul smacked the table with his open palm. "He may have walked right out with the guards looking the other way. If enough dhans change hands, even a respectable man might be tempted. And there are many less than respectable men at Far North prison."

"But where would Ved get the money?" Kayla fussed with the hem of her shirt, twisting and untwisting the rough cloth. "The Council took nearly everything from him."

"There were many who felt his imprisonment was unjust," Zul said. "That a high-status trueborn should never be subject to judgment, particularly when the only ones harmed were lowborns and GENs."

Kayla had always worried that Ved knew about her and

Mishalla's connection to his being sent to prison. What did his escape mean? Was he only interested in regaining his lost power? Or did he have some plan to come after her and Mishalla?

The tables were filling up, a GEN boy jostling against Kayla as he took his seat. No one had the temerity to sit close to Zul. The space next to him remained empty.

Servers brought out bowls of kel-grain topped with slivers of synth-protein and thick slices of fried patagobi and other root vegetables. Zul waved off a serving. Kayla shook her head, her stomach too roiled.

"Where do you think he is?" Kayla asked, raising her voice against the rising noise.

"Calling in favors, I suspect," Zul said. "Looking for ways to rebuild his adhikar. Certain Judicial Councilors and high-status members of Congress no doubt fear what he knows about their corrupt practices. He'll take what he can from them in exchange for silence."

Bad enough Ved was out and free. Ved regaining his power frightened her. Her fingers still twisting in her shirt hem, Kayla felt something give. She realized she'd put her fingers through the cloth. Another mending job.

She forced herself to relax her hands. "I don't see what he could do from someone's adhikar. As well known as he is, he can't let himself be discovered. He'd only be sent back."

Zul made a face, as if he was tasting something bitter. "Ved's compatriots have been working behind the scenes to have him pardoned. Memories are short amongst the high-status. If he can stay hidden until the proper strings are pulled, he can walk free."

"The last time Ved was free, he turned lowborn babies into GENs," Kayla said.

"He won't do that again," Zul said. "The Kinship wouldn't let him."

"Would he go after Mishalla?" Kayla asked.

"Ved doesn't even know Mishalla exists. She's safe enough as a lowborn."

Kayla's mind turned to a new worry. "Is Mishalla safe from Scratch? She still has tankborn genetics. Could she get it?"

"I wouldn't think so," Zul said. "The only GEN sector she visits is Chadi and they haven't had many cases there."

"But that could change now that she's joined the Kinship."

"I suppose," Zul said.

He had only half his attention on her. The lowborn house manager was motioning to him from a doorway between the sick room and one of the escape tunnels. Larger safe houses like this one included meeting rooms where the Kinship could gather.

Zul rose, gesturing to the manager that he'd be there in a moment. Kayla got to her feet too, realizing she only had a few more moments with Zul. "Was it you who persuaded her to join?" she asked.

"It was her choice." Zul started across the open space, threading through the crowd still gathering around the tables.

But he'd sworn he'd keep her out of the Kinship. Outrage flooded her at yet another broken trueborn promise.

She caught up with him. "You have to tell her she can't join." Her heart pounded in fear of Zul's reaction to her defiance.

The old man spun back to her, an imperious light in his face. Most of the time, Zul treated her like an equal now, a full member of the Kinship. But with him stretched to his full nearly two-meter height, she saw the difference between them was more than their disparate size. He was still a high-status trueborn, privileged from birth. And she was still just a nothing GEN.

No, not a *nothing* GEN, she acknowledged. Just a rude one, making demands of Zul when he'd had no part in Mishalla's joining.

Zul could have dressed her down, but he didn't. "I told Mishalla about the risks, but she made up her own mind."

Kayla couldn't leave it. "But why would she?"

"You'll have to ask her that. She wouldn't tell me."

Whatever else he might have said was cut off by the beeping of his wristlink. He read the message on the device's display, then turned away again. "I have to get to the meeting."

He walked off. As he disappeared into the chamber beside the sick room for his meeting, Kayla realized she'd never told him about her circuitry problems. Should she ask one of the medics to check her out? Maybe one of the two was more tech oriented. But they were so busy with the Scratch victims. The sick needed the medics' help more than she.

So she set off another self-check. As the check completed all thumbs up, her stomach rumbled. Despite Zul's unsettling news, she found she was hungry after all. She returned to the trestle table to look for a place to sit.

The tables had been laid out in rows perpendicular to the kitchen alcove. Because of the limited space, there weren't enough tables for everyone to eat at once. While Kayla stood wondering if she could squeeze in, three GENs vacated the bench in front of her. Before she thought to move, two boys jumped for the space, and a third boy would have too if a golden-skinned GEN woman with chestnut hair hadn't hissed at him to try elsewhere.

The woman patted the space beside her, inviting Kayla to sit. Then she called out, "Another bowl, Tisch!"

Tisch, a stocky lowborn man, hurried from the kitchen with a bowl mounded high with steaming kel-grain, synth-protein, and vegetables. The lowborn man not only didn't scowl at a GEN's demand, he gave the woman a one-armed hug and kissed her on the forehead.

"Yes, we're joined," the GEN woman told Kayla at her wondering glance. "At least we are here in the safe house, me being a GEN and him a lowborn. I'm Maia."

"Kayla." She put out a hand for Maia, then Tisch, to shake. "My friend Mishalla married a lowborn boy, but she's been restored and isn't a GEN anymore."

Maia gave Kayla a once over. "You're the one who was Assigned to Zul. The one who saved those lowborn children."

"It wasn't just me who saved them."

Tisch's gaze lingered a moment on Kayla's tattoo. "Rumor is you haven't always been a GEN. That you were trueborn."

Kayla couldn't help herself—she touched her right cheek. "I was almost four when they put me in the tank. So I really don't remember being anything but a GEN."

That wasn't strictly true. Kayla used to have the occasional nightmare about her time as a minor-status trueborn, flashes of memory about her trueborn mother. Until Zul revealed the truth to her four months ago, Kayla thought those dreams and memories were just something her imagination concocted.

Tisch hurried away to answer another summons, but Maia

continued to stare at Kayla. "Why haven't you been restored?" the redhead finally asked.

"Because the treatment isn't available," Kayla said.

"I would think you'd be top of the list," Maia said. "Knowing Zul like you do. Being former trueborn. Not a real tankborn like me."

Kayla bristled at the word *real.* "I have the same circuitry running through me as you do."

"But I wager you'll be restored long before the likes of me," Maia said.

What could she say to that? Maia seemed ready to pick apart whatever defenses Kayla might come up with. She turned away from the redhead, focusing on her bowl of kel-grain instead.

The slivers of synth-protein that striped the top were a far more generous portion than her nurture mother, Tala, had ever been able to provide. Kayla felt a pang of homesickness, a longing to see Tala and her nurture brother, Jal, again. It had been nearly six weeks now since she'd seen them. Since neither Tala nor Jal were free to leave Chadi sector, Kayla would have to go there to see them. But after she and Risa left Beqal sector, they'd be going north, not south where Chadi lay.

Her appetite had faded again, but she could imagine Tala scolding her for refusing good food. So Kayla spooned up her breakfast, washing down the warm kel-grain with some soy milk she poured from a communal pitcher. Finally Maia left, replaced by a skinny GEN boy with light, close-cropped hair. Another boy, a scruffy GEN who looked to be an eleventh-year like her nurture brother Jal, sat opposite.

The skinny boy nodded and introduced himself as Beph and his scruffy friend as Fashi. "You new here?" Beph asked.

Kayla shook her head. "I'm just here to make a delivery. Are you here with family?"

"Nah," Beph said. "Fashi and me, we were due for a reset. Fashi said one wrong thing too many to an enforcer, and I defended him."

Fashi nodded. "Got a problem with my mouth."

"How'd you get away?" Kayla asked.

"Kinship enforcer," Beph said. "Stepped in and did this thing with a datapod."

"Knocked us out," Fashi said. "When it all went black, I thought I'd never wake up."

"Came to here," Beph said. "Been here two weeks."

"Don't know what's next," Fashi said. "We help with the Scratchies sometimes."

Beph and Fashi then launched into a detailed description of a complicated gambling game they'd created to pass the time, something involving stones and squares of plass. Kayla's attention drifted, so she was only half-listening to their chatter when something Beph said caught her interest.

"The lowborns think she's some kind of goddess," the boy said.

"Think who's a goddess?" Fashi asked.

"Some GEN girl," Beph said.

"Where'd you hear this?" Kayla asked.

A guilty look flashed across Beph's face. "One of the Scratchies. That one that died this morning. Before he came here, he heard it from an allabain lowborn passing through."

Kel-grain dribbled from Fashi's mouth. He swiped it away, then shoved his thick hair away from his face. "Why would they think she's a goddess?"

"How would I know?" Beph said, then he lowered his voice. "Those allabains believe some crazy stuff. Like the twin suns joined to become a god and the moons are their children."

Fashi's pale skin flushed. "My nurture-mother believes in Iyenkas."

Beph guffawed. Kayla would have liked to hear more about the GEN girl goddess, given the rumor that Risa shared the other day, but the boys changed the subject back to the gambling game.

Risa had told Kayla that allabain lowborns didn't believe in the Lord Creator, the god that trueborns and most lowborns worshipped. But other than mentioning the dual god, Iyenkas, a joining of the suns, Iyenku and Kas, Risa never said much else about allabain beliefs or which god she followed. She saw beliefs in a God or gods as a private thing, not something to be blaring to the world.

Kayla finished her kel-grain, then tracked down Zul just as he was about to leave. As Kayla handed Zul the DNA packet she'd brought, she tried to catch his eye, but he was deep in conversation with another high-status trueborn. She didn't like leaving things between them the way they had, but she wasn't about to force herself into a conversation between two trueborns.

She left the safe house via a different exit than the one she'd entered through, then zigzagged her way up and down the local streets and alleys back to the extrusion factory. The lorry was there, but no Risa. The back doors of the lorry bay were shut, although the left latch wasn't quite pushed home. Odder still, the big roll-up door to the factory was still shut.

As Kayla puzzled over that, Risa came around the side of

the building. "Were you waiting for me?" Kayla asked. "If I'd known I would have gotten back sooner."

"Can't raise anyone. Pounded on that door three or four times." She poked a thumb over her shoulder at the factory's delivery door. "Was around to the front even, but no one here. Like they've all been sent on holiday."

Kayla trotted down the alley to Beqal's main street. When there should have been dozens of GENs abroad by now, the street was deserted. When she would have expected to hear voices, it was quiet and still.

A cold chill rushed through Kayla's body. She ran back to the lorry. Her gaze shot to the loading dock door, scanned it quickly from top to bottom. A few GENscrib insults were scrawled in black on the beige paint, the same sort of thing they'd seen in Qaf.

Her heart pounding, she turned in a slow circle, looking around her. A mural decorated the wall of the building across the alley, a GEN worshipper with her hands extended up to paradise, prayer mirror shining in her hands.

There was something written on the silvery-white of the prayer mirror. "What's that building?" Kayla asked Risa.

"Foodstores," the lowborn woman said. "Problem?"

Kayla didn't answer, just reached for the ladder she and Risa used to access the top of the lorry bay. Her hands shaking, she pulled it down and climbed up, then walked along toward the cab to get closer to the part of the mural featuring the mirror.

Even standing on the edge of the bay, she was still at least three meters away, and the letters were small. But the pattern was familiar now that she'd seen it twice before.

"We have to get out of here," she shouted down to Risa as she ran back toward the ladder. "Now."

Risa trusted Kayla enough not to ask questions. While Kayla hurried down the ladder and shoved it back into the storage position, Risa whistled for Nishi. Whether the seycat heard the urgency in Risa's summons or was ready to return, Nishi appeared almost instantly, the tail of a rat-snake in her mouth.

Risa scooped up Nishi and both she and Kayla ran to the cab. Nishi growled with displeasure, but luckily the seycat didn't struggle free. The moment they were all in the cab, Nishi leapt from Risa's arms and into the sleeper.

Risa had the lorry engine started and in gear in seconds. She reversed out of the alley, turning in a backward arc into the access road. The lowborn woman gunned away, traveling fast along the narrow lane between the rows of warehouses and factories. They'd passed a half-dozen of the blocky buildings before Risa stopped, the Plator River crossing their path.

Risa switched on the console vid screen so they could see down the lane behind them. Kayla peered hard at the screen as someone emerged from the alley. Her heart seemed to freeze in her chest. It was the GEN boy she'd seen earlier, the one with the red-brown skin who'd smiled at her. He was steps away from the foodstores warehouse.

"Oh, no." Kayla groped for her prayer mirror.

"Denk, denk, denk," Risa muttered. "Are you sure—"

Cutting off whatever else Risa had been about to say, the foodstores warehouse exploded, sending debris high into the overcast sky. The GEN boy's body flew with the debris and crashed into the unforgiving pavement.

8

Kayla pushed open the lorry door. Before she could jump out, Risa grabbed her wrist. "Can't get mixed up in this."

Kayla could have wrenched free in an instant, but she only gave a token tug. "He's hurt, Risa."

"Someone else can help."

"Like the Brigade?" Already she could hear the alarms from across the Plator in trueborn Tef sector. "The boy is either dead or dying. How can we leave him for the Brigade, let him get chopped up for his DNA?"

Risa's grip loosened slightly. "Still not our business."

"How is it different from rescuing a Scratch victim? Giving them a dignified death in safety?"

Risa mulled that over for a moment, then let go. "Be quick."

Kayla raced toward the explosion site. Already GENs were reappearing on the street and staring at the destruction. The Brigade couldn't be far behind.

If enforcers found her loitering there, they would arrest her first and ask questions later. They might download her on the spot, setting off the Kinship failsafe. Destroy her in an instant.

Behind her she could hear the lorry engine as Risa backed the big vehicle along the access road. When she reached Kayla, Risa slowed enough that Kayla could jump onto the back bumper and ride the rest of the way.

The GEN boy moved a little and groaned. His face was smeared with blood, soaking into his shoulder-length black hair. His right wrist lay at an odd angle. The fingers of his left hand strained to reach a carrysak a meter away from him.

When she got to his side, Kayla hesitated. She'd done nothing wrong yet. Other GENs were starting to cluster closer. There was still time for her and Risa to escape.

But the gaping gash across his forehead into his hair, the pasty look to his red-brown skin, and his rapid, shallow breathing told her he hadn't much time before he'd be stepping into the Infinite's broad hand. The Brigade would take his body to the gene-splicers and recycle it into future GENs. Even if he wasn't dead yet, the gene-splicers would just take his "meat" as they wished. So it was worth the risk to get him out of here in a hurry.

Kayla lifted him as carefully as she could in her arms. She gritted her teeth against his shout of pain.

When she turned toward the lorry, he rasped out, "Carrysak."

She went down on one knee to hook the carrysak strap in her fingers. As she was about to straighten, a silvery glint caught her eye. She spotted a prayer mirror wedged under some of the rubble. The palm-sized metallic mirror had to be the boy's.

She pinched it between two fingers of her other hand,

registered that it was oddly thick and heavier than the usual prayer mirror. Clutching it tightly, she ran for the lorry. Risa had one of the bay doors open and there was just enough room between the door and the stacks of crates to put the boy.

Kayla set him down, then squeezed inside with him, dropping the carrysak at his feet. His prayer mirror she tucked in her waistband pocket. She rolled him toward her to keep him out of the way of the door while Risa shut it and closed them in darkness. A few moments later, the lorry started to move, then the bay illuminators came on.

The boy thrashed in the narrow space, muttering, "Chut it. Chut it."

"It'll be okay," Kayla said, even knowing it wasn't. "We'll get you to a healer."

The lorry shuddered as Risa must have reached a rougher road. Kayla slammed a hand against the inside of the door to keep her balance. The GEN boy grunted, squeezing his eyes shut, his pain clear.

"I'm Kayla 6982," she said. "What's your name?"

"Abran 9416," the boy said, his voice slurred.

Not a GEN name she'd heard before. "Are you from Beqal sector, Abran, or just Assigned here?"

He didn't answer. His chest rose as he inhaled, taking in a stuttering breath. She stared, sure it would stop at any moment. Blood glistened across his forehead and nearly covered one eye.

Kayla unlocked and shifted a few crates aside so she could sit. Leaning against the tower of crates beside her, she was glad they'd taken the boy with them. His last minutes should be in friendly hands, not on a rubble-strewn street, or stuffed in the boot of a Brigade Dagger.

She considered searching his carrysak to see if there was any evidence of who he was, but she was uncomfortable going through a stranger's personal things. Once he died, she would. But while he was alive, he deserved his privacy. She'd had her personal things searched far too often by the Brigade to feel right doing it herself.

The blood dripped slowly, stickily toward his ear. She wanted dearly to clean his face. But what if she went up to the cab for sani-wipes and he died while she was gone? Tala's partner Xan had passed into the Infinite's hands that way, breathing his last just after Tala and Kayla left the room. Kayla had felt bad about that, but Tala said sometimes the souls wait until they're alone. They want to save the family that final pain.

She should give the boy that chance to die in private safety. Meanwhile, she'd go up and get the sani-wipes, so she could clean him after death if not before.

She scaled the stack of crates, then squirmed through the slim space between the top of the stacks and the bay's ceiling. They'd left an area clear around the hatch, both to give them quick access between the bay and cab, but also to leave a space for Nishi to curl up. Risa must have let the seycat into the bay because the five-legged feline was there in her cubby, spitting at Kayla.

No help for it, Kayla had to drop down next to Nishi to crawl through the hatch. Usually the seycat tolerated Kayla, but the creature must have been agitated by Abran's presence. Nishi lashed out, two painful love taps that would likely bleed into Kayla's leggings.

As Kayla twitched aside the sleeper curtains, Risa glanced back over her shoulder. "How is he?"

"Breathing, barely." Kayla found the first aid box tucked into one of the built-in shelves surrounding the sleeper bed. "Took a denking big ride when the bomb went off. Bleeding from the head, and his wrist is broken, I think. Who knows what kind of internal injuries."

Risa's jaw worked at a hunk of devil leaf. "Long as he's alive, Grid could ping him. Send the Brigade after us."

"Do you think we're already outside his Assignment area?" Kayla peered through the windscreen to orient herself. They were hurtling along on a cross-sector road, already back out in the scrap grasslands. Beqal central ward shrank in the rear display.

"Depending on his Assignment, could be," Risa said. "Either he dies soon, or we find a place to leave him."

Kayla, digging through the first aid box for the packet of sani-wipes, turned back toward Risa. "We can't just drop him at the side of the road."

Risa looked back over her shoulder. "Could have left him in the street."

Her attention back on her driving, the lowborn woman exhaled heavily, flecks of devil leaf spattering the back of her hand on the wheel. "We'll keep him for now. Until he dies or we talk to Zul. But if Brigade boards us, I won't hide the boy. Just turn him over. Tell 'em we just found him, couldn't get signal to call Brigade."

Anger burned inside Kayla at the necessity of that, but what else could they do? They had to protect themselves. "I did get his name and ID. Abran 9416. Maybe that'll help when you contact Zul. At least find his nurture parent so we can notify him or her about his death."

Kayla scooted over to the hatch, swinging her legs through into the bay. "Call off Nishi, would you? She already got me once."

Risa whistled. Nishi didn't obey the summons, but when Kayla dropped down into the cubby, the seycat didn't claw her again either.

She squirmed her way back through the narrow passageway between the crates and the lorry ceiling. Before she came into view of Abran, she steeled herself for him already being gone. As much peril it put them in if Abran was still living, she realized she wanted quite desperately to be at his side when he breathed his last, as she hadn't been able to with Xan.

She swung off the crates, still not looking. So when she turned to face Abran, she nearly lost her grip and fell.

He was alive. He was *sitting up.* And he looked a long way from a boy about to die.

9

Her first response was joy, the next worry. She stripped a sani-wipe from the packet and started cleaning blood from Abran's face.

"Hey!" the boy protested.

Abran tried to ward off her hand but she persisted. She cleared away the blood from his cheek, exposing his uninjured GEN tattoo. When she cleaned what had been a gaping head wound on his forehead, she saw it was now closed into a fat, black scab nearly as long and as wide as her index finger.

Great Infinite, he'd been healed at as rapid a pace as she'd been. What did it mean that GENs were suddenly healing faster?

Without finesse, she snatched up his right arm. Hadn't it been bent wrong at the wrist? She'd been sure it was broken.

"Can you move it?" she asked.

He flapped his hand up, then down, wincing a little. It clearly still hurt, but although it was badly bruised and swollen, it was only slightly crooked. And if he could move it like that, it wasn't broken.

She poked at his head wound. "Does this hurt?"

"Not much."

She squeezed his belly, and his red-brown face flushed redder. "Any pain here?"

"No!" He grabbed her wrist. "Can you lay off?"

"Denk it," she muttered. "I've gotten us all into trouble." She dropped the packet of sani-wipes in his lap.

She scaled the crates again and hustled back toward the cab, thoughts tumbling in her mind. Yes, she was glad the boy wouldn't die, but what would they do with him now? Every option put all of them or at least the boy at risk.

The bay rocked from side to side, the crates groaning with the motion. Good thing the stacks were locked together and crammed in so tight they couldn't tumble and take Kayla with them.

In response to Nishi's hiss, Kayla gave the seycat a warning growl before dropping into the cubby. Her quick, careless squirm through the hatch netted her a scraped elbow. With a kick, she slammed the hatch shut before dropping into the seat beside Risa.

"He's alive," Kayla said.

"You mean, still alive?" Risa asked.

"I mean he's awake, sitting up, and in no real pain," Kayla clarified. "He must not have been hurt as much as it looked at first." Yet he'd looked nearly dead. How could her judgment have been so wrong?

"Chut it." Risa rubbed at her face with one hand. "Big problem, then."

"We can take him back to Beqal," Kayla said. "There's still time to get him back to his Assignment area."

Risa laughed darkly. "Zul checked. Boy's Assignment area isn't Beqal. It's Nitha."

Nitha, nearly a hundred kilometers from Beqal. A roaring started up in Kayla's ears and panic clutched her throat. "A runaway? The boy's a denking runaway?"

Risa nodded. "Zul had Devak check. Boy was pinged four days ago."

Which meant he'd be pinged again in another day, discovered missing, and tracked to the lorry. "What do we do with him?"

Risa was polite enough not to point out that Kayla's impulse had gotten them into this mess. "Devak can push out the next ping another five days. Give us time to drop him in Taq." Taq was a GEN sector next over from Beqal. "Zul can arrange Kinship transport back to Nitha."

"But Devak will need his passkey to change the Grid database," Kayla said. "Which means you'll have to download him."

Kayla knew how to operate a datapod and could have done it. But GENs weren't allowed to use datapods, so it would be stupid to let a non-Kinship GEN like Abran see her handling one.

While Risa looked for a wide enough shoulder to pull the lorry over, Kayla made her way back to Abran, simmering with a mix of irritation at the GEN boy and self-contrition for her part in creating their current crisis. As she climbed down the crates, she blasted him. "Are you so sanaki stupid you didn't think they'd find you on the Grid?"

His eyes widened. "How did you know—"

"The lowborn driver has to protect my patron's interests."

Kayla sat on the crates and faced him, her diminutiveness and his lanky height bringing them nearly eye to eye. "She used your name and ID to check on you."

"How dare you—" He clamped his mouth shut, stopping the flow of words. "I left Nitha three days ago, the day after I'd last been pinged."

"Stop your lying. GENs can't sense a Grid ping."

"I was a few centimeters outside my area that day. Grid tech reported it to my patron, and my patron punished me. Leaving the next day seemed like my best chance to get somewhere safe."

The bay swayed as Risa pulled the lorry over, and Kayla had to grab the crates on either side to stay upright. Still sitting on the floor, Abran flung out his right hand at the bay door to balance himself, banging his wrist on the latch. He sucked in a breath, wincing in pain.

Kayla refused to let herself feel sympathy. "There's nowhere a GEN is safe from the Grid, GEN boy. Sometime tomorrow, they're going to ping you. They'll track your movements back to where you've been since you left Nitha, and then they'll find you here with us."

"The Humane Edicts—"

"—forbid GENs being monitored by the Grid every moment," Kayla said. "Except they do monitor you. And store that data away. They just don't look at it until you go missing."

"But after that explosion, they might think I'm dead," Abran said. "Wouldn't I be safe then?"

"Them *thinking* you're dead won't help you," Kayla said, exasperated by his ignorance. "The Grid will still be monitoring you."

Suddenly, a suspicion sprouted in her mind. She gripped his shoulder hard enough that it had to hurt. "Did you have something to do with that bomb? Is that why they might think you were dead? Did they expect you to kill yourself?"

"They? Who's they? I had nothing to do with the bomb!" He tried to shove her hand away, but she held fast.

Outside, Risa's footsteps approached, crunching in the roadside gravel. Kayla heard a hiss above her and spotted Nishi crouched on top of the crates, her tail whipping.

Sure the seycat would bolt outside the moment the bay door opened, Kayla released Abran and tried to catch the door before it swung too wide. But even though her fingers missed the latch and the door yawned open enough to allow Risa to heave herself inside, Nishi didn't move.

Risa straddled Abran in the small space as she latched the door again. She spied Nishi hunkered down on the crates above. "Seycat's got better sense than me."

Kayla settled back on her crate seat. "Cold outside?"

"Bhimkay." Risa shivered as she shifted to sit beside Kayla. "Already had its prey—wild drom. Lucky."

"They can't get in here, can they?" Abran asked, his voice rough.

Now Kayla saw his face had paled, turning the ruddy color of his skin gray and pasty. She considered a dark joke about leaving him off in the scrap grass and letting him take his chances with the massive spider predator. But Abran looked truly terrified.

"We're safe here," Kayla said.

Risa was the one with the problem. She'd either have to take a stupid risk with the bhimkay by going outside again, or use Kayla's tight route back to the cab.

Kayla tipped her head toward Risa. "We've been talking about the explosion, and why he was there."

"Boy had something to do with it?" Risa asked.

"No!" Abran said.

"So he says."

Abran, trembling, groped for the hem of his shirt. That was where GEN boys tended to keep their prayer mirrors, and he looked to be searching for it.

He glanced up at her. "My prayer mirror. I had it in my hand when the explosion happened."

"I found it," Kayla said. "At least I'm guessing it's yours. Why did you have it out like that?" Most GENs prayed in a safe, private place, to avoid exactly what had happened to Abran—loss of their mirror.

"I was . . . asking the Infinite for His protection."

Risa leaned toward him. "Against the bomb you set?"

"I had nothing to do with it!"

"Still to be proved," Kayla said. "Could be the Infinite didn't grant you protection because you set the explosion."

Abran's dark eyes glittered with frustration. "Why would I stop to send a prayer to the Infinite if I'd just set a bomb nearby? Why wouldn't I have waited and gotten far enough away to be safe?"

"Unless you'd intended to be a martyr," Kayla said.

He threw up his hands. "For what cause? And how the denking hell could a GEN get explosives anyway?"

That, of course, was the sticky point. After the lowborn insurrection thirteen years ago, anything remotely explosive had come under tight trueborn control. A GEN was the least likely to be able to get their hands on the makings of a bomb.

"Still," Kayla reached over and gave his shoulder another little squeeze. "When the lowborn downloads you, it won't just be for your passkey. She'll be pulling everything she can from your annexed brain." For instance if he was connected to the graffiti she'd seen on the warehouse, that could give them clues to the source of those mysterious words.

Risa pulled the datapod from the bandeau around her breasts and held the device pinched between her fingers. Reflexively Abran slapped his hand over his left cheek.

Risa gestured with the datapod. "You know GEN girl here can pin you down. You want that?"

He shook his head and lowered his hand. But still his eyes tracked the datapod as it approached his tattooed cheek. He flinched as the extendibles bit into his skin, a reaction Kayla had finally learned to suppress. Still, he stared cross-eyed down at the device until the last moment when the light turned from green to red. Then his focus went blank as the datapod temporarily took control.

Kayla couldn't suppress a shudder. "I hate downloads."

"Wouldn't like it either, datapod making me black out like that."

"It's not the blacking out. It's the giving over control."

After a few minutes, the green ready light flashed again. An instant later, the datapod fell into Risa's hand. Abran's eyes came alive again, and he gasped in a breath as if he'd been holding it the whole time.

Kayla gestured at the sani-wipes still in his lap. "You'll want to clean the blood off that cheek." The extendibles had left behind six little dots of red.

He fumbled for a sani-wipe with a shaking hand. She felt

a speck of grudging sympathy. Fishing his prayer mirror out from her waistband, she handed it over.

"It's pretty damaged. So scratched up you can hardly see your reflection." Which would make it harder to send the prayers up to the Infinite.

"I don't mind."

After using the mirror to clean his face, he tucked it under his shirt, in the pocket she'd guessed was there. Girls, if they weren't allowed a carrysak, would slip a prayer mirror into their bandeau, or into a pocket in the waistband of their leggings, like Kayla did.

Risa stuffed the datapod away. "Left wristlink in the cab."

She'd use the wristlink to upload whatever data she'd gleaned from Abran. But she'd also want to contact Zul to discuss what happened next with the GEN boy.

Risa rose, using the bay door for balance, and peered up at Nishi. The seycat was perfectly relaxed, licking its front paw.

"Bhimkay's gone," Risa said, unlatching the door.

Abran gasped, shrinking back against the tall stack of crates behind him. He seemed to vibrate with fear as Risa dropped to the ground and latched the door behind her.

"Risa trusts her seycat," Kayla said. "If Nishi doesn't sense a bhimkay, there's no bhimkay nearby." Still, Kayla listened for Risa's retreating footsteps, the sound of the cab door opening and slamming shut.

Abran's hands shook, and his red-brown skin had turned pasty. Being nearly blown up by a bomb hadn't rattled him much, but he'd all but crumpled at the mention of the bhimkay.

Kayla still didn't trust him one iota, but she gave in to an impulse to distract him. "I can make you a new prayer mirror. Risa has some milled metal she uses for repairs. If you polish it, it makes a good mirror. You could get it blessed by an Intercessor later."

"No thank you. My mother gave this one to me."

Mother. Not *nurture* mother. Kayla never referred to Tala as just plain mother. Tala hadn't birthed her, she'd *nurtured* her, far more important. Since Kayla had been trueborn once, she had been birthed. But that woman, Aideen Kalu, meant nothing to Kayla beyond being a name Zul had once mentioned to her, nor did Elana Kalu, the trueborn child Kayla had once been.

How much could the woman who had nurtured Abran mean to him, if he called her only *mother*? Despite his sentimental attachment to the damaged prayer mirror, they couldn't be as close as she and Tala were.

Risa would be learning plenty about Abran from the download, but it couldn't hurt to confirm truth or lies from the boy himself. "Where were you nurtured? What sector?"

Color rose faintly in his cheeks. "In Jassa."

His embarrassment made sense. Even by GEN standards, Jassa, with its muggy heat and prolific vermin, was the most unlivable sector on Svarga continent.

"I've never been to Jassa," Kayla lied, "tell me about it."

His mouth twisted as if in distaste, then he reeled off a description. "Thick with sticker bushes. I lived close to the Sheysa River and we were overrun with sewer toads in the winter and rat-snakes in the summer."

Kayla and Risa had been in eastern Jassa a few months ago when it was still blistering hot. They'd thought to escape the oppressive heat of the lorry cab by camping outside along the Sheysa River. It was just as stifling and they'd had to pick rat-snakes out of their blankets all night long.

But Jassa was legendary. His knowing about it didn't prove anything.

"What's your nurture mother's name?" Kayla asked.

"The lowborn must know it by now from the download."

"I want to hear it from you," Kayla said. "To see how many lies you've told me."

"I'm not lying!"

He said it stoutly enough, but there was a hint of hesitation. How much was truth then, and how much lie?

"You can't stay on this lorry unless we know who you really are." When he still hesitated, she said with exasperation, "Don't you think we know how to ask the question without bringing the Brigade down on us?"

He pulled his knees to his chest and wrapped his arms around them. "My mother is Dieta."

The lorry engine rumbled to life, and the lev-truck eased out onto the highway, rocking as it traveled from gravel shoulder to pavement. If Risa was on the move, that meant she'd uploaded the data to Zul. She couldn't have talked to him yet, though, since not enough time had passed. Did she want Kayla to make the call?

She poked a thumb toward the cab. "The lowborn woman will want me up front. But one last question and you denking well better tell me the truth. Why were you stupid enough to run away from your Assignment in the first place?"

He barely hesitated with his answer. "My patron beats me. With his fists, with a club, whatever is handy. He's burned me too, on my skin and even on the inside by using a shockgun on my tattoo."

Kayla scanned his unmarred face. "How do I know this isn't just a story?"

His cheeks darkened. "I can show you."

Kayla wasn't sure she wanted to see, but she nodded.

He lifted his shirt. Scars, like white worms, crisscrossed the red-brown skin of his chest and belly. Some were as skinny as a bit of rat-snake web, some as wide as that scab on his forehead. The wounds had to have been bad if his circuitry couldn't erase those scars.

"This too," he said. He dropped his shirt and held out his left pinky finger. For the first time, she saw the end jogged outward at the joint. "After he broke it, he wouldn't let the healer straighten it. He said he wanted it to heal that way so I would remember what he'd done."

"But why?" Kayla asked. "Why keep hurting you that way if it could keep you from doing your Assignment?"

"The only thing I'm good at is numbers. My patron has me keep his books on an old sekai. I count things, keep track of stock," Abran said. "As long as I can operate a sekai, his work gets done. But I was afraid he would kill me sooner or later, or hurt me so bad the gene-splicers would take me apart. I had to run."

"Even so," Kayla said with a twinge of regret. "We'll be dropping you in Taq. The lowborn woman knows another driver who can take you back to Nitha."

"No," he all but whispered. "Please, no."

Uneasy with the distress in his face, Kayla climbed the crates and made her way back to the cab. Nishi had already returned to her cubby and she was polite enough to express her displeasure at Kayla's passage with only a hiss. Kayla got back through the hatch without a new claw mark.

As she lowered herself from the sleeper to the cab, a sticker bush, ripped from its roots, rolled across the lorry's path. Risa slammed on the brakes in reflex, although the bush bounced harmlessly up over the nose of the cab, past the windscreen and out of sight. Kayla barely avoided smacking into the dashboard.

"You already scared that boy with your bhimkay story," Kayla said, settling into her seat. "Your driving may finish him."

"Uploaded the data," Risa said, tossing over the wristlink. "You call Zul. Wind's throwing the lorry all over the road."

With the wristlink laid across her left palm, Kayla tapped its screen to wake it. To the unsuspecting eye, the device was a clunky older model a lowborn might typically own. It looked battered and well-worn, maybe a hand-me-down from Risa's mother or father, or she'd scrimped to accumulate enough dhans to buy a used one.

But in reality, the thick four-centimeter square display on the wristlink boasted better resolution than what anyone less than high-status had access to. Despite the scratched and dented case, the wristlink's internals were cutting edge, able to amplify even the weakest network signals out here in the back of beyond.

Kayla pressed in the code for Zul's wristlink. The SEEKING CONNECTION displayed for so long, she wondered if even Risa's high-tech wristlink was foiled by the lack of network out here in the barrens of Nafi sector.

Then the message vanished and the crystal clear display refreshed. Except it wasn't Zul's face on the small screen. It was Devak's.

He seemed stunned for a moment, then something passed across his face she couldn't decipher. He glanced to one side, then back at her. "Sorry, Pitamah left his wristlink behind. I thought I better answer it."

"Is he gone again?" Emotions whipped through her, longing mixed with despair, frustration at her own weakness woven through.

"He's meeting with Councilor Mohapatra, and they're cooking up some kind of plan for that GEN boy."

Devak's image, despite the small screen, was beautifully rendered by the hi-res, from his expressive dark eyes to that perfect kelfa-colored skin. An ache settled in her heart and she wished she could hand the wristlink back to Risa. But as the lorry shook and fishtailed, she knew that wasn't an option.

"Are you okay?" he asked. "I heard about the bombings in Qaf and Beqal."

"We're fine. We were plenty far away. But Abran—the GEN boy—was right in the middle of it."

"I got the passkey and GEN ID Risa sent," Devak said, "and got the GEN boy's next ping extended out. It's all forwarded to Pitamah and the councilor for their meeting."

His tone was neutral and businesslike, but he kept looking away. She thought there might be someone else there, like Junjie, or the lovely trueborn girl Kayla had imagined. But his gaze went everywhere, up, down, left, right.

She burned to know what was running through his mind, but forced herself back to the problem with Abran. "I need to know if what he told me matches what you can find out from his download. He says he was abused."

Now he looked straight at her. "Most GENs are, one way or another."

True as it was, it surprised her to hear him say it. When she'd been Assigned to Devak's family, his mother had never laid a hand on her, but she'd been cruel in other ways, belittling Kayla every chance she got, making clear her disgust at having a GEN in her house.

"In any case, we need to know what to do with him. Drop him off in Taq to have a Kinship driver return him? He can't go to a safe house without being brought into the Kinship. I don't know near enough about him to suggest that."

"I'll have Pitamah pass on what he and Councilor Mohapatra decide." Another glance to the side, then squarely back at her. "Anything else?"

Devak's gaze was so intent, it seemed to burn her. Why was he staring at her that way? Was he that eager to sign off?

Then a message displayed across the bottom of the small screen. Go private?

A mix of dread and anticipation churned in her stomach. She nodded, then glanced over at Risa.

"We're going to talk a while longer," Kayla said, "but I don't want to disturb you. Okay if I take the wristlink into the bay?"

Risa smirked a little. "Yeah, GEN girl."

Kayla scrambled across the bed and through the hatch again. She wedged herself in Nishi's cubby, as far from the seycat as she could get. The feline had apparently become resigned to Kayla's frequent intrusions into her territory and ignored her.

With Risa secure in the cab and Abran at the far end of the bay, Kayla was certain she and Devak wouldn't be overheard. Even so, she kept her voice down.

"What is it?" she asked.

He looked away once more. Kayla would have given anything to have a holo-enhancer on the small wristlink screen that would enlarge the image. But that was one extra the Kinship hadn't seen necessary for Risa's use.

Finally Devak looked back at her. "I've been thinking a lot about what you said at the safe house. I want to apologize for letting things go so long without me talking to you."

His impassive tone, the bland neutrality of Devak's expression pushed the air from Kayla's lungs. She caught herself about to send a foolish prayer up to the Infinite, and squelched the impulse. Not even the Infinite could change a human heart.

"When we were together," Devak went on, "I let myself forget. Who I was. Who you were. How big a gap there is between us."

She couldn't breathe. Too much pain. Too little will.

"But now I'm back in my world again, without you. And I realized we shouldn't really expect anything between us," he said.

"Not even friendship?" Kayla forced herself to say. At least that would be some connection between them.

"Do you really think GENs and high-status trueborns can be friends?" Devak asked.

She wondered if she was bleeding, the way it felt as if her heart had been wrenched from her chest. "I thought I had your respect at least."

Another glance away. "You do. I'm still Kinship. I still want for you . . ." A flicker of misery crossed his face, then vanished. "I know we'll still see each other. Talk to each other. I just didn't want you to think that there was any chance."

"Of course not," she said. "Risa's calling. I have to go."

She shut down the connection, then the wristlink slipped from her nerveless fingers. Dimly she was aware of Nishi pouncing on the device and batting at it like prey. She ought to take it away, but she couldn't move.

She dropped her head in her hands, a knife cutting her throat. Tears pushed themselves free and she sobbed silently, the tears wetting her hands, her face, the plass of the crates.

When she felt Nishi butt against her, she let the creature crawl into her lap. She cried all the harder as she cradled the seycat's purring warmth.

10

Devak stared down at the wristlink in his hand for a long, long time, wishing in spite of himself that Kayla's face would reappear on the screen. He only needed to tap in Risa's number to get her back. But that would defeat the purpose of what he'd just done.

And what purpose is that?

His heart aching, he scanned the close confines of Pitamah's sleeproom, but there were no answers written on the plain white walls, or in his great-grandfather's usual clutter. The room was claustrophobic to Devak, the wind chimes, glass ornaments, stacks of old paper books crammed into an even smaller space than Pitamah's previous room in the Foresthill house.

He couldn't stay there a moment longer. Devak arrowed out the sleeproom door, his hip banging against Pitamah's lev-chair crammed in the corner. Two strides brought him to his own tiny sleeproom where his bed and bedside table took up all the space on one end, and two chairs for the computer took up the other.

Thankfully, the computer's display and keyboard were holographic, the guts of the machine installed within the wall. Otherwise, he really wouldn't be able to turn around. But the room had the same blank walls as Pitamah's, since Devak's mother had taken the valuable woven hangings from their old rooms. The one window was so high, he had to stand on the bed to get a fragment of a view of the Chadi River a quarter-kilometer away.

He flopped back on his bed, still tortured by his conversation with Kayla. It had seemed clear two days ago when he'd dropped off Junjie at the lab. He couldn't stop thinking of Kayla that day, but he couldn't figure out a way to be with her, either. He kept imagining how trueborn society would treat her—with disgust like his mother had, or contempt the way his father had. Or violently like the Brigade would, enforcers dragging her away to be reset.

And it wouldn't be much different once she got restored and became a lowborn. Even marriage between a high-status and a demi-status horrified trueborn society, let alone the unthinkable match of trueborn with lowborn.

So he'd decided he had to let her go. Release her to be with someone more suitable than him. Even if it felt like someone had carved out his heart, it was better this way. Because now she could forget him.

The sound of brisk footsteps across the front porch snapped Devak out of his haze. The front door rattled as the electronic lock released, then he heard Pitamah's familiar tread inside. The living room of the house they shared was barely bigger than the sleeprooms so it would take only seconds for his great-grandfather to reach the front sleeproom. He might wonder where his wristlink was, the one Devak still held tight in his hand.

Denk it, why hadn't he ignored the wristlink's summons? Pretend he hadn't heard?

Devak got slowly to his feet and retraced his steps to Pitamah's room. As he walked in, the old man's gaze strafed him, taking in the wristlink Devak held out. "A call?" Pitamah asked. "Risa, or . . ."

"Kayla," Devak said.

He tried to hide his misery, but it must have been transparent in his face. Sympathy softened Pitamah's eyes. "You finally talked to her."

"For the last time. Unless it's unavoidable Kinship business." Devak slanted a look at his great-grandfather. "It's what you told me I should do."

"I never told you that," Pitamah said. "I only said you should get things straight with her."

"She's a GEN, Pitamah," Devak said, despair making his voice raw. "I don't know what to do about that."

Now his great-grandfather's dark gaze narrowed on him. Devak wasn't sure what that sharp look meant. He didn't see anger or disappointment in Pitamah's eyes, the two emotions Devak dreaded most from his great-grandfather. It wasn't sympathy, either.

Then it hit Devak—Pitamah hadn't left behind his wristlink by accident. He'd meant for Devak to answer it. He'd been prodding Devak to clear things up with Kayla for weeks now. Pitamah knew that Risa would call again about the GEN boy's data and must have hoped that Devak would have asked to talk to Kayla, too.

Of course, his great-grandfather would never admit such a thing. Zul plucked the wristlink from Devak's fingers. "Did you learn anything more?"

Devak wasn't sure if he was relieved or irritated by Pitamah's change of subject. "The boy told her he was abused. That's why he ran."

Pitamah fastened the wristlink to his wrist. The device was snugger than it used to be, back when his great-grandfather was nearly skin and bones. "Does she think Abran should go to a safe house?"

"Become Kinship, you mean?" Devak shook his head. "I don't think she trusts him yet."

Zul nodded. "Kayla has good instincts. The Kinship is lucky to have her."

Those words seemed loaded, adding to the stew of guilt and misgivings inside Devak. Was Pitamah passing judgment on Devak for ending his friendship with Kayla?

As he was working up the courage to ask, Pitamah gestured Devak out of the room. "I need your computer skills." Pitamah strode from his sleeproom toward Devak's.

His great-grandfather's robust gait was still a surprise. As long as Devak could remember, Pitamah had been a weak and unsteady man, bedridden more often than not. Drugs like crysophora would give him a temporary boost, but leave him weaker than ever.

But now Pitamah's lev-chair gathered dust in the corner of his room, even though he'd celebrated his hundred-and-third birthday just last month. Where before he'd hobbled and struggled to walk—if he even had the strength to stand—now he marched. His great-grandfather's new treatment these past few weeks had given him not only strength, but seemed to have added years to his life.

"Are we hacking the Grid database?" Devak brushed his fingertips against one of the holo projection boxes jutting from the wall of his room. A display flickered to life.

"The GEN Assignment database. Councilor Mohapatra is going to steal Abran from his current patron."

That brought Devak up short, his fingers hovering over the activation panel of the holographic keyboard. "Can he do that? Won't he get censured by the Assignment specialists or Social Benevolence?"

"I know Abran's patron. Cruel doesn't begin to describe Ehimay Baadkar. He's killed more than one GEN Assigned to him. Two GENs brave enough to report him ended up reset, realigned, and Assigned elsewhere. That's discouraged any others from speaking up."

"So if Councilor Mohapatra transfers Abran's Assignment—"

"Baadkar won't dare say a word," Pitamah said. "He's been under Judicial investigation for his cruelty not only to GENs, but even minor-status trueborns in his employ. We'd only need to show the Judicial Council Abran's scars and Baadkar could have his other GENs confiscated."

His computer ready, Devak seated himself in one of the room's two chairs. Pitamah stayed standing, looming over Devak's shoulder.

The system installed in Devak's sleeproom wall wasn't cutting edge, but the software it ran was. Using it, Devak could look up GEN data in the Assignment database or hack into the monitoring Grid to track tankborn locations. His access limited him to the Central Western and Southwest territories, but that encompassed everything south of the Plator river clear to the southern coast of Svarga continent. Because he knew how to decrypt and re-encrypt the data, the Assignment and Grid computers accepted Devak's input as if it had come from a legitimate tech.

Devak readied one of the computer's data ports. "Where will the GEN boy go after his Assignment is transferred? To the councilor's household?"

"He'll stay with Risa. Work with her and Kayla on the lorry. We want to keep him under Kinship control, use him as a witness when we bring judgment against Baadkar."

Devak's stomach twisted at the thought of the boy staying with Kayla. "How long will that be?"

"A few weeks, perhaps as long as a month," Pitamah said, pressing his wristlink against the computer's data port. "We're lucky the boy fell into our lap like this. Baadkar is one of the worst, and if we can get judgment against him, we think we can start really changing things from the inside. Change the whole trueborn culture of excusing abusive treatment of GENs."

"But how can Risa and Kayla continue their mission with Abran underfoot? He's not Kinship."

Pitamah's dark gaze felt like a spear in Devak's gut. "And so he's not worthy of being saved from abuse?"

Devak's cheeks heated. "Of course he is. That's not what I meant."

Pitamah stared at him another long moment, then said, "They'll have to be careful. Stay out of the safe houses. We'll try to get the word out that Risa's lorry is no longer a haven for the Scratch-infected. For the time being, keeping Abran with them is their mission."

As the wristlink finished uploading, the display flashed with what Risa had sent. Armed with Abran's designator ID, passcode, nurture mother's name, and home sector, Devak initiated a search for the GEN boy's record.

Abran's GEN record popped up on the holographic screen. He was a seventeenth-year, and his current Assignment was his first according to the record. In the looped animated image of the boy included in the record, Abran turned to his right to expose his left cheek, pausing there so someone with a sekai could scan his tattoo from the screen and learn basic information about him.

Abran was good-looking, never mind that his red-brown skin was the wrong shade. Devak gave himself a mental poke. What did skin color matter in a GEN? Then the poke became a kick. Why did skin color matter so much to him anyway?

"The councilor's GEN account information should have uploaded with Risa's data," Pitamah said.

Devak scanned the display, using swipes of his fingers across the holo screen to transfer Abran's GEN record from Baadkar's account to the councilor's. An acknowledgement message popped up declaring the transfer was complete.

Pitamah tapped a call code into his wristlink. "Vagish will want to know it's been done."

While Pitamah paced the hall, speaking to Councilor Mohapatra, Devak watched the image of Abran on the holo-screen. The GEN boy's face turned slowly, over and over, showing the tattoo, then returning to stare directly from the screen. There was a rebellious look to those dark eyes that reminded Devak of Kayla.

The full significance of this boy traveling with Kayla struck Devak. Abran was good-looking and a GEN. There was nothing like status blocking an alliance between him and Kayla. And why shouldn't they become close, two young GENs thrown together like that? Wasn't that what GENs did, crowded together in their warrens, uncomplicated couplings without concern for status or pregnancy?

The nastiness of that last thought burned in Devak's gut. Shame warmed his face, and he turned away as Pitamah returned so his great-grandfather wouldn't see the color likely staining his cheeks.

Pitamah didn't seem to notice as he sagged into the second chair. For the first time in a long time, Devak realized his great-grandfather looked tired, a gray pallor bleaching his skin.

"I'm afraid I've over-estimated my energy level," Pitamah said in response to Devak's concern. "I was scheduled for another treatment this afternoon, but then this business with Abran came up. I don't like asking you to drive me to the lab, when it was my own foolishness that put me in this state."

"I'll take you," Devak said. "Junjie has been bugging me to share a meal with him. We can go to one of the lowborn Houses for dinner while the medics give you your treatment."

Devak would have helped his great-grandfather to his feet, but Pitamah waved him off. He'd never liked needing assistance all those years he was so infirm. Now that he had a hope of a normal life, even at his advanced age, it had to be especially bitter to take his great-grandson's hand.

Pitamah walked carefully, Devak hovering beside him,

using the excuse of his wristlink call to Junjie to explain his slow pace. His great-grandfather made it without mishap to the AirCloud parked in its carport. Not even a closed garage here at their Two Rivers home, so anyone who drove by could see the old lev-car with its dented, faded finish. It irritated Devak that he still cared about such a trivial thing.

The skyway cut directly across the Central Western Territory to southern Plator sector, at its highest point traversing that territory's adhikar land. Central Western had the second largest stretch of adhikar after Southeast, the irrigated parcels comprising a fifth of the territory. Swaths of vivid green kel-grain fields alternated with scrap grass pastures filled with droms, the genetically engineered versions towering over the few wild cousins that shared the grazing.

He and Pitamah owned similar adhikar land in the Southwestern Territory, just enough acreage to maintain their high-status rank. A team of lowborns managed the drom herds and kel-grain fields, most of them Kinship and paid under the table by others to conserve Devak's and Pitamah's meager funds.

They reached the far edge of the expanse of adhikar and crossed into south Plator. Devak took the first exit, piloting the lev-car in a lazy arc as the roadway circled back on itself. Before they dropped completely to street level, Devak spotted a Jahaja backing up to the rear of the genetics lab where Junjie worked. The bhimkay emblem of the Brigade gleamed in black and red on the sides of the multi-lev.

There weren't any empty lev-car docks close in to the lab, so Devak dropped off Pitamah near the door before searching for a place to dock the AirCloud. There had been a time when the Manels could have arranged a reserved space for two or three lev-cars down in the lab's underground parking so they would never be inconvenienced. No more.

But maybe that was just as well, Devak thought as he hunched his shoulders against the encroaching chill of late afternoon. If he could attach such importance to as minuscule a thing as a prime docking slot, maybe he needed to do some soul-searching to figure out the kind of person he'd let himself become.

Junjie was waiting out front, grinning and waving as if Devak might miss him otherwise. "Zul already went in," Junjie said as he ushered Devak inside. "It's early yet for dinner. The curry house I wanted to take you to doesn't open for a couple hours. Want a tour of the lab?"

"I thought I wasn't allowed to see the labs," Devak said.

Junjie shrugged. "We'll skip the confidential stuff. But I can show you where I work."

A guard was seated out front, a minor-status trueborn woman with short frizzy hair and what looked like a perpetual scowl. She took Devak's name and locked a visitor tag to his left wrist. Junjie explained the tag would allow him to pass through certain sections of the building, but would set off alarms if he entered a forbidden area.

Just as they were about to step through the security door, the front door opened and Junjie nudged Devak back out of the way with a none too gentle elbow. The guard beamed at the newcomer. "Garud-Mar. Good morning."

The man was clearly high-status, with his perfect skin tone and neatly trimmed black hair, his understated navy uttama-silk korta and chera pants. But as the man turned toward Devak and Junjie with idle curiosity, Devak was shocked to see the man's bali earring. If he was high-status, it should have been a diamond, but the man wore a large demi-status emerald.

The man held the security door open for them, his lean, handsome face serious but not unfriendly. Once Junjie had the door, the man went inside, then Junjie entered with Devak following, an upside-down procession since Devak was the most high-status of the three. Past the security door a long hallway stretched to the back of the building with doors on either side.

Devak waited until the man had gotten ahead of them, then whispered, "Who is that?"

"Akhilesh Garud," Junjie murmured. "He's head of GAMA. The one who designed Zul's treatments. And the one we all work for."

Devak gestured at his right ear. "Why is he—"

Junjie shushed him. Akhilesh stepped inside a door halfway down the hall. Junjie exhaled in a rush, as if he'd been holding his breath. He started down the hall, leading the way.

Devak followed, persisting with his question. "Why is he demi-status? He's got high-status looks."

"Family scandal," Junjie said. "An ancestor who might have been minor-status."

As he passed each lab, Junjie named off the techs who worked inside, some of them gene-splicers working on GEN modifications, some medic-engineers working on treatments like what Pitamah was receiving that day. The doors were all solid, so Devak couldn't see into the labs Junjie identified. He wasn't sure he wanted to.

"The Scratch-infected GENs they bring here, are some of them still alive?" Devak asked.

"Yeah." Junjie stopped at a door four down from where

Akhilesh went in. A tiny nameplate on the wall read GURU LIANG LING. "I've been told there are beds upstairs for them. That they're medicated for pain. I've never seen them though."

"What happens when they die?"

Junjie made a face. "Akhilesh and his crew experiment. They say it's to study the disease, but the rumor is they use the GEN tissue after to make new GENs."

"Couldn't that end up making more GENs with Scratch?"

Junjie shook his head. "They sterilize it. Test it a hundred times over." He made another face. "They wouldn't want to waste all that effort making a GEN."

"Why are they the ones experimenting with Scratch victims over there?" Devak asked. "I thought you and Guru Ling were the only ones working on a Scratch cure."

Junjie pushed open the lab door. "Something about cross-contamination. I don't get it either. It's like they care so little about the GENs they don't care if Scratch is ever cured." Junjie gestured around the cramped lab. "This is it. Scratch central."

It wasn't much to look at. A bank of microscopes along one wall, one of them with a magnified holographic image floating above it. Clear plasscine beakers and concave dishes covered a countertop, some of them half-filled with oddly colored liquids and gooey substances. No windows, so harsh illuminators lit the room.

"Guru Ling is busy in her office," Junjie said, pointing to a closed door. "I'll have to introduce you to her another time. She's the best. Stern, but just crazy smart."

Junjie dragged Devak over to a cluttered desk jammed into a corner. "Where genius happens." Junjie spread his arms to encompass the cramped space. "Which reminds me."

Junjie swung into his chair and activated his computer. He tapped away at the holographic keyboard, then dug a datapod from his chera pocket that he fit into the physical interface. Images popped up on the screen, two graphs, side by side. The title across the top read *DNA Analysis—Subject A, Subject B.*

"What's that?" Devak asked.

"That GEN girl's DNA profile," Junjie said. "Gemma."

"And whose is the other one?" Devak didn't have the expertise in DNA that Junjie had, but he could see the two graphs were entirely different.

"That's just it," Junjie said. "Both of those are Gemma's. Or rather, I guess one is Gemma's and one of them is Gabrielle's, the other personality in Gemma's brain. Except it isn't just another personality upload. It's actual double DNA."

"You can tell all that from her passkey?" Devak asked. He knew a lot of information was encoded in that twenty-digit number, but to be able to find two DNA profiles in one passkey seemed hard to believe.

Junjie shook his head. "When Coria took Gemma to a safe house, she got a DNA sample and brought it to me."

"Is it really possible for the gene-splicers to build her with two entirely different DNA profiles?" Devak asked, although the answer was right there in front of them.

"They use animal DNA in GENs, why not other human DNA?"

"But why would they," Devak asked, "when it obviously causes her problems?"

Junjie made a face. "I don't think most gene-splicers care much about GEN problems." He cleared the screen, then snatched out the datapod and tucked it away in his pocket again.

"Could . . ." Devak had to force himself to ask the question. "Could my father be involved? Could it be something like what he did before with the lowborn children?"

"The children only had circuitry installed," Junjie said. "Their DNA wasn't jiggered like this GEN girl's was. I can't see what Ved or anyone else could gain by messing up a GEN like this."

That was true. Gemma's double personality had been confusing enough for the poor GEN girl. Who knew what the mix of DNA could be doing to her body?

"Was it just careless work, then?" Devak asked. "Could it have been a black-market gene-splicer who messed up a reset on a stolen GEN?"

Junjie considered, then nodded slowly. "Might be. It would make sense that she would just be dumped."

While Devak tried to wrap his mind around Junjie's revelations, his wristlink beeped. Devak read the text on the screen. "It's Pitamah. There's something the medic wants to go over for after his treatment."

"He'll be in the genetics lab," Junjie said, "where Akhilesh went in. I can take you over—"

"Junjie!" Guru Ling poked her head out of her office, her sharp demi-status features reminiscent of Junjie's. "I need you." She vanished back into her office, seemingly oblivious to Devak's presence.

"I remember where to go," Devak said to Junjie. "Fourth door on the right."

He stepped out and started down the hall. At the fourth door, he reached for the latch, but although it clicked in response to his tag, it didn't release. Devak tried a couple more times, then finally knocked.

A muffled voice called through the door, "Just a minute. In the middle of something."

While he waited, a noise down the hall past Guru Ling's lab caught Devak's attention. Instinct prompted him to press himself nearly out of sight into the doorway to Akhilesh's lab. At the far end of the hall, two enforcers emerged in the stairwell, no doubt coming up from the underground parking area. They carried a burden between them.

They were too busy angling their load up to the next flight of stairs to notice Devak. He nearly gasped when he realized what the enforcers were carrying.

A body. A GEN body, from the faint glitter of a tattoo on the left cheek. Devak could see the angry marks of Scratch on the pale skin of the man's face and arms. Considering the careless way the enforcers knocked the GEN into the railing as they made the turn at the landing, the man must be dead.

The enforcers disappeared upstairs with the body. Devak's curiosity drove him from his hiding place, hurried him down the hall to the stairwell. He hid out of sight until the enforcers reached the second floor and stepped out of sight again. Then he climbed the stairs two at a time, treading as quietly as he could.

When he got to the second floor and could take a look, he spotted the enforcers three doors down the hall. The man holding the GEN's feet dropped them and waved his wrist at the door. The lock release clicked, but the handle wouldn't turn. The other enforcer swiveled the GEN around, then waved his wrist at the lock. No luck, same as when Devak had tried to open Akhilesh's door. Maybe the whole security system was down.

The enforcer holding the dead GEN's shoulders muttered something about the chutting lock and gave the door an angry kick. When no one answered, the enforcer unceremoniously let go of his load, and the body hit the floor with a dull thud.

The enforcer's callousness sickened Devak. The GEN man might be dead, but his body should be treated with dignity.

Devak took a step from his hiding place, intending to use his high-status rank to chew out the disrespectful minor-status enforcer. Then something stopped him in his tracks.

The GEN groaned, his eyes fluttering open. *He was still alive.*

The shock hit Devak's belly with a wave of nausea. It rooted him to the ground as the door finally opened and the enforcers shoved the suffering GEN through.

As the door started to swing shut, Devak ran down the hall. He caught the door noiselessly with the toe of his shoe.

Carefully, he edged the door open enough to see. Junjie had said there were beds for GEN Scratch victims who were brought in still alive. Maybe that was why the enforcers had brought him here, however brutishly. But Devak could only see banks of scientific equipment—microscopes, surgical lasers, and computer arrays more numerous and complex than what his father used to use for the Monitoring Grid. Maybe the beds were on the other end, hidden by the door.

Devak pushed the door open a little farther to get a better look. The two enforcers were stripping the GEN man of his clothes, leaving him in only his skivs on the plasscrete floor. A tech, a minor-status dark-skinned woman, bent to apply a datapod to the GEN's cheek, which meant he still clung to life. You couldn't upload or download a dead GEN. You had to use other methods to extract the data in a deceased GEN's annexed brain.

The tech poked and prodded the GEN's tattoo, searching for a Scratch-free place to apply the datapod. The tech's fumbling must have hurt the GEN, because his eyes widened, his head jerking from side to side as he scanned the room. Maybe he was seeking his god, the Infinite.

The man's gaze finally fell on Devak. The GEN mouthed silent words, *Help me*. Then he convulsed, a brief ugliness before lying motionless, his half-open eyes unseeing.

As the tech tossed the datapod on a nearby workstation in disgust, she spied Devak. "What the denking hell are you doing here?"

In for a half-dhan, in for a dhan. Devak pushed the door open and stepped inside. "I'm lost."

He took a quick look around. At the end where he'd thought the beds might be placed were rows and rows of gen-tanks, and in several of them Scratch-marred GENs floated. Tubes crisscrossed their bodies, leading out of the tank to a clear box filled with pale yellow liquid. The GENs were motionless—sedated? Was that yellow liquid an experimental treatment for Scratch?

One of the enforcers left off manhandling the GEN and confronted Devak. "You don't belong in here." The enforcer had a hand on his shockgun, but as he noted Devak's diamond bali, he dipped his head. "Young mar, you'll have to leave."

"Sorry, wrong room," Devak said. "I was looking for Akhilesh's lab."

An impatient voice at the door claimed Devak's attention. "There you are." A pale-skinned minor-status woman in a medic's tunic gestured out to the hall. "Your great-grandfather is downstairs."

"Sorry." Devak took a last look at the bank of gen-tanks, the peculiar yellow liquid, then followed the medic.

The minor-status woman led him back down the stairs, then to the fourth door down. Inside this first floor lab, Devak saw that as head of GAMA, Akhilesh was far more well-funded than Guru Ling. His lab was quadruple the size of the one in which Junjie worked, and bustling with techs. There was even more equipment than he'd seen upstairs, workstations along the walls and in the middle of the room, with comfortable-looking float chairs for the techs.

Akhilesh glanced over at Devak and nodded in greeting, then returned his focus on something a tech had up on a computer display. Devak could see some of the same colorful DNA patterns Junjie had been showing him, but from that distance it was impossible to make out any details.

The medic nudged Devak toward the curtains on the left side of the lab. "In here," she said curtly, all but pushing Devak behind the curtain.

Pitamah lay in a reclining float chair, his eyes closed. The medic blathered on about being careful with his great-grandfather on the trip home, that he should insist on Pitamah getting some rest and a good night's sleep. Devak only listened with half an ear since his great-grandfather would do what he wanted, medic's instructions or no.

Finally the woman left, and Devak leaned close to Pitamah, whispering, "Are you awake?"

Pitamah's eyes slitted open. "Barely. Haven't got a denking bit of strength left."

"They brought in a Scratch victim. Still alive." He explained how he'd followed the enforcers to the second floor and what he'd seen.

His great-grandfather's gaze sharpened on his. "Could you tell if the ones in the tanks were alive?"

He thought back to that sickening view of a dozen or more tank-bound GENs, their bodies filled with tubes. "Why put a dead GEN in the tank?"

"To experiment, I suppose," Pitamah said. "I don't like it either, but we need GAMA's help in tracking down a Scratch cure. Our friends can't do it all." Pitamah had taken to using coded language whenever he couldn't speak openly of the Kinship.

"So there aren't beds for the Scratch victims who are brought in alive?" Devak asked.

Pitamah's gaze hardened. "That's why we bring as many as we can to safety." His great-grandfather squeezed Devak's shoulder weakly. "I've spoken to Akhilesh about his treatment of GENs, and he swears he's working to improve the way his staff handles them."

"You couldn't tell that from what I saw upstairs."

"Akhilesh doesn't command the Brigade," Pitamah said. "But he does do a great deal of good. My treatment. Research to ensure healthier GENs, including finding a cure for Scratch."

Except according to Junjie, Guru Ling was the only scientist working on that. But maybe Junjie didn't know everything that was going on in here or upstairs.

Pitamah drifted off to sleep just as Junjie came looking for Devak. "That curry house should be open."

Devak glanced at his great-grandfather. "Should I leave him?"

"He usually sleeps a couple hours after a treatment," Junjie said.

Devak could see the logic in that, so he and Junjie headed out. The curry house was close enough it wasn't worthwhile to unplug the AirCloud from its dock to drive. So they walked, dodging heavy vehicle and pedestrian traffic as lowborns and minor-status trueborns headed home from work. The moment passersby, trueborn or lowborn, saw Devak's diamond bali, they gave him plenty of space on the walkway. Junjie they jostled against, even one or two lowborns bumping against Devak's friend.

Devak told Junjie what he saw upstairs. About the GEN who'd died right in front of him.

"That's Akhilesh's main lab, where the real work gets done," Junjie said. "I know he's been sequencing Scratch up there, seeing if there's a genetic component. Something to explain why some GENs get it and others don't. Why lowborns and trueborns seem immune."

"Then he is helping with a cure." Devak body blocked a lowborn from barreling into Junjie.

"More like he's studying it to death," Junjie said. "Guru Ling is actually testing vaccines."

The curry house was packed, but when the lowborn owner saw Devak's diamond bali, he booted out two customers who'd barely finished their meal to offer up their seat. The place was steaming with body heat despite the chill outside, redolent with cinnamon and cumin. Devak splurged, choosing a bowl of curry with thinly sliced prime-grade drom and a scoop of rice. He would have paid for the same for Junjie, but his friend insisted he preferred curried vegetables and kel-grain.

Stomachs full with good curry and plenty of hot tea, they made their way back through quieter streets to the lab. Junjie cradled a box of gulab jamun, a favorite of his that Devak had insisted on buying.

Pitamah was waiting in GAMA's lobby, so Devak returned his visitor tag and said good-bye to Junjie there. Pitamah's energy had improved, so he walked to the AirCloud rather than Devak bringing it around.

As they drove past the lab on their way to the skyway, Devak got a glimpse of someone just arriving at the GAMA lab. As they continued on, Pitamah turned in his seat to look back. "Is that Hala?"

Hala was one of his great-grandfather's old friends from back when GENs were first engineered. Hala was Kinship, and along with the old medic Jemali, had helped rescue the lowborn children who'd had GEN circuitry installed in them through Devak's father's despicable scheme.

Pitamah settled back against his seat. "What business would Hala have with GAMA, I wonder?"

Then his great-grandfather fell asleep again, leaving Devak to brood over what he'd seen on the second floor.

11

Just as Junjie turned from giving Devak a final wave goodbye, Hala Hamia creakily pulled open the GAMA lobby door and stepped inside. The guard, Deha, smiled at the elderly high-status trueborn, even as she scowled at Junjie. Junjie suspected that Deha, minor-status like him, resented his higher-paying, more respected position as a genetic tech. She liked to make Junjie wait before she'd buzz him through the security door.

But with Hala here, she quickly snapped a bracelet with its visitor tag around the old man's wrist, then hit the door's release button. Tucking the carton of gulab jamun under his arm, Junjie jumped to open the heavy inner door. He stepped aside as Hala walked through, then proceeded slowly behind the old man as he walked to the last door on the left. Junjie waited a few more moments to make sure Hala gained entry to Akhilesh's private office, then he entered Guru Ling's lab.

Junjie heaved a sigh of relief once he was in his familiar workplace. He always felt so awkward around high-status trueborns. Except for Devak, of course, who Junjie had known since they were second-years rolling around in the mud together. But even when his family had been demi-status, Junjie never quite knew what to say or how to act around high-status like Zul and Hala and Jemali. In a way, they seemed almost god-like by comparison to someone as lowly as himself.

Junjie returned to his computer, setting the carton aside on his workstation. He should have been done for the day, but he wanted to spend a little more time puzzling out Gemma's dual identity. Plus he had the call to make once Guru Ling left, and this lab was the most secure place he could make it.

Junjie found a clean Petri dish and served himself one of the small, syrupy dough balls from the carton of gulab jamun. It had been hard to let Devak pay for dinner and this small treat, but it also wouldn't have been fair to his friend *not* to take the gift. Devak never lorded his status over Junjie. Sometimes he'd let slip his dismay that Junjie was now minor-status, like the day of the Qaf sector explosion. But that was more Devak seeing injustice in Junjie's fall.

Still, he wondered if someday even Devak, once he grew older and became as exalted as the adult high-status trueborns Junjie knew, would let their friendship fade. Junjie was surprised Devak hadn't abandoned him already. But their connection still seemed strong.

One overly-sweet gulab jamun was all Junjie could manage, so he took the other three to Guru Ling's office. She was packing up to leave, her expression preoccupied but not overtly unfriendly, the way the security guard Deha's always was. Usually, with her brilliant mind and brusque manner, Guru Ling reminded him of his father, dead more than a decade. Now, with her long black hair loose from its braid, the messy strands and her clear exhaustion softening her face, he could nearly see his mother.

"Would you like to take the rest?" Junjie asked, opening the carton to show her.

She shook her head. "Thank you, but too sweet for me. Garud-mar enjoys them."

Akhilesh might be demi-status through happenstance, but he scared Junjie just as much as any high-status. Still, it couldn't hurt to take him an offering. That would give Guru Ling time to be well and truly gone, and Junjie would be alone for his call.

They departed the lab together, Guru Ling turning left toward the entrance and Junjie right toward Akhilesh's office. Junjie turned to watch her go, wondering not for the first time if Guru Ling used pub-trans because she didn't *want* a lev-car, or because, like Junjie, she couldn't *afford* one. She might be minor-status like Junjie, but she deserved enough salary to buy at least a used AirCloud or WindSpear.

Junjie heard the rumble of conversation and realized the door to Akhilesh's office was ajar. That made it a little easier. It would have been more intimidating to knock on a closed door.

Junjie lifted his hand to tap at the door, when Hala's words froze him. "These are *adult* GENs whose cells you're altering? Not the under-fours?"

Akhilesh's answer was an inaudible buzz. He must have been on the other side of the room, maybe behind his desk.

Hala spoke again. "And these have been successful changes?"

As Akhilesh's voice blurred again, Junjie remembered his

datapod. He'd installed a tiny amplifier and receiver in it, handy both for gathering gossip for the Kinship and for his other compatriots.

Junjie dug the datapod from his pocket, thumbed on the amp/receiver, and held it up close to his ear. Hala's voice would be too loud, but now Junjie could hear Akhilesh.

". . . several trials," the GAMA head said. "Some failures, but it's to be expected."

"And you're using upload programming?" Hala blasted out. "Not the tank?"

Upload programming to alter GEN genetics. Junjie was so astounded by that revelation, he nearly missed Akhilesh's response.

"With the problems we've encountered creating and gestating GEN embryos, we need a reproducible method to repurpose adult GENs, to alter their skill sets when possible to address critical needs. In fact, we're considering re-engineering selected GENs . . ." Akhilesh's words faded out, and for a moment Junjie feared his device had failed. But then the GAMA head continued, his voice taking on a dramatic flair. ". . . to allow them to reproduce."

Junjie couldn't suppress a gasp, but luckily, Hala had responded with the same surprise, and neither Hala nor Akhilesh seemed to have heard Junjie's inadvertent slip. Junjie looked around the hall just to make sure once again that he was still alone.

"Can it be done?" Hala asked, excitement clear in his tone. It was well-known amongst the Kinship that Hala fervently wanted GENs to have the freedom and ability to procreate.

"I believe it can, and must, if we are to keep the GEN

supply steady," Akhilesh said. "Unfortunately, there's been a problem with my most promising subject."

"What kind of problem?" Hala asked. "Surely it's something solvable."

"Ah, well." Akhilesh cleared his throat. "The GEN girl was in the midst of alterations. She'd volunteered, mind you, expected changes. But agitation was a side effect of one stage of the treatment. She panicked one night when she was alone in the lab and slipped out. Sadly, she's not only gone missing, but I've heard from sources she may have contracted Scratch."

"Oh, dear." Hala sighed heavily. "Then there's no hope for her."

"There may still be if we can find her quickly enough," Akhilesh said. "I understand the Scratch infection is recent, so we might still be able to counteract it. We've made recent strides in our experimental vaccines."

"Surely you can locate her via the Grid," Hala said.

"We . . . ah . . . had her temporarily removed for the course of the experiment," Akhilesh said. "Stupid now in retrospect, but the pings were interfering with our uploads. Our last visual report from the Brigade told us she's been traveling with the allabain, although they hustled her away before she could be returned to safety. The allabain mistrust trueborns and they dislike the Brigade even more, so extricating her from them will be difficult."

"Then we send a lowborn out to search for her," Hala said, his raspy old voice bright with enthusiasm. "I know exactly the person to ask."

"You would be doing a tremendous service not only to trueborn society but to GENs too."

"Yes," Hala said. "I've never agreed with GEN sterility. They deserve to procreate as much as any trueborn or lowborn."

Junjie's jaw dropped at Hala's passionate statement. It was no surprise that he held that position, but to state it so blatantly outside a Kinship meeting seemed terribly risky.

After a long moment of silence, Akhilesh finally spoke again. "I forget sometimes that you were involved at the beginning, Hala. I suppose you can be forgiven your . . . eccentric views. But I would truly appreciate your help. We do have someone else out in the field, but thus far that hasn't borne fruit. Here, come take a look at this."

They moved farther away from the door, likely to Akhilesh's computer system that was installed in the back corner of his office. Junjie might have been able to increase the gain on his amplifier and still hear them, but the need to make his call pressed on him, especially with this new information in his possession.

He took the carton of gulab jamun back to the lab with him. He'd take them home, give them to his auntie. She liked them well enough.

Activating the security lock on the door so he would get a few extra seconds' warning before someone entered, Junjie tapped out the call code on his wristlink. The person answering used audio only, their secrecy too tight to let a field agent like him become familiar with the faces at headquarters.

"Yeah, s'me," Junjie said. "Is she there?"

"Yes," the boy responded, all business. "I can get her for you."

"Thank you."

There was a long pause and Junjie figured the boy had left.

But then he asked, "How have you been?" in that familiar warm and friendly tone that Junjie liked.

"Good, thanks. How about you?"

"Fine," the boy said.

Another silence stretched and Junjie hoped the boy would say a few more words, but this time it seemed he'd gone off to find *her*. Junjie sighed, wishing the boy would at least give his name. But none of them did, including *her*. Junjie had taken to calling her Neta—"leader."

Whoever Neta was, Junjie knew she was important. He knew she and her compatriots were taking Loka in the right direction in spite of some of their methods.

While Junjie waited, he rolled around in his mind what Akhilesh had said. Not about GENs being allowed to have babies, but the other part—about using upload programming to change genetics.

That part was far too close for comfort. He should be letting the Kinship know about the conversation too, not just his other compatriots. But he didn't like what that use of upload programming might reveal. He'd decided months ago which loyalty superseded which, and it wasn't the Kinship that won out.

So he wouldn't be telling Devak or Zul what he'd heard, despite a stab of guilt for not confiding in Devak at least. Maybe he'd get permission to share it all later.

The boy's voice interrupted his thoughts. "Here she is."

"Junjie," Neta said in the cultured tones of a trueborn. "What do you have for us?"

He gave his report, not leaving out a single detail.

12

Abran!" Kayla shouted across the loading dock, "Lock down those crates!"

Abran, halfway back to Peq sector's foodstores warehouse, made an abrupt about-face and raced back to the lorry. He got into the bay just in time to catch the stack of crates as it started to sway. He palmed the magnetic catches on the top two crates he'd just loaded. The tower steadied into place.

He grinned at Kayla as he hopped back out of the lorry bay. "That was close."

Abran had a habit of using that brilliant smile to squeak his way out of trouble. Surprisingly, it worked with Risa, since it turned out Abran bore a faint resemblance to the son she and Kiyomi had fostered. But for Kayla, her mistrust of him built a sturdy wall between them and made her immune to his seemingly irresistible good looks.

She grabbed Abran's arm as he started past her, using enough of her strength in her grip to be sure he was paying attention. "You will denking well lock those latches down on the crates before you walk away. If any of that kel-grain gets scattered and spoiled, it's me and Risa who take the heat."

Abran gave her a dark look. "I forgot, once."

"It's not the first time, Abran," Kayla said. "You know how many times Risa or I have had to follow behind you these past two weeks, fixing your mistakes? And with a sket like yours, a brain-worker, I would have expected better."

His jaw worked, resentment flickering in his eyes. "I'll be more careful."

"And you'll do your share," Kayla said. "I don't expect you to carry what I do, but I want you ready to work when we are."

"I was only gone five minutes," Abran protested.

"That was five minutes too long," Kayla snapped.

She knew she was being unfair. He'd asked to hop out of the lorry just as Risa was about to turn into the alley that ran along the warehouse. Kayla had thought he wanted a public washroom since he seemed to feel so awkward sharing the lorry's small unit with two women.

But instead he managed to find a pretty young GEN girl with near-high-status color skin selling sweet kel-grain bread. No doubt he'd gotten his pastry just on the force of that smile of his and kept the quarter-dhans Risa had been paying him in his pocket.

"So while we were working, you were eating," Kayla said.

"I was right behind you when you were carrying your first crates," he pointed out.

"You jiks!" Risa shouted from the back of the lorry. "Chut on your own time. Get back to work."

Risa was only putting on an act, using the coarse word to make her anger seem more real for Abran's sake. But Abran didn't know that. His cheeks turned darker, and when he flicked a glance over at Kayla, she could see his unease.

It made sense that a GEN boy as good-looking as Abran wouldn't be interested in a drab-colored girl like her. That still stung, despite her disinterest in him.

Except for Devak. But that had never made sense. And now she understood that it had never been real in the first place.

Sweet Infinite, her heart still felt in a million pieces after the conversation with Devak. Having an outsider like Abran here just made matters worse. His presence complicated everything. She couldn't use the wristlink. She couldn't go to safe houses. She and Risa had to watch every word they said.

Zul had effectively put their mission on hold while they babysat Abran. Yet again, he had made a pronouncement, and Kayla and Risa had to deal with the consequences.

It didn't help that Risa had taken to Abran so quickly, when it had been weeks before the lowborn woman lost her dislike of Kayla. Kayla knew Risa didn't trust Abran any more than she did, but Risa *liked* him nevertheless.

And it wasn't just Risa. Every GEN female they came across in their travels, from a thirteenth-year to a thirtieth-year, seemed to fall in love with Abran the moment he directed that brilliant smile on them.

But Kayla sensed something behind that ready smile, those good looks and easy charm—a hollowness, a darkness. Likely that sprang from the mistreatment by his patron, and she ought to be sympathetic. But intuition—or maybe the Infinite's own voice—told her to be cautious.

They resumed their mindless work, toting crates from warehouse to lorry, the dampness of a sullen mist soaking their clothes and chilling their skin. The work warmed them, but nothing, not even GEN circuitry, could dry the soddenness from their rough duraplass rain gear.

Since she was keeping her eye on him, she realized Abran shivered quite a bit as he worked. She'd also noticed it when they'd started loading, but she'd been cold at first too. Did he not want to utilize his GEN circuitry to warm himself? Some GEN boys were like that, insisting they were tougher than the cold, or pain. They considered using the circuitry the easy way out and would instead gut it out through discomfort. And since Kayla could out-lift Abran almost four-to-one, he probably was looking for a way to prove himself.

At least after her scold, Abran managed to finish the rest of the loading without forgetting to lock crates in place. Kayla didn't take that on faith, assuring herself that not only were the magnetic locks on the crates in each tower engaged, but each tower was locked to the next, and adjacent walls of crates were securely fastened to each other.

Despite her lecture about spoiling kel-grain, they'd all tracked a fair amount of kernels across the loading dock. With all the spillage in the warehouse, it was impossible to avoid picking up kernels in the soles of their shoes. Trueborns didn't waste the sealed plasscine sacks used for their own stores on GEN food. Instead, the kel-grain went into the cheaper, reusable crates.

But kel-grain didn't pack as well in crates. The small kernels leaked through the crates' loose joints. No wonder GEN foodstores warehouses were overrun with rat-snakes. Nishi was in seycat heaven chasing vermin.

As their feet crushed the kel-grain kernels into the

plasscrete dock, their sweet, malty scent teased Kayla. Because of the timing of this load and the Kinship pickup scheduled, she and Risa hadn't had so much as a moment to grab a nutra before starting work. She was so denking hungry even the kel-grain smelled enticing.

Kayla locked in one last stack of crates, then jumped from the bay. She spotted Abran and Risa crossing the loading dock with what would be the last part of their load, a few sacks of raw plassfiber. But where Risa wore thick duraplass work gloves and made sure to have the sleeves of her rain gear pulled down over the glove cuffs, Abran was toting his sack barehanded.

"Idiot boy!" Kayla said. "You're going to have plassfiber splinters all over your hands."

"I told him," Risa said. "He was too lazy to get the gloves from the cab."

"It's only twenty sacks," Abran said, heaving the plassfiber in behind the towers of kel-grain. "I don't need gloves for such a small load. It'd be even smaller if you'd help."

She took a step toward the front of lorry for her own work gloves, but Risa stopped her. "Get the delivery signature." Risa tossed her sekai at Kayla.

Abran's gaze fixed briefly on the sekai. Kayla waved it at him. "A problem, GEN? Do you think I'm too stupid to know how to use a sekai?"

His gaze narrowed on her a moment, then he shrugged. "When you get back, I bought extra pastries for the two of you. I know you and Risa haven't eaten."

She nodded her thanks, then watched Abran go for another sack. To her exasperation, she had to squelch the urge to run for a pair of gloves for him. Better he should learn his own lesson.

She stepped inside the warehouse, puzzling over how a GEN as careless as Abran could have made it this long without being reset. But maybe he was so good with numbers, even someone as evil as Baadkar could put up with Abran's shortcomings.

Maybe as a brain-worker, he'd never toted plassfiber sacks. But what about growing up? He would have lived in a cheaply built warren like any other GEN. The plasscrete walls would have been just as substandard where Abran had been nurtured, with raw unprocessed plassfiber used as a filler in the mix. You only needed to brush bare skin against a wall to get splinters in your hands or arms or face.

It had been a nightly ritual in Tala's flat. Kayla's nurture mother would check Kayla and her nurture brother Jal before they bathed, and she'd pluck out plassfiber splinters. Sometimes Tala would miss one and it would fester a bit until Kayla's GEN self-healing would push it out. If Abran had ever experienced that once, he'd never pick up a plassfiber bag barehanded.

He'd better not expect her to pluck out those plassfiber splinters when they finished loading. He'd have to figure that out on his own.

His gift of pastries for her and Risa should have tempered her irritation, but it just annoyed her more. Somehow the generous gesture seemed calculated. Maybe Kayla was just being too suspicious—it was hard not to be when she lived a life with so many secrets. But she couldn't help but think that the boy cared more about twisting women around his little finger than working hard the way a GEN should.

Deep in the gloom of the warehouse, she was glad to be out of the damp, glad enough not to be handling the plassfiber.

Something made her glance over her shoulder and she saw Abran had followed her part way into the warehouse. He seemed to be searching, so maybe he hadn't spotted her. Kayla's empty stomach tumbled in anxiety as she wondered what that GEN boy might be up to.

Moving out of sight of Abran, Kayla found Feyda, the warehouse manager, just outside her office. The medium-skinned GEN woman nodded as Kayla approached. "Want to double-check your records. You might have taken cargo intended for Mendin sector."

That likely meant Feyda had a datapod upload for Kayla. Sometimes Kayla could just take the datapod itself and upload in the privacy of the lorry, but sometimes the datapod couldn't be shared that way. Since the Kinship came by most of their datapods illegitimately, there were usually shortages of the device.

Unless it was just another Kinship membership roster, there didn't seem to be much point in this particular upload. Kayla wouldn't be able to use the safe house passwords since she wasn't free to enter a safe house. Risa could deactivate the Kinship failsafe, then download Kayla and do the safe house runs herself. But that would present other problems.

Feyda led Kayla deeper into the warehouse, to what would be the one dead spot where the trueborn netcams didn't cover. She and Feyda chatted inanities along the way, commenting on the weather, the new style of prayer mirrors that were too ornate for Feyda's taste, the kel-grain shortages in Tinga and Jassa sectors.

They stopped just short of the front corner of the warehouse, just behind a tower of crates. Feyda kept up her chatter; the cameras' audio would record them even if the video couldn't. She dropped the datapod in Kayla's hand and waited while Kayla put the device to her cheek. So accustomed now to uploads, she barely paid attention to the stream of data and code.

She'd put up her hand so she could catch the datapod when its extendibles retracted when a last stream of code arrowed into her annexed brain. Just like the upload from Coria, it moved to a different location than where the rest of the data and programming had stored. About to trace that path to check the code, she heard footsteps approaching.

She fumbled the datapod off her cheek. It hadn't quite retracted its extendibles and the little metal feet clawed at her tattooed cheek. Denk it, now she'd be bleeding and that could invite questions.

She quickly passed the datapod to Feyda, then rubbed her right cheek against the rough corner of one of the crates, hard enough to make the wound worse. Now her cheek really stung.

"Kayla?" Abran's voice reached her an instant before he did.

She rounded on him, all her ire spilling into her words. "What are you doing here?"

He took a step back. "I brought you one of the pastries. What happened to your cheek?"

"Is that any of your business?"

His dark gaze hardened a little. "I'm just asking."

She realized her evasiveness would just increase his suspicion. Using her circuitry, she heated her cheeks to feign embarrassment. "I stumbled and fell against the crates." She pointed to the corner where a little of her blood was smeared.

He looked around at the floor, bare except for the towering

stacks of crates. "What could you have possibly have tripped on?"

Now real mortification flooded her. "I'm clumsy, okay? I don't need something on the floor to tangle my feet."

Even Feyda, as startled as Kayla at Abran's intrusion, gave her an odd look at her sharpness with the GEN boy. Of course, Feyda didn't know the strange circumstances of how he came to be with Kayla and Risa. Still, Tala would have given her a severe tongue lashing if someone witnessed her being so unforgivably rude.

"Sorry." She took the pastry he held out to her. "Thank you."

He held his palms toward her. They were angry red and slightly swollen. "You were right. Hurts like denking hell."

"Learned your lesson," she said, then when he seemed to want to wait for her, she added, "tell Risa I'll be out in a few minutes."

Finally he walked away. Now so hungry that the knots in her stomach vanished in anticipation of food, Kayla took a big bite. The sweet bread was dry and spiced too heavily with ground qerfa root, but it quieted the ravenous rumbling.

As she wound back around through the obstacle course of crates with Feyda, she returned her focus to that odd final upload. She tried to track where it had stored itself, but it wasn't there. Had she forgotten the neural path? Or had it been another glitch like what had happened with the one Coria had loaded?

Or . . . could it be neither one was a glitch? Could the two programming uploads have hidden themselves? Gone somewhere in her annexed brain that even she couldn't access?

She denking well didn't like the idea of the Kinship stuffing programs in her brain, then concealing where they'd been stored.

But how to ask Feyda with the netcams watching? It took her until they reached the warehouse entrance to work something out.

"That prayer mirror you were talking about," Kayla said, "did the seller tell you anything about the decorations?"

Feyda looked at her blankly for a moment, then realization lit her hazel eyes. "I asked, but they wouldn't say. A family secret."

Of course Feyda didn't know what had been in the datapod. Because the Kinship liked their secrets, at least with GENs. Trueborn and lowborn Kinship members who were given information had it spoken to them or sent over the network in written form via a wristlink or sekai reader. They might not understand it all, but at least they were conscious receivers.

But GENs just had the data and programming dumped into them. The upload content was often incomprehensible. Sometimes it seemed like GENs were nothing but pack-droms for the Kinship, drones to ferry information.

Kayla had lost her appetite, but she forced down the last of the pastry Abran had given her. She'd never shaken Tala's admonitions not to waste food. As she swung down from the loading dock, she spotted Abran trotting down the alley toward the lorry with a bag tucked under his arm and three plasscine bottles in his hands.

"Those pastries were awfully dry," he said as he caught up with her at the lorry. "I got some fruit-meld from that same vendor."

More likely he'd wanted to see the pretty GEN girl again. She kept her uncharitable thoughts to herself. "You better get those splinters out. They'll fester if you don't."

"Risa gave me tweezers." He handed her a bottle filled with bright orange juice. Then his gaze fixed on her face. Could he see the tell-tale pricks of the datapod?

"You have a few crumbs." He pointed in the direction of her right cheek.

She turned away to brush them off, heading to the front of the lorry. She kept her back to him to keep him from getting a closer look.

Risa was already behind the wheel. Kayla had to let Abran go in first, since he would be crawling through the hatch to share Nishi's lair. As he passed her, she kept her face turned away. She wanted desperately to take a look at herself in her prayer mirror, but she'd left it stowed in one of the sleeper shelves. She'd have to wait until Abran was in the bay.

Kayla pulled herself up into the lorry after Abran and settled beside Risa. The lowborn woman spied the scrape on Kayla's cheek, but at Kayla's quick head shake, Risa waited until Abran squirmed his slender body through the hatch.

Once the hatch shut, Kayla said, "I had to hide the datapod marks from . . ." She hooked a thumb toward the bay.

"Made a hash of your tattoo." Risa unearthed a sani-wipe from a storage pocket in the door.

Kayla took the wipe and dabbed at her face. "Just the surface. It'll heal. Denking boy surprised me in the warehouse just as I was finishing." She mimed applying a datapod to her tattoo.

"I tore into him for that. Shouldn't have followed you." Risa turned her focus on the rear vid display as she backed from the alley. "As drom-headed as he is, he's a hard worker. Tries."

"Yeah," Kayla admitted, then lowered her voice. "Still think it's a bad idea having him along."

Risa gave her a brusque nod. "Told Zul as much. But with him and the councilor taking Baadkar to trial, no real choice."

Risa got the lorry out on Peq sector's main street. As they rumbled along crowded Ciele Road, Kayla stared out the window at the passing warehouses and warrens, all too aware of Abran just on the other side of the hatch.

She was tired of thinking about the GEN boy. Tired of worrying about her every word, about revealing too much to him about Kinship business.

It was a two-day drive to their next destination, Skyloft, the most northeast on Svarga continent. And to minimize trueborn notice, Risa would have to stay close to the perimeter of Northeast Territory's adhikar. That would keep them on the outskirts of the trueborn sectors along the way, which would make the trip even longer. They'd lay over in the northern tip of the GEN sector, Nafi.

Closing out thoughts of Abran, Kayla shut her eyes and made herself comfortable. Instead of fretting over the GEN boy, she'd puzzle over that disappearing string of code at the tail end of Feyda's download.

In the last few weeks, she'd noticed changes in herself—a little better control over her body heat, the ability to trace individual strands of code and pockets of data within her annexed brain. She didn't understand all the programming or what the data signified, but she could follow where it went within her annexed brain.

As much as she appreciated her new, sharpened abilities, she was uneasy about where they might have come from. Were they a consequence of the unusual number of uploads she received via the Kinship? Was her neural circuitry compensating for the near constant traffic by increasing efficiency? Or had specific Kinship programming been uploaded to cause the changes?

It ticked her off to think of Kinship trueborns subjecting her to uploads that mucked with her internal programming. Next chance she got to speak with Zul, she'd tell him no more denking changes to her without her express permission.

But for the moment, Kayla would take advantage of what she'd been given. She went within, only half-aware of the lorry bouncing along potholed Ciele Road, then steadying as Risa reached the well-paved highway. Methodically, Kayla followed strand after strand of the newly uploaded information. In her mind's eye, each string of new code stood out from the older uploads, almost as if it glowed within her mind.

Was it possible she'd always had this ability to see uploads, but just didn't know what to look for? Now the difference between old and new information seemed obvious. If it *had* been Kinship collusion, how did they think these abilities would help the cause? *And why not tell her?*

At least this ability was useful to *her*, because she wanted to know what all those uploads were and where they got stored. She also wanted to add them to the mental checklist that she kept in her bare brain.

As they always did, the paths she tracked faded with her discovery of them. She could still find them, with time, patience, and those mental tags she'd stored, but it was more of a challenge. But clearing that fresh information away would make it easier to find anything hidden.

Sure enough, there it was, a tiny grain of *newness*. She followed along her circuitry, diving deeper into her annexed brain than she ever had. The paths got so interwoven, she had to be extra careful to stay on the right one.

Deeper. Deeper. Closer. It seemed to get darker except for that one speck of bright newness she followed. She'd never been here before.

Her mental process slammed to a halt, as if a barrier stopped her progress. She could still sense the new fragment ahead, just on the other side.

Could she get through? She pushed against the mental wall and realized it was permeable, not as solid as she'd thought at first. She forced her way through.

The circuitry was gone. There was nothing in all directions but elusive, disorganized thoughts and memories. And that faint newness still ahead.

And then it hit her. No circuitry.

She was in her bare brain.

The upload had stored that hidden code in her bare brain.

It should have been impossible, but there it was. And one way or another, she was going to read what had been written.

It was harder here in her bare brain. The code she chased had been stored in scattered bits and pieces. Not knowing what she was looking at, she had no idea if she was even reading it in the right order.

Then she hit what she recognized as the header, the beginning. She'd read enough of the uploads to know what that looked like. It was three letters in a character string.

F. H. E.

It was her bare brain that figured out what that meant. She jolted upright, gasping, her eyes flying open.

Risa spared her a glance. "Bad dream?"

"Yeah," Kayla lied.

She settled back in her seat, afraid to close her eyes again. The three letters felt like a brand burned into her bare brain. *F. H. E.*

Freedom. Humanity. Equality.

13

The first segment of the drive to Skyloft seemed endless, despite Risa's decision to take the more direct northern route past the adhikar expanse rather than the southern way. The lowborn woman had sighed and glanced over at Kayla more than once, no doubt wishing Kayla could spell her during the ten hour driving stint. But they didn't dare, not with Abran on board.

As the only driver, Risa had to stop a few times to get out and stretch her legs, and for Abran to unfold himself from the cubby he shared with Nishi. One of those times Abran didn't shut the hatch quick enough and Nishi escaped, then refused to return to Risa's whistle. It took nearly an hour to cajole the seycat back to the lorry. Nishi leapt into the cab with a sewer toad in her jaws, completely unperturbed that she'd delayed them.

Abran was more careful when Risa pulled over later so the three of them could share a meal. It turned out the bag Abran had been carrying in Peq sector held meat pies he'd bought from the pretty GEN girl who'd sold him fruit melds. The pies were a welcome change from the nutras they usually ate on the road. Kayla was grateful for the more appetizing dinner, but she did wonder how long his dhans would hold out if he spent them so lavishly.

As they stood beside the deserted northern highway eating their meat pies, Risa and Abran chattered away, their conversation a blur to Kayla. She was too preoccupied by what she'd found in her bare brain to register whatever they were talking about.

While Abran's and Risa's talk went on and on, Kayla wandered over to the high, electrified fence that bordered the adhikar along which the highway ran. Both suns had already set, although Kas's glow still lightened the sky. Within the adhikar, Kayla could see the well-groomed pasture of a drom farm in the approaching dark, the vivid green of the scrap grass a sharp contrast to the brown tufts on the northern side of the fence. Two scruffy droms grazed maybe twenty meters from the barrier and a third lay on the ground, six legs tucked under it, its large dark eyes half-closed.

Kayla's thoughts tumbled over and over as they had been these long hours on the road. FHE inscribed in her bare brain. Mysterious additional programming being uploaded into her, code that seemed to have nothing to do with the Kinship.

The words that FHE represented seemed to equate destruction, based on what she'd seen in Qaf, Fen, and Beqal. What did it mean that they'd been written in her brain?

In her bare brain. The only private part of her. The only place she thought was safe from datapod uploads.

The only uploads she received these days came from the

Kinship. Bad enough the Kinship was apparently "improving" her through uploads, now some mysterious entities had breached her bare brain and dumped their code there.

Who or what was FHE anyway? A branch of the Kinship, one that wasn't happy with the pace of GEN reforms? Or could the source be amongst lowborns, sympathetic to the Kinship, but not members? The issues that had led to the lowborn insurrection thirteen years ago had never really been resolved. The trueborns and the Judicial Council gave nothing but lip service to lowborn rights. Even the Kinship was focused more on GENs than lowborns.

What if those letters had an even darker source? What if Ved truly was connected to the bombings in the GEN sectors? What if his machinations had infiltrated the Kinship? He could have planted manipulator spiders in the datapod programming Feyda and the others had had Kayla upload.

It was horrifying to think that something of Ved's might be in her bare brain. This had certainly gotten too big for her to handle on her own. It was time she contacted Zul. She would demand that he tell her about the extra programming the Kinship was installing in her annexed brain, and if they had anything to do with the intrusion in her bare brain. If it turned out Ved had been the one to inscribe those initials, the Kinship would have to know.

With Abran around, it would be all but impossible for her to get to a Kinship meeting or even use the wristlink. But she had to find a way.

Risa called to her and Kayla returned to the lorry. The lowborn woman pointed a thumb to the sleeper. "You could take a rest."

Kayla shook her head. She wouldn't be able to sleep anyway.

"Abran?" Risa asked. "Stretch out? Have a rest?"

Abran glanced over at Kayla. "If that's okay."

It wasn't. Kayla didn't want him there at all, let alone sleeping in her and Risa's bed. His place was back in the bay. But even thinking that, Kayla could see her nurture mother Tala shaking a finger at her mean-spiritedness.

So he settled in on the bed, and Kayla hunched on the seat, arms wrapped around herself. She tried to lean against the door and shut her eyes, but her thoughts kept bouncing back to the illicit upload in her bare brain.

Kayla did doze a little, finally waking as the lorry came to a stop. "Where are we?"

Kayla's internal clock told her it was nearly midnight. All three of the trinity moons had risen, Avish and Ashiv slender crescents, Abrahm full and fat, bleaching out the stars in the black night sky. Risa had parked alongside a ditch and Kayla could just make out what looked like the edge of a lowborn village on the far side, nearly hidden by a patch of sticker bushes.

"In Esa sector," Risa said. "Couldn't drive anymore."

Esa was a mixed sector where lowborns lived alongside minor-status trueborns. Risa had to have been plenty tired to stop here rather than push on to the safer GEN sector, Daki.

There was no legal reason Risa couldn't overnight the lorry in a mixed sector like Esa. But the trueborn residents wouldn't like her stopping here without prior permission.

"If any minor-status trueborn sees you've got GENs with you," Kayla said, "they'll likely roust us."

"Be okay," Risa assured her. "That village is Kiyomi's sister's clan." She gestured across the ditch.

Kiyomi's sister was allabain. Most of the lowborns in a mixed sector were respectable businesspeople who lived in cheaper versions of trueborn houses. But there would often be a gathering of allabain lowborns who would settle on the outreaches of a mixed sector, in ramshackle structures they could tear down and carry to their next encampment.

To a trueborn, wherever lowborns lived was a shantytown, even in a mixed sector when the lowborn neighborhood was often a well-kept row of houses a half-kilometer down from the trueborns' own homes. Kayla herself had grown up calling the thrown-together dwellings shanties. But Risa had taught Kayla that lowborns called a gathering of their homes a village, whether they were perma-built or portable like the ones she glimpsed in the darkness.

Kayla twitched aside the sleeper curtain just enough to see that Abran was sound asleep. Then she gestured to Risa to come outside with her. Kayla shut the lorry door as quietly as she could and Risa did the same. Risa paused long enough to ease open the rear bay door and release Nishi.

Nishi streaked past them, slowing long enough to sniff the ditch that the lorry was parked alongside. Then she dashed into the village. Kayla watched until the feline vanished in the dark spaces between the shacks.

"I've never seen her go anyplace where people are," Kayla said.

"Nishi likes a rat-snake over a sewer toad any day," Risa said. "Better chance she'll find rat-snake in the village." Risa shrugged. "Anyone sees her, she'll scare them, sure. But she'll run before they do."

Kayla and Risa walked away from the village and Nishi's

nighttime hunt. The black water in the ditch below them stank of sewer toads, human waste, and decay. Abrahm's bright glow created strange dark shadows that stretched across the narrow path, concealing bumps and dips and other hazards. At one point Kayla's foot caught on what she thought was a rock, but it was a dead sewer toad, and she sent it flying into the ditch. Its compatriots below complained at the interruption of their sleep, their scratchy croaks punctuating the silence.

They stopped beside a tall junk tree, its wide trunk casting a black shadow on the ground. Plenty of distance now between them and the lorry.

Kayla turned to Risa. "I have to talk to Zul."

The lowborn woman huddled against the junk tree, hugging herself against the cold. "Can pass along a message."

Kayla was cold too, and was about to activate her circuitry to warm herself. But suddenly, she didn't trust it. For the moment, it seemed better to feel the same chill Risa did.

"I have to talk to Zul directly," Kayla said.

"Too late tonight," Risa said. "I'll take the GEN boy with me for supplies tomorrow. Leave you the wristlink. Work for you?"

"Yes, thanks."

They pushed off from the junk tree and started back to the lorry. Twenty or so meters away, a shadow detached itself from beside the bulky vehicle and Kayla realized it was Abran. He had his arms wrapped around himself like Risa had. His carrysak made a lump at his hip.

"Where'd you go?" he called out, his voice loud and demanding in the quiet.

His imperious tone surprised Kayla. Risa might be Kinship and used to Kayla's familiarity with her, but even she had her limits. In the absence of Councilor Mohapatra, Risa saw herself as in charge, and she demanded respect from those that worked for her. Risa might have let it go as simple rudeness if Abran had been a lowborn, but she wouldn't stand for insolence from a GEN. Not until she knew the GEN better, anyway.

Risa closed the distance between her and the lorry. "Don't know it's any business of yours, tankborn." As angry as Risa sounded, Kayla suspected that if she hadn't been there, *tankborn* would have been *tat-face* or even *jik*.

His expression stormy, Abran pushed off from the back of the lorry. His hands were closed in fists.

A big miscalculation, because even if an easy backhand from Kayla wouldn't put him in the dirt, Risa was a scrapper. She wouldn't hesitate taking on even a bigger, younger boy like Abran.

But then Abran remembered himself. "Sorry." He relaxed his hands but rebellion still lingered in his gaze. "I was worried when I woke up and you two were gone."

"Just wanted to stretch our legs," Risa said.

"I could use a walk." He trotted off along the ditch, his carrysak bouncing against his hip.

Risa shook her head. "Never seen a GEN so careless of his skin." She nudged Kayla. "Go with him."

Kayla moved along the ditch, this time taking greater care not to stumble. Ahead of her, Abran veered to his left at the junk tree, heading into a thick patch of scrap grass that was studded with fat sticker bushes.

Just as Kayla reached the junk tree, Abran glanced over his shoulder. The tree cast its dark moon-borne shadow over her, so he couldn't see her, and instinct told her to keep it that way for now. She suspected Risa's scolding had embarrassed him, and he needed time alone to soothe his pride. Better if he didn't know she was following.

When he pushed between the sticker bushes, she followed, picking her way carefully through the long thorns. The thick scrap grass muted her footsteps, and he still didn't seem to realize she was behind him. She was about to call out when it suddenly occurred to her he might be looking for a place to relieve himself. Better stay quiet to save him the mortification. If that was what he was up to, she'd slip out of sight and wait for him beside the junk tree.

But he didn't unfasten his breeches. Instead he pulled out his battered prayer mirror and pressed it to his lips. It was an odd way to pray—you usually wanted to see your reflected image when speaking to the Infinite. But he might have felt closer to the deity that way.

She should have walked away then, but now she feared he would hear her in the quiet. So she stood still, but with her back to him.

"It's me," he said.

She heard what almost sounded like a faint whisper. But it was just the breeze rustling the sticker bush spines against one another.

"I have to know they're okay," he said. "Please."

It didn't matter who he meant. His nurture family. Not likely a GEN girl he'd left behind, since he'd said they. But it was someone he loved, that he prayed to the Infinite to protect. She did it herself with Tala and Jal.

"If you could just show them to me, somehow." She heard the desperation in his plea.

Another long hesitation, while the breeze filled in the silence with its whisper. Then he said, "I don't know if I can do this anymore."

That brought Kayla back around. She didn't like the desolate sound of that. GENs did sometimes find ways to kill themselves, condemning themselves to damnation, with no chance of returning to the Infinite's hands.

Abran stuffed his prayer mirror back in the hem of his shirt, a mix of fear and anger twisting his face. Would it be better to confront him now, or should she wait until he'd calmed himself? She didn't want to make things worse for him.

Then he bent to the carrysak at his feet and pulled something from it. When he pushed up the left sleeve of his shirt and held his arm up into a beam of moonlight, she suddenly realized what he was doing. What he held in his right hand clinched it—a clear, palm-sized vac-seal filled with something milky yellow. Before she had the wit to step in and stop him, he'd thumbed the activator tab on the vac-seal, pressed the circular package to the crook of his left arm, and rubbed it into his skin.

Kayla's heart turned to stone. Her feet felt leaden as she stepped in close enough for Abran to see her.

"You're a jaf-head," she said.

He jumped, but he kept that vac-seal against his arm. "It's not what you think." His speech slurred a little.

"If that's not jaf buzz, what is it?"

He staggered a little, wincing as he backed into a sticker bush thorn. Then he looked back down at his arm and squeezed the last of the jaf from the vac-seal.

"That stuff is denking expensive," Kayla said. "No one

outside a high-status trueborn could afford to use it. How could a GEN like you get your hands on some?"

Still, he didn't answer. But Kayla figured it out and she felt even sicker. "You stole it. From your previous patron."

"No." He shook his head as if to clear it.

"Do you have a better explanation?" Kayla asked. "And have you been doing that in the bay all this time? Risking all of us with your habit?"

"No. This is the first time."

He shoved the empty vac-seal back into the carrysak at his feet. When he straightened again, she searched for the blissed out look jaf users got. Other than a slight unsteadiness, she couldn't see much difference in Abran.

"That stuff is made for trueborns," she said. "To make them happier when everything is dark for them. How do you know it will even work on a GEN?"

"I just wanted to try it," he said. "Just this once."

"So you stole a million dhans worth of drugs—"

"I didn't steal it! He . . . he gave it to me."

"You expect me to believe that?"

He set his mouth, looking stubborn as a drom. Then he shook his head.

"Tell me the truth. All of it."

His gaze flicked to the left, then back at her. When he spoke, there was only the slightest slurring. "My patron ordered his youngest son, Ekavir, to transport four carrysaks across the border into Shafti sector. My patron lives in the far north of Nitha sector, right up against the adhikar, and a long way from the Shafti border. Ekavir hadn't earned the right to a lev car yet. So he could ride a drom, or he could walk. He wasn't about to arrive in Shafti with his best korta smelling of drom, but he wasn't about to carry those carrysaks himself on foot either. He talked his father into lending him me. So I toted the carrysaks, but I had no idea what was in them."

"How'd you end up with this one?"

"We were walking along the electrified adhikar fence. No one knew, but the power went out in a section. A bhimkay climbed over. It got hold of Ekavir . . ." His throat seemed to close off.

"I remember that story, about a bhimkay killing a trueborn," Kayla said. "But no one said anything about a GEN being with him."

"Who would mention the GEN?" Abran asked, and Kayla knew he was right. "I was terrified. Of the spider, of what they'd do to me once they found out Ekavir had died and I hadn't."

"They would have reset you," Kayla said, "Even though none of it was your fault. You were there, so you should have somehow saved the trueborn."

"He would have beaten me first," Abran said. "I knew I'd be reset whether I went back without Ekavir, or if I ran. So I ran. I dropped three of the carrysaks along the way, but held onto this one. I don't even know why. But I kept running, keeping close to the adhikar, until I cut across Shafti, then Maf sector to Fen."

"So when you said your patron might not have known for a couple days that you'd escaped . . ."

"He'd expected us to be away close to a week," Abran said. "So they wouldn't have started looking for Ekavir right away."

That made sense. And even after the week had passed, it might have taken the jaf buyer some time to realize Ekavir wasn't going to show up. "And you thought the Grid might not find you because they might think you were dead?"

"Once they found Ekavir, they might have thought the bhimkay carried me off."

It all fit. Except she didn't like the fact that he'd kept so much from her and Risa. "When did you find out what you had?"

"I knew it was something illegal. But I didn't dare stop until I was well out of Nitha sector. Then I opened the carrysak."

"Why not leave it behind?" Kayla asked. "All this time, you've put me and Risa at risk. Do you know how often we're boarded and inspected by the Brigade?"

"I was afraid if I dumped them, they'd detect my DNA," Abran said. "Know where I'd gone."

"They'd only need the Grid for that," Kayla said. Of course, at the moment he was safe from the Grid, the Kinship's machinations fooling it into thinking Abran legitimately worked for Councilor Mohapatra. "How many vac-seals have you used?"

"Just the one," Abran said, then at Kayla's skeptical look, he added, "I promise. Just one. I pretend everything is okay, but sometimes I feel eaten up inside, worrying that Baadkar will find me and take me back."

"Well, you won't be using anymore," Kayla said. "The rest of the vac-seals and the carrysak they came in are going into the lorry's incinerator." She grabbed the carrysak from between Abran's feet.

"No!" Abran said, trying to take the carrysak from her.

Between his unsteadiness and her strength, she easily kept her grip on it. "You might be feeling pretty good right now from that hit of jaf, but without the proper stim to follow it, you'll be crashing soon."

He looked like he wanted to argue with her, but in the end, he let go of the carrysak. Even still, he looked pretty worried as Kayla tucked it under her arm.

"Let's go," Kayla said. "Risa will be worried."

As they emerged from the sticker bushes then along the ditch, he kept eyeing the carrysak. He wasn't swaying anymore, but he seemed edgy, not at all like the mellow jaf users she'd seen.

"How do you know so much about jaf?" he asked.

"Doctrine school. Weren't you paying attention?"

It was also a drug Zul told her he'd tried instead of crysophora. Crysophora was a super-charged stimulant, but he risked damaging his internal organs using it. Zul said jaf gave him at least the illusion of well-being, helping him cope with his debilitation mentally, but not physically. She guessed he didn't use either drug now with his new treatment.

She still felt uneasy about the mysterious regimen that had so improved Zul's condition. It was hard to trust any trueborn gene-splicers, inside or outside the Kinship. Sometimes it was hard to trust trueborns at all.

Abran slanted a look down at her. "How long were you hiding there?"

"I wasn't hiding." Kayla winced at the lie. "Well, I was. But Risa sent me off after you. I was there long enough to hear your prayer. I didn't want to interrupt."

"Oh." The one word came out strangled.

"I heard you pray for your family. It's hard to leave them behind when you're Assigned. Has it been a long time since you've seen them?"

"Yes." Now he had that desolation in his eyes again. "They're not . . . in a good place."

She couldn't help the sympathy that washed over her. "I'm sorry."

He nodded in acknowledgement. He seemed to want to share more, but he pressed his lips together as if to block the impulse.

When the lorry was in sight, she put out a hand to stop him. "For your own safety, you ought to think before you mouth off, even to a lowborn like Risa. And you risk an awful lot being out here alone where an enforcer could see you."

He shrugged. "You came out here by yourself."

"I'm guessing I have a lot more experience handling the Brigade than you do, Abran. And I have Risa at my back. She knows I'm too valuable to my patron to let me get reset."

"You don't think Risa would protect me?" Abran asked.

"Maybe not, when you bring this—" She held up the carrysak. "—into our home."

His hand twitched as if he wanted to take the laden carrysak back from her. He wouldn't have been able to and had to know that. Could he already be that hooked after one hit of jaf? Or had he lied about how many he'd used?

When they got back to the lorry, Kayla found Risa sprawled across the bed, sound asleep. She backed out of the cab quietly. "I'll have to tell her about the jaf in the morning. And Councilor Mohapatra will have to know."

"No." Abran shook his head. "He might send me back."

"He won't."

Abran gripped her arm. "Please, I have to stay with you."

"I told you, he won't send you back." At least she didn't

think the councilor would, not with the judgment he was building against Baadkar. But Abran didn't know about that. Zul feared the boy would run off if he knew he would have to testify.

Abran let go of her, his gaze strayed again to the carrysak. "Will you have to wait until morning to incinerate those?"

Kayla gave him a narrow-eyed glare. "I'm dumping the vac-seals now. The carrysak can wait until later. Go get in the bay. Leave the door open for Nishi."

She waited until the lorry rocked with his weight as he climbed inside. He'd have to sleep in the back by the doors, where he had that first night. She was small enough to crawl over the freight to Nishi's cubby, but Abran wasn't. And she wasn't letting Abran scramble across Risa to the hatch.

Kayla hopped back into the cab. The bigger incinerator in the bay was blocked by crates of kel-grain, which left only the mini-cin in the washroom. She'd be able to feed the vac-seals of jaf in there one by one. Once she and Risa dropped their load and had access to the bigger incinerator, she'd destroy the carrysak.

She shut the door of the washroom behind her, hoping the whomp of the mini-cin wouldn't wake Risa. Then she unfastened the carrysak's latch and pulled out the first vac-seal.

Now that she was in the brighter light of the washroom, she realized the jaf had an odd color to it. Where the jaf she'd seen Zul inject was a creamy yellow, this batch was a little brighter, pale, but almost golden like Nishi's eyes. The vac-seals were the right shape—circular—but there was no encoding mark on the plasscine.

Could this be bootleg jaf? Something that Baadkar had his

people cook up? If so, Abran had put himself at even greater risk using it. She'd have to keep her eye on him, to make sure he didn't have any adverse effects.

It occurred to her that Zul and the councilor might want her and Risa to keep the bootleg jaf as further evidence against Baadkar. But besides the peril of them hiding and transporting the drugs, the crime of making and selling jaf seemed like such a trivial thing compared to the way Abran's former patron had abused him. In fact, she could easily imagine the Judicial Council slapping Baadkar on the wrist for the bootleg jaf, and ignoring completely the issue with his treatment of GENs.

Better to destroy it, she decided, dropping the vac-seal into the mini-cin, then following with the other eighteen. She searched the carrysak, looking for any hidden pockets, but there was nothing else inside.

That job done, she performed her nightly routine in the washroom, then nudged Risa aside to climb in beside her. As Kayla tried to relax into sleep, her conversation with Abran gnawed at her. To have been beaten by his patron, seen a man killed by a bhimkay, run for his life, then been in so much despair over his family he used jaf from a questionable source—he wasn't the carefree boy he pretended to be.

Maybe it was time for her to be kinder to him. Maybe what he really needed was for her to be a friend. She had to admit it—after Devak's abandonment, she could use a friend herself.

14

The next morning, Abran seemed to be back to his old self—at least the self he chose to show the world. While Kayla took her turn in the lorry's washroom, she heard his light tenor voice singing a bawdy song to Risa. The lowborn woman's guffaw rattled the washroom door. Risa had been ready to tear Abran's head off earlier when she found out about the jaf, but the boy's abject apology had apparently turned her around.

When Risa shared out the last of the nutras, Abran revealed his surprise. While Kayla and Risa were still sleeping, he'd crept out and gone down to the sticker bushes to gather a couple handfuls of pale blue berries to add to their breakfast.

Of course the sticker bush thorns had scratched his hands and forearms while he'd harvested the berries. Abran didn't seem the least bit fazed by the thin red lines criss-crossing his brown skin, but they reminded Kayla far too much of Scratch. Her stomach clenched at the thought of him contracting the disease.

In that moment, as the sweet-tart berries all but melted on

her tongue, she realized that she wasn't completely indifferent to Abran's well-being. Last night she'd made a conscious choice to stop resenting his presence and to feel empathy for him instead.

There was still the call to Zul to make about the drugs and her own problem. But if things turned out as she expected—that Abran would continue with them—she would find a way to accept the boy.

"Abran," Risa said, startling Kayla out of her reverie. "Need you with me at Streetmarket."

"What about Kayla?" Abran asked.

"That your business?" Risa asked, staring down Abran. "After you bring jaf buzz onto my lorry, you think you can ask questions?" So she hadn't forgiven him completely.

He shook his head. "Sorry." Apparently the boy was learning to respect Risa.

"Go change," Risa said. "Can't have you wearing your worst at Streetmarket. Councilor likes his GENs looking tidy."

"Use the new clothes?" Abran asked.

One of the councilor's aides had sent three changes for Abran. He had the extras tucked away on top of one of the crate towers to keep Nishi from sleeping on them.

"What else, GEN?" Risa snapped. "Be quick."

Kayla could see the questions in Abran's eyes. One hard stare from Risa kept him silent. He crawled through the hatch to Nishi's cubby and pulled the hatch door shut behind him.

"Councilor Mohapatra doesn't give a rat-snake's hind leg what we wear," Kayla said.

"Gives us some private time, doesn't it?"

One eye on the hatch to make sure Abran didn't pop his

head through again, Risa handed over her wristlink. Kayla slipped it under the sleeper mattress.

"After your call, want you in the village," Risa said, nodding in the direction of the lowborn encampment. "Find Aki. She's Kiyomi's sister, and Kinship. GEN boy and I will meet you there."

Kayla and Risa stepped out into the chill morning to wait for Abran. A thicket of sticker bushes pierced with junk trees concealed all but a couple of the lowborn bhaile—tents the allabain built of sticker bush branches covered with plasscine sheets. Kayla could hear faint voices calling out—women reciting morning prayers to the twin god, Iyenkas, children's excited squeals, a booming man's voice ordering someone to go to the GEN well for water.

Behind Kayla and Risa, on the other side of the sticker bushes, a row of warehouses and factories shielded the sector's central ward from the ramshackle lowborn village. Kayla caught the stink of molten plassfiber wafting on the air, which meant one of those factories processed raw plass. The mixed sector warehouses stored food and dry goods, much higher quality than anything found in a GEN sector. GENs would be the main workforce, helping to produce and package what they'd never consume themselves.

"This okay?" Abran asked, sliding down from the cab to stand between Kayla and Risa.

Kayla couldn't help herself—she scanned him from head to foot. The boy certainly cleaned up nicely.

His broad shoulders looked even wider in the deep-green tunic, his legs longer and leaner in the matching chera pants. Gold piping, the stylized initials of Councilor Mohapatra, decorated his long sleeves and the cuffs of his cheras. Despite that declaration of ownership, Abran carried himself with an almost trueborn-like pride and arrogance. You would have thought he wore uttama silk instead of cheap woven plass threads.

The defiance sparking in his eyes alarmed Kayla. She leaned close to whisper in his ear, "Don't forget who you are, GEN."

He turned his fierce expression on her. "Who are you to tell me who I am?"

Risa heard, because she sucked in a breath, about to reprimand him. But then his gaze dulled, and the sharp lines of his face softened.

Risa snapped, "Let's go, GEN boy." Abran fell in behind her without argument.

But he gave Kayla one last look over his shoulder. The enigmatic message in his eyes teased her to decipher it. Apology? Resentment? Before she could figure out which it was, he followed Risa around the lorry and disappeared from view.

Earlier, she'd thought he'd straightened out his attitude. But it was almost as if when he went in to change his clothes, he'd transformed himself back into the insolent boy he'd been last night. Was this how he usually acted around his trueborn patron? Abran must realize his arrogance gave Baadkar an excuse to beat him. He was lucky not to have been reset.

Kayla's stomach tightened with sudden anxiety. Maybe he still had a stock of jaf buzz hidden somewhere. They only knew about what had been inside his carrysak. What if he had more, secreted away amongst the cargo? He could have taken another hit when he went to change, and that was what made him edgy and rude again.

Her blood ran cold. She climbed back into the cab, switched on the bay illuminators, then slipped through the hatch.

The niche they'd created for Nishi was ill-lit, but she could see well enough to know there was nothing concealed in the corners. But as a GEN, she knew enough about hiding things to believe the vac-seals of jaf could be right under her nose and she might not see them.

Or maybe she wasn't seeing anything because there was nothing there to see. Maybe she'd made too much of Abran's brief moment of rebellion. How often had she wanted to lash out at the tight controls trueborns kept GENs under? More times than she could count. And it had had nothing to do with a jaf buzz.

Jumping to conclusions about Abran wasn't productive. It would be more worthwhile to keep her mind open, see if he showed any more signs of having taken a hit. And she'd look sharp as they finally unloaded the kel-grain to make sure none of the seals were broken, and scrutinize all the tight corners of the bay for anything illicit.

Putting aside her unease about Abran, Kayla slipped back into the sleeper and closed the hatch and curtain. She took a breath to settle her thoughts, then dug out the wristlink and tapped in the code for Zul.

He answered quickly enough, but she could tell from the way his words were muted that he wasn't talking to her. There were other voices in the background, voices raised just short of shouting, a contentious back and forth between them and Zul. She made out a few words—*Scratch* and *GENs* and *explosions*—and guessed that he was at a Kinship meeting. From the voices drowning his out in the background, it didn't sound as if he was winning the argument.

The image in the wristlink display, dark and indistinct as if

Zul's hand was resting in his lap, blanked out completely as he shut off the vid-screen. Then he must have raised his wristlink to his mouth before murmuring, "In a meeting."

By deactivating the video, he no doubt wanted to keep her from identifying whoever was in the room with him. The cultured tones of high-status trueborns boomed through the receiver of Risa's wristlink as the argument raged on.

"Can we deal with this later?" Zul asked over the noise.

"It took some doing to get time alone," Kayla said. "I can't use the wristlink while Abran's around."

"Junjie's here. Can he handle it?" Zul said, his exasperation clear.

She was tempted to say yes, a knee-jerk reaction for her to back off when Zul was irritated. But even though she liked Devak's lively, hyperactive best friend, it was Zul she needed to pass her news to.

"Someone has encoded me," she told him. "Written in my bare brain. The letters *FHE*."

Without the video, Kayla didn't know how to interpret his lack of response. The rowdy discussion rolled right on in the background.

Then she heard the scrape of a chair and Zul saying, "Excuse me," then, "Junjie. With me."

As they moved away from the shouts, she could hear their footsteps, Junjie's light tread and Zul's heavier one. The door rattled as it opened and closed; silence fell.

The video feed came back on and Zul's serious face regarded her from the display. She could see Junjie over Zul's shoulder.

"The discussion was going nowhere, anyway. Sometimes

it seems they've abandoned the mission." Zul shook his head. "What's this about your bare brain?"

She explained about her last datapod upload at the Peq sector warehouse. How something seemed off about it, how she'd managed to trace a path back to her bare brain.

"I want to know if someone from the Kinship put it there," Kayla said. "Is there some splinter group you haven't told me about called FHE?"

She heard Junjie suck in a breath. His eyes widened slightly.

"Absolutely not," Zul said. "What the devil is FHE, anyway?"

She glanced away, guilt sharp within her that she'd kept this from Zul so long. But at the same time, annoyance bubbled up that she felt such obligation to tell him everything.

"It stands for Freedom, Humanity, Equality," she said finally. "I've seen the words written in GENscrib on warehouse and warren walls in GEN sectors." She hesitated, then decided she might as well tell him all of it. "It was written on both the warehouses that blew up, the one in Qaf sector and the one in Beqal. I also spotted it on some rubble of a warren in Fen sector. I think it's a warning to the GENs who work or live there to clear out."

"Then whoever they are," Zul said, "they're not trying to hide that they're responsible."

"If they're not Kinship—" Kayla said.

"They're not," Zul said flatly.

"You'd tell me if they were?" Kayla asked.

"Yes, damn it, I would!" He looked away and she heard him drag in a long breath. "I do keep secrets from you, Kayla. I imagine you do the same with me. As do a few of those damned idiots in there. In some cases it's wrong-headed and over-cautious. But this is the first I've heard of FHE."

For the first time in a long time, she felt as if he was telling her the truth. "If it isn't the Kinship . . . it can't be GENs. Where would they get bombs?"

"Lowborns blew a few things up during the riots fourteen years ago," Zul said.

"And the chemicals they used to make the bombs are all under lock and key now," Kayla pointed out.

She could see Zul wanted to argue against where they were inevitably headed. She cut off his objections. "It could be trueborns. I've been thinking it could be Ved's doing."

She could see from his troubled gaze that he'd already gotten there. "But why? It makes no sense. Why would he do something so openly when he's in hiding?"

"Because he hates GENs," Kayla said. "He wants to make life worse for us. Take away our food, our homes."

"Then why would he put up a warning?" Zul asked. "Why not let the GENs die in the explosion?"

"Because we're valuable?" Kayla guessed. "Because it's getting harder and harder to make more of us? Or maybe whoever is working for him, the one setting the bombs, feels guilty enough not to want to kill GENs."

"We'll double the effort to find him, then," Zul said. "We've been scouring the most likely adhikar parcels, the ones owned by cohorts of his. We'll expand the search."

His mention of searching reminded her of what she'd been looking for in the lorry. "That boy brought drugs with him. A carrysak full of jaf vac-seals."

"Denking hell." Anger blazed in Zul's eyes, visible even

in the tiny wristlink screen. "He stole them from Baadkar."

"How did you know?"

"Apologies for not telling you before now," Zul said. "I didn't think it was relevant. Baadkar's been in the drugs business for years."

"I destroyed the vac-seals. I'm sorry if you wanted them for evidence." She held her breath, expecting Zul's disapproval.

But he just shook his head. "He's had GENs creating knock-offs for years, and the Council has looked the other way. Even when some batches have sickened dozens of people."

Anxiety squirmed inside Kayla. "Abran took at least one hit. Will he be okay?"

"If he hasn't shown effects yet, he should be fine. Keep an eye on him."

"I have been. His behavior changes from day to day. I can't be sure he doesn't have more than what I destroyed." She hesitated, then threw out the question, "Do we jettison him? Dump him in Skyloft or even here in Esa? Baadkar must know one of his carrysaks went missing. Doesn't that increase the risk someone will come after Abran?"

Zul rubbed his face, as if trying to summon the right decision. "We're so close with the judgment. The drugs business only strengthens our case. I think Baadkar would weigh one carrysak of jaf against the perils of disclosure of his illegal actions and let it pass."

"And if the Brigade were to find more of it on board?" Kayla asked.

"We'll do everything we can to save you, Kayla."

Stop the Brigade from resetting her, he meant. Or from

attempting to download her and setting off the Kinship failsafe before it performed its own reset.

Zul's eyes narrowed in the small screen. "I want to go back to you finding those initials in your bare brain. I'd be interested to hear how you learned that trick of tracing the datapath."

"I meant to ask you the same thing," Kayla said. "I don't mind carrying your data around, but for the Kinship to reprogram me via uploads that change my basic abilities without my permission—"

"The Kinship had nothing to do with it," Zul protested. "Our uploads are mostly just data. If there's programming, it's not meant to work on your neural system."

"How do you explain the changes, Zul? This ability to see the data and follow strings of code."

"I swear to you—"

"I've heard of other GENs who can do that," Junjie blurted out, leaning in closer. "The brain sort of teaches itself. Kind of a protective thing when there have been a lot of uploads."

She certainly got more uploads than the average GEN thanks to the Kinship, so that made sense. She still wasn't completely convinced that the Kinship wasn't directly involved, but Junjie's assurance that other GENs could do the same made her feel a little better.

"I've also been healing faster," Kayla said. "Maybe two or three times as fast as the average GEN."

Junjie looked at her blankly a moment, then shrugged. "No idea. Could be all the uploads have your brain working at a higher rate, even in healing."

"I've never heard anything like that," Zul said, "in all my years of working with GENs."

Junjie's eyes lit as if he'd just figured something out. "I know a way to erase the FHE in your bare brain. Where are you and Risa now?"

"Esa sector, but only for half a day," Kayla said. "We drive to Skyloft this afternoon to unload, then spend the night there."

Junjie fidgeted behind Zul, his eagerness to try his idea coming out in excess energy. "I could meet you tomorrow at the Daki safe house. It's not far across the Skyloft-Daki border."

"How do I manage a trip to a safe house with Abran along?" Kayla asked.

Junjie only hesitated a moment. "Tell him the truth. Risa's under orders to send you for some reprogramming. Abran doesn't have to know where you're going for that."

Zul considered, then nodded. "Junjie could download whatever new data you've been carrying around. They can always use updates out in the hinterlands."

Kayla couldn't hold back her irritation. "No one is poking around in my brain, Junjie included, until I agree to it."

Zul stared at her as if she'd grown a third arm. Junjie seemed to be holding his breath, maybe because he was shocked that Kayla would speak that way to Zul.

A faint smile curved the old man's mouth. "Is that acceptable to you, Kayla? Having Junjie try to correct the problem?"

Of course it was. The idea that someone, maybe Ved, had put something into her bare brain disgusted her. "Yes. I'd like that."

"I have to get back," Zul said. "Have Risa contact Junjie to arrange a meeting time."

Zul switched off. Kayla found she was shaking as she shoved the wristlink back under the bed.

She climbed from the sleeper and out of the lorry, locking the door behind her. It took a few deep breaths to calm her.

So she'd stood up to Zul. She'd done it before, back when she lived in the Manel household. He hadn't bitten her head off then.

But it felt different now. As if something had changed inside her. As if she'd gained more control over herself, her destiny, even with GEN circuitry still running along her nervous system.

It must just be all this time with Risa, living a life far more independent than most GENs. And the way those frequent uploads had changed her brain's function, like Junjie said. She was growing up a little.

Satisfied with that realization, she started along the footpath toward the lowborn village. As she crossed the ditch via a narrow plasscine bridge, the second sun rose and the blue-green sky grew brighter. The added light lifted her spirits and she headed toward the village filled with an unexpected joy.

15

Devak piloted his AirCloud along the Northeast Skyway, the roadway descending as he approaching the exit for Esa sector. The adhikar below the skyway was a blur of green and brown and drom-colored gray in the early-morning light. Ahead of them, the neighborhoods of Esa sector sprawled in an eclectic assortment of brawny minor-status mansions alongside tall lowborn multi-residences. The row of factories and warehouses where GENs worked marked the sector border.

Mishalla sat beside him, the red-headed, pale-skinned girl as much a mix as Esa sector. Like Kayla, she'd been born a trueborn, but with a crooked right leg. When the gene-splicers couldn't correct the defect, Mishalla's parents let her be converted into a GEN.

But Mishalla was now a lowborn girl, thanks to Kayla giving her friend the restoration treatment that she herself had been meant to use. He ought to resent Mishalla for that, but she was the sweetest girl he'd ever met, trueborn, lowborn, or GEN, and it was impossible to harden his heart against her. And he was in awe that Kayla could have made such a tremendous sacrifice for her friend.

Mishalla stared avidly out the AirCloud's passenger window, looking back over her shoulder to get a last glimpse of the adhikar as they took the Esa exit and crossed into the mixed sector. She turned to him, her smile brilliant. "Thanks for bringing me. I wasn't looking forward to using pub-trans for the trip from Plator."

"You're welcome."

Devak felt a twinge of guilt at her gratitude. He hadn't planned to transport Mishalla today. He'd been given the duty to drive to Daki sector's safe house to collect DNA packets and pass on new datapod uploads. But then he saw the schedule that Pitamah kept of Risa's and Kayla's route. They stopped in Daki yesterday to spend the night before continuing on to Skyloft sector. It worried Devak that he might cross paths with Kayla in the Daki safe house.

Then Eoghan contacted him about Mishalla needing transportation to Esa for her first Kinship mission—seeking out information on a GEN girl who had been traveling with the allabain lowborns. Devak figured he would spend the morning with Mishalla in Esa, help her as he could, then she would come along with him to Daki. Kayla and Risa would likely already be on their way to Skyloft by the time he got to Daki sector.

He docked the AirCloud in the factory district, not far from the first of the shacks in the lowborn shantytown that was their destination. Devak was supposedly here to do a census of allabain lowborns, with Mishalla along as an intermediary. Lowborns who lived on the fringes, and particularly the allabain, barely trusted the minor-status trueborns they shared the sector with, let alone a high-status like him.

He'd worn his best—a deep purple uttama-silk korta, heavily embroidered with gold thread, and matching chera pants. The lowborns wouldn't notice that the pattern of the embroidery was out of fashion or that the cuffs of the chera pants were slightly frayed. Still, his finery would likely put the lowborns off, which was his intent. That way they would focus on Mishalla and tell her what she wanted to know.

Devak cut through the alley between two warehouses, Mishalla following a respectful two paces behind him. She'd dressed in a traditional Plator sector gown, light green and nearly ankle length, a plaited belt cinched around her waist. It was nice enough to show that she was prosperous, so they would respect her, but not so rich to cause resentment the way Devak's peacock clothes would.

Devak reached the muddy ditch and waited by the plasscine boards that formed a rickety bridge across it. Mishalla lifted her skirt as they reached the slippery borders of the ditch, taking slow careful steps, dismay clear in her face. Sewer toads crawled through the thick, filthy water that oozed along the bottom of the ditch.

Kayla wouldn't have hesitated across the bridge. He doubted she'd be wearing a skirt, no matter what role the Kinship had chosen for her to play. In fact, the only time he'd seen Kayla wear a dress was at Mishalla's and Eoghan's wedding and that had been at a distance because he hadn't wanted any of the guests to see him. But even from the far periphery of Plator sector's central green, he'd known it was Kayla in that billowing gown, beautiful and fierce.

Devak held out his hand to Mishalla. "I'll help you across."

She shook her head. "Someone might see us."

"You're not a GEN anymore," Devak said.

She looked up at him, her eyes flashing. "There's no shame in being a GEN."

"I never meant there was," Devak said, although he could never seem to erase that last grain of instinct that GENs were somehow inferior. Which was why severing ties with Kayla had been right. "I meant no one will give a rat-snake's tail if I hold your hand."

"It still won't look right, a high-status like you and a lowborn like me," Mishalla said. "Go on across. I'll be fine."

He tested one skinny plasscine board with his foot, not sure if it was sturdy enough to carry his weight. Because of their nomadic lifestyle, foraging for their food, allabain lowborns tended to be shorter and slighter than other lowborns, let alone trueborns. The flimsy bridge might be a way to keep outsiders from their village.

But it held him, which meant it was safe enough for Mishalla. If not for her bad leg, that is. As she put one cautious foot in front of another on the wobbly boards, he saw her intense focus to keep her balance. He reached out for her when she was halfway across, and despite her independent streak, she took his hand when it was within reach.

They resumed their proper ranks as they started toward the shantytown, Mishalla a few paces behind him. They followed a dirt path that ran between two long rows of shacks. The shacks had been put up parallel to the ditch, and they followed its bends and curves.

The allabain lowborns were truly nomadic, their homes

constructed of the coarsest, cheapest plasscine cloth, an ingenious arrangement of rods giving each shack its shape. From the irregular shapes of the rods, he guessed they were harvested from the sticker bushes, the evil thorns carefully clipped to leave the flexible, nearly indestructible branches.

Easy to take down, easy to carry. Just like the sticker bushes, the allabain connection to where they were rooted was fragile, despite their inner strength. Sticker bushes let go when Loka's powerful winds strafed them, scattering their seeds as far as they were blown. The allabain lowborns gave way to the enforcers the same way.

The cloth doorways to each shack had been tied open. Devak checked inside each one as they passed. "Where is everyone?" he asked.

It was late enough in the morning that the lowborns ought to be abroad, cooking for the mid-day meal, carrying clean water from the GEN wells to do washing. Yet every shack was empty.

They followed the curve of the ditch that ran parallel to the line of shacks. "There they are," Mishalla said.

It seemed every resident was crowded in a cleared space, their backs to the ditch, their faces tipped up to the warm suns, arms stretched up to the sky. The women's brilliantly-colored dresses made Mishalla's look plain. The men's black leggings and white shirts were brightened by sashes as gaudy as the women's clothing.

A frame had been constructed in front of the crowd and a sheet of plasscine cloth hung from the frame. The twice-life-sized image of a girl had been painted on the cloth, her skin near black, her arms reaching skyward just as the lowborns' were. Her hair lay in myriad beaded braids around her shoulders.

"The girl in the painting," Mishalla said, "she's a GEN."

Now Devak saw the DNA mark on the dark girl's left cheek. The lowborns, as one unit, bowed low in the dirt toward the mural.

"They look like they're worshipping her," Devak said. "Who is she?"

"The one who's been traveling with them?" Mishalla guessed. "The one I'm supposed to find. But he never said—" Her words cut off with a gasp. "She's here!" She took off toward the crowd at a limping run, skirt hiked up, red hair streaming behind her.

Devak thought maybe Mishalla meant the black-skinned girl in the painting, although he couldn't understand why that made her so happy. He squinted against Kas's growing brilliance to see who Mishalla had spotted.

In an instant, his heart both rose to the heavens and squeezed into a painful knot. The person Mishalla threw her arms around wasn't the girl from the mural.

It was Kayla.

Devak's first impulse was to turn and run the other way, to return to the lev-car and wait there for Mishalla to return. Kayla hadn't seen him yet. She would never have to know he was here.

But surely it would come out that he had brought Mishalla here. And if the allabain saw him racing away, it could impact Mishalla's first Kinship mission. All because he was too much a coward to face Kayla.

He started around the back of the crowd of worshippers,

keeping his gaze fixed on Kayla. So he knew the moment she spotted him, just as she drew back from her friend's embrace. Her joyous smile faded, then vanished as he closed the distance between them.

Her gray eyes narrowed on his face. "Why are you here?"

She'd pitched her voice low, but her tone was barely civil. He'd seen GENs reset for less. Yet his judgment of her shocked him. She had every right to be angry with him, GEN or no.

"I brought Mishalla," he told her.

"Then you can go," Kayla said. "Risa and I can take Mishalla back to Plator when she's ready."

"I thought Risa's lorry was packed to the rafters with kel-grain," Devak said. "Not to mention that GEN boy with you. Would Risa really want to take a side trip to drop off Mishalla?"

He could see Kayla working herself up to another argument. But the lowborn worshippers had lost their patience with the interruption of their service. A few had broken off their prayers to glare, and one shushed them.

Kayla tugged Mishalla away from the crowd, moving down the rows of lowborn shacks. Devak hesitated, then he followed, unable in spite of himself to let Kayla out of his sight. When she pulled Mishalla between two of the plasscine tents, he stepped into the sheltered area with them.

Mishalla pressed her nurturer-enhanced ears against the side of first one tent, then the other. "No one inside. We can talk here."

Kayla ignored Devak, keeping her gaze on Mishalla. "You look so good. And so happy. Is Eoghan treating you well?"

"More than well," Mishalla said. "He tells me he loves me a hundred times a day."

"I'm so glad you're here," Kayla said, "but it's such a surprise."

"I'm on Kinship duty. I'm looking for her." Mishalla hitched a thumb over her shoulder in the direction of the mural. "Devak's my cover, pretending to take a census of the village."

At the mention of his name, Kayla tossed an unfriendly glance in Devak's direction, then said to Mishalla, "Why does the Kinship care who the allabain worship? Why does the Kinship need you at all? It isn't safe, Mishalla."

"You think she can't do the Kinship's work?" Devak asked. "Don't you think she's already proved myself?"

"That's just it, she has. Mishalla's done more for the Kinship than anyone." She took her friend's hands. "But I wanted you to stay in Plator with Eoghan, live a good life with him and the children."

Mishalla shook her head. "All those babies we restored to lowborns are gone."

"How?" Kayla asked.

"The Kinship used DNA matches to return them to their parents," she said.

"That's good, then," Kayla said. "But what about the others? The ones who weren't at the crèche?"

They'd found twenty children at the hidden crèche, lowborn babies and toddlers who had been converted into GENs by Devak's own father, much to his shame. But many more transformed lowborns had already been sent out to Assignments.

"The Kinship has found most of them," Devak said.

Kayla speared Devak with a glance. "And restored them?"

At his nod, Kayla asked, "But they weren't sent on to Mishalla to foster?"

"They were at first, but I'd get so attached." Mishalla sighed. "Every time they would take one away, it would be harder. So Zul thought—"

"Zul thought it would be easier for you not to care for the children." Outrage bubbled up inside Kayla. "Because Zul and the other trueborns, they always know what's right for the lower classes."

"It was a kindness," Devak said in defense of his great-grandfather. "So it wouldn't be so painful for her."

"But did he ask Mishalla what she wanted? Or was it just another case of Zul making decisions for other people?" Kayla turned to Mishalla. "Is that why you've joined the Kinship? Because you haven't any children to nurture?"

Now Mishalla looked away. "Not exactly."

"Then why, when it would be better to stay safe in Plator?" Kayla asked.

"Because I wanted to be a part of the Kinship," Mishalla said. "I wanted to go to meetings, do what I could. I didn't plan to leave Plator, but then I got a mission I couldn't turn down."

"From who?" Devak asked. "Pitamah? He told me he tried to talk you out of becoming active in the Kinship."

Mishalla shook her head. "Another high-status. Hala."

"Zul's friend?" Kayla asked.

Mishalla smiled and nodded. "After a meeting, he walked with me to the square and we talked. He saw how I couldn't keep my eyes off the lowborn children playing on the green. I ended up telling him how much I wished for one of my own. He said he might be able to help me."

"Does Hala know of children who need fostering?" Devak asked.

"No, not that. Even better." Joy lit Mishalla's face. "There might be a way he can fix me. Fix all GEN girls, really. So we can have babies of our own."

16

Kayla let the thought into her mind before she could stop it. *That would mean I could create a child with Devak someday.*

It was stupid to even think. She wasn't sure she even wanted a baby, ever. Not considering how GENs were treated by trueborns. And certainly not now when she was so young.

Even if she took the step of being restored like Mishalla and became a lowborn and there *was* a way to have her body fixed so she could bear a child, there was the little problem of Devak being a high-status trueborn. A trueborn who wanted nothing to do with her.

Maybe with time, she might find someone else, but . . . that train of thought was too much right now. Better to focus on Mishalla's mission.

"Did you know about this?" she asked Devak.

"No," he said. "Pitamah never said anything. Although something else makes sense now."

"What's that?" Kayla asked.

"Pitamah saw Hala at GAMA headquarters a couple

weeks ago, just as we were leaving. If Hala has figured out a way to give GENs the ability to reproduce, he must be working on it at Akhilesh's lab."

"Zul *doesn't* know," Mishalla said. "Hala said it's only in the very experimental stages and it may not even pan out. Even if it does happen it will take a few years, time for me and Eoghan to be ready for a child of our own."

"You're willing to take the chance?" Kayla asked. "Hala would probably have to put you back in the tank, Mishalla. He could do things to you, make changes you can't control."

"I know that," she said. "But it's worth the risk to me. To be able to bring a child into the world with my own body, a child that's mine and Eoghan's. I love the fosters, but they're so easily taken away from me."

"But why make you work for the Kinship in exchange?" Kayla asked. "Why not just fix you when the treatment is ready?"

"Because completing the mission is the first step," Mishalla said. "A GEN girl who volunteered to try the uterine restoration had a bad side effect and panicked partway through the experiment. Before they realized what was happening to her, she escaped from the lab. Even worse, she may have caught Scratch after she ran away."

Kayla zeroed in on that word *volunteered*. Why would a volunteer run away? Kayla didn't believe that for an instant. "How long ago was that? With Scratch, she'd have to be dead or dying by now."

"Hala said the Brigade has seen her recently and she looked well," Mishalla said. "So it's possible she never had Scratch at all."

Kayla's suspicion sharpened even more. "What's so important about this one girl?"

Now Mishalla's eyes lit with excitement. "They were growing a womb inside her. It had failed in the other GEN volunteers, but in her it was working, Kayla. The girl is few years older than us, but they were getting close to being able to reprogram her body enough to make her fertile."

"So, you're looking for the girl," Kayla said. "Why here?"

"Because that's her." Mishalla pointed again to the hanging of the dark-skinned GEN that the allabain were worshipping. "Her name is Raashida. And Hala says she's our best hope to have our own babies someday."

"That's why you're here in Esa?" Kayla asked.

"Hala heard she'd been here."

"I assumed Pitamah sent you to Esa," Devak said.

Mishalla shook her head. "Eoghan called Zul, asking for transport, because he didn't want me taking the pub-trans here. Don't tell Zul. Hala would rather keep this from the other Kinship until we have Raashida back safe. They've been so hard-pressed with the bombings and other issues that he didn't want to bother them with it until we knew for sure."

The chanted prayers had stopped. The clatter of the plasscine sides of the bhaile tents flapping in the breeze broke the silence. Then lively voices rang from the open space in ordinary conversation.

"I'll go see what I can find out." Mishalla started to step away.

"Wait." Kayla put a gentle hand on Mishalla's wrist. "You're willing to give this GEN girl back to a trueborn gene-splicer so you can maybe have a baby some day."

Guilt flitted across Mishalla's face. "I think it's for the greater good. I truly do. And this is Hala we're talking about, not just any gene-splicer. I need to at least talk to her."

Kayla could see from the determined look on Mishalla's face that there was no talking her out of it. She let go of her friend's wrist and Mishalla slipped from between the bhaile, heading back toward the gathering area. Leaving Kayla alone with Devak.

His dark gaze pierced her, and she couldn't help the wrench in her heart. His cruel words should have killed what she felt for him. They hadn't.

"I thought you'd be in Daki," he said, "not Esa."

"Risa was too tired to drive any farther. Would you have come if you'd known I was here?"

She could see the answer in his eyes. He had hoped to avoid seeing her. She tipped her chin up, refusing to let herself feel hurt. "I have to go. Risa asked me to find Kiyomi's sister, Aki."

"I don't know if you've heard," he said before she could walk away. "Two more explosions in GEN sectors—one last night up in Cati, one this morning down in Giaqi."

"I just spoke to Zul. He never mentioned it."

"That's what they were discussing when you called him," Devak said. "After you signed off, he realized you should know. He had Junjie call me, and asked me to relay the information when I spoke to you next."

"Did Junjie tell you I think it's Ved who's setting off those bombs?"

"It can't be," Devak said. "Why would he?"

"Because he hates GENs and wants us to suffer. Were those kel-grain warehouses the bombs destroyed?"

He looked reluctant to answer, but he nodded.

"Is there enough GEN feed anywhere to replace it?"

"Just what's growing," he said. "But the winter cycle crop won't be ready to harvest for two more months."

"So what do you suppose Social Benevolence will use to feed the GENs in Cati and Giaqi and Qaf and Beqal?" Kayla asked. "They won't offer up trueborn supplies to make up for the loss. They'll take from other kel-grain warehouses. So everyone is a little more hungry. And where a warren has been taken down, GENs will be that much more crowded together. Don't tell me you think your father isn't evil enough to do this."

He looked away, grief and guilt in equal mix in his face. "He is. But he doesn't do anything that doesn't profit him. Where are the dhans in destroying GEN warehouses?"

"The people helping him might profit and work harder to get him pardoned," Kayla said. "They own kel-grain farms on their adhikar. The shortage will drive up prices. They have interest in the plass mines. Social Benevolence will need plenty of plasscrete to rebuild the warehouses and warrens. Some of those dhans will filter back to your father one way or another, either in favors or wealth. Not to mention that if Ved gets pardoned and gets his adhikar back, he'll profit the same way."

"If it's him."

She couldn't bear that sorrow in his face. He didn't want to believe her, probably couldn't handle one more drom-load of shame delivered by his father.

He reached out for her, but not far enough to touch her. "I handled things so badly with you, Kayla."

"It doesn't matter," she said, keeping her voice flat.

She started off to look for Aki and Mishalla, hoping he

would go his own way. But he walked right alongside her. She ignored him, dodging a line of lowborns who had started up a quick-paced dance. Someone blew on a uille pipe, another dragged a drom-hair bow across the strings of a fiddle, the music's pace challenging the dancers.

When she finally got free of the ever-growing file of dancers, she spotted Aki. A short and dainty version of Kiyomi, Aki was nevertheless a near look-alike to Risa's wife. She was rolling up the plasscine mural with two other lowborn women, one of them Mishalla.

Devak caught up with her, the lowborns parting for him and giving him wide berth. "My intent was not to hurt you."

Yet he had, badly, as surely as his father had hurt the GENs by destroying their warehouses. "You didn't hurt me," she lied. Now she all but shoved through the remaining milling bodies between her and Aki, desperate to get away from Devak.

But he doggedly kept pace with her. "You have to know there was no real hope for anything between us. I was trying to save you pain."

Kayla stopped abruptly and whirled to face Devak. He couldn't stop in time and bumped lightly against her before he withdrew. That brief contact had every nerve-ending zinging within Kayla. She half-worried her circuitry would short with the electricity of it.

She pitched her voice low. "You trueborns can't ever seem to leave off controlling GENs. The enforcers want to reset us, our patrons want to order us around, but trueborns like you and Zul are the worst. You want to make things easier for us, or softer, or less painful. But you never seem to ask what we want."

"I just want what's best for you, Kayla."

"After all we went through together, don't you think I can figure out on my own what's best for me?"

"It's what I'm supposed to do," Devak said. "I'm a high-status trueborn. I'm supposed to make the decisions."

"For everyone? For GENs, for lowborns?"

"Yes. And for trueborns. It's what I was taught to do. By my father, by Pitamah. I'm the one who's supposed to be in charge."

"And you think that's right?" she asked. "To decide for everybody?"

He looked desolate. "I'm supposed to."

"So you decided I'd be better off without your friendship. Without . . ."

She raised her hands, wanting so desperately to rest them on his chest, to feel his warmth, the beat of his heart. But she wouldn't let herself touch him.

"You're just a boy, Devak," she said, trying to put her anguished thoughts into words. "Like any GEN or lowborn boy, like any demi or minor-status. Whatever the rules might be, you don't have to choose for *anyone* except yourself. And most especially, I don't want you choosing for me."

"We can't be together, Kayla. There are a million reasons why."

"That's your choice," she said. "Only yours. Not mine. I won't let you take what *I* wanted away from me."

"We can't—"

"We won't. Because you don't want what I want."

She caught a flash of movement from the corner of her eye. Risa was approaching along the pathway between the rows of bhaile.

"Don't do me any more favors," she said to Devak, then she turned her back on him. Dipping below the joined arms of a pair of dancers, she hurried over toward Risa.

"That didn't take very long," Kayla said as she caught up to Risa and fell in beside her.

"Just bought necessities. Some produce, synth-protein, kel-grain for ourselves. Tired me out keeping an eye on that boy. Looks ready to bolt every moment."

"Do you need me to pick anything up from the square?" Kayla asked.

"GEN boy carried all of it to the lorry. Can work hard when you get him focused. Invited him here, but GEN boy wanted to stay back, get the sleeper to himself."

"You're not afraid he's going to run without one of us watching him?" A few days ago, Kayla would have been relieved to have Abran gone. Now she wasn't as sure.

"Calmed down back at the lorry. Just didn't like being out. Afraid of being seen, I suppose."

Kayla couldn't blame him, despite Zul's assurances that Baadkar was unlikely to tip the kel-grain kettle by searching for Abran. She brought Risa up to date on what Zul had said, including the revelation about what had been written in her bare brain and that Junjie would be fixing it in Nafi sector.

It seemed nearly everyone was up to dance now as the musicians picked up a lively jig. Kayla and Risa had to skirt the gathering place to avoid the dancers' flying elbows.

Risa's sharp eyes widened when she spotted Devak on the far side of the clearing. He stood beside a few oldsters too decrepit to dance, making a show of entering data into the sekai reader in his hands. Risa's gaze shifted to Kayla in a silent question.

"He's supposedly taking a census of the village," Kayla said. "But Mishalla's the one on Kinship business."

"Looks like Aki's got her working already. Woman doesn't like an idle pair of hands. Like her sister."

Mishalla and Aki were with a group of women seated under the frame where the mural had hung. Risa headed that way, Kayla following.

Now Kayla saw what the mural had hidden—a massive flat stone set in the ground. Mishalla and Aki sat with several other women around it, each of them using a palm-sized rock against the surface of the stone to grind something pinkish-gray into a pulp. Kayla recognized the thick branches that had once been the base of a sticker bush. Fragments of pinkish-gray root were still attached to some of the branches.

Aki spotted Risa and called out, "Sister!" She put aside her rock to come give Risa a hug.

From across the stone, Mishalla motioned Kayla over. She handed Kayla a rock and a piece of sticker bush root.

Kayla's attention strayed to Devak on the far side of the gathering place. His fingers tapped the screen of the sekai, but his gaze was on the circle of women. For an instant, those dark eyes connected with hers, then she looked away.

Worried she might pulverize the rock along with the sticker bush root, she took care to moderate her strength as she rolled the rock against the stone. With little effort she crushed the chunk of fibrous root. The long fibers released their hold on the pulp, creating an unappetizing mess that stunk faintly of rat-snake dung.

"Do they eat this?" Kayla asked, smearing the fibrous blob across the stone.

Aki returned to her place, nudging Kayla aside to make room for herself. Risa settled next to Mishalla and stuffed a wad of devil leaf in her mouth. Aki picked up her rock and a chunk of root.

"We eat the pulp, and weave the fiber," Aki said. "The bhaile fabric used to be made from sticker bush roots before plasscine sheets got cheap enough we could trade for them."

Kayla poked a finger into the pink-gray paste and dabbed it on her tongue. It took everything in her not to spit out the bitter tasting stuff.

"It's poisonous raw," Aki said, a trace of laughter in her light tone. Risa, on the other side of Mishalla, guffawed, spewing bits of chewed devil leaf.

Now Kayla did try to get the nasty stuff out of her mouth. But the paste coated her tongue, numbing it.

"That little bit won't bother a GEN," Aki assured her, her eyes still bright with humor. "You're here about Raashida?"

"That's the girl on the mural?" Kayla asked, pretending Mishalla hadn't just told them her name. "The one they were praying to?"

"They worship Iyenkas here, the dual sun gods become one," Aki said. "They're convinced that Raashida is Dhartri, the daughter Iyenkas promised to send to earth. Dhartri the healer."

"Risa and I have been hearing stories," Kayla said, "but I figured that was all they were. Made up stories."

Aki leaned close to Kayla. "Do you remember two . . . no, three storms ago? A lowborn woman in Dika sector had a young son dying from an infection in his foot. She'd gone to sleep that night sure her son would be dead by morning. But when she woke up, she found Raashida dead of Scratch, lying beside her son."

So Raashida *had* had Scratch, and long enough ago, she would have had to have died of it. Kayla glanced over at Mishalla, and she could see from her friend's face she was making the same calculation.

"Anyway," Aki went on, "the boy not only wasn't dead, he'd been healed completely. The village decided to bury Raashida to honor her. But when the lowborns went to collect the body after preparing a grave, they discovered Raashida had risen from the dead."

Kayla stared at her, unbelieving. "She can't have really been dead. They only thought she was."

Mishalla said, "Maybe her circuits overloaded and put her heart and lungs on standby. I've heard of that happening to GENs."

Aki tipped her head toward the others at the stone. "They're all convinced. Because they've seen what she can do with their own eyes."

"She's here?" Mishalla asked eagerly.

"Not anymore," Aki said. "They're moving her to keep her safe. She stays in a village long enough to heal those that need it, then she travels to the next with a handful of trustworthy allabain."

"Then she's healed more people than that boy?" Kayla asked.

"Everyone she touches," Aki said. "I saw her myself. I had a deep scratch from a sticker bush thorn here." She held out her right arm. On her inner arm, a jagged line, faintly white against her golden skin, stretched nearly from wrist to elbow. "It was bad enough, I'd planned to ask a Kinship medic for some anti-germ. But one touch from Raashida and it had healed within an hour."

Kayla's stomach lurched as she remembered how quickly she had healed that night they found Gemma. But she'd never met Raashida, never had the GEN girl touch her. Still, the reminder of her possibly malfunctioning circuitry unsettled her. And what did it mean that other GENs' healing systems—Abran's, Gemma's, now this Raashida's—had also gone awry?

Aki hooked a thumb across the gathering place to where Devak stood. "Is that trueborn one of us?"

As much as a trueborn can be. Kayla left the thought unspoken. "That's Zul's great-grandson."

"That's Devak?" Aki asked. "So Zul's brought him into our fellowship at last."

From under her voluminous dress, Aki produced a black DNA packet, although she kept it out of sight under the grinding rock. "Raashida wouldn't let me download her passkey, but she allowed me to take a DNA sample. I thought Zul could see if it can be cross-matched with the Grid database. If Raashida's been removed from the Grid, that's one less worry for her and the lowborns protecting her."

Kayla took the packet and passed it to Mishalla. "You and Devak will be able to get this to Zul quicker than me."

He was too far away to have heard her speak his name over the noise of the crowd. Still, his attention sharpened on her and he seemed to lean in her direction as if to get nearer to her.

Or it was her imagination? Now he was moving through the crowd, nearly a head taller than the diminutive allabain, no more aware of her than the rock in her hand.

A rock she'd managed to break in two with the pressure of her fingers. "Sorry," she muttered. "My sket." Kayla tossed the pieces and brushed aside the dust.

Mishalla asked. "Where is Raashida now? Somewhere near enough that we could follow her?"

"I don't know," Aki said. "They kept their next destination a secret. For safety."

Mishalla's face fell. "No idea at all?"

Aki shrugged. "Could be anywhere. No way to know where any allabain might end up."

The disappointment was sharp in Mishalla's face. She got up, wiped sticker bush root from her hands and rounded the stone toward Devak.

Kayla got to her feet and followed. He and Mishalla had already untangled themselves from the crowd and had started back through the village, opposite the direction where Risa had parked the lorry.

"Devak!" Kayla called.

They both stopped, but when Kayla caught up, she said to Mishalla, "I need to talk to Devak."

Mishalla smiled, surely with some kind of romantic notion on her mind. She moved out of earshot along the pathway.

"I know she asked you not to, but would you talk to Zul about this?" Kayla asked. "About this procedure Hala is promising?"

"I will." Devak gazed down at her. "I wish . . ."

"What?"

"Sometimes I don't know what the right thing is. I only know what other people have told me is right." His fingers found the diamond bali in his ear. "I thought I knew four months ago. Then I went back to my life."

A life that didn't include her. "You need to figure out what you want, instead of what other people think you should want."

"Do I get that privilege?" he asked.

For a moment, anger spurted inside her at his talk of privilege. But then she remembered that in some ways he was as boxed into his world as she was in hers. She was the one who'd found ways to punch holes in her prison walls.

"You can have whatever you want," she told him. "And not just because you're a trueborn. But you're the one who has to fight for it, not wait for someone else to tell you it's okay."

She wanted so much to take his hand, to feel it against her cheek again. But he'd told her in so many ways he didn't want that anymore.

Abran's familiar voice called out to her. "Kayla!"

She looked across the now near-empty gathering place. Abran had come from the lorry and stood beside Risa on the path. He waved, a broad smile lighting his face.

"Abran's waiting," she said.

Kayla turned her back on Devak and walked away. When she reached Abran, she stepped in close to him, hoping it would look to Devak that there was some intimacy between them.

Abran seemed startled, but he didn't move away. With a rusty laugh, Risa started back toward the lorry, leaving Kayla alone with Abran.

He lowered his mouth to her ear. "I got you something in one of the shops on the square."

Kayla couldn't stop herself from looking back at Devak. He hadn't moved from where she'd left him. His face might as well have been set in stone.

"Don't you want to know what it is?" Abran asked.

She returned her attention to Abran, although she could still feel Devak's gaze on her. "Yes. I do."

Abran reached into the secret pocket inside the hem of his shirt. He kept his hand closed a moment before opening his fingers to reveal a necklace fashioned of dark red glass and polished brown wood beads. An intricately carved wood pendant of the same soft brown color as the beads hung from the center.

He reached around her neck to hook the necklace on. "The pendant is only carved sticker bush, but it looks perfect against your skin."

Her fingertips idly tracing the pattern on the pendant, she glanced back again to see if Devak was still there. He was, but no longer looking her way. He was moving off to catch up with Mishalla. The two of them walked away.

"You don't like it?" Abran asked. She could hear the tension in his voice.

She forced a smile, one finger running over and over an imperfection in the carving. "I do. It's beautiful."

"Good." Relief relaxed his face.

They started off again, hurrying to catch up with Risa.

17

Risa pulled into Skyloft late, traveling through the quiet, night-dark local streets to the mixed sector's warehouse district. The kel-grain they would unload in the morning would be stored here to be doled out to the two closest GEN sectors, Daki and Ret. Then they'd backtrack into Daki sector to meet at the safe house with Junjie, who would hopefully erase the intrusion from Kayla's bare brain.

The last several hours had been an awkward dance between her and Abran. He wanted her to sit up in the sleeper with him as they traveled, and when Kayla refused his request, she felt his fingers stroking her hair. She jerked away and glared at him, hard enough that he retreated into the bay with Nishi.

The next morning, while Abran took his turn in the washroom, Risa pulled Kayla from the lorry. They walked along the access road behind the warehouses and lowborn factories, a drizzle seeping through their cheap duraplass hats. Parallel to the road, sluggish muddy water meandered in a creek too small to have a name. On the other side of the creek, Nishi stalked prey in a grove of junk trees, the seycat's red-orange coat visible then concealed by the sticker bushes clustered around the taller trees.

Risa hooked an arm in Kayla's, a familiarity the lowborn woman rarely risked. "That necklace mean you're choosing the GEN boy? That you're forgetting the trueborn?"

"I'm not choosing Abran. All of a sudden, he seems to want to choose me." She fiddled with the beads on the necklace. "An alliance with a GEN like Abran makes a lot more sense than the foolish dream I was hoping for. Devak's forgotten me, Risa. That dream died a long time ago."

She shrugged. "If Nishi can't find rat-snake, she doesn't bring home scrap grass instead."

Outrage bubbled up at the comparison. "So it's always better to love a trueborn than a GEN?"

"Course not." Risa flicked her free hand with impatience. "Better to admit the one you love, not pretend with the one you don't."

"Sometimes scrap grass is your only choice," Kayla said.

"If you're a drom," Risa said. "That what you are? And willing to settle for what a drom settles for?"

Kayla sighed, her breath curling out from her mouth. "I thought you liked Abran."

"And I thought you didn't."

Did she? Still not much. Him touching her hair had made her shudder, and not with any joy. "I don't dislike him. I guess I've come to feel sorry for him."

Risa snorted. "Almost love."

Up ahead, a cluster of lowborn and GEN workers lingered around the rear door of a plass extrusion factory. They seemed focused on getting out of the cold to start their work, but Risa dropped Kayla's arm and took a step away from her.

"Not sure about that boy, still," Risa said once they'd passed.

"Yesterday, you said he worked hard."

Risa's mouth compressed in a thin line. "Disappeared on me yesterday. Just a few minutes. Worried he'd got his hands on some more buzz."

Kayla's heart sank. "I wondered that too, yesterday. He went in to change his clothes, then came out kind of different."

Risa shrugged. "Find him with it again, he's gone. No more chances."

"What if it's the damage that patron of his did to him? It could have broken his circuitry and made his moods more changeable than usual. It might have nothing to do with him getting more jaf buzz."

"Could be. Still has no right to treat either of us the way he does."

No, he didn't. "Maybe he'd gone off to buy the necklace." Kayla drew her fingers across the pendant and its flaw.

"Maybe."

They reached the end of the row of factories and warehouses. The access road ended at a thicket of sticker bushes, scrap grass, and junk trees. A couple of narrow plasscrete boards made a bridge across the creek, likely how Nishi had gotten to the far side.

Risa turned back the way they came, whistling for the seycat. Nishi answered with an impatient rasping scream.

"Hasn't fed herself yet," Risa said. "Best we go unload. Check on the GEN boy."

The first sun had sliced through the overcast, shutting off

the drizzle. Kayla took off her hat and shook the moisture from it as they retraced their path.

"Would it be so terrible for me to be with Abran?" Kayla asked. "He's good-looking. We're both GEN." She wasn't even convincing herself.

Risa walked a little faster. "Loading dock's open. Better get to it."

Abran had already opened the bay doors and was up on the loading dock with a couple of crates in his arms. He caught sight of them and smiled, his gaze locking on Kayla. She forced a return smile, wishing she could create a warmth for him as easily.

Why couldn't she fill up that hollow place in her heart with Abran? Was her mistrust of him warranted, or was she still clinging to her longing for Devak, and Abran couldn't match up?

She'd think about it later, when there wasn't work to be done. She hurried to join Abran and Risa on the loading dock.

It took only an hour to unload the kel-grain, but triple that to take on a load of plass bars at the extrusion factory. As practiced as Kayla and Risa were shifting at crates and sacks of goods from the lorry bay to a warehouse, carrying and loading the ten-meter-long plass bars proved to be a challenge. The bars were flexible enough to take some bending without damage, but they lacked something the factory techs called tensile strength, and too much pulling could break them.

If it wasn't for the lowborn woman, Japara, and two lowborn

men, Garai and Crevan, who pitched in to help load, Kayla was sure she would have broken the lot. It wasn't a matter of Kayla using her sket to carry as many of the bars as her strength would allow. The six of them had to work together in teams of three, one on each end, one in the middle to support the half-dozen or so they took at a time. They only half-filled the bay with the entire load, but it was slower than taking on crates of kel-grain or plasscine bags of plassfiber.

Japara had a boy with her, Petiri, an active seventh-year who had sense enough to stay out of their way, but ran up and down the alleyway as they worked. Japara scolded him when he waded in the creek and got his shoes wet. Then the boy nearly toppled off the plasscrete bridge that Nishi had used before his mother's cry called him back.

Competing with the tediousness of loading the plass bars just right, Kayla had to contend with Abran's flirtations. He'd touch her as they worked, nudging a strand of hair behind her ear when her hands were full securing a layer of bars, or brushing a trickle of sweat from her neck. She would smile in response, thinking she might start to feel something for him. But the only heat she felt was from the unexpected early winter sunshine.

Just past midday, Abran volunteered to seek out the GEN food vendor that had passed by earlier. With GENs working alongside lowborns in Skyloft's factories and warehouses, the vendor did a brisk business in meat pies and fruit melds. Risa doled out enough dhans for him to bring back food for the three of them.

Japara, Garai, and Crevan returned to the extrusion factory. Kayla climbed into the bay and checked the straps they'd used to secure the plass bars. They'd been piled against the walls on either side of the bay, leaving ample space in the middle for Abran to bed down. Nishi had already claimed her territory atop one of the stacks, three rat-snake babies she'd rousted from a nest beheaded and half-eaten.

Risa watched her from the bay door. "A girl shouldn't have to work so hard to like a boy."

Kayla tugged on a strap that didn't need tightening. "I like him fine."

"You pulled away every time he touched you," Risa said. "Looked pretty glad just now when he left."

"I'm just taking things slow." She moved toward the doors, her gaze following the length of the plass bars.

"You don't want to take things at all. If the *thing* is that GEN boy."

Just then, lightning sizzled across the sky, striking close enough that the explosive thunder was almost instantaneous. A drift of smoke in the junk tree grove told her where the bolt had hit.

Then the skies opened up, swift-moving dark clouds dumping a flood of rain. A handful of lowborns and GENs who had stepped outside for a break reversed direction and dashed for shelter.

Risa shouted, "Time to get moving." She took off at a run to the front of the truck.

Kayla shut one door of the bay, then stood just inside watching for Abran. The access road was deserted. The lazy creek along the road had filled alarmingly high in the short time it had been raining. Water gushed over the top of the plasscrete bridge.

Finally, she spotted Abran at the far end of the access road. She set aside her uncharitable wish that he'd run away and she tried to be glad he hadn't. He pelted toward the lorry with his head down and his arms wrapped around something. When he got close enough, she saw him cradling a lump under his shirt. His rough drom-wool shirt wouldn't do much to keep their midday meal dry.

He was grinning as he reached the lorry and shouted her name. She gave him a hand up into the back of the bay, overusing her strength enough that she pulled him off his feet. He rolled across the floor, one of the meat pies flying. He came up laughing, then shook his drenched head at her and sprayed her with water.

She laughed in return, hurrying to pull shut the second door, then helping him gather up the food.

He held up the meat pie he'd dropped. "This one's a little squished, but I'll eat it."

"No, you won't," Kayla said. "It's my fault you fell. That one can be mine."

He took a bite of it. "I've claimed it."

He produced two unblemished meat pies from under his shirt, then tossed her a fruit meld. "I'll take Risa hers."

The lorry shook as Risa pulled out and Abran stumbled, half-falling into Kayla. She steadied him, a hand around his arm, her face so close to his, she could see the moisture still beaded on his eyelashes.

His lazy smile captivated her, and her skin prickled at the heat in his intense dark eyes. She had a little trouble catching her breath. It was only a physical reaction to him, but it made her stop and wonder.

Then the lorry shuddered again, this time coming to a stop. A few moments later, the hatch door opened.

"Kayla, Abran!" Risa shouted.

At Risa's urgent tone, they both abandoned the food and ran for the hatch. Kayla grabbed the ladder and took a step up. "What is it?"

Now Kayla saw the fear in Risa's face. "That lowborn boy fell in the creek."

"Petiri?" Her heart froze in her chest. By now the creek must be roaring from the downpour.

"Boy's hanging on tight, but he's about to be washed away."

Kayla and Abran raced for the rear doors, Kayla hitting the latch and opening the door in one motion. She and Abran leapt out, then ran forward along the lorry. She peered through a downpour so thick she could barely see two meters. Using her hands to shield her eyes, she scanned the raging creek.

Petiri had been washed to the other side, where he clung to a junk tree stump. Japara burst out of the factory door, screaming as she raced for the creek. Garai and Crevan, close on her heels, grabbed her before she jumped in after her son. Kayla could already see the black roots of the tree Petiri clutched as it loosened from the soil, the force of the flash flood undermining its grip on the bank.

Kayla searched frantically up and down the bank for a way to cross to the other side. There was no wading in that chin-high water, and swimming in that current was out of the question. The plasscrete bridge was under raging water. If there was another bridge anywhere near, she couldn't see it. Likely flooded as well.

"We need to make a bridge," Kayla shouted above the

creek's roar. "I can grab hold of him if I can get to the other side."

The tree stump lurched as more of the roots gave way. Garai groaned, Japara screamed. The junk tree's deep tap root, which should have held it firmly in place, was likely rotted, with the tree good and dead. Now only half of the roots seemed to be holding on.

"Petiri!" Japara sobbed. Garai held her close. "I told him! I told him to stay away from the creek!" she howled. "It's too dangerous!"

Crevan looked frantic. "Some plasscrete boards?" He started toward the factory.

"There's no time for that," Abran said.

He swept his prayer mirror from his shirt hem and tossed it in Kayla's direction. As she fumbled for a grip on it, he ran along the bank and leapt into the water. It was more stupid than heroic—the moment he hit the thrashing brown foam, it threw him downstream so fast he tumbled past the boy between one heartbeat and the next.

Kayla didn't even have time to feel grief at his loss before Abran slammed into a rock near the far shore and held on. He hugged the rock, his red-brown skin tinged with a ghastly gray, crimson blood smearing his untattooed right cheek.

Just then, the junk tree stump gave way completely, tumbling into the water. Japara screamed as Petiri went under. Kayla found herself running as if she could catch up with the boy.

Then Abran, one arm precariously clutching his rock, flung his other arm out in hopeless effort. His body went taut, then jarred as if something had hit it. He pulled his arm in, and a moment later, Petiri's head bobbed above the water. Abran gathered him in close, wrapping himself around the rock again.

Abran struggled to lift his head above the water's rush. He had Petiri propped up so the boy's head would stay above the creek's swollen flow. But Abran himself kept slipping lower, water slamming into his face for several moments until he could drag himself higher.

She realized she was gripping the prayer mirror so tight, it gave a little in her hand as if she'd cracked it. "Risa!" When Risa, a few meters behind her, turned her way, Kayla lobbed the prayer mirror at her.

"The plass bars!" Kayla shouted to the men. "Can we use those to reach across?"

Garai and Crevan looked at each other, then Crevan said, "They're not strong that way. They'd likely snap if he pulled on them."

"What about three or four bound together?" Kayla asked.

Another exchanged look. "Maybe," Garai said.

A yell from Abran sent Kayla's heart in her throat. He'd slipped partway off the rock. She watched as he crawled his fingers along it, got himself secured again. The bank was too steep for him to climb up on the other side, even if he could get free of the current.

"We have to try," she said, running for the lorry, not even caring if the men heard her or if they'd help.

But they followed her and between the three of them, they got a trio of plass bars out of the load. Using several straps, they bound them together. "You two hold tight to the far end," Kayla said.

They held on while Kayla used all of her sket's strength to pull in the opposite direction. "It's holding!" Crevan shouted.

Now they hurried along the creek, Kayla in the lead. Where she drew even with Abran, the water was nearly level with the top of the bank.

Between the driving rain and Abran's focus on keeping his grip on the rock, Kayla doubted he even knew she was there. Petiri had revived and he'd all but climbed onto Abran's shoulders, driving Abran even lower in the water.

"What now?" Kayla shouted.

Garai motioned her to retreat along the bank. "If we send it straight across, the GEN and the Petiri's weight might take us all in once they let go of the rock and the water takes them. We should feed it to them at a shallower angle. There'll be less stress on the bars that way."

Following Garai's guidance, they started paying out the long plass bars. The two lowborn men backed her up, walking forward as she fed the lifeline toward Abran like a rigid rope. But the distance was such that eventually the two lowborn men had to let go. It was only her hanging on to one end, directing the other toward Abran. Garai stood behind her, gripping the back of her shirt to steady her.

Despite the bars' greater strength with three bound together, they sagged once the bundle was halfway across the creek, enough that the tips would strike the water and be flung high. Each time they made contact, the contraption threatened to fly from her hands. The rain made her grip slick, but Garai had wrapped extra strapping around each end, giving her something more to hold onto than slippery plass. Abran would have the same grip on his end.

Two more meters to go, and she saw with horror that Abran's grip was weakening. He was sagging from the rock and Petiri looked terrified. Japara screamed again, the sound going on and on.

Risa hovered close, looking miserable that she couldn't help. Kayla flung over her shoulder at her, "Tell the woman to shut up!"

Risa ran toward Japara and grabbed her, dragging her bodily away. Kayla lifted her voice, shouting against the storm. *"Abran!"*

Somehow her cry reached him. He repositioned himself, wedging his shoulder against the rock to free an arm while keeping the boy between him and the rock. As quickly as she could, Kayla sent out the rest of the length of bar to Abran.

The end of the bars kept dancing away from Abran as he tried to reach for it. Kayla pulled the bundle in, then fed it out again upstream, once, twice. Abran finally lunged for it and got hold, but lost Petiri, only grabbing the boy's shirt at the last moment.

Abran was turned toward her; she had no idea if he could see her. His face was a dark blur in the downpour. He had to give up the slim safety of the rock now, to trust her strength to be enough against the raging pull of the creek. He wrapped his arm more securely around the boy. And pushed away from the rock.

The jolt seared along her muscles and tendons, tore at her shoulders. Despite Garai's hold on her, she tipped precariously forward, felt her feet slip forward on the muddy bank. Her joints roared with pain.

I can do this. I can do this.

She pulled against the driving creek and Abran and Petiri's weight. Hand over hand, she reeled in the lifeline a centimeter at a time. Abran and Petiri bounced in the water and she was terrified Abran would lose his grip.

Would the bars hold? Three together had to be enough.

Then with a sudden lurch, the bank gave way under her feet and her shirt tore from Garai's grip. She was neck deep in water, and only her fingertips thrust into one of the straps wrapped around the bars had kept her from letting go. Trash beneath the surface of the creek—pieces of fallen tree limbs, rocks small enough to be pulled along by the water—slammed into her and threatened her grip on the plass bars. Something hooked the necklace Abran had given her and snapped it off her neck, nearly toppling her under the water.

Infinite help me.

Behind her, Garai flung himself onto the muddy bank and wrapped his arms around her chest. His mouth close to Kayla's ear, he said, "Save my boy. Please."

Garai lifted her so the water only reached her waist. Ignoring the debris smashing against her, Kayla dragged at the plass bars again, pulling, heaving their length in as Crevan caught what she fed him. Abran came closer, closer.

Petiri rode on Abran's shoulder, fear-filled eyes fixed on his father. But Abran looked barely alive, as if his every resource were being used up in saving the boy.

Finally, they got close enough to the shore that Crevan could snag the boy. Risa rushed over to help Garai get Kayla and Abran from the water. Garai flung Abran over his shoulder and ran for the truck.

Kayla swayed, her cold-chilled legs betraying her. With an

arm around Risa's waist, she and Risa stumbled along to the bay of the lorry. The others were already inside.

"Use your chutting circuitry, girl," Risa yelled as they flopped into the lorry bay and out of the sullen downpour. The doors clanged as Risa shut them, cutting them off from noise and the day's dim light.

Her brain must have been made stupid by the cold. She turned on her warming system, then slumped against the nearest stack of plass bars. Risa vanished, then a few moments later the illuminators came on in the bay.

Kayla spotted Petiri in his mother's lap, heaped with some of Risa's store of packing blankets. He shivered violently, but his eyes were bright. Garai had his arms around both his son and wife.

Abran sprawled several feet away. Crevan had piled blankets over him.

Kayla's circuitry had warmed her enough she felt merely cold, as much as she could hope for until she could get into dry clothes. But she didn't like how still Abran lay.

She pushed herself up and woozily made her way over to him. Crevan shot her a worried look.

"Thought that circuitry of his would toast him right up," the lowborn said.

"It should," Kayla said.

She dropped beside Abran and took his hand under the blankets. It felt like ice in her relatively warmer fingers.

"Warm yourself, Abran," Kayla said.

He turned his face toward her, but seemed confused. "Can't," he said. "Nothing there."

Now a new chill shivered up her spine. "Your circuitry isn't working?" she asked. "You can't warm yourself?"

"Nothing there," he muttered. His gaze strayed to her neck. "Lost it. Better that way." His eyes drifted shut.

She thought at first that he meant that the water had somehow damaged his circuitry. Then she realized he meant the necklace. But why was it better that she'd lost it? She was sorry it was gone. Although keeping the necklace would have meant nothing if she hadn't saved Abran.

And if she couldn't get him warm, she might still lose him. He was in far worse condition than Gemma had been. And Gemma had had her circuitry to help.

"Give us some privacy," Kayla said to the lowborn man.

Crevan walked over to where the others were focused on Petiri. Risa was squirming through the hatch with a large flask, likely filled with kelfa drink heated in the flash oven.

"Hand that off," Kayla said as Risa passed her. "I need a dry shirt and leggings."

Risa gave the flask to Crevan, then went back to the sleeper. Meanwhile Kayla tugged off Abran's sodden clothes. She was about to pull his clout from his hips, then decided to leave him a little dignity. She piled the blankets on top of him again, but he still vibrated with the cold.

When Risa returned, Kayla stripped off her own shirt, leggings, and socks. She left on her wet skivs as well, unwilling to strip naked with such an audience. Those last scraps of fabric were soaked, but her circuitry-augmented body heat would dry them eventually. She tugged on the thick tunic and winter leggings Risa had brought.

Risa held out Abran's prayer mirror. "He'll want this."

Abran might not be able to speak to the Infinite in his current state, but the Creator of the creators would be able to see Abran through its reflective surface. Kayla took it, then noticed the mirror's odd plasscine backing had indeed cracked. She wondered if there was storage for a small keepsake inside, if that was the purpose of the case. Maybe a lock or two of hair from his nurture mother and sister.

"Best you take care of that boy, the way you did with Gemma," Risa said.

Kayla knew she had to, knew her warmth would restore him better than a hundred plasscine blankets, but she hesitated. The reality of lying beside him, so intimately close to his near-naked body, seemed impossible.

Risa poked her. Then as if sensing she needed the privacy, walked off toward the hatch. Kayla lifted the blankets and slid under them.

She fit herself against him. He felt like ice, not like a living thing at all. He'd stopped shivering too, but not because he'd warmed up like Gemma had—his body was so cold it was shutting down.

She moderated her temperature higher and higher until she felt nearly feverish from it. His violent shivering started up again until she almost couldn't hold him. She nearly sobbed with relief when the shuddering slowed, when his skin lost its clamminess.

His circuitry must have finally kicked in. He felt nearly as warm as she. So warm, so comfortable that she couldn't resist the tug of drowsiness brought on by exhaustion.

She was startled awake by Abran's voice. "They told me I didn't have to."

His eyes were open and turned toward her, but he still seemed dazed. "*Who* told you?" she asked. "Told you what?"

He reached a trembling hand up and pressed it against her cheek. It still felt cool, but quickly warmed against her hot skin.

His gaze roved across her face, lingering on her tattoo. "It's beautiful."

His fingertips traced its pattern on her cheek. Her breath caught in her throat. Then he leaned closer, pressing his mouth against hers.

It seemed strange and wrong at first, especially knowing the lowborns were there, and maybe were watching them. But then she shut off her mind and let her body take over. Her heart thundered in her ears and she felt so impossibly hot she feared she would burn him. But he didn't seem to notice. He kept his body pressed against hers, the kiss going on and on.

"GEN girl!" Risa's voice calling from the hatch jolted them apart. "Going to drop this crew off, then on to Daki sector. For that reprogramming."

Kayla glanced up at Risa, caught the worried look on the lowborn woman's face before she shut the hatch. The sense of wrongness settled again in the pit of Kayla's stomach, even as her body still tingled from Abran's nearness.

She realized he'd sagged back and fallen asleep. His chest rose and fell with deep even breaths. He shivered a little with her having pulled slightly away from him.

She lay down again and wrapped her arms tightly around Abran. Setting his prayer mirror where his hands were clutched to his chest, she increased her already feverish heat. Abran's shuddering eased.

The lorry bumped as Risa pulled away. The motion jostled Abran even closer to Kayla, and her stomach churned. Abran's kiss seemed to still cling to her mouth.

As a thirteenth- and fourteenth-year, she'd let more than one GEN boy steal a kiss from her in a Chadi sector alley. She'd been too young for it to feel good or bad—mostly it felt silly. The boys would sometimes grope her, but they were her age, and just as ignorant as she.

Then along came Devak. His kiss had been serious business. She'd not only felt it with her body, but with her heart.

Why not with Abran? Her body had said yes, had wanted it. But somehow it hadn't seemed right. Because she had no real feelings for Abran? Or because she still had too many for Devak?

She couldn't, wouldn't think about it for now. Instead she turned her mind to the intrusion in her bare brain, welcoming the distraction. Like probing a sore tooth, she followed the familiar neural pathways within her to that infuriating brand on her bare brain. Then she explored the other lines of programming that seemed to weave within her annexed brain like a tightening net.

She felt helpless to solve the problem of Abran. But she would demand answers from Junjie in Daki sector. And if Junjie couldn't help her, she'd go all the way to Zul himself.

18

Devak upped the speed of the wiper blades on his AirCloud's windscreen, squinting through the buckets of water the heavens flung down at him and Junjie. He'd programmed the route into the lev-car and was letting it handle navigation, but the vehicle's onboard computer could only adjust so well to the buffeting of the fierce winds. He'd grabbed the wheel more than once, just to have something to hang onto.

Beside him, Junjie seemed to be handling the rough ride by fidgeting with a datapod, flipping the thumb-sized device over and over in his fingers. Devak's gaze kept straying to Junjie's nervous gesture, a distraction from the way the lev-car rocked and yawed its way across storm-ravaged Daki sector.

It wasn't so much Junjie's twiddling fingers that distracted Devak, it was that datapod. It contained the upload for Kayla, to correct the intrusion in her bare brain. Once they got to the Daki safe house, Junjie would meet up with her, would press that datapod against the tattoo interface on Kayla's cheek. He'd probably touch Kayla since Junjie didn't give a rat-snake's tail about the rules against trueborns touching GENs. Or maybe he'd just hand over the datapod and let Kayla do it herself. Their fingertips might still brush.

Junjie's gaze narrowed on Devak. "You're thinking about her."

"I'm not," Devak lied.

"Then why not come with me?" Junjie asked. "Why not see her?"

Devak side-stepped the question with one of his own. "Why risk being seen entering a safe house when I have no business there?"

Junjie swapped the datapod to his other hand and resumed flipping it through his fingers. "Yet you drove all this way, just to give me a ride here."

Because Devak couldn't resist being at least that close to Kayla, even if he wouldn't actually see her. "If Jemali had brought you, you would have had to go with him on his rounds, attending to the Scratch-infected. Or he would have left you stranded in Daki safe house."

Junjie smirked. "Too bad you can't take my place, so you could be stranded in Daki with Kayla."

Great Lord Creator, he could think of nothing he'd like more. But then the memory of Kayla walking so close beside that GEN boy intruded. Devak could see Abran fastening that necklace around her neck, as clear as a vid in his mind's eye. "I doubt Kayla even wants to see me. We've completely cut ties."

It was what he'd wanted. What they both wanted apparently.

Junjie glanced over at him and Devak could see his friend formulating a new line of attack. Devak cut him off. "Anything new with Guru Ling?"

Junjie frowned, but went along with Devak's dodge. "Yes, as a matter of fact. Guru Ling's been studying Scratch-infected GENs' lymphatic systems."

"I thought Akhilesh wouldn't give her any biological samples."

"Right. Too high a risk of infection, da, da, da. Even when he's using the tissue to generate new GENs." Junjie's mouth twisted with disgust. "Akhilesh is a chutting pain in the kulhe. We went around him. Got samples from our own GENs."

"*Our* GENs?" Devak asked.

"*Kinship* GENs. I would never, even if I had the adhikar, be patron to a GEN. It's just so . . . so wrong." Junjie shuddered. "A few GENs from the safe houses gave permission to experiment on their tissue. It violates the Infinite's liturgy, but we know what that liturgy is worth. The Infinite Himself would praise the sacrifice."

Since when did Junjie know so much about the GENs' religion? Devak was about to ask, but Junjie barreled on.

"So Guru Ling discovered this extra fluid in the infected GENs' lymphatic system. Really gross stuff, kind of pus-like. She calls it duwu. Anyway, the scratch marks are the body's reaction to duwu. It messes up a GEN's blood, making more and more tiny clots form in the veins and arteries until it's nothing but clots and fluid too thin for the heart to pump. That's when they die."

Devak gripped the wheel again to ride out a blast of wind. Junjie grabbed the door handle as the lev-car whipped from side to side.

The wind eased, and Devak sat back again. "What I don't get is why the GENs' super-immune system doesn't counteract the Scratch."

"Guru Ling hasn't figured that part out," Junjie said. "She says it's like the virus mutated to a form that fools the GEN programming into thinking Scratch is a natural process. GEN bodies just leave it alone. Almost like the way jaf buzz can make an addict's stomach feel full, so they stop eating and eventually starve themselves."

Devak thought of his mother and the damage she did to her body with her vac-seals of BeCalm and crysophora. Thank the Lord Creator she'd never tried jaf buzz. At least she hadn't before she deserted him, after his father went to prison. Who knew what she was trying now?

Devak tuned back in to what Junjie was saying. "Guru Ling has some promising trials going that focus on the duwu. The best one counteracts the duwu's build-up and clears it from the tissue. She went to Akhilesh just yesterday for more funding."

"And maybe some legitimate biological samples too," Devak said.

"Just as soon use ours," Junjie said. "At least we get permission."

Just then, the AirCloud arrived at the northwest corner of Daki sector, where the safe house was tucked away beneath a nearby warren. The north coast of Daki faced the Uttaraa Sea, but the sheets of rain were so thick Devak couldn't distinguish the gray of the rolling waves from the downpour.

Taking manual control of the lev-car, he left the well-paved cross-sector road for a local road. Jouncing along for a good kilometer across the potholes, he finally pulled in behind a row of rain-lashed warrens.

Lord Creator, what a dismal place to live. Skyloft got some protection from The Wall, the mountain range that divided the livable part of Svarga Continent from the Badlands. But Daki was just thrust out there into the sea with nothing to shield it from the bad weather.

"This is as close as I dare get," Devak said. "You never know who's watching." Although any enforcer out in this storm would have to be especially dedicated.

"You're sure you won't come with me?" Junjie asked one last time.

Kayla was so close, somewhere in the tunneled safe house beneath the third warren over. A quick dash through the rain and Devak could see her.

His weak moment was interrupted by a summons from his wristlink. From the pattern of beeps, he could tell not only that it was Pitamah, but it was an emergency.

Devak said to Junjie, "You might need to get a ride back with Jemali after all."

Junjie waved goodbye and slipped from the lev-car. He dashed off toward the third warren over.

Once Junjie had disappeared inside, Devak pressed the wristlink's answer button. "What is it?"

"I need you in Nafi," his great-grandfather said. "Another bombing. Right above a safe house."

"Denking, chutting hell," Devak muttered as he swung the AirCloud away from the row of warrens. "Anyone hurt?"

"We don't know yet. But that's the safe house we sent Gemma to."

Mercifully, the rain that had pounded Daki and Skyloft gave

way to a drizzle across the Northeast Territory adhikar, then stopped entirely when Devak arrived at the bombed warren in Nafi. Rubble from the explosion had scattered across the roadway, so Devak parked the lev-car one street over.

As he threaded his way through the clot of GENs gathered along the street, they parted for him just as the lowborns had in Esa. Before he met Kayla, he'd convinced himself that they moved aside out of respect.

Now he knew it was resentment and fear. Resentment of the GEN enslavement that he represented as a trueborn, and fear of what he could do to any one of them.

Even the allabain had reason to be wary of him. With one wristlink call to the Brigade, he could have their bhaile tents torn up and burned and all of them driven out, the way the enforcers were now doing while searching for Raashida.

He turned back toward the gathering of Nafi GENs. A mix of emotions played out on their faces, grief, despair, and in one tall, pale-faced GEN man, he saw anger. And no wonder—their home, such as it was, had been destroyed. It occurred to Devak that this was how the lowborn riots started. Life got worse and worse for the lowborns, trueborns treating them with more cruelty day by day—until the lowborns struck back.

As he eyed the group, some of them retreated, nurturers pulling their charges farther away. But the tall, angry-faced GEN didn't back away. He said loudly enough that he must have known Devak could hear, "He'll find a way to blame us. Punish us for our own misfortune."

A woman beside him shushed him, flicking a worried glance toward Devak. Devak walked away, ignoring the man's dangerous words.

He continued toward the dozen or so enforcers clustered opposite the rubble from the GENs. A plass sheet had been wrapped snugly over a man-sized shape lying still and silent on the ground. Nearby, a plasscine cloth had been thrown more haphazardly over a body half the size of the other.

Ignoring the enforcers' stares, Devak went to the smaller body first. Steeling himself, he twitched aside the sheet. His heart sank at the sight of the lifeless face. No more than a sixth-year, Devak guessed. Her long dark hair was a bloody tangle, her blue eyes half-lidded. She was gray with dust, but she had likely been pale-skinned.

Shifting to block the view of the enforcers, he closed the girl's eyes. Across the rubble, he caught the gaze of the angry GEN man. As Devak watched, the man dropped his face and his hands tightened into fists. The woman beside him sobbed. Could this have been their nurture daughter?

Devak arranged the sheet more respectfully, then rose and strode over to the enforcers. Minor-status, all of them, even the captain. There was resentment in their faces too, that Devak's high status alone made him better than them. He couldn't blame them for that. Doubtless there were plenty of high-status ready to lord their rank over these enforcers. They didn't know that Devak never would.

Off to one side, a single GEN enforcer looked at Devak sidelong, his light brown eyes a near match for his face. Once Devak met the GEN enforcer's gaze, the enforcer looked down at his own right hand spread flat on his black shirt front. Pinky finger tucked in, the GEN had stretched out his thumb and other fingers as wide as they would go.

It took Devak a few seconds to register the crude letter K.

He was Kinship. And maybe he knew the fate of those in the safe house.

"I'm Devak Manel." Devak said to the captain, letting the still-powerful Manel name sink in. "I was asked to assess the situation."

The captain stepped forward, and in an instant sized Devak up. High-status, but young, his clothes modest for someone of his rank. Any respect the captain might have shown Devak dropped several notches.

"We have the situation handled, Manel-Mar," the captain said, his tone barely polite. "Your presence isn't needed."

"Six of the residents of this warren were scheduled to be Assigned to one of our kel-grain processing factories in Peq sector," Devak said, hardening his tone. "I need to know if they survived."

The captain pulled out his sekai, his pale-eyed gaze fixed on Devak. Would he dare insult a trueborn from the high-status Manels by checking Devak's story? The factory didn't exist. Pitamah said he'd try to get a tech to add the fictional facility to the industrial database, but on such short notice, it might not have been done.

Ved Manel's imperiousness might have been the only useful thing he'd bequeathed to his son, and Devak used it now. It was a tilt of the chin, a looking down the nose, eyes narrowed. It was a careless lifting of his wristlink, fingers reaching for the com button as if readying to report the captain to his commander.

The captain shoved the sekai back in his pocket. "Only one death. An enforcer on patrol near the warren."

"And the GEN kit," Devak said.

The captain shrugged. "The nurture mother thought her mate had taken the kit, her mate thought the nurture mother did. A pity. The kit had a tech sket. Expensive jik to lose."

Anger burned inside Devak at the captain's heartless attitude. "You won't mind if I look for my workers, then." He motioned toward the GEN enforcer. "And I'll take him with me. For protection."

The captain smirked. "He's lazy and useless, but you can have him. And I'll ask you to wait until my men question and download the lot of them before any of them slither away."

The captain gestured to two of his squad members and they moved off around the rubble. Devak and the GEN enforcer took the longer route on the other side of the wreckage.

The GEN man kept a respectful pace behind Devak, but stayed near enough that his low voice was audible. "I'm Waji."

Glancing back, Devak saw the moment it clicked with Waji that Devak was Zul's great-grandson. A familiar worshipful look sparked in the GEN man's eyes.

Devak supposed that connection was better than the one most trueborns made—to his father, Ved. "Do you know what happened with the safe house?"

"The underground structure survived the explosion," Waji said, "so they were able to initiate the evacuation procedure."

The two members of the Brigade squad that the captain had sent over had the former warren residents lined up. One of the enforcers questioned the adult GENs verbally. The other went down the line and slapped his datapod against each GEN's cheek, man, woman, and child, downloading their annexed brains.

Even from a distance it was easy to see when the datapod's

extendibles connected with the facial tattoo's circuitry. The GEN being downloaded would flinch from the pain of the extendibles piercing the skin, then go blank-eyed when the download began.

Devak and Waji stood just out of earshot of the enforcers while Devak made a show of searching for those supposedly Assigned to the Manel's factory. He had his sekai out as if to scan through it and a datapod in his hand ready to use when the Brigade had finished.

Waji's light brown eyes narrowed as one of the enforcers tore his datapod from a child's cheek before the extendibles had completely retracted. The GEN enforcer's hand dropped to his shockgun, fingers toying with the holster snap. The GEN-issue weapon was lower power than the trueborn version, but its blast would knock the trueborn enforcer unconscious for several minutes.

Devak positioned himself between Waji and the cruel enforcer. "Did everyone get out of the safe house?"

"Most of them." Waji flicked a glance over at Devak. "Have you heard about the updated evacuation procedures?"

"I know that the sick sometimes have to be left behind." Devak felt sick at the thought. "That the enforcers take them."

"This goes beyond that. It's a recent decision. Because of the number of safe houses discovered by the Brigade." Waji leaned to one side of Devak, his gaze on the other enforcers. "Once as many as can have evacuated, they destroy the safe house."

"They? You mean the Brigade?"

"The Kinship," Waji said. "They've started booby trapping them to implode and collapse before an enforcer gets inside. Nafi was the first."

Devak stared at Waji. "That can't be true."

"When those enforcers find the safe house entrance," Waji said, "every tunnel will be buried. They might find the access point under the warren, but they'll likely assume it's just a hiding place for contraband goods."

"But the ones left behind . . . wouldn't it mostly be GENs killed? Because they're the only ones with Scratch?"

Emotions flickered across Waji's face, anger, outrage. It mirrored the anger on the tall GEN man's face. Again Devak thought of the lowborn riots, how people could only bear so much misery before they struck back.

Then a bleak mask fell over Waji's face. "Yes, only GENs killed. Although not crushed to death, thank the Infinite. Before they left, the medics would have helped them into His great Hands."

Help them. Inject them with something to hasten their death, more like it.

"I can't believe Pitamah would sanction this."

Waji met his gaze. "He may not. I've heard . . ." The GEN glanced away, then back at Devak. "He has less sway now with the Kinship than he used to. Ever since . . ."

Since they lost so much status. Anger burst inside Devak at the realization that Junjie was entirely right. The Kinship was just as fixated on status as trueborn society at large. For them to callously allow the death of sick GENs, when their mission was intended to save lives, to improve GEN rights, made the Kinship no better than these arrogant enforcers.

He had to speak to Pitamah about this as soon as possible. This was what came of avoiding attending Kinship meetings with his great-grandfather. He might have seen before now that Pitamah was losing influence. Maybe he could have done something.

The two enforcers finally signaled to Devak they'd finished their inquisition of the GENs. Devak went along the line, using his datapod on the cheek of each adult male, then pretending to check the download against a list on his sekai reader. He took care to place the datapod on each GEN's cheek in a spot that hadn't already been savaged by the enforcer, then waited to be sure the extendibles had retracted when the download had finished. Even so, he wished he could have apologized to each man.

The man whose nurture daughter had been killed in the explosion was the last one to be downloaded. He was tall enough to meet Devak's gaze, and his unguarded rage startled Devak. He hesitated putting the datapod to the man's cheek.

"Why are you bombing our warrens?" the man asked, his voice so soft Devak was sure the enforcers couldn't hear.

"I had nothing to do with it," Devak said.

"You trueborns—haven't you made our lives wretched enough? But to take our homes, kill our . . ." The GEN man swallowed convulsively.

"It wasn't trueborns. And you'd better not let them hear you say such things." He held up the datapod. "I have to download you. If I don't, they'll wonder why."

The man's dark gaze burned into Devak. Then he turned slightly, offering up the GEN tattoo on his left cheek. "By the Infinite, take what you want."

Devak applied the datapod, and as the download initiated, the GEN man's eyes went blank as he blacked out. What kind of strength this man must possess to speak out that way. He'd made himself so vulnerable to Devak when he clearly would as soon have wrenched Devak's head off.

Devak looked down the line at the gathered GENs, at Waji, a Kinship stalwart. The placid, despairing acceptance with their lot he saw in so many GENs was missing in this group. It might be difficult for GENs to communicate across sector borders, but they managed it, when GEN Assignments moved them from one place to another, or when an itinerant GEN like Kayla passed on news.

As more GENs heard about the bombings, as their anger grew, then what? They couldn't all be reset to keep them under control. Some would surely escape, some might strike back.

The datapod dropped from the man's cheek into Devak's palm. The GEN man's eyes regained their sharp intelligence. He reached out his hand, although he didn't dare touch Devak.

He said softly, "Thank you. For covering her properly."

Devak gave a brisk nod and turned away. His throat felt tight.

He narrowed his gaze on the smirking captain and his arrogant squad. Why couldn't the trueborn enforcers see the humanity of these GENs? Or the worth of Waji, a faithful member of their ranks despite their dismissive treatment of him?

And Kayla, the best of them. Courageous, strong, kind, but fierce. Protective of those she cared about.

Yet these trueborn enforcers would abuse her at the least imagined transgression. They would reset her, turn her into someone else, at the slightest impression of disrespect. Even he would not be able to protect her if she fell into the hands of the Brigade.

And the Kinship, the one place he thought he and Kayla might have cobbled together a friendship—now he saw the truth. Even within the Kinship, he and Kayla couldn't be together. There was judgment even there.

It had to change. Someday, surely it would be different. A few trueborns would first accept, then embrace equality, then a few more. Someday, all of Svarga would see nothing wrong with a marriage or joining between a GEN and high-status trueborn.

But not now, and not for a long, long time. And the only way to save Kayla from trueborn judgment would be to give up even the least dream of any alliance between them. To let her be with Abran, or someone like him.

His wristlink beeped, signaling a message from Pitamah. He dragged himself from his despair to read what his great-grandfather had sent.

They took Gemma to Ret sector, the first message read.

Then, *She died along the way.*

Devak's heart fell, even though he'd never met the girl. Then the next message came through, and he read it over several times in hopes it would somehow make sense.

She's alive again, and healing everyone she touches.

19

Junjie galloped as fast as he could to the Daki sector GEN warren, but he was still soaked by the time he reached the blocky building and got under cover. As he headed down the warren's first-floor hall, his teeth chattered so hard he bit his tongue. When he got to the communal washroom at the end of the hall, his stiff fingers twice flubbed the code to the safe house trap door hidden in one of the showers. A third time would have locked him out.

To his infinite gratitude, the moment he emerged from the access tunnel into the safe house, Xiana, a lowborn kitchen worker, spotted him and ran for a cup of hot kelfa drink. Xiana shouted to a GEN assistant for a blanket, which the GEN, Zo, threw across Junjie's wet shoulders, at the same time offering a towel to dry Junjie's drenched hair.

He turned down the towel, but asked for a quiet corner to work, explaining he was there to correct a small programming problem in Kayla 6982. Xiana's and Zo's faces lit up at the mention of Kayla. All the safe house people seemed to know her, and idolized her almost as much as they did Zul. Junjie wondered if Kayla even knew what it meant to Kinship GENs and lowborns alike that she'd helped save those lowborn children and had sacrificed the restoration treatment in lieu of her friend.

They led him into the meeting room where the Kinship usually convened. Carved out of Daki's red rock, the roundish space was just big enough for a two meter by three meter table and ten chairs. More important, the room had a door for the privacy Junjie would need.

Xiana refilled Junjie's kelfa cup and Zo fetched a plate of kel-grain rolls that he set on the table. Then they went back to their work of cleaning up from the morning meal, conscripting some ninth- and tenth-year boys and girls to help. They scolded anyone who so much as looked Junjie's way.

From the doorway to the meeting room, Junjie could watch for Kayla's arrival from any of the four entrances. As he waited, sipping the kelfa, he ran through his mind the sequence of uploads and downloads he'd be doing via his datapod and wristlink. It would be a lot to add all at once, but with Kayla already so self-aware of what had already been done to her, they might not have another chance to install everything else.

Despite his needling of Devak to come with him, Junjie never expected his friend to say yes. It would have been awkward to have Devak along. He might ask questions. But Kayla was so used to uploads and the occasional download, she likely wouldn't say a word.

When she finally stepped from the tunnel on the far side of the safe house main room, he waved her over. Then she got close enough for him to make out the serious, determined look on her face, and unease prickled up Junjie's spine. But maybe she was just preoccupied with some detail of her work with Risa, or the inconvenience of having that GEN boy, Abran, with them, or Daki's nasty weather.

He motioned her into the meeting room and shut the door, then waited for her to sit. But as he took a chair facing her, her eyes narrowed on him and the words spilled out.

"I'm fed up with being programmed, Junjie, without anyone letting me know what or why. That stops right now. I want to know everything you're doing today, before you do it."

Everything. *Everything.* He couldn't possibly reveal all of it, at least not yet. His compatriots weren't ready for that, most especially not Neta.

"I . . . ah . . ." He offered up his datapod. "First I need to turn off the Kinship failsafe. So I don't, you know, fry your brain."

She plucked the datapod from his fingers. "The only reason to turn off the failsafe is if you plan to download me."

"Sorry, I have to." Truth. "I have to know what all might have gotten stored in your brain." Mostly truth. "So I can clear out what shouldn't be there." Mostly a lie.

She waggled the datapod at him. "That's all that's in the first upload?"

"Yes. I swear."

She stared at him a few moments longer, then activated the datapod. "I'll do it." One last suspicious look at him and she applied it to her tattooed right cheek.

She didn't even flinch at the bite of the extendibles into her skin. He supposed with all the uploads she got, she was used to the momentary pain of the needle-like extendibles.

She kept her gaze on him and Junjie felt like she was stripping his thoughts right out of his mind, the way an enforcer would download a GEN's annexed brain. He wanted to tell her, *It wasn't me that programmed you.* But that wasn't exactly a hundred percent true.

And would be even less true after today's session.

The red light on the datapod flashed green and Kayla caught the device as the extendibles retracted. He reached for the datapod, but she closed her hand around it.

"What else are you going to do?" she asked. "Step by step."

Oh, sweet Infinite, he was a terrible liar. But if he didn't say something, she might use her sket and crush the thumb-sized datapod with her fingers.

His mouth went bone dry as he cast about for a story. Something he could tell her with a straight face that might persuade her to go through with everything.

But what if he said the wrong thing and made her mad? She wouldn't hit him, would she? Take a swing at him with one of her powerful fists?

No. Kayla wouldn't hurt *him.* But the datapod, with all the culminating programming on it, might not survive.

He made the leap into some more partial truth. "Okay," he squeaked. "It *was* me."

"What was you?" Kayla snapped.

"The extra programming," Junjie said. "I created it. I had it added to the datapod uploads you've been getting." Mostly a lie. He'd only written a small part of the code, and someone else distributed it.

Kayla's fingers flexed around the datapod. "Why?"

Careful. "Sometimes it seems the Kinship moves so slow."

That was nothing but the honest truth. "I think GENs deserve more. Sooner. Now. And especially you."

"Why me?"

A lump lodged itself in his throat. Because *she* wanted it, that's why. But he couldn't say that. "Because of everything you've done. Because I think you deserve better."

"What's this *better* that you decided I should have?" She pinched the datapod between thumb and index finger. "Without asking my permission?"

He wanted to beg her forgiveness. Because he hadn't liked it one bit that his compatriots were deciding for her, just like Zul and the rest of the Kinship did. But sometimes trueborns just couldn't seem to help themselves. It was as if they were genetically engineered to run things. For the first time, Junjie sort of wished he'd been demoted to a lowborn instead of a minor-status when his mother died.

"You've already noticed some of the changes," Junjie finally said. "You're better able to see what's being uploaded. And it improves some of your GEN abilities, like the speed of your circuitry. You can warm yourself faster and more efficiently. You can track data and make mental computations and such much quicker."

"And the healing," she said.

He hadn't a clue why she might be healing faster. "Yeah, sure. But Zul doesn't know," he said hastily. "No one knows but me." That last word almost got stuck in his throat.

Her hand closed around the datapod again. "You're not changing my genetics, are you? Your programming can't do that, can it?"

Suddenly he remembered the overheard conversation

between Hala and Akhilesh. How Akhilesh implied his experiments were using upload programming to alter GEN genetics.

"No," Junjie said emphatically. "The uploads have only altered or replaced the programming in your annexed brain. Anything genetic, like your strength sket, I can't change."

"And how did the letters FHE get stored in my bare brain?" She asked.

That was a stumper. Some hotshot programmer thought he or she was being cute.

"I don't know," Junjie said. "Truly. My stuff didn't put that there."

Quicker than he might have expected, her free hand shot out and grabbed his wrist. "Then there's someone besides you involved."

He gaped at her. "I don't—"

She shook him. "Who?"

Her hold didn't hurt, but it felt a little like being in the clutches of a bhimkay. "No one." Another shake. "Please—"

"We're done then." She got up and stuffed the datapod into the pocket in her waistband.

"Wait, please." He grabbed her shirt as she turned away. "Let me explain."

She stared down at him, then with a sigh, sat down again. "Talk. No more chutting around with me."

"Okay. Right." He locked his hands together in his lap. "I can't tell you everything. But everything I say will be the truth. You decide what to do." That was how it should have been. They should have brought Kayla in at the start. Let her choose.

She waved at him to continue. "Okay," Junjie said. "Everything we've done so far is to make you better."

"That remains to be seen. Who's 'we'?"

He shook his head. "Can't say exactly. Based on the uploads you've gotten, you can guess who some of us are."

He could see the calculation in Kayla's eyes. "Celia? The trueborn woman who picked up Gemma?"

"Yes."

"And everyone who's uploaded me since then?"

"Not all of them are FHE," Junjie told her. "Some of them gave you our programming without knowing it."

She was silent a long time. Then she gestured at him to go on.

"We're trying to free the GENs," Junjie said. "Just like the Kinship is. Only differently. With the programming." What he was leaving out, their other tactic, weighed on him as heavy as a thousand kilos of plasscrete. But it wouldn't take Kayla long to put those pieces together.

"What else is on the datapod?" she asked.

"Some stuff I know. A substitute for what the Kinship does to protect you from the Grid. A way for you to store bare brain memories into your annexed brain. I helped with those. But the rest they haven't told me."

"So it could be anything," she said, her hand going to her waistband where she'd tucked the thumb-sized device. "It could reset me for all you know."

"No! It wouldn't. I trust these people. They only want to help."

Her mouth twisted in a smile. "Maybe I don't want their help. Can you really erase those letters in my bare brain?"

"Yes."

"Can you do it without uploading the rest of that stuff?"

He sighed. "Yeah. I have another datapod and the algorithm is copied on my wristlink." She'd be ticked. But maybe she should have been here explaining it to Kayla.

"I'll keep this one then." She patted her secret pocket.

He'd handled this about as badly as he thought he might. Well, if they'd done this the right way, Kayla would have willingly taken what the FHE had to offer.

He dug his spare datapod from his pocket. Kayla plucked it neatly from his hand. "How do I know this doesn't have more of that programming on it?"

Junjie grimaced, then unlatched his wristlink and passed it over to her. "Know how to clear a datapod?"

"Of course."

She flipped over the wristlink and after pressing the tiny button on the datapod to engage the extendibles, she snapped the datapod into the port on the back of the wristlink. Her fingers flashed across the small keyboard on the front of the wristlink, then the display declared, *Data flushed. Content zero.*

For a non-tech GEN, Kayla *had* learned a few things during her time with the Kinship. Even before his compatriots started dumping all that new programming into her.

Junjie brought up the list of software on his wristlink. "JT8840 is the one that'll erase the code in your bare brain."

"How do I know you're not lying?" she asked.

"By the Infinite's hands, I'm telling the truth."

He saw the shock in her eyes at his invocation of her deity. His deity now. He'd dug deeper into the false prophets' made-up liturgy and discovered they'd lifted much of it from ancient Earth documents. Documents with far more truth and majesty than anything he'd learned about the Lord Creator.

When she still stared at him, Junjie said, "Read through JT8840 if you're not sure."

"Purging a datapod is one thing. I can't understand programming code."

"You can now," Junjie told her. "That's part of what got uploaded in your annexed brain. Bring JT8840 up on the display and read through it."

She gave him a dubious look, but did as he'd asked. He watched her eyes grow wider as she scrolled through the code.

"Is this a trick?" she asked.

He gave a little shriek of exasperation. "It's a simple program. You've just read it. If you still don't trust me, you'll just have to live with the letters in your bare brain."

Her thumb tapping on the wristlink, she sat silent for a good long time. Then she looked up at him. "Do you swear by the Infinite's hands this is the only thing you'll upload?"

"I do." His hand went to the prayer mirror tucked in the hem of his shirt. She didn't miss the now automatic motion.

"Can I see it?" she asked.

"Sure." He rarely pulled it out, but he put it in Kayla's hands. "I made it myself."

He'd used a reflective mirror from a defunct microscope. The etching on the back of the Infinite's cupped hands was clumsy, but Kayla admired it nonetheless.

She gave it back to him and he put it away. "I'm ready," she said.

He had her copy the JT8840 program herself onto the datapod, then double-check that that was the only thing loaded on it. Then she released the datapod from the wristlink and pressed it to her tattoo. The light flashed red as the extendibles bit.

And her eyes went blank.

"Wait!" Junjie jumped to his feet. She wasn't supposed to be downloaded. What was going on? "Kayla!"

She didn't respond, her gaze empty. Great Infinite, he wasn't accidentally resetting her, was he? Horror filled him at the thought. But he didn't even possess the GEN reset program.

Then her eyes started flickering to life, but they didn't stay alert. They flashed from glassy to aware, strobing back and forth so quickly he was sure he had damaged her. He reached for the datapod, thinking to tear it from her cheek, but he feared he would catch it at that moment of download emptiness and somehow ruin her even worse.

Finally, in quick succession, her eyes filled with life again and the datapod light flashed green. Kayla slapped the thing away from her cheek and it rattled across the table.

Her hands covered her face. She stared at him, but in that moment didn't seem to be seeing him.

"Please, Kayla," Junjie pleaded, sinking into his chair. "Oh, dear Infinite, you're not reset, are you?"

20

Kayla slowly shook her head. She could barely keep in check her rage at the . . . invasion? Not strong enough. The *rape* of her mind.

She tightened her hands into fists to keep herself from wrapping them around Junjie's neck. "Did you do that?"

Terror and horror mixed in equal amounts in his face. "No, I would never have. Not after I promised you." He gasped in a breath that sounded like a sob. "I don't even know what *that* was."

"It downloaded me," Kayla said. "And I could *feel* it. Feel it stripping everything from me."

"But you blacked out," Junjie said. "I could see it in your eyes. They . . . flickered in and out."

She remembered that. Paralyzed, but aware. Then switching back and forth between that frozen download state and awake as she was uploaded.

Junjie really was crying now, his eyes wet, one tear spilling. "I was only uploading the one program. Did it even work?"

She followed along the pathways as she'd learned to do,

retracing the neural network to where FHE had been stored. Just as Junjie had promised, the letters had been erased.

"Yes. But there are hundreds, maybe thousands of new programs running in my annexed brain."

Understanding flashed on Junjie's face, tightening the knot inside Kayla's stomach. "I think . . ." Junjie gulped. "There are two possibilities. One, someone hid those programs on my datapod. But it was my own personal one. I bought it new from a tech shop in Plator."

"Or . . . ?" Kayla prodded.

"The programs have been in you all this time. Maybe since you got that first FHE upload from Celia. Probably compressed or distributed throughout your annexed brain, so you wouldn't recognize them. Something must have triggered the download, expanded the programs, then installed them in your annexed brain."

Kayla leaned closer to Junjie. "And what could have triggered that, except you?"

He slapped his thighs. "It wasn't me! Maybe the programs on my datapod detected me deleting them, and set off a secondary protocol. They must have known I might get cold feet. So they made sure."

She wanted to believe him. Of all the trueborns she'd met, she'd been certain that Junjie, more than Zul, even more than Devak, had seen her as his equal. "Tell me why, Junjie. And no denking lies."

In a motion as natural as any GEN's, Junjie swept his prayer mirror out again. He held it up against his heart and his lips moved in some brief silent prayer.

When he'd finished, he said, "The FHE wants to bring

you in." He wrapped his fingers more tightly around his prayer mirror. "To make you part of us. So they wanted you prepared."

Prepared against my will. Her outrage seemed to fill the small meeting room, to pound against the granite walls. "*What* did they put inside me?"

"They don't tell me everything." *Just like the Kinship,* Kayla thought. "I don't know the names of anyone. I've only spoken to two people, a boy, and a woman I call Neta." He lowered his voice a little. "Our leader."

"I don't care about that, Junjie. What's the programming?"

"I'm not sure," he wailed. "I can only guess. First, a way to hide their programming if you're downloaded. Then, a way for your brain to write its own programs you might need, and to hide those. A way to increase your memory capacity. All of it's to your benefit—"

She slammed her hand on the table, denting the surface. "But no one asked me! You trueborns think I'm some kind of animal slave, the Kinship acts as if I'm a child, and now the FHE treats me like a denking machine."

"You're not an animal to me, Kayla," Junjie said quietly. "If I'd known they planned this, I wouldn't have done it. I swear to you."

Her stomach hurt, she was so angry. But she could see the remorse in Junjie's eyes. He reminded her of her nurture brother, that time Jal had broken a carved plasscine doll she'd treasured. Jal had begged for her forgiveness, as close to tears just as Junjie was now.

She let go of her rage; it was useless anyhow. Junjie wasn't the enemy. She'd never heard him speak a negative word against any GEN. Even when suspicion of every trueborn urged her to mistrust him, instinct told her Junjie was telling her the truth, at least as he knew it. She saw it in his unflinching gaze, and the way his fingertip traced the etching of the Infinite's hands on the back of his prayer mirror as he still whispered to the great deity.

She sucked in a long breath. "How do I get all this out of me?"

Her heart fell at his miserable expression. "I don't know," he said. "It's probably so distributed, I'd have a hard time finding it all. And if I only managed to erase part of it, the broken pieces of programming would really mess up your thinking."

Denking hell, to have to live with these unwanted uploads. Yet she'd agreed to myriad other uploads from the Kinship. Until the FHE programming had allowed her to read what had been stored in her annexed brain, she hadn't given much thought to what the Kinship might be shipping along her neural circuitry.

"Um . . ." Junjie glanced sideways at the datapod she'd thrown. "Do I put the Kinship failsafe back in place?"

"Only if you can do it with a datapod *you* had nothing to do with."

She was tempted to just do without it, to take the risk. But if an enforcer downloaded her without the failsafe and got that treasure trove of Kinship data, she'd be reset anyway. She still had enough loyalty to at least some in the Kinship—Risa for instance, and Mishalla—to want to protect them.

So Kayla sought out the resident safe house tech, a twentieth-year GEN woman, and explained that the contents of both of Junjie's datapods were corrupt. Curiosity sparked in the tech's eyes, but used to Kinship secrets, she didn't question Kayla's excuse. She just sorted through her datapods for the right one and handed it to Kayla.

Kayla applied the device to her tattooed cheek and waited for the brief failsafe activation to complete. Except the upload seemed sluggish, as if her annexed brain were resisting the process. It seemed to take forever for the short string of text to travel along her circuitry to where the failsafe algorithm was stored.

"Not done yet?" the tech asked, eyeing the red light on the datapod.

Kayla shook her head. It reminded her of that first Kinship upload from her friend Skal, before her first Assignment. But that one took longer because of the message the Kinship was passing to her. This reactivation upload was just twenty or so characters of text.

Just as she panicked at the thought that this was some other FHE programming, that the tech was one of them too, the activation clicked into place. Kayla did a quick survey of her annexed brain and found nothing new hiding.

Kayla handed back the datapod and she and Junjie started back to the meeting room. Along the way, a naggingly familiar buzzing started up in Kayla's ears. When she recognized the sound, new panic shot through her. She drew Junjie out of the press of bodies and whispered, "I can't possibly be back on the Grid, can I?"

"Uh uh. No way." Junjie shook his head. "I guarantee you, that would be the last thing they'd want."

"Because what I'm hearing is the same as what I heard right before I was taken off the Grid that first time. A buzz I wasn't even aware of until it suddenly got quiet."

Junjie lowered his voice so he could barely be heard over the safe house noise. "It might be all those programs competing for processor time. That can cause some static."

She crammed her hands over her ears, but the noise was internal. Then from one heartbeat to the next, the static coalesced to one word.

Kayla!

She jumped, heart racing as she looked around her. "Who was that?"

Junjie gaped. "Who was what?"

"You heard it, didn't you? Someone called my name."

Junjie looked uneasy. "I didn't hear anything."

"I'm not crazy." Now she squeezed her eyes shut, listening hard. The buzz was back in her ears. But she was sure she'd heard—

"Kayla!"

She jumped again, this time knocking Junjie into the wall. Then she saw the elderly high-status trueborn heading toward them.

It was one of Zul's old friends, the medic, Jemali. "Kayla, I'm glad I caught you. We need you at Ret sector safe house."

"Junjie and I aren't finished." Kayla speared the minor-status boy with a hard look. "He's been telling me all about—"

Junjie waved his hands at her, just about turning himself inside out to stop her from speaking. She turned her back on him. "He's telling me about—"

Her throat seemed to close. *FHE* dangled at the tip of her tongue, but she couldn't speak the letters out loud.

She rounded on Junjie, but he seemed as alarmed as she was. He whispered in a sort of terrified awe, "They've blocked you."

"Can your conversation wait?" Jemali asked, oblivious to their byplay. "There was another warren explosion in Nafi sector. A sixth-year GEN girl was killed."

"No," Junjie moaned.

The last piece fell into place, the truth that had been staring her in the face, that she'd tried to ignore. She kept her gaze steady on Junjie, and saw the confirmation. *FHE has been blowing up warrens and warehouses. And Junjie is neck deep in FHE.*

But did FHE have some connection to Ved Manel? Or was this Neta the key player? Maybe Neta and Ved were working together. Or did Ved Manel truly have nothing to do with the bombings?

She wanted to grill Junjie about FHE and the bombings, but she couldn't get the words out. After a few frustrating moments of trying, she instead asked Jemali, "Why do you need me in Ret and not Nafi?"

"Ret is where we evacuated Gemma and some of the others from Nafi," Jemali said. "But Gemma died along the way."

That was a jolt. "I'm sorry to hear that."

"She resurrected, Kayla," Jemali told her. "Shortly after she arrived in Ret."

The stories from Esa sector about Raashida came back to her. "Or she wasn't truly dead, and she revived."

"That may be. In any case, after she revived, a few of the sick who she touched were healed completely of their Scratch. It terrified her. She's begging for you and Risa to come back for her and take her away. She said she felt safe with you."

I hardly know her, Kayla wanted to say. But then she felt ashamed of herself. Gemma was a GEN, her double identity likely the cause of some trueborn mischief. If Kayla could help her, she ought to.

"Will you come?" Jemali asked. "At the least, I think it would comfort the girl to see you."

"Yes," Kayla said, then grabbed Junjie's arm. "You're coming too." She pulled the trueborn boy along as she followed Jemali.

They rode to Ret sector in Jemali's WindSpear in near silence. Silence, that is, except for the unrelenting buzz in her head. Several times she tried to thwart the block FHE had installed, but she could never get out more than a few stuttering words. She finally gave up.

As she stepped clear of the access tunnel into the common room of the Ret safe house, she could see nothing but a wall of bodies between her and where she guessed the sick room lay. "What's going on?" she asked over the roar of voices. "Where's Gemma?" Jemali, a head and a half taller than Kayla, straightened to see over those packing the space.

"Lord Creator!" Jemali exclaimed. "They're attacking her."

He started pushing through the crowd, Kayla following in the old trueborn's wake, Junjie behind her. She could see nothing but Jemali's back until they finally broke through into the sick room.

Even then, she could scarcely believe what she was seeing. A mob of forty or fifty Scratch-afflicted GENs, their Scratch wounds suppurating and seeping, were out of their beds and surging toward one end of the sick room. Twenty or so lowborns and healthy GENs faced the sick and formed a barricade against them, arms locked, their bodies in two rows. And behind them, Gemma cowered, squeezed into a corner of the sick room, her back to the carved-out wall. She had her hands up to ward off anyone coming close to her.

"Don't touch me," she moaned. "Don't anyone touch me."

With sick GENs trying to spill around the human barricade, Kayla forced her way in to help. As she reached for the first person in the line to join the chain, she half-stumbled when she realized whose hand she took—Devak's.

Devak spared her only a brief glance before a roughly shoving GEN recaptured his attention. Jemali went for the far end, Junjie with him. Just as he took his place, Junjie got slammed into the wall by an eager GEN, but he recovered quickly. Now they pushed the seething bodies back, trying to give Gemma more space. What they would do next, Kayla had no idea.

Kayla craned her neck around at Gemma. She looked better than she had when Kayla and Risa had last seen her—much better. Her short dark hair was thick and lustrous, she had some color in her pale face, and the few Scratch scars that had been visible on her arms had vanished. In fact, Gemma all but glowed, as if the Infinite had shaped her body with His hands, making her beautiful and vibrant.

It was impossible to believe she had *died*. She must have fallen into a brief coma, then awakened. Yet how could she look so healthy, so radiant, if she'd been ill enough in the last few hours to fall into unconsciousness?

When the crowd shifted enough for Kayla to see past them, she spotted a few Scratch victims, near death, who remained in their beds. A few more knelt nearby, prayer mirrors out, calling out praise to the Infinite. The kneeling GENs were healing from their Scratch just as Gemma had, the marks starting to scab over.

The crowd shifted again and now Kayla could see a brown-skinned GEN man on hands and knees all but crushed between the packed bodies. As people jockeyed for position in the crowd, more than one GEN stepped on him. She wondered why he didn't stand, then it registered—he had no feet. They'd been eaten away by Scratch.

He squirmed along the floor between the legs of the crowd, then through the chain of people holding back the sick. Looking behind her, Kayla saw him reach toward Gemma with hands missing half their fingers. Gemma pressed herself even farther back against the sick room wall in horror, but the man touched her. He cried out in ecstasy and moved back from Gemma again, looking at his wounded hands as if expecting a miracle.

Kayla spied a mixed group of lowborns and GENs in the common room gaping at the scene. "Someone come take that man back to his bed. The rest of you take our places so we can get Gemma out of here."

At first they didn't budge, making Kayla angry enough to wrench a few arms. Then a tall, stout lowborn woman, the safe house manager from her demeanor, barreled down on the awestruck audience.

"Get in there and do what she says," the lowborn woman thundered, "or I'll be knocking heads together!"

The gawking GENs and lowborns finally seethed into the sick room. Two GENs gently picked up the brown-skinned man and carried him to a bed. Six burly lowborns replaced Devak, Junjie, and Jemali in the barricade. The safe house manager took Kayla's place.

Kayla moved to Gemma's side, Devak, Junjie, and Jemali backing her up. Kayla would have taken the girl's hand, but Gemma waved her off.

"I can't let you touch me, Kayla."

"But we have to get you out of here." Kayla looked over at Jemali and Devak. "Is there somewhere else we can take her?"

"No door on the meeting room here," Devak said, "so it would have to be one of the access tunnels. The openings are narrow enough we can keep this chutting lot out."

Kayla would have called him on his insult against her fellow GENs, but she was sickened by them herself. It was frightening the way they'd trampled the brown-skinned man and were scaring Gemma. The crowd had shown no respect for elderly Jemali, nearly knocking the old trueborn off his feet.

"Can the boys help you up?" Kayla asked Gemma.

The girl nodded and Devak and Junjie moved in to take her hands. The lowborns holding back the crowd pushed harder against the sick to make a path. Jemali led the way, then Gemma and the boys, then Kayla as close as she could behind Gemma to shield her from the crowd. Just as they'd escorted Gemma from the sick room to the common room, a GEN man lunged toward them, his Scratch marks oozing and ugly. "I just want to touch her!"

Kayla planted a hand on the man's chest and he sprawled backward onto the stone floor. "Anyone else?" Kayla shouted.

A GEN woman, her face marked with the angry red of an early Scratch infection, dug her fingers into Kayla's arm. "Don't you see?" the woman said, her pale eyes wide in her face, "she's the Infinite's daughter, come to save us."

It was like what the allabain were saying about Raashida in Esa sector. Except the allabain had called her Iyenkas's daughter, not the Infinite's. Other Scratch-infected GENs in the sick room tried to reach Gemma, but the lowborn and GEN volunteers blocked the way out. The crowd in the common room parted as Jemali pushed through and finally the way was clear to the tunnel they'd entered from.

Another ten meters, then they were able to duck into the tunnel. Jemali switched on a borrowed illuminator to give them more light. A phalanx of lowborns in the common room closed off the tunnel entrance.

Kayla backed up to the damp tunnel wall to give Gemma her space as best she could. "Why is it Devak and Junjie can touch you, but I can't?"

Gemma's voice shook as she spoke. "Because they don't follow the Infinite."

Junjie jolted, pulling his hand away from Gemma. "What does that have to do with anything?"

"They were all dying," Gemma said. "Or would be dying soon enough when the Scratch got bad enough. They would be stepping into the Infinite's hands. But the ones I touched . . . I healed them. I've stolen their chance to rejoin the Infinite."

Junjie rubbed his hands together, worry in his dark brown eyes. "Your healing them just means they'll live a little longer, then die of something else. They'll get their chance to meet the Infinite." His hand strayed to where he'd tucked away his prayer mirror.

Gemma stared at him, tears filling her eyes again. "I don't think so. This was their chance. What if I cut them off from the Infinite forever?"

"But you've already healed me, Gemma, remember?" Kayla said as the pieces clicked together in her mind. "When we first picked you up, I had a gash on my cheek that you healed."

Now Gemma looked even more horrified. "No."

Kayla softened her voice. “Your healing hasn’t cut me off from the Infinite. There’s nothing in the liturgy like that.”

She couldn’t seem to help herself—Kayla glanced over at Devak. They both knew that the liturgy of the Infinite was pure fiction created by trueborns. But most GENs didn’t know that. It had taken long hours of soul-searching for Kayla to abandon the beliefs she’d been raised with, clinging only to what her heart told her was true—the existence and omniscience of the Infinite.

“I think He would understand, Gemma,” Kayla said. “He’ll find their souls again.”

“I didn’t know what I was doing,” Gemma said. “When I woke, I was just going bed to bed, offering them water. Then the ones I touched rose from their beds, and they were calling me daughter of the Infinite. It’s sacrilege. The Infinite has no daughter.”

“They’ve been sick,” Kayla said. “They didn’t know what they were saying.”

But the same had not been true for the allabain. Even the ones who had never been healed by Raashida were worshipping her. Would these GENs do the same with Gemma now that they’d seen what she could do?

“They all wanted me to touch them,” Gemma said. “To heal them. Even Mephi.”

“The one we saw on his knees?” Kayla asked.

Gemma squeezed her eyes shut. “He was nearly dead. Feet gone. Nothing but sores and ooze and stink. I tried not to let him touch me because I knew the Infinite was waiting for him. Then I realized He was waiting for all of them, but I had interfered.”

Kayla looked over at Jemali. "Can Mephi live like that? Healed of the Scratch but the rest of him . . ."

Jemali looked troubled. "He's probably lost more tissue than we saw. He must have internal organ damage. Whatever it is Gemma's doing, I can't help but think there are limits, that Mephi will die soon anyway, Scratch or no Scratch."

Kayla glanced from Jemali to Devak. "You were here before us. Did you see any of the Scratch-infected before she touched them? Is it possible the ones healing had already started to heal?"

"No one heals from Scratch," Jemali said.

"I healed them," Gemma said.

"Like Raashida—" Kayla cut herself off as three pairs of trueborn eyes turned her way.

Of course, Devak knew the GEN girl's name. What he hadn't learned on his own at the allabain camp in Esa sector, Mishalla would have told him. Jemali seemed in the dark, and she expected the same about Junjie, considering the way the Kinship compartmentalized information.

Except what if Junjie knew about Raashida because FHE had something to do with her and Gemma's healing ability? FHE's programming had speeded up Kayla's healing process, long after the effects of Gemma's touch had worn off. What if another FHE tweak could transfer that healing from a GEN to others?

Jemali turned his sharp focus on her. "Is there another GEN healing people? If there's more than one, it's something the Kinship should know."

Why *didn't* the Kinship know? Even if Mishalla hadn't reported to Zul, wouldn't Devak, despite Mishalla's plea not to?

But then, knowing Zul, if he'd been informed about Raashida, he might just keep her and her healing abilities secret.

"Raashida was just a GEN I knew in Chadi." If Zul could keep secrets, so could she. At least until she knew if FHE was involved. "What if the healing has nothing to do with Gemma? What if the Scratch virus has changed and now GEN healing works against it?" Kayla turned to Junjie. "That's possible, isn't it?"

"Sure," Junjie said readily, maybe because he was glad to deflect FHE involvement. "Viruses mutate all the time. Although Guru Ling and I haven't seen any mutation in the lab that responds to GEN self-healing."

"But it's possible," Kayla said.

"No," Gemma said, then she took hold of Kayla's hands. Gemma shoved up the long sleeves of Kayla's shirt. Devak's eyes narrowed and anger flickered in them. "Where did all those bruises come from?"

She'd barely paid attention to them when she'd dressed that morning. But now several of them had purpled up impressively. Her circuitry had healed the cuts, but the blood still pooled under the skin.

"I had to rescue someone from a creek yesterday in Skyloft sector," Kayla said, leaving it at that.

Gemma gripped her more tightly. "Do you feel it?"

Kayla did. Warmth traveled up her arms, the heat throbbing within each purple bruise. She could feel her ramped-up circuitry speed the process even more until she felt light-headed.

Gemma's eyes were closed, her face rapturous. Kayla watched as the bruises on her arms faded before her eyes, and she felt even woozier. Even the aching soreness of her muscles vanished.

Kayla was too stunned to react quickly enough when Gemma's grip loosened and the GEN girl collapsed. Devak caught her before she hit the hard stone of the tunnel.

Kayla took a step toward her. "I'll take her."

"I think touching you is what made her pass out." Devak lifted her in his arms. "Better to not take a chance."

"What if she tries to heal you?" Kayla asks.

"I'm not sick."

"What about wounds, like what I had?" Kayla asked.

"Nothing for her to heal," he said. "Jemali, do I take her back to the sick room?"

Jemali rested his wrist against Gemma's forehead. "She's a little feverish, but I don't know that she'd be safe in there. I don't think she can control when she heals, and it seems the more ill someone is, the more it takes out of her. Someone ill enough could hurt her badly."

"Then I'll take her to Two Rivers," Devak said. "Pitamah will know what to do."

Jemali looked from Gemma to the sick room beyond the tunnel. "I should stay here. See what I can do to ease Mephi's pain. Devak, can you take Kayla and Junjie where they belong?"

She'd rather walk the seventy or so kilometers back to Risa's lorry in Daki sector than ride in Devak's lev-car. But Junjie smiled with relief, no doubt planning to use Devak as an excuse to clam up about FHE. If Kayla wanted to pull more of the truth out of Junjie, she was going to have to figure out a way to get him alone. Maybe she and Risa should kidnap the boy.

For now she had no choice but to endure the close quarters with Devak. She followed him and Junjie down the tunnel.

21

As they walked through the misty night air from the alley where they'd exited the tunnel to the AirCloud, Devak calculated all the ways he could avoid sitting next to Kayla. Junjie could drive so Devak could sit in the back with Gemma. The two GEN girls could sit together, but that wouldn't fly after he'd insisted Kayla not touch the fragile Gemma. There wasn't enough room in the front passenger seat for both Junjie and Gemma, and the half-conscious girl shouldn't be up there alone. Which meant Junjie and Gemma in back and Devak up front with Kayla.

All those mental machinations of who should sit where only showed how turned inside out he was about Kayla. He even completely forgot to take much care to conceal himself and the others from possible onlookers as they exited the safe house.

Both suns had set, and although the rain had stopped, thick clouds concealed most of the trinity moons' light. And although the warehouse district was ill-lit enough obscure them, if an enforcer had happened along, Devak would have had a denking hard time explaining what he was doing carrying around a sick GEN.

Still, they made it to the AirCloud without being seen—or at least no one confronted them. Junjie helped Devak get Gemma situated in the back, arranging the girl as comfortably as they could on the narrow seat. Junjie even offered his lap as a pillow for her.

Devak was about to pull out when Junjie said, "Wait. Turn up the illuminators."

Devak did, then went up on his knees to see over the seat. Junjie pushed aside Gemma's short dark hair. New red marks striped the girl's face. "The Scratch is coming back," Junjie said.

Kayla leaned between the two front seats to see, her shoulder only millimeters from Devak's left arm. "Was she never really recovered? Her body just fought it off enough that she seemed healthy?"

Devak caught himself leaning closer to Kayla and pulled away instead. "Could she have caught it again from all the Scratch-infected in the sick room?" he asked.

"It can't have been that," Junjie said. "Scratch isn't infectious person-to-person."

Kayla tipped her head to one side, bringing her closer again. "Could the sickness have somehow boomeranged back on her when she was healing?"

Junjie scrunched up his mouth. "There's nothing scientific about that."

"There's nothing scientific about her being able to heal either," Devak said.

"Yes there is. We just haven't figured out the process yet."

Junjie sighed. "I wish I could have tested her when she was well. To see if her body had cleared the duwu out of her lymphatic system." For Kayla's benefit, Junjie explained, "That's a fluid that collects in GEN systems when they're Scratch-infected."

Devak faced forward again and powered on the AirCloud. "We'd better get going."

Kayla hadn't settled in her seat yet and as the lev-car jostled on the pocked road, she was thrown against Devak. She quickly moved away and strapped on her restraint, but sensation lingered all along Devak's arm where she'd touched him.

"She's not glowing anymore," Kayla said.

"Why in the Inf— Lord Creator's name would she glow?" Junjie asked.

"You didn't see it before? When I first saw her in the sick room, it seemed like she was giving off kind of a light. Energy of some kind. I felt it when she touched me. Heat shooting up my arm."

Like he'd felt when Kayla brushed against him. "I didn't feel anything like that when I was carrying her."

"She might have used the last of that healing power of hers on my bruises," Kayla said. "What about earlier, when you walked her from the sick room?"

Devak considered. "I might have felt some warmth, but there wasn't anything in me to heal." At the time, he'd thought it had something to do with Kayla being so near.

From the back, Junjie said, "I know I felt it. I didn't know what it was. But look at my hand." He thrust his right hand between the seats. "I cut that second knuckle on a broken flask yesterday. Some reagent splashed into it, so it got a chemical burn too."

Devak glanced over. Junjie's knuckle at the base of his middle finger was as smooth and unmarked as the others.

"Then she can heal GENs, lowborns, and trueborns alike," Kayla said. "Or could. If you can't feel anything from her now, Junjie, maybe she can't anymore."

"She just feels feverish," Junjie said. "Can you kill the illuminator? I think it's bothering her."

Devak did, plunging them into darkness. He could hear Kayla breathing beside him, and a fragrance drifted from her—flowers? A hint of qerfa spice? Or was it just *Kayla*, a scent unique to her?

As he guided the lev-car up the ramp to the northbound skyway, Kayla turned toward him. "Are you taking me to Risa first? Gemma needs care sooner than I need to be back at the lorry."

"It's only a short drive to Daki sector. If I took you to Two Rivers with me, I doubt I'd be able to get back this way before morning. I'm sure Risa wants to get on her way."

"And I'll be out of *your* way," she said quietly.

He got as far as taking a breath, the words on his tongue. Then he shook his head. "I was going to say, 'It's for the best.'"

"Do you think it is?" she asked.

He glanced in the rear viewer and saw Junjie slumped against the window, his mouth sagging open. Hopefully asleep.

"I think," Devak said softly, "that it's all getting too heavy for me to carry. I think you were right."

"About what?" Kayla asked.

"That by making decisions *for you* I'm making you *less*. And that's wrong."

She stared out the windscreen. "I suppose that's your way."

"It has been. But I've been rethinking a lot of what my parents taught me. Even what I learned from Pitamah. Between some things that Junjie made clear to me and what I found out tonight in Nafi sector, I've realized even the Kinship isn't what I thought it was."

She turned back to him. "I've been seeing that too."

"Do you know about the new evacuation procedures for safe houses?" he asked. When she shook her head, he related what Waji had told him.

"Oh," was all she said at first. "But Zul—"

"He was against it, but they ruled him down."

"I think I heard a little of that the morning you and I and Mishalla met in Esa. I called him on Risa's wristlink and interrupted him at a Kinship meeting. Can't Zul do anything to change it?"

"He's lost power," Devak said. "That's what happens to trueborns when their status slips."

"And GENs are always the pawns."

"Yes, more than anyone else," Devak agreed. "But sometimes I feel like a piece on a sarka board too, always moved by someone else's hand."

"All the more reason for you to leave all of us to our own choices," she said. "GENs. Other trueborns like Junjie. Anyone you feel you have to *guide.*"

He knew what she said was right, but still anxiety clutched at him. Fear that if he didn't control his world, it would shatter around him.

But hadn't it anyway?

Devak groped for a way to explain it to Kayla. "I've been so afraid of being like my father, but I think I've become too much like Pitamah. Nudging others, *guiding* them. With all his years, I always thought he *does* know better what we all should do, so it made sense to live by his example. Except now, I'm not so sure."

He could feel her gaze on him. "Even if he did know better," she said, "Zul ought to have left it for people to choose for themselves. GENs, lowborns, trueborns. Give them all the information and let them decide."

"You don't think some things should stay secret?"

He heard her sharp inhalation. When he glanced over, her mouth was open as if she was about to say something. She looked over her shoulder at Junjie, her eyes narrowed.

Finally, she said, "There's power in secrets, power it seems Zul doesn't want to share. There was a time, back when GENs were first created, that Zul might have changed things if he hadn't been holding back so much about GENs. By keeping things secret, it made things worse for us. Have you ever thought of that?"

"I know he was grief-stricken over great-grandma Fulki. Not thinking as clearly as he should have."

"But that didn't last forever. He saw which way things were going." Kayla sighed. "I know he was ill. But he could have spoken out."

Devak let that idea settle inside him. "Yes. He should have."

She swiped the air with her hand. "Water down the Chadi River. He's doing what he can now."

"I wish I could do more."

One corner of her mouth quirked up in a half-smile. "As long as *more* doesn't mean deciding for others. For me."

"No, that's not what I meant. But . . . what if I think that you're making a mistake?" He could see her walking close beside that GEN boy.

She was quiet a long time. "It's my mistake to make, Devak. And sometimes it's not a mistake at all. Sometimes it's just making the best of things."

As they pulled onto the skyway toward Daki sector, Devak worked up his courage. "I made a mess of things that day you called after picking up the GEN boy. Now I want to be honest with you. Truthful."

A wary look lit her eyes. "About what?"

He let out a long breath. "I'm finally facing reality. I hate it, but I've figured out that trueborn society isn't ready for GENs and trueborns to be together."

Her gaze dropped to her lap. "Okay."

"I don't like us sneaking around to make sure no one sees us. I can't stand to think of the way you would be treated by trueborns if they did know about us. You could even be reset."

"Yes." Her breath seemed to catch. Her voice grew fainter. "So we shouldn't be together."

"Do you really agree? Or is that just what you think I want?"

"Is it really what you want?" she asked.

"No. But I think it's all we can expect." He took the last Daki exit, gunning the accelerator harder than he should have. "And it seems like change is a million years away."

It was dark and deserted in the Daki warehouse district, so Devak pulled right up alongside Risa's lorry. He expected Kayla to jump out of the AirCloud the moment it stopped, but she hesitated.

"It hurts inside, Devak. But I think you're right."

She might as well have ripped at his heart. He realized he'd wanted her to reject that hard truth. Even now he wanted to pull her into his arms for a last moment of closeness. But then she did pull the door latch and slip out of the lev-car. Devak watched her dash through the light drizzle to the cab of the lorry, and he felt desolate as she disappeared inside.

He didn't dare linger, both for Gemma's sake and for Risa's and Kayla's, since his presence might draw attention. He wound his way back to the southbound skyway, taking the entrance too fast. As they arched over the Northeast Territory adhikar, he dodged in and out of the light traffic.

Junjie cleared his throat. Devak wondered how much his friend had heard of his and Kayla's conversation. "Yeah?"

"It occurred to me," Junjie said, "if Gemma is relapsing, then Raashida might be too. Which means we have to find her."

"How do you know about Raashida?"

A few moments of silence ticked away. "I heard Akhilesh talking about her with Hala. She was part of an experiment—"

"—to give GENs the ability to reproduce," Devak said. "Mishalla told us. She's looking for Raashida too. Hala asked her to."

"That makes sense. Akhilesh told Hala he needed Raashida back. So if Mishalla finds her, that means Raashida will end up back with GAMA."

Devak remembered the half-dead GEN he'd seen on the second floor of the GAMA facility, the others in the gen-tanks. "Would that be good or bad?"

Junjie let out a puff of air. "If Akhilesh only uses her for that fertility experiment, not as good. But if Raashida heals people the way Gemma does—"

"She does. Mishalla told me that too."

"She could be a key to eradicating Scratch," Junjie said.

"Do you think the Kinship gene-splicers will make it a priority if we find Raashida?" Devak asked. "That they'll use what they learn from her to help the Scratch-infected?"

"Why wouldn't they?"

"I don't know anything anymore." He unlatched his wristlink and tossed it back to Junjie. "Tell Risa to look for Raashida. Make sure Risa knows to take her to the Kinship and not Mishalla."

Guilt twinged inside Devak at that. Was he deciding for Mishalla now? For Raashida? But he had to make some choices, or he'd never do the right thing.

As Junjie started to tap out the code, Devak added, "And make sure Mishalla knows what we decided. That we can't let Raashida be returned to Akhilesh."

After Junjie spoke to Risa, he asked for Kayla. As he asked Kayla to speak to Mishalla, Junjie kept glancing over at Devak. When he was done, he dropped the wristlink on the passenger seat. "It's wrong the way things are. I mean, with you and Kayla."

"Because we decided not to be together?"

"Because you had to decide at all," Junjie said. "I just think it could be different. Should be."

Devak didn't see how it could be, at least not for years to come. As they continued on toward Two Rivers, Devak couldn't help but think of Kayla, and every maddening image seemed to include that GEN boy traveling with them. He kept seeing Abran's handsome face, the GEN boy pulling Kayla close and kissing her, doing what Devak wished he could do himself.

When they got to Pitamah's small house in Two Rivers, a

Kinship medic was there waiting for them. Devak didn't know the woman, a demi-status who gave her name as Iskra, but if Pitamah had called her, she was good.

Gemma was thrashing and moaning as Devak carried her inside, her body burning with fever. So whatever healing capacity she'd had, it seemed to be gone.

Devak set Gemma on his bed, then he and Junjie cleared out for the medic. Devak sank to the sofa, exhausted by the day, but Junjie paced, clearly upset by Gemma's decline.

"Do you want to go home?" Devak asked.

Junjie shook his head. "I'd like to stay awhile. See what the medic says."

"You could spend the night. I can take you home in the morning to change, then to the lab."

"Thanks. Yes," Junjie said. "That would be good."

Devak would have given Junjie the sofa, but his friend refused, saying since he was shorter he'd be more comfortable in a float chair than Devak would be. Devak found an old sleep shirt of his and unused supplies in the washroom for Junjie, so they got ready for bed, always with one ear for the medic.

It was nearly two hours later before Iskra came out with Pitamah. Devak's heart sank seeing his great-grandfather's grave expression.

Junjie jumped to his feet, nearly upsetting the float chair. "She's not—"

"No, still hanging on," Iskra said. "But it's an especially bad case of Scratch."

"Because she had it before?" Devak asked.

"Could be," Iskra said. "I can't bring down her fever. She's so hot, when I touch her, it's like she heats me too."

Devak's gaze met Junjie's. "She was doing that—"

Junjie cut him off. "Do you think she'll be okay?"

Iskra held out both hands, palm up, as if she was weighing Gemma's chances. "Scratch always kills, but this girl survived it once. Maybe she will again. We'll see in the morning. I've given her all the crysophora and fever meds I dare. Any more and the drugs might do what the Scratch hasn't."

Iskra went off to another emergency and Pitamah went to bed. Devak turned off the illuminators again and he and Junjie lay there in the dark.

"Why didn't you want me to tell the medic about Gemma healing?" Devak asked.

"I don't know. Maybe afraid I'd jinx Gemma," Junjie said. "She healed herself once before, maybe she will again."

"Why do you suppose Gemma healed herself from Scratch in the first place? And Raashida? Why them and not all the other infected GENs?"

"Don't know," Junjie said sleepily. "Wish Akhilesh would share more data with me and Guru Ling."

"But why is he experimenting at all?" Devak asked. "When it's Guru Ling looking for a cure?"

"I think Guru Ling knows, but she won't tell me," Junjie said, his words slurred. "She just keeps saying she'll have the cure soon, and then she'll be able to stop Akhilesh."

A few moments later, Devak heard Junjie's rough snoring. He didn't think he'd ever fall asleep himself with everything that was roiling in his mind, Gemma's dire illness, Akhilesh's cruelty, his longing for Kayla. But sleep did take him, dragging him into a frightening dream of being plunged into a gen-tank and held under until he drowned.

He half-woke, gasping for breath, then dropped off again, this time not waking until morning. Junjie's chair was empty. Devak found him at Gemma's side, dressed in his clothes from the day before.

"How is she?" Devak asked.

"Breathing easier, I think," Junjie said. "Maybe not quite as feverish."

"Pitamah says there's some rice and curry left over from dinner last night. We ought to eat and get going or you'll be late at the lab."

Junjie reluctantly pulled away from Gemma. Devak changed into fresh clothes in Pitamah's room, then he and Junjie wolfed down breakfast.

There was a mist on the Chadi River as they crossed over it traveling north. Junjie was quiet as they pulled onto the skyway, his attention straying out the window to the blur of GEN warrens in Mut sector below them, then the vivid green of the Central Western adhikar.

They crossed Plator's southern border. The GAMA lab was a kilometer or so ahead, but they had to continue on the skyway to north Plator to get to Junjie's house.

They were just passing the lab when Junjie grabbed Devak's arm. "What's that?" Junjie pointed toward the GAMA building just in view.

Devak swerved, earning an angry klaxon blare from the lev-car behind him. "What are you looking at?"

"Enforcers at the lab," Junjie say, pressing against the side window.

"You have enforcers there all the time, bringing in Scratch-infected GENs."

"They're bringing stuff out." His neck was craned back now as they passed the lab.

"You want me to take the next exit?" Devak asked. "Double back?"

After one last look, Junjie turned forward in his seat again. "Take me home first. When you drop me off at the lab I'll ask Guru Ling."

But about six kilometers from the last Plator exit, the one Devak would take to get to the small house where Junjie lived with his aunt, the traffic slowed to a near crawl. As they crept along, Junjie opened his window and leaned out to try to see what was happening up ahead.

Junjie sat back down. "Just take the next exit. I'll tell you how to get to Auntie's house."

But when they pulled off the skyway, all the smaller local streets were blocked off, each barricade manned by a couple enforcers. When Devak peered past the blockade down the side street, he could just see the Plator river beyond.

Junjie bounced in his seat, agitation coming off him in waves. "I don't like this. Can you park the AirCloud somewhere? It's not that far to walk from here."

"Denking hell, I forgot to plug in last night." Devak had been focused on Gemma and not his power usage. "I'm going to need a dock."

Devak found a public power dock and tapped in his account code. Pitamah wouldn't be happy with the sky-high rates Devak would be paying to charge up his AirCloud.

Junjie motioned him to hurry up. "I know a shortcut through the alleys. Hopefully avoid the Brigade."

The narrow walkway between two long rows of lowborn

flats was an obstacle course of opportunistic chaff head bushes and ancient incinerators. Some of the incinerators must have been malfunctioning because the alleyway stank of unburned garbage.

Junjie plowed right past the crossroad where Devak expected him to turn left. "Isn't your aunt's house that way?"

"I want to see what's going on by the river."

"I don't think that's such a good idea with all the enforcers." But Devak followed right behind Junjie out of the alley to the rocky stretch of land that ran along the river bank.

At least twenty enforcers were gathered near the bank about fifty meters down from the alley. Their focus was on what looked like a bundle of sodden rags laid out on the rocks.

Junjie stumbled and Devak had to steady him. "I think I see a hand," Junjie said. "I think that's a body."

A chill skittered down Devak's spine. "If it was a GEN, drowned in the Plator, you wouldn't see one enforcer here, let alone twenty."

They continued toward the enforcers, Devak hoping that as a high-status, he would be able to bluff his way through some excuse for being here. But it turned out he didn't need to manufacture a story when a few of the enforcers stepped aside and a man started toward them. Devak was startled to see Akhilesh.

"Junjie!" Akhilesh shouted. "Lord Creator, I'm not sure you want to see this."

"What's he doing here?" Devak asked.

"Good question," Junjie said, a note of disgust in his voice.

Akhilesh fumbled along through the rocky footing. "Go back to the lab, Junjie. You don't need to be here."

"Who is that?" Junjie tried to see around Akhilesh.

"Don't blame her," Akhilesh said as he reached Devak and Junjie. "She'd convinced herself she'd found a solution to the Scratch problem. When it turned out to be based on faulty data, she couldn't bear it."

"Who?" Junjie asked. "Who are you talking about?"

Devak knew who, and he guessed that Junjie did too. Junjie's cheeks were flushed and his eyes shiny, as if he were fighting back tears.

Akhilesh patted Junjie's shoulder. Devak wanted to slap the man's hand away before he said anything else. "It's Guru Ling," Akhilesh said. "She threw herself into the Plator River and drowned."

Junjie shook his head. "I don't believe it."

"We don't always know what is in the hearts of others," Akhilesh said.

"That wasn't in her heart," Junjie said.

Akhilesh looked ready to offer another platitude, but a Brigade enforcer called out his name. One more unwanted pat on Junjie's shoulder, then Akhilesh walked back to the body.

Junjie gave Akhilesh a hard look. "He's lying. Guru Ling didn't throw herself in the Plator."

"But if her research went wrong—"

"Her research went wrong a bunch of times. Faulty data, mistake in methodology. She just started over." Junjie shook his head. "The only way Guru Ling ended up in the Plator is if someone threw her in."

22

Is it much farther?" Abran asked, walking alongside Kayla down Liku Street in Chadi sector's main ward.

"Another half-kilometer or so," Kayla said. "Not far."

The ten days since she'd last seen Devak had blurred together, the endless trips up and down the Western Territories a fog of lifting and carrying cargo. They'd finally ended up in Mut sector this afternoon, where they took on a load of drom wool. And with Chadi the next sector over to the southwest, Kayla could finally come home again. She'd sent a message ahead to let Tala know she was finally coming home for a visit.

Risa, planning to drive south across Mut's border into Two Rivers for a Kinship meeting, sent Abran with Kayla. There was no time to give Tala advance notice that the GEN boy was joining them, which might mean shorter dinner rations, but Tala was always glad to welcome another guest.

Kayla's heart trembled in anticipation. It had been two and a half months since she'd last seen her nurture mother, Tala, and her nurture brother, Jal. Kayla had had nothing but messages passed in a long oral chain of GENs from Tala in Chadi to Risa. Kayla flung a prayer of gratitude up to the Infinite to be home.

Abran nudged her arm and gestured toward what had now become an all too familiar sight—another bombed warehouse. With the setting of Kas, the second of the brother suns, a golden light softened the ugly edges of the rubble.

There'd been at least one site of destruction in every GEN sector they'd been through, a half-dozen over the last ten days. But she'd hoped Chadi would have been spared.

"That used to be kel-grain stores," Kayla said. She could still smell the sickly sweet stink of burned grain. "There's one other foodstores warehouse in Chadi, but it's smaller."

"Hopefully no one was hurt," Abran said. So far, FHE's evil deeds had only killed the young GEN girl and the enforcer in Nafi sector.

Kayla had spent several sleepless nights tortured by the need to tell Zul what she knew about FHE. She'd slip out of bed, filching Risa's wristlink from the cubby the lowborn woman kept it in. But the programmed block FHE had placed in her annexed brain stopped her from even tapping out Zul's number. She just couldn't summon the will.

Even worse, she hadn't even been able to speak to Risa about FHE. She'd wait until Abran was out of earshot, would formulate the words in her mind. But she couldn't voice them. She couldn't type them even when she asked to borrow Risa's sekai.

Thank the Infinite, the neural block was only for what she knew of FHE. She could take in other new information and tell Risa or Zul about it. But she couldn't reveal anything about FHE or its connection to the bombings.

She'd become an unwilling party to Junjie's deception, to FHE's dealings. And it was tearing her up inside.

At least the incessant noise in her head had faded as the competing programs settled in her annexed brain, just as Junjie had said they would. But the voice still intruded, sometimes clearly calling her name, sometimes muttering just out of comprehension.

She assumed the voice was just an artifact of the FHE programming. But then it occurred to her—what if it was someone trying to communicate with her? The FHE programming had done everything but turn her into a flash-oven. Had it built a communication device within her too?

But every attempt to find an answer met with failure. She'd trace the path of her circuitry to what seemed to be the source, send mental messages back through that conduit. But there was never a response. Just that mindless blabber or that occasional clear cry of her name.

She got so frustrated, she'd been tempted to let Junjie have another try at quieting it. But she wasn't sure the block would even let her ask him. Not to mention, there was no guarantee he wouldn't just make things worse.

So she tried to ignore the voice, told herself it was just extraneous noise. But perversely, even though it irritated and sometimes startled her, there was also something about the timbre that filled her with warmth when she heard it. That surrounded her with a sense of security and love. Which angered her all the more, since real security and love lay just ahead, in Tala's flat.

Kayla's pace quickened as the twenty-ninth warren came into view. "Almost there."

Tala was waiting outside, Jal dancing beside her with his usual impatience. Kayla ran the last thirty or so meters, taking care to leap over Liku Street's potholes and ruts.

She threw her arms around Tala, giving her as tight a hug as she dared. Jal did a silly jig beside them, then joined in the embrace, uncaring that a few of his eleventh-year pack loitering across the street could see him.

Kayla finally let go of Tala. Had time added a few lines to her light brown face, or had Kayla just not noticed them before? Tala's waist-length hair was just as golden as it had always been.

Kayla smiled at Abran and motioned him forward. "This is Abran. He's been traveling with us."

"Good to meet you," Tala said, then passed a speculative glance from him to Kayla. Whatever questions she might have, Tala kept to herself. Just as well since Kayla didn't have any answers.

Jal, on the other hand, grinned, looking eager to tease. For the moment, he just dashed past them and into the warren.

Tala tucked her arm in Kayla's, and they followed. Abran hesitated before crossing the threshold, then trailed behind as they climbed the narrow stairs to the fourth floor. Jal, of course, bounded ahead, leading the way.

A girl of about Jal's age was waiting in Tala's flat. Jal announced loudly, "This is Betia. She helps Tala sometimes."

Betia was as light-skinned as Jal was dark, her brown hair long and silky instead of tightly curled like Jal's. She had one quiet toddler boy in her arms while another raced around the living room as frenetically as Jal used to. A sixth-month baby, towhead Pren, sat beside the sofa, pounding a toy hammer on the floor. Pren had arrived at Tala's just days before Kayla's first Assignment.

"Then the dhans I send are making their way to you?" Kayla asked. Without the extra money, Tala wouldn't be able to hire a helper.

"Yes, thank you." Tala pressed a quarter dhan in Betia's hand.

As Betia left, she gave Jal a lingering look. He grinned in response, then dropped his smile when he caught Kayla looking. Well, that would squelch any impulse in her nurture brother to tease her about Abran.

"How much time do you have?" Tala asked.

"We can stay for dinner and a while after," Kayla said. "But the lowborn woman will want us back tonight. We're heading to Mendin at dawn."

"I'll get dinner started then. Jal," Tala called as the boy dragged Abran toward his room, "I'll need another handful of patagobi root. Qeti upstairs will have some to borrow."

Sketching a quick promise to Abran that he'd be right back, Jal dashed off. Abran stood awkwardly in the living room as the quiet toddler tapped on his shins.

"That's Pik," Tala said. "Kayla, would you—"

"I've got him," Abran said. He picked up the boy and nestled him in the crook of his arm. "He kind of looks like me." Abran seemed unsettled by the notion.

Kayla laughed. "Always strange to see another GEN with some of your DNA." She saw Pren had nodded off. She carried him to the crib in Tala's room.

Minutes later, Jal thundered back down the stairs and into the flat with two handfuls of patagobi. He dumped them in the kitchen, then all but bounced out of his skin as he urged Abran into his bedroom. Abran followed with little Pik still in his arms. Kayla stayed behind to keep active Choti entertained while Tala worked in the kitchen.

It was an evening like so many Kayla remembered from her childhood. Tala made a stew of kel-grain, adding the patagobi root and some actual chunks of drom that looked like more gristle and fat than meat. Jal's rapid-fire patter drifted out of the thin walls of his room as he showed off the new sekai he'd been issued as a tech GEN. She could hear Abran's occasional laughter in response to some silly thing or another Jal said, and she felt a warmth inside that for the moment, Abran was happy.

Tala must have collected some wild herbs for the stew because despite its humble ingredients it was delicious. Abran took his first bite tentatively, then he all but licked his bowl clean. His effusive compliments brought a flush to Tala's cheeks.

For the first time in the nearly five months since she'd been traveling with Risa, Kayla relaxed. While Tala bottle-fed Pren, Kayla helped feed the hyperactive Choti. Abran spooned stew into quiet Pik's mouth. Abran nodded every once in a while at Jal's constant chattering about bleeding edge tech, occasionally sending a smile Kayla's way.

Kayla so dearly wanted to tell her nurture mother about the work she'd been doing for the Kinship. Because of the extra dhans Kayla sent to Tala and the extraordinary communication chain that the Kinship had worked out, Tala had to know there was more happening in the lorry than delivering goods. But Kayla had never been able to spell it out, and certainly couldn't now with Abran at the table.

When Kayla remembered her promise to the woman in

Fen sector, Tala sent Jal to a warren two streets over to find Lis, the woman's nurture daughter. When Kayla delivered the nurture mother's love and warm wishes, quoting what the Fen woman had said as best she could, Lis cried. But her gratitude for the message was clear, and she returned to her warren smiling. Tala glowed with pride at Kayla's simple deed and Kayla's heart spilled over with her own thankfulness.

Later, Tala took her aside when they went into Jal's room to put Pik and Choti down for bed. Tala had tucked baby Pren in his crib an hour before.

While they gave the sleepy boys a quick wash with sani-wipes, Tala asked, "Do you still dream of her?"

"My nightmares?" Kayla asked. "I haven't had one in months."

"But you know who she is now."

A shock ran through Kayla. "Do you?"

"A message came two weeks ago. Delivered by a GEN woman I've never met. Not the usual person who brings your messages."

"What did she say?" Kayla asked.

She could see the distress in Tala's eyes. "She said, 'Kayla knows her true name is Elana Kalu. And she knows her true mother is a trueborn named Aideen Kalu.'"

"That's not right," Kayla said hotly. "*You're* my true mother. My nurture mother. I don't care about *her*."

She pulled Tala into her arms and stroked her back. Who could have passed along a message like that? Zul? But why would he when he had to know it would hurt Tala?

"I never came to love a nurture child so quickly as I did you," Tala murmured.

Even now, Kayla could feel the love radiating from Tala. "And I'm so lucky to have you as a nurture mother," Kayla said.

They tucked the boys into their bed, chatting about the inconsequential—Jal's first crush, which GENs were planning their joining ceremonies, where Kayla's fifteenth-year friends had been Assigned after she left. But it was exactly those tiny details that Kayla had missed most about home.

Kayla couldn't stand it when it was time to leave. They all went downstairs together to delay their parting. When Kayla spied the tears in Tala's eyes, she couldn't speak from the lump in her throat. And Tala squeezed her so tight, Kayla could barely breathe.

"When can you come back?" Tala asked.

"I don't know." Kayla took a shuddering breath. "I love you."

"I love you too," Tala said.

Kayla lifted her head from Tala's shoulder and in the dim streetlights caught Abran staring at her. He seemed surprised. That she was crying? That she wasn't eager to get away from her nurture mother and back to her Assignment like some GENs would be?

She gave Jal a quick one-armed hug, then she and Abran started back down Liku Street. She turned twice to wave goodbye. The third time, Tala was gone, no doubt to check on the sleeping toddlers. Jal had joined his pack, the group of ten or so including one girl—Betia. Jal had his back to her.

Liku Street ended as they drew closer to the Chadi-Mut border, transitioning to gravel-topped dirt, then a mere footpath. Two of the trinity moons, Avish and Abrahm, had risen, but their crescents provided an unreliable light. Sticker bushes thrust up here and there, their shadowy branches looking like clusters of bhimkay. Kayla shuddered at the image.

Abran walked close behind her on the narrow path. "It wasn't like I expected."

"What wasn't?"

"The flat. Your mother. Your brother." He reached a hand out to her when she stumbled on a rock. "The food."

"The warrens in Jassa don't look much different."

He was silent a moment. "I guess not."

Their feet crunched in the gravelly dirt. "Are you worried about the judgment?" The councilor had contacted them a couple days ago to say that Abran's testimony would be taken next week.

"I can't face him again," Abran said.

"Baadkar won't be in the room when you testify. He'll be watching on a vid screen."

"He'll know I'm there. He'll know I haven't—" He cried out, startled as he tripped and fell, landing hard on all fours.

"Are you okay?" Kayla asked, offering a hand.

"Yeah." He let her help him to his feet.

His pants were torn at the knees and she could see a dark smear through the tear. "Your knee—it's bleeding."

"I'll be fine."

Risa had parked the lorry not far from the border and stood leaning against the cab chewing devil leaf. As Abran limped along, he shook Kayla off when she tried to support him.

As he headed for the rear of the lorry, Risa called, "Seycat's out, GEN boy. Keep that door open!" He waved a hand in response before disappearing around the end of the bay.

Abran had been traveling in the cab with them instead of in the bay, trading with Kayla between the passenger seat and the sleeper. He'd been stretching out on the cab seats to sleep. He must be even more upset than she thought to go hide himself amongst those smelly bales of drom wool piled high in the bay.

Kayla and Risa swung up into the cab. "What rat-snake got up his behind?" Risa asked.

"The judgment next week, I think." But there seemed to be more to it, something about being around Tala and Jal.

Kayla and Risa took their turns in the washroom, Kayla pounding on the hatch to let Abran know when he could use it. When he didn't come out immediately, Kayla sent a questioning glance at Risa. The lowborn woman wagged her chin at the hatch and Kayla opened it.

Her eye caught the reflection of his prayer mirror and she heard Abran saying in a rough voice, "I need it now . . ." just before he spotted her face in the hatch opening. He shoved his mirror in his hem so quickly, she could hear stitches rip.

He craned his neck up at her. "What?"

"You can use the washroom."

She dropped back into the cab to give him space to get to the washroom. After he finished, then returned to the bay, Kayla and Risa moved to the sleeper.

"That was odd," Kayla said softly as she dropped beside Risa. If he was inclined, Abran could press his ear to the bay wall and be able to make out ordinary conversation, but they were safe if they kept their voices low.

The lowborn woman arranged her voluminous, ankle-length sleep dress around her like a tent, then pulled her dark, gray-threaded hair forward over her shoulder. "What's odd?" Risa divided her hair into thirds and started braiding it.

"His prayers. I didn't mean to eavesdrop, but . . ." Kayla

undid her own braid, dropping the ribbon in the bedclothes, then brushed out her kinky hair. "He makes demands of the Infinite. *I need it now!* As if the Infinite serves him instead of the other way around."

Risa stole Kayla's ribbon and tied it on her braided hair. "Suppose the boy is arrogant enough to think so. But then, some don't like the way their prayers are answered either."

Kayla's fingers stilled halfway down her braid. "You mean me? And . . ." She hooked a thumb back toward the bay.

"Thought you two might find a way to be together." Risa cleared her throat. "After that kiss."

"You didn't look very happy about us kissing."

Risa shrugged. "Wasn't at first. But when you gave up the impossible, I thought that one might be good for you."

Kayla had told Risa what had passed between her and Devak that night in Daki, had sobbed in the lowborn woman's arms. "I thought he might be too. Abran's a GEN. Good-looking. Seems to like me even though . . ." Her mouth twisted as she gestured at herself.

"You're as beautiful as any GEN girl," Risa said. "Or lowborn, come to it."

Kayla took in a breath to deny Risa's compliment, but the lowborn woman's scowl stopped her. "Anyway," Kayla said. "There's no reason we shouldn't fall in love."

"But?"

Now Kayla shrugged. Maybe she still clung to the idea of Devak. Maybe that kept her from feeling more for Abran.

Risa reached behind her and unearthed another ribbon from one of the cubbies. "As much time as that GEN boy's spent with us, still don't really know him."

Kayla resumed braiding. "We know that his patron abused him so badly his GEN circuitry is broken. We know he ran, which was both stupid and brave."

Risa held out the ribbon. "Seen more stupid than brave from that boy."

"I've been wondering about his nurture mother and sister," Kayla said, tying the end of her braid. "He said they're in a bad situation. Could our friends"—she meant the Kinship—"get them re-Assigned somewhere? Or to a seycat den?" A safe house.

"Could ask," Risa said cautiously. "Don't know how interested our friends would be after the boy gives testimony."

Kayla let that hard reality sink in. "I thought our friends would change things. But it seems like they don't care about GENs anymore."

"And they don't give a rat-snake's ass about lowborns. I can tell you that." Risa's barking laugh was so loud, it likely woke up Abran. She lowered her voice. "It comes down to dhans. Some of them have started to think how much GEN freedom would cost them."

Just then, Risa's wristlink beeped. She glanced down at it. "Mishalla. Best take it outside. Around the front."

Kayla tugged on her shoes, then slipped out and took a seat on the lorry's front bumper, her back against the suspension engine. She had to suppress a shriek when Nishi rushed out from under the cab, growling and feinting at Kayla's ankles. The sharp scent of their drom wool cargo irritated the feline, making her crankier than usual.

While Nishi trotted off into the brush behind the warehouses, Kayla raised the wristlink. "Hey, Mishalla."

Mishalla smiled at Kayla from the wristlink's small screen. "Sorry to bother you. I wanted to ask if you and Risa were going anywhere near Amik sector?"

Kayla had memorized Risa's delivery schedule in her bare brain, then stored it in her annexed brain. That hell-forsaken FHE programming was good for something.

Kayla accessed the schedule. "Day after tomorrow."

"Thank the Infinite," Mishalla said. "Hopefully that will be soon enough. Raashida is in an allabain village there. I'm certain of it this time."

Even knowing Raashida would be going to the Kinship and not Akhilesh, Mishalla had continued to give Risa and Kayla tips about the GEN woman. Kayla suspected her friend hoped Hala would persuade Raashida to return to the fertility experiment after the Kinship had learned what it could about her healing ability.

In any case, all of Mishalla's tips had turned out to be dead ends. Twice, Risa and Kayla had been in the area anyway, so not much time had been lost. The third time, they'd had to arrange for a significant detour, which had severely tried Councilor Mohapatra's patience, especially when it turned out to be for nothing.

"I'll let Risa know. I'm sure we'll be able to take the time to look for her." Although the way Kayla felt about the Kinship these days, she wasn't even sure it was best to give them Raashida.

They said their goodbyes and Kayla went back inside. Risa was already snoring. Kayla climbed into the bed and pulled the drapes closed. Easing herself under the covers, she let Risa's warmth lull her to sleep.

Kayla!

She jolted upright, confused and muzzy. She'd never been awakened before by that inner voice. Or had it just been part of a dream? Buffets of wind shook the lorry. Maybe that was what had roused her, and she'd only imagined being called.

Her internal clock told her just over an hour had passed since she'd fallen asleep. She lay back down, exhaustion and the warmth of the covers irresistible.

Before she could drift off, footsteps moving past the lorry brought her awake again. She tweaked aside the curtain on the sleeper and squinted into the shadows. Outside, the night was ill-lit by two of the trinity moons, half-faced Avish and a sliver of Abrahm. She spotted Nishi in a strip of moonlight, trotting across one of the warehouse's plasscrete aprons into the thick nest of sticker bushes that ran along the back of the warehouse district.

Then she caught sight of a shadowy figure moving away along the alley. An enforcer?

With a shock, she realized it was Abran disappearing into the shadows. Was this it then? Was he running, so frightened about giving testimony against Baadkar that he'd leave the lorry and the only ones keeping him safe? He was never taken off the Grid. Baadkar could find him if he wanted to take his revenge.

If she went out there after him, she'd put her own self in peril. No GEN should be wandering the warehouse district at night. Any passing enforcer would want to know what she or Abran were doing there.

She couldn't quite bring herself to let him go. She had to at least try to bring him back. She quickly pulled on dark leggings and changed her sleep shirt for a matching day tunic. Shoving her feet into shoes, she jumped from the cab of the lorry and shut the door quietly behind her.

She followed Abran's path along the alley between the weaving factory and the foodstores warehouse. Halfway down the dark, narrow alley, she spied movement at the other end. She recognized Abran's silhouette, his broad shoulders, just before he moved out of sight.

She hurried after him. If he doubled back, he would see her, but hopefully he wouldn't bolt. She stopped at the corner, leaning out far enough to see him duck into the next alley over.

As she hesitated there in the shadows, another dark figure approached along the line of factories and warehouses. A man, from his stride and build. Dressed in black.

A fist seemed to grab hold of her stomach. A moment later, her unease became terror as the approaching man stopped at the alley Abran had entered. Avish's moonlight picked out the emblem on the man's chest. The red stylized bhimkay glowed like fire from the enforcer's uniform.

Move on, move on, move on! Kayla chanted silently.

The enforcer took one more look around him. Then he walked into the alley.

Kayla stood frozen for a moment, her mind moving in a hundred directions. Imagining Abran beaten, arrested, reset.

That last thought pushed her from her hiding place. She hurried along the front of the foodstores warehouse, keeping to the shadows as best she could. When she got to the next alley, she dared a look around the corner.

The enforcer and Abran stood halfway down the alley, beside an incinerator. The enforcer had his back to Kayla, and Abran's attention was on the enforcer. They were talking, but too softly for her to hear.

Any second the enforcer was going to pull out his datapod. He might do something as harmless as download Abran, but he could reset him just as quickly. Kayla tensed, ready to attack the enforcer and thrust him aside before he raised a datapod to Abran's cheek.

But then Abran turned away, his voice drifting toward her. "Let's go down to the other end. Less light there."

The enforcer followed Abran deeper into the darkness, not seeming the least put out by a GEN leading the way. Was it a GEN enforcer then? Kayla hadn't noticed a tattoo. But she'd been so fixated on the glittering bhimkay emblem, she'd never looked at the man's face.

GEN or trueborn, the real question was, why was Abran meeting an enforcer in the middle of the night? She ran through every conversation with Risa that she could remember, or had stored in her annexed brain. They'd never mentioned the Kinship in Abran's hearing. Could he be here to betray them?

Now they both had their backs to her and were well past the incinerator. She slipped into the alley, keeping to the warehouse wall as she got closer. With her gaze fixed on Abran's and the enforcer's backs, her clumsy feet caught on something. An empty fruit meld bottle went flying and slammed into the side of the incinerator with a metallic clang.

She scrunched herself against the wall beside the incinerator, praying the darkness would hide her. Footsteps approached, heavy enforcer boots. The enforcer stopped even with the incinerator. His toes were no more than a meter from where she hid.

Abran called out, "What is it?"

A rat-snake squirmed from beneath the incinerator, its myriad beady eyes glittering in the faint moonlight as it paused to stare at her. She had to suppress a shudder as the rat-snake's eight arachnid legs tippety-tapped closer, its abdomen wriggling left and right as it approached.

But then it ran out into the alley, all but crawling across the enforcer's boots. The man yelped and leapt back. He kicked out at the creature even though it was well out of reach of his boots as it scrambled out of the alley.

"Rat-snake," the enforcer said with disgust.

She'd been so focused on hiding, she hadn't thought to look up at the enforcer's face to check for a tattoo. She took the quickest glance around the incinerator, but could only see the back of the enforcer's head again.

Then Abran started up the alley to meet the enforcer part way and Kayla ducked back to safety. But now she would certainly be able to hear them, even if they whispered to each other. If betrayal was Abran's plan, she'd race back to the lorry, try to get her and Risa out of here before the Brigade could arrive in full force. But they'd been so careful—he shouldn't know enough to betray them. Did he?

She eased herself right up against the incinerator and tried not to think about the possibility of a rat-snake nest beneath it. The smooth metal was just the slightest bit warm from its last use. The lid had been left open and the metal box amplified the enforcer's voice when he next spoke.

"A big risk meeting me here."

"I nearly died in that river," Abran said. "Nearly died after from the cold."

"Why jump in at all?" the enforcer asked.

"I couldn't let the boy drown," Abran said.

"Chutting idiot."

"Maybe so. Do you have it?"

"Cost me a pile of dhans," the enforcer said. "But I got two vac-seals' worth, just like you asked."

Abran was buying more jaf buzz? Was he truly an addict after all? She supposed it was better than betrayal. But how could he continue to hurt himself this way?

"I might not have enough to cover it," Abran said. "But I'll give you all of what I've got."

Kayla crept out again, far enough to see Abran dig in the pocket where he kept his prayer mirror and produce a crumpled handful of dhans. He took the two vac-seals the enforcer handed over in exchange, tucking one inside his waistband. Abran thumbed the activator tab on the other and pressed the circular packet to his inner arm.

That he couldn't even wait for the drug, that he took a hit in this dirty alley, sickened her. As it took effect, he staggered as he had in the sticker bush thicket, bumping into the alley wall and losing his balance. He fell, thwacking his head against the wall as he landed on his butt.

The enforcer stood over Abran, his left cheek hidden from Kayla. No tattoo on his right, which made sense since few GENs had tattoos on their right cheek like Kayla did.

"You going to be able to make it back to that lorry?" the enforcer asked.

Abran didn't lift his head or open his eyes. "I'll manage."

"Because I have to go," the enforcer said. "Have a patrol to get to."

"Go. Thanks."

The enforcer turned and continued down the alley, away from Kayla, so she had no chance to check his left cheek for a tattoo. Not that it mattered now. Even a minor-status trueborn might deal drugs to a GEN if it meant a few extra dhans. It wasn't as if the GEN would report him.

She had to confront Abran, as tempting as it was to leave him. Even knowing how terribly vulnerable he was, and how angry the councilor and Zul would be if Abran ended up being arrested if another enforcer found him, she was tempted to just walk away.

Just then, Abran's voice drifted her way. "I sent him away so he wouldn't see you. Maybe you could give me a hand in return."

She stepped clear of the incinerator. "How'd you know I was here?"

"I heard your footsteps behind me earlier. Caught a glimpse of you." He reached out for her.

She didn't move. "You weren't going to take the jaf anymore."

He sighed, his outstretched arm sinking back down. "It's not jaf. I swear." He fumbled under his shirt. "Take a look."

He tossed the unused vac-seal and she caught it. The third trinity moon, Ashiv, had risen, its three-quarter face adding to Abrahm's half-circle. She stepped toward the end of the alley where the moonlight spilled in.

The only jaf buzz she'd seen had been at Doctrine school during a dull dry lecture about dangerous drugs. The teacher had passed around a vac-seal of genuine jaf, let them handle the duraplass packaging under her watchful eye.

The lectures weren't to warn them off using jaf—no GEN could afford to buy such a high-priced narcotic. Not to mention they'd be reset and their genetics recycled if they were caught using.

But their patron might take jaf, so a GEN would have to know the signs of overdose, know to get help right away. Zul had only started trying jaf after Kayla had left her Assignment with him, so this was the first time she'd seen the stuff outside of Doctrine school.

So she knew the vac-seal was circular, like this one. The drug was a creamy yellow, thick and opaque. It tasted sweet, but she wasn't about to break the activator tab to test it.

"Hold it up to the moonlight," Abran said.

She did as he asked. The pale yellow contents of the vac-seal was translucent, not opaque. It was more that light golden yellow of the vac-seals he'd had before. As she manipulated the vac-seal, the stuff felt thinner, almost watery.

"What is it, if it's not jaf?" Kayla asked.

"Can you help me up?" Abran asked. "I'll tell you on the way back to the lorry."

"Why are you so much worse than when you took it back in Esa sector?"

"Was used to it then," Abran mumbled. "Hits hard the first time. Or if you haven't used in a while."

Still half-tempted to abandon him in the alley, she nevertheless tucked the vac-seal into her own waistband and pulled him to his feet. His arm around her shoulders, they walked slowly from the alley. Not wanting to risk an encounter with the Brigade, Kayla kept to the shadows.

As they neared the lorry, a blur of red and gray rushed past toward the rear of the bay. Nishi, with a rat-snake in her jaws. Kayla wondered if it was the one in the alley that had startled the enforcer.

Kayla helped Abran into the bay, the thick, rank funk of drom wool rolling over her. The bales of wool had been piled to either side, leaving a valley in the middle from the doors to the hatch ladder. Nishi had climbed the bales and started in on the rat-snake, its legs cracking as she broke them from the body.

Kayla let go of Abran to reach for the rear door, but he didn't quite have his legs under him. As he swayed, she grabbed for him, ending up with a handful of shirt where his prayer mirror was hidden. The pocket tore loose and the mirror smashed to the floor of the bay.

"Oh, Infinite, I'm sorry," Kayla said. She could just make out the pieces of the mirror in the moonlight that streamed through the open door.

Abran, half-slumped against the wool bales, flailed out with his foot at the fragments, as if to knock them closer to him. As angry as she'd been at him, she felt wretched having broken his prayer mirror.

Abran lost his balance and fell to his knees against the pile of bales. Kayla gathered up the two main halves of fractured glass, the thick, heavy backing. She brought them to the door to get a better look at the damage.

The two pieces of mirrored glass maybe could be patched together if glued to another piece of glass. The backing—

She sucked in a sharp breath when she saw inside it. The thick backing was packed with electronics.

"What is this?" Kayla asked.

Abran sagged against the oily drom wool. "Give it back, please." He reached out.

Kayla marched past him, dropping the broken mirror pieces in his hand, but keeping the rest of it. As she mounted the hatch ladder, she felt explosive enough in that moment to hope he cut himself.

Once she had the hatch open, she shook Risa. The lowborn woman came instantly awake. "What is it?"

"Turn on the bay illuminators. We have a problem."

Kayla jumped down to the bay floor as the illuminators flickered on. Keeping a secure grip on the prayer mirror backing and its electronic guts, she crossed the length of the bay again and latched the rear door.

Risa came through the hatch in her night clothes. Kayla brought Risa the bit of electronics in her hand. "Is this what I think it is?"

Risa looked it over, fingering the tiny transmitter and receiver. "Comm device."

"Thought so," Kayla said. "Even a non-tech like me learns a little bit about electronics in Doctrine school." She rounded on Abran. "So you haven't been praying to the Infinite. You've been . . . what? Spying on us?"

He stared at his feet. "I had to. Baadkar has my mother and sister."

Risa came up beside Kayla and handed back Abran's communicator. Kayla crushed the circuitry between her hands. A few broken bits fell to the floor.

Despair filled Abran's face. "He has them trapped somewhere. Says he'll kill them if I don't do what he wants."

"Why kill them?" Kayla asked. "Why not just reset them?"

Abran hesitated before answering. "He knows killing them would hurt me more."

It seemed like a waste of GENs, from a trueborn's point of view. But Baadkar had killed GENs before, so maybe it was worth it to control Abran.

"So you've used the communicator"—Kayla tossed aside the crushed case—"to keep tabs on us."

"Yes." There was something about the way he drew out the word that set off an alert inside her. Then Abran's glance up at her throat clinched her suspicions.

His words that day he'd nearly drowned came back to her. *Lost it. Better that way.*

"The necklace was part of it too, wasn't it?" Denking hell. And she'd been sad that the gift had been lost. "What was it supposed to do?"

His gaze shifted away. "Track your movements since they couldn't get access to your Grid data."

The faintest gasp from Risa, but Kayla kept her voice cool. "Why wouldn't they be able to access my Grid data?"

He shrugged. "Something about Baadkar being on the wrong side of Social Benevolence. He wasn't allowed to request Grid locations anymore."

So Baadkar didn't know anything about the Kinship's adjustments to her location data. If the trueborn had compared Kayla's Grid location report with Abran's first-hand account of where Kayla and the lorry really were, that would put an end to her Kinship mission. She'd be banned to a safe house.

"Why tag me and not Risa, if you only wanted to keep track of the lorry?" Kayla asked.

Abran flushed. "I couldn't have given a lowborn woman a gift. Especially one so—" Discretion cut off the word *old*.

Unoffended, Risa barked out a rusty laugh. She pulled a bale of drom wool off the pile, threw a plasscine blanket over it and sat on the tight-packed bale, knees close to Abran's. "What's Baadkar want with a lorry delivery driver and her GEN helper anyway?"

Abran sank farther against the bale he leaned against. "Because Baadkar collects Scratch-infected GENs. Gives them to a trueborn scientist he deals with, gets a couple hundred dhans a head."

"Again, GEN boy," Risa said, leaning even closer to Abran, "why us?"

"Because it came to Baadkar's attention how often you've turned infected GENs over to the Brigade," Abran told her. "The trueborn scientist Baadkar works with wants the Scratch GENs you find turned directly over to him. The Brigade doesn't always follow orders and bring them to him, not if they get better bribes. I was supposed to report right away when you picked one up."

Now Risa looked Kayla's way, worry in her eyes. Kayla could almost read the lowborn woman's mind—if Baadkar had noticed how often they picked up Scratch victims, they weren't being nearly as careful as they thought they were.

Kayla dropped down on the bale next to Risa. "Haven't had much to report to Baadkar since you started traveling with us, have you?" Thanks to the Kinship getting the word out that the Scratch-infected should stay away. "Looks like he had bad information."

Abran shrugged. "And now he wants me back. I'm a waste of his time, he says."

"Who's the trueborn scientist?" Kayla asked.

"Akhilesh."

Risa's worried look deepened. "Head of GAMA? Don't like GAMA knowing anything about us."

Anxiety burned in Kayla's gut. "What about your nurture mother and sister? Do they even exist, or was that another lie?"

"They're real." Abran's despair deepened into desolation. "Baadkar won't say where they are. He won't even let me talk to them."

"What about the drugs?" Kayla pressed. "The ones you say aren't jaf buzz?"

At Risa's startled look, Kayla handed over the vac-seal. The lowborn woman held the palm-sized circular packet up to the light. "Not jaf."

"It's called punarjanma," Abran said. "It's a substitute for GEN healing, to replace what my circuitry can't do anymore."

"I know he beat you," Kayla said. "But I don't see how that could damage your circuitry."

"It wasn't the beatings. Baadkar-Mar liked to use a shockgun on me." His trembling hand went up to his left cheek. "Low power so he wouldn't kill me. But he'd shoot the energy directly into my tattoo. Eventually, my circuitry stopped working."

Horror filled Kayla at Baadkar's cruelty. "It doesn't work at all? Surely you can access your annexed brain?"

He glanced off to the left, then back to her. "Barely."

"You can't heal yourself?" He shook his head. "Warm yourself?" Another negative.

"That's why I have to use the punarjanma," Abran said.

"How'd you figure the enforcer could get you more?" Risa asked.

Abran's shaky hand rubbed at his eyes. "I met him a few days ago when we passed through Mendin going south. I arranged with him about the drug then."

"How did you even know about it?" Kayla asked. "That punarjanma even existed?"

He dropped his hand to his lap as if the weight was too much to hold up. "I heard about it from one of Baadkar-Mar's other GENs. He'd been damaged too, so he knew about the drug."

"But how did you get a whole carrysak full of it?"

"Told you."

She remembered his story—how his patron had asked his son to transport four carrysaks to Shafti, how the son had brought along Abran to carry them, and the son had been killed by a bhimkay. In Abran's previous version, the contents of the carrysaks had been jaf buzz and not this punarjanma.

But it didn't make sense. How valuable could punarjanma be if it was only to be used for GENs? And only GENs whose healing systems didn't work. There couldn't be that many in that situation. Any why not just put the GEN back in the tank and fix him or her that way? Yet Baadkar had sent his son to go sell the punarjanma, in expectation of some profit.

Maybe the punarjanma *did* work on trueborns, but in a different way. Jaf buzz and crysophora acted as stimulants for trueborns, but made GENs sick and crazy, revving up their circuitry until they collapsed. Maybe for trueborns, punarjanma was another stimulant like jaf or crysophora.

But punarjanma's stimulus would supplement a GENs healing process when it failed. Instead of electrical impulses from a GEN's circuitry stimulating the cells to heal, the drug would do it directly. Punarjanma's greatest value would be as a trueborn stimulant, but if it was cheaper and less time-consuming a treatment for GENs than the tank, that gave it a little extra worth.

Abran had shut his eyes and looked to be sleeping sitting up. Kayla muscled him to his feet, and walked him to the bed he'd made for himself near the hatch ladder. He was out before she even got him prone.

Risa fingered her wristlink. "GEN boy has to go. Too dangerous to keep him anymore, nosing into our business."

Kayla stared down at the sleeping Abran. He'd spied on them, betrayed them. Lied so many times, it was hard to be sure if they knew the full truth even now.

Yet his scars were real. His despair over his family was utterly convincing, as was his terror of Baadkar.

"I've never quite trusted him," Kayla said. "I tried, but I couldn't."

"Nor me," Risa agreed.

Kayla's fingers sought out her prayer mirror tucked at her waist. "I'd like to think he hasn't lost his place in the Infinite's hands. That it would take more evil than what he's done." The kind of evil Baadkar had committed.

"Only a few days more until the judgment," Risa said. "Boy can stay with the councilor until then."

And what about after? Would he go back to Baadkar? Once, she would have thought, *Of course not*, but did she really know the Kinship anymore?

"When you call," Kayla said, "see if anything can be done for his nurture family."

Risa called Zul, loathe to contact Councilor Mohapatra

directly. Zul, thank the Infinite, agreed with Risa and promised to send someone to pick Abran up.

After Risa signed off, she jerked her chin toward the hatch ladder. "I'll wait here. You get some sleep."

Kayla felt the slightest twinge of regret at not saying goodbye to Abran. But she turned her back on him and returned to the sleeper.

Despite her exhaustion, she was restless at first. She kept thinking of Abran's dilemma, his broken circuitry, and imagining it happening to her. Some might think that would be a good thing. If *she* couldn't access her annexed brain like Abran, then neither could an enforcer with a datapod.

But Kayla had come to appreciate what her circuitry could do, in spite of—or maybe even because of, she admitted grudgingly—FHE's improvements. From the simple convenience of her internal clock and the Svarga continent maps programmed in her annexed brain to the way she could warm herself and access far more data than a non-wired trueborn or lowborn. Not to mention her quicker healing from injury or disease.

Abran had none of that anymore. It could be that if Councilor Mohapatra sent Abran back to Baadkar, the trueborn would realize the GEN boy was so broken, he'd be sent off to the gene-splicers to be broken down for his DNA. Abran wouldn't be worth as much as a live, functioning GEN would be, but Baadkar would pocket a small fee in exchange for the boy's genetics.

Despite Abran's treachery, Kayla felt a little sick inside that the boy might end up sold to gene-splicers. Her hands tightened into fists as she considered the myriad ways trueborns controlled GENs—mentally, physically. They'd turned Abran against his own, and Risa had had no choice but to cast him out.

Kayla relaxed her hands with an effort. She'd figured out the first time they'd had to turn over a Scratch-infected GEN to the Brigade, they couldn't save everyone. If they lost this GEN boy, she'd have to learn to live with that.

She retrieved her prayer mirror from the cubby she'd placed it in for safety. With the reflective surface pressed against her lips, she prayed for all those GENs whose lives were cut short by trueborn cruelty. And when she couldn't quite bring herself to pray for Abran, she prayed instead for his soul.

23

His back aching from hours in his chair, Devak stared at the flood of data scrolling past on the holographic display of his computer. Tapping the keyboard, he sent the infiltration spider he'd programmed a little deeper into a data storage unit tucked away somewhere in Dika sector. He'd lost count of how many databanks he'd hacked into over the last eleven days, first in Guru Ling's home sector, Plator, then when that search came up dry, in the surrounding trueborn and mixed sectors. So far, not a clue as to where Guru Ling might have hidden her research off-site, or if she even had.

Junjie sat on a chair beside Devak, feet up on Devak's bed, using a sekai Pitamah had loaned him to sort through the data Devak collected. Pitamah had kept himself as scarce as possible the last week and a half, remaining intentionally ignorant of what Devak and Junjie were up to.

Gemma had survived after a rough few days, and had been moved to Foresthill sector to stay with the old medic, Jemali. If she could still heal others as she had at the Daki sector safe house, no one knew. Although she'd allowed Jemali to take tissue samples for research, she stayed alone in a room at his small house, refusing to see anyone but him, touching no one. She'd died again two days ago. When she revived, she was weaker than before, and had yet to gain her strength or fully fight off the Scratch. Jemali said it was only a matter of time until she had another relapse that she couldn't battle back from.

Junjie was sure that Guru Ling had left something behind that could cure Gemma and all the other sick GENs. But after eleven days of failures, Devak knew it was a hopeless quest. He hadn't yet scraped *every* likely database of contents that might connect to Guru Ling's research, but he was nearly out of options.

"Nothing," Junjie said, his thumb moving quickly across the sekai screen as he scrolled through Devak's last data dump. "What's next?"

"Not much." Devak retracted the infiltrator spider with the data it had collected, and routed the data to Junjie's ID.

"Then we'll go farther out." Junjie tapped and scrolled, peering at the sekai screen.

Devak was pretty sure that wouldn't help. If Guru Ling had tried to leave anything behind, Akhilesh had probably purged it.

The GAMA director never did let Junjie get any closer to Guru Ling's body that day at the riverside. Akhilesh had suggested kindly enough that Junjie go home, that he should take a few days off. But he had enforcers escort Devak and Junjie back to the AirCloud—for their safety, he said. And when Devak took Junjie home, he found his aunt gone. When he called her, she'd told him she'd moved to Sheysa sector.

Since he'd turned out to be such a troublesome boy, she had no room for him anymore in her home.

Another half-dozen enforcers crawled all over the small Plator sector house. Everything inside was turned upside down and torn apart. Junjie had told the Brigade that Guru Ling had never been to his house, and that he never took home any of the studies he did in the lab. But still they followed him while he packed some clothes and personal items and escorted him from his own house.

It was the same at Akhilesh's lab. Enforcers blocked Junjie's way while one Brigade officer after another carried crates and equipment out. All of it went into the back of a lorry they'd brought in.

Junjie hadn't had much at the lab—a couple sekais, a beaker full of broken datapods, a few tricky mind teasers he'd kept on his desk to fidget with. But the one thing that really mattered to him—a holo of his mother, the only image he had of her—nearly went into a crate along with a bunch of other odds and ends from Guru Ling's lab.

An enforcer had found the little thumb-sized self-powered projector in the back of Junjie's desk drawer where he'd hidden it. Junjie had had to beg the enforcer to give it back. The enforcer must have had at least a tiny grain of a heart. After checking to be sure the device only displayed a holo, she'd tossed it to Junjie instead of into the lorry.

"Nothing in that batch either," Junjie said, dropping the sekai on the bed. "It isn't even tech data. Just a bunch of IDs for dead GENs."

"The Scratch victims the enforcers bring in?"

"Can't be. The IDs are from GENs who died ten years ago

and more. There must be some other storage areas we could search."

"There are plenty I could hack into if I went continent wide," Devak said. "But if Guru Ling was putting her data off-site in a sector besides the ones surrounding Plator, how would we ever guess which one?"

"Why didn't she leave me a clue?"

"Because she killed herself."

"She didn't," Junjie said emphatically. "That's a lie Akhilesh made up."

"She left a note," Devak pointed out.

"Which *I've* never seen. We only have Akhilesh's word on that."

Devak pushed away from the computer. "We're getting nowhere. We might have to give up."

"But there might be a cure for Scratch out there." Junjie scrubbed at his face. "I can't believe all of Guru Ling's work is lost."

"Didn't she tell you anything about what she was researching?"

"Not all the details. She didn't like sharing until she was confident her methodology was correct." Junjie turned and propped his feet up on Devak's desk. "I knew about the duwu in the lymph system and the way Scratch kills. She was trying a bunch of methods to counteract the process and ways to inoculate. But she never told me she found a way that worked."

"You were doing work for her," Devak said. "How could you not know more?"

"Because what she had me doing for her was just little pieces." Junjie huffed with exasperation. "Little side studies to prove her theories. I never really knew what the theories were."

"Maybe just as well," Devak said. "Considering what the enforcers put you through. You could be dead if you knew more."

They'd taken Junjie into custody for several hours the day after Guru Ling died. "That's true. I couldn't answer what I didn't know."

"Maybe that's what she wanted."

Junjie just shook his head. Devak's stomach rumbled and he realized it was nearly time for evening meal and they'd never even stopped to eat at midday. With Pitamah at some Kinship meeting with Jemali and Hala, Devak and Junjie were on their own.

Devak rummaged through the kitchen cupboard, then the coldstore. "Can you stand more kel-grain?" he called to Junjie. "There's a little ground drom meat and some patagobi to mix in."

Junjie came to the kitchen doorway. "Kel-grain is fine. Auntie and I have certainly eaten plenty of it."

Devak was eating quite a lot of kel-grain too. The rice his mother used to buy was a luxury far beyond his and Pitamah's means, now that they barely had the adhikar to maintain their high status. But he'd also eaten a fair amount of it back in the days when Kayla was Assigned as Pitamah's caregiver, when he shared meals with her in his great-grandfather's room or in her small shack.

Denk it. He never should have let her into his mind. He'd struggled to avoid thinking about her these past several days. That was one good thing about the mind-numbing data search he and Junjie were doing. It distracted him from dwelling on

Kayla and the terrible ache in his heart that came with thoughts of her.

Devak set the bag of kel-grain on the counter beside the radiant stove and filled a pot with water. He scooped out the proper measure of the gray oblong grains. They were half the length of the kernels of rice he and Pitamah could no longer afford, with less than half the flavor if they weren't spiced up.

Junjie sat at the table, the holo of his mother in his hands. He thumbed it on and stared at the brief animation of his mother smiling at him. The image flickered partway through its display, Mrs. Tsai dissolving momentarily into static each time through the animation.

Devak gave the pot a stir, then covered it and lowered the heat. "Did you figure out how to fix the corrupted image data?"

Junjie shook his head. "I wouldn't have thought a mini-holo would get damaged so easily. The case is intact." He held it out for Devak to see.

"Maybe it was defective to start with."

"Maybe. But it's only been doing this since I got it back from that enforcer. Maybe she dropped it bringing it out."

Junjie lent a hand with dinner, slicing the patagobi leaves into narrow strips while Devak browned the drom meat. He was pretty sick of drom, particularly since the only ones he and Pitamah could afford were the beasts from their adhikar that were past breeding age. They couldn't butcher the droms reserved for their premium wool, or eat the young ones sold for their tender meat to the high-status trueborn market. That left the stringy elderly beasts. They split the gamey meat with the lowborn family that cared for the herd.

Junjie picked at his dinner portion, punctuating each bite

with heavy sighs. Kayla kept intruding in Devak's mind, the look on her face just before she'd climbed from the AirCloud that night, what she said about mistakes. *Sometimes it's not a mistake at all. It's just making the best of things.*

But he could never figure out whether his decision to stay away from Kayla was the right thing for both of them or a big mistake on his part. If pain were a gauge, the way he felt inside meant he'd made a huge error in judgment.

To his surprise, his bowl was empty. Between his hunger and his preoccupation with Kayla, he'd eaten his way through his portion of kel-grain and couldn't remember even tasting it.

Junjie had barely touched his. "Do you think there was a note? I'd really like to read it. Maybe I could make sense of this."

"I've been all through Akhilesh's public files. I suppose Guru Ling's letter could have been in Akhilesh's private database, but not even my hacking could get through his firewall."

"If a letter exists," Junjie said, "why hide it? Even if he wrote it himself, he would want the Brigade to know about it." Junjie's expression brightened. "What if it's in the Brigade database?"

"It could be," Devak conceded.

"You could find it there."

"Hack Brigade files? That wouldn't be easy," Devak said. "They've probably got even stronger firewalls than the Grid does."

"But you know how to hack into the Grid," Junjie said. "How much harder could it be?"

"Plenty harder. And if their sentries detected me, we could have the enforcers on our doorstep pretty denking quick. And

I doubt the Kinship would want to step in to save us and risk that much exposure."

Junjie poked at his kel-grain with his spoon. "What about someone else in the Kinship? Could one of the other data techs do it?"

"The question is, would I want to ask for help?" Devak nudged his empty bowl from side to side. "I personally know five techs at least as good as me or better at system infiltration. A few weeks ago, I wouldn't have hesitated contacting them. But this power shift in the Kinship . . . I'm not sure who we can trust."

Junjie scooped up a bite, then set it down again. He looked up at Devak. "I think this is important. Even though it's risky. Will you try?"

Devak was going to say no. But somehow Kayla's face intruded again. He could see her disapproval, imagine what she'd think of him if he backed down from Junjie's challenge.

"Okay. I'll see what I can do."

Junjie whooped. "I'll clean up. You go get started."

So Devak returned to the computer. He guessed that if there had been a note and Akhilesh had turned it over to the Brigade, it would have most likely been the Plator-based division. The trick would be to find some sort of weakness or back door to the Brigade computers. His spider needed a vulnerable path to infiltrate.

Three hours later, his eyes burning with exhaustion, Devak thought he'd explode from frustration. He kicked the wall in irritation, the noise startling Junjie, who was dozing on Devak's bed.

Junjie sat up, rubbing his eyes. "What's the matter?"

"There's no way to break through," Devak said. "They're too well-protected. Not the slightest crack for my spider to crawl through."

Devak shoved back from the holographic display. He could see that Junjie was trying to hide his disappointment, which made Devak's failure sting that much more sharply.

To make things even worse, there was Kayla in his mind's eye again. He was remembering how impressed she'd been that night he'd hacked into his father's computers. He'd been such a hero to her when he'd updated the programs and data to keep her and her friend Mishalla safe from the monitoring Grid.

Now it was a routine job for him to access the monitoring computers. It took him seconds to ghost in GEN locations to fool the Grid into thinking the tankborns were where they should be instead of off on Kinship business. Sometimes he went a step further to keep safe even non-Kinship GENs by deleting Brigade alerts that notified the enforcers a GEN had strayed outside his or her allowed radius.

Brigade alerts. He felt like a ton of plasscrete had just fallen on his head.

"I am a chutting idiot," he muttered as he pushed back toward the computer.

"You have an idea?" Junjie scrambled off the bed and into the chair beside Devak.

"Of course I know a back door to the Brigade system." Devak's fingers flew over the holographic keyboard, sending his spider back in. "The path I use to overwrite the alerts."

"So you can find the letter?"

"If it's not behind a different firewall."

He shut off his awareness of the ache in his shoulders, of

the burning in his eyes, of the fresh hope in Junjie's face. This time when he sent in the infiltration spider, it was as if his own mind followed it, crawled into his computer, crept along the electronic pathways. The system's circuitry became his own, like the annexed brain of a GEN.

Was this what it was like for Kayla? he wondered. Being so hyper-focused, as if he was following the synapses of his own brain? As if it was no longer an algorithm that brought the infiltration spider into existence, but his own thoughts? And now he reached into the Brigade system with mental spider feet that would pluck out exactly what he was looking for?

And there it was. The search terms seemed to glow brilliant white—*Guru Ling, suicide, death report, final note.* Embedded in the note, a Brigade system tracking spider crouched, ready to report an intrusion. Devak's infiltration spider sent the Brigade's tracker a red herring, sending it scurrying off to defend some other part of the system. Then with a sweep of his physical fingers on his keyboard, Devak had the note downloading to his own computer.

"Do you have it?"

Junjie's question nearly startled Devak off his chair. He looked at the computer clock in stunned disbelief—nearly another hour had passed. He'd been so focused on the single task of finding Guru Ling's letter, it had seemed like only minutes since he'd started.

His legs felt as wobbly as a rat-snake belly. His experience following his spider's crawl into the Brigade computer might have been similar to how Kayla felt when she used her GEN circuitry, but it took far more effort for him than it ever seemed to for her. He was only human, and she was—GEN.

For the first time he realized that in some ways she was more than human. Better than human.

Except she wouldn't want him thinking she was anything but human. Even though some of her GEN abilities were so far beyond anything he could do.

He realized something else. All evening he kept thinking of her. That wasn't unusual, since he had a hard time keeping her from his thoughts. But by remembering the two of them together that night he first reprogrammed the Grid computers, he'd found the key to hacking into the Brigade system.

Beside him, Junjie was reading the letter displayed on the holo-screen. His face was screwed up with confusion.

"I can't believe she wrote this." Junjie read aloud, "*I wanted you to know, Junjie Tsai, if I don't see you again, I hope you think of me as you think of your mother. That seeing your mother's face will remind you of me, no matter what the flaws.* That's crazy. First, she didn't look a thing like my mother. Second, I didn't know if she even liked me, let alone thought of me like some kind of son."

"Except she's not exactly saying she wants you to think of her as if she was your mother." Devak read the letter again. *Your mother's face . . . no matter what the flaws . . .* "Sweet Lord Creator! Where's the holo of your mother?"

"The kitchen table." Junjie ran to retrieve it and handed it over to Devak.

Devak closed his fingers over the black holo case. "It doesn't have an interface jack."

"Of course not. You send the image to the holo tech company and they load it and seal the case."

"Do you suppose it's just a mag-connector holding it

together?" Devak studied the case. "Because you'd have to open it to upload anything else onto it."

"Why would you . . ." Junjie's eyes grew wide. He snatched the holo projector from Devak and switched it on.

Junjie's gaze softened as he watched his mother's smiling image. At the moment it briefly dissolved into static, the light went on in Junjie's eyes.

He gave it back to Devak. "Break it open if you have to."

"I should be able to save your mother's image, but if I can't—"

"I don't need a holo of her to remember her," Junjie said.

Devak found a demagnetizer in his desk and passed it over the seam in the holo case. It fell open and the holo image vanished. "I'll try to fix it if I can," Devak said.

He'd never worked much with holo units, and never with one as small as this. He was looking for the data chip where the image and the instructions for its display were stored. Devak nearly missed it, the chip was so tiny, nothing more than a glimmer of metal inside the case.

It was too small to connect to the computer, but there was a miniscule port in one of his datapods that the data chip fit into. Then he snapped the datapod into one of the computer interfaces and copied the chip contents onto the computer.

The image of Mrs. Tsai was even more degraded on the computer display. And when Devak imported the holo code into a data translator, it stopped looking like a picture at all.

"Oh," was all Junjie could muster. Devak himself couldn't say a word.

There, neatly listed on the screen, was file after file of Guru Ling's research. Including, if the last file could be believed, a cure for Scratch.

24

Abran had been long gone when Kayla woke the next morning, leaving her and Risa to unload the drom wool on their own. Kayla hadn't realized how much Abran's labor lightened hers until he wasn't there to lend a hand. She missed his strong back even more when their next load was plasscrete rubble from a bombed out Mendin warren. A GEN crew helped Kayla and Risa pile the chunks in the rear half of the bay. It would go to their next stop in Amik where it would be crushed to make road base.

Risa must have called her wife during the night, because Kiyomi arrived via pub-trans from their Cayit sector home to join them. Yomi would travel with them up to Amik sector, help unload the plasscrete, then go stay with her still-ailing auntie in Amik.

When they stopped in Qaf sector for the night, Risa offered that she and Kiyomi could bed down in the bay. But Kayla insisted she'd sleep there, despite the oddness of lying in what had so recently been Abran's bed.

Nishi, who sometimes would share the sleeper bed with Risa if Kayla wasn't there, was jealous of Kiyomi and would bite Risa's wife while she was sleeping. So the seycat had been banished to the bay where she grudgingly curled up in Kayla's blankets.

The seycat was too smart to sleep on the pile of plasscrete mounded in the rear of the bay, wary as she was of the plassfiber splinters that flaked out of the rubble. Kayla herself made sure to clear away the chunks that had tumbled from the pile while they drove to give her a safe spot to bed down.

They got an early start the next day leaving Qaf. With Risa driving and Kiyomi in the passenger seat, Kayla sat up in the sleeper, watching the night-dark sky lighten as Iyenku pushed above the horizon. Kas made its appearance as they pulled into the Amik sector warehouse district.

The sky was a cloudless blue-green, a rarity for early winter in the northern territories. But puddles in the packed-gravel roadway spoke of recent rain.

Her gaze fixed on the rear view vid display, Risa backed the lorry along the alley between the plasscrete processing plant and a foodstores warehouse. Their slow pace gave Kayla plenty of time to search for the FHE inscription, a habit now for her. Thankfully, the beige walls on either side were bare.

"Mohapatra hired helpers here," Risa said around a mouthful of devil leaf. "A few factory GENs, mostly allabain lowborns. Same ones might be protecting that GEN girl, Raashida. After unload is done, you go with them to their village."

"If I find Raashida?"

"Bring her here," Risa said. "Allabain won't like us taking

her, but she's likely took sick again by now anyway, like Gemma. Sick more than once, I'll wager. Needs help they can't give."

The rear of the truck cleared the back of the processing plant. Creeping even more slowly, Risa turned the wheel of the lorry to navigate behind the building. The lorry suddenly lurched and tilted as the rear right lifter sank.

"Denking hell?" Risa muttered, as she jammed on the brakes.

In the console vid, Kayla could see a slice of the wide space that stretched behind the processing plant and the warehouses beside it. Her view included a dozen or so allabain standing in yellow muck.

"Best I get back on the roadway," Risa said, gunning the suspension engine. Since only one of the six lifters had tilted into the mud, the lorry righted itself pretty easily.

Risa killed the engine and they all climbed out, Kayla following Kiyomi through the passenger door. They had to squeeze between the lorry and the wall of the processing plant, keeping close to the lorry so they could stay on the relatively firm roadway.

As they got clear of the blocky building, they could see the mess first hand. The factories and warehouses all had the usual plasscrete loading docks jutting out from the backs. But where there should have been a plasscrete apron to drive the lorry on, there was nothing but yellow mud. The allabain and GENs stood shin deep in the stuff.

They'd made the best of the nasty conditions. The GENs and the allabain men had rolled their loose pants up to the knees and the allabain women had brought the backs of their skirt hems between their legs to tuck up into their waistbands. Kayla guessed none of them had bothered to wear shoes.

A lowborn man, dressed more plainly than the allabain in brown shirt and pants, slogged through the mud toward them. "I'm Keita," he said, dipping his head at Risa. "Plant supervisor."

Risa spat a stream of devil leaf juice into the mud. "Denking hell. What happened here?"

Keita grimaced. "We had a few cracks in the plasscrete apron. Lowborn sector board decided to replace rather than repair. Tore out the apron last spring, but then couldn't get funding from the trueborn board."

Kayla spied the hopper that fed the crushing machine on the opposite side of the processing plant. She visually measured the distance between the lorry bay and the hopper with dismay. "We can't get any closer?"

"Not and get out again," Risa said. "Saw how we sank in it."

Resigned, Kayla helped Kiyomi unlatch the doors. Nishi made a mad dash for freedom, then skidded to a stop at the end of the bay when she saw the mud. The seycat seemed to judge the driest spot, then leapt to the relatively solid roadway. She ducked under the lorry, seeking firmer ground.

With a sigh, Kayla shed her shoes and traded them for the work gloves she'd tucked into an empty corner by the back door. Following the allabain example, she rolled her leggings up above her knees. Then she adjusted the hinges on the right hand bay door so it swung flat against the lorry and out of the way.

Spitting out her devil leaf, Risa shouted at the work crew, organizing them in two lines stretching from the bay to the hopper. Kayla headed one line and Keita, the supervisor, headed the other.

Risa and Kiyomi climbed into the bay and tossed out

plasscrete chunks, Risa to Kayla and Kiyomi to Keita. Kayla passed her load to a dark-haired, blue-eyed allabain girl named Lak, who passed it to the next in line.

The two long lines worked as efficiently as any factory machinery, quickly delivering the plasscrete from the back of the lorry to the hopper of the processing plant. An hour later, Kayla was surprised to see half the load was already gone. "Faster than it took us to load it, that's for sure. We had a few helpers in Mendin too."

"No job ever takes long with allabain," Lak said. "We have so much kin."

With that last word, Lak fixed her gaze on Kayla. The allabain girl quickly motioned with her fingers, making the crude K that stood for Kinship. Kayla wanted to ask her about Raashida, to confirm that the GEN girl was at the village. But with the supervisor right there, Kayla didn't want to take the chance.

The last chunks of plasscrete traveled down the lines by mid-afternoon. Risa and Kiyomi swept the last of the dust to the road. Kayla tugged off her gloves and slapped them against the bay door, dislodging as much of the raw plassfiber as she could. Risa and Kiyomi did the same, then Kiyomi tucked all three pairs in a storage box by the top of the hatch ladder.

Risa was busy paying off the workers with a stock of dhans Councilor Mohapatra had sent on. A few of them received many times what the others had, including Lak. Which meant they were all Kinship. Lak and the others would keep only some of their wages. The rest would be used for Kinship business.

After they'd been paid, the GENs headed into the processing plant. Kayla wondered how much of their extra pay would line the lowborn supervisor's pocket.

The allabain started off together through the mud, some of them arm-in-arm, moving in the direction of a holo hedge that marked the border between Amik sector and trueborn Sarada sector. Despite their efforts to stay clean, the men's flowing pants were spattered with muck up past the knees, and the women's skirts were heavy with mud.

Lak hung back, catching Kayla's eye. Kayla looked to Risa for confirmation and the lowborn woman nodded. Kayla snagged her shoes from where she'd left them and hurried to catch up with the allabain girl.

Lak hooked her arm in Kayla's without hesitation. "Raashida is still with us," Lak said.

"How is she?" Kayla asked.

Lak grew serious. "She falls ill, then recovers, over and over. I'm told she died again, then resurrected."

"And they think she's a goddess?"

"If by *they* you mean the other allabain," Lak said, "some do. *I* think there's something wrong with her circuitry that makes her heal, then lets her get sick again."

They reached the berm the holo hedge had been built on. Here the packed gravel pathway had shed the recent rain and the going was firm. A relief not to have to slog through the mud even though the gravel pricked Kayla's mud-caked bare feet.

The path meandered roughly parallel to the warehouse district, then gave way to a wilder area where the road ended and junk trees competed with sticker bushes and chaff heads. On the trueborn side of the hedge, the larger growth had been cleared away, a few junk tree stumps still poking up through expanses of manicured scrap grass.

The line of allabain threaded through a break between two

massive sticker bushes. Kayla and Lak slipped through last and into the village.

The allabain had pitched their tent-like bhaile amongst the junk trees and sticker bushes, a natural barrier of Lokan scrub surrounding their village. The ground was as well-drained as the path beside the hedge, and the bhaile clustered in a circle around a central open space dotted with a junk tree or two and three or four sticker bushes. The scrap grass had been beaten down by many feet.

Kayla waited her turn behind the others at a cistern made of plasscine sheets around a frame of cleverly bent sticker bush branches. Kayla sighed with pleasure as she finally rinsed the yellow mud from her feet and legs. Then she slipped her shoes on.

Across the open space, a crowd knelt around a bhaile that was slightly larger than the others. A tall allabain man stood guard at the door flap.

"That's the headman, Tekin," Lak said. "He decides who sees Raashida."

They started across the open space. "Do they all want her to heal them?" Kayla asked. "That's what made Gemma ill, healing too many at once."

"I heard about Gemma," Lak said. "Some of the ones near Raashida need healing, some just want to worship her. It's Raashida who insists on touching all of them. Even though it makes her sick."

"The ones she heals—do they sicken again like she does?" Kayla asked. "Or do they keep their health?"

"She's been here two weeks. Early on, someone brought in a Scratch-infected GEN. That's him." Lak pointed to a powerful looking GEN toting a large bucket of water in each hand. "After she touched him, it took a day for his Scratch scars to heal. He seems almost better than he was before."

Tekin spotted them approaching and nodded a greeting to Kayla. When she came up alongside him, the gaunt, gray-haired man towered over her, although he was aged and slightly built. No match for Kayla's strength if she'd been inclined to push him aside and carry off Raashida.

Tekin might have seen some of Kayla's calculation in her eyes because he planted his feet wider and threw back his shoulders. "Are you here for a healing? Dhartri is resting."

Kayla recalled what Aki had said in Esa sector. The worshipers of Iyenkas, the dual gods become one god, considered Raashida their daughter, Dhartri. The healer. Tekin was clearly a believer, zeal burning in his eyes. Kayla wondered how she would persuade Tekin to let her take Raashida back to Risa's lorry.

As she puzzled over that difficulty, someone grabbed her arm and pulled her around. To her utter shock, she saw it was Abran. What looked like the mark of a sticker bush thorn slashed through the tattoo on his left cheek.

Kayla yanked her arm free. "What are you doing here? How did you even get here?"

"It doesn't matter." He looked back over his shoulder, toward the warehouses. "You have to leave, now."

"You don't have the right to tell me what to do," Kayla said. "When you're such an idiot. You ran away, didn't you? You ran away from the only people who could keep you safe."

"You're in danger," Abran said, glancing back at the warehouses again. "Please, come with me."

He tried to take her arm, but she backed away, colliding with Tekin. The gaunt lowborn gave Abran an appraising look. "Are you here for healing?"

"No, he's not," Kayla said. "He needs to leave." What was he doing here anyway? Especially right when they'd found Raashida?

Just then, a dark, slender hand pushed aside the door flap of the bhaile. Raashida, tall and slim and beautiful, emerged from the tent and approached Abran. The beads braided in her hair clacked softly as she moved.

The GEN girl must have been in a well cycle, because there was no sign of Scratch on her dark face. She tipped her head up to Abran, and she appeared even more radiant than she had in the mural the Esa allabain had painted of her. Like Gemma, Raashida glowed with whatever process burned inside her.

"You've hurt yourself," Raashida said, reaching for Abran's left cheek.

Abran shouted, "No!" and tried to pull back.

But Tekin had moved behind Abran, his hands on Abran's shoulders to hold him still. The crowd had surged to their feet, forming a wall around Abran. As Raashida's hand cupped Abran's cheek, he cried out as if in pain.

Kayla yanked Tekin's hands off Abran and pushed against the crowd to make space. But Abran was still crying out. He pulled away from Raashida, and his hands flew up to where hers had been on his face.

"Let me see," Kayla said, taking his wrists and tugging at them.

Abran resisted. She managed to get his right hand clear. She could see nothing wrong, no wound or mark.

But his tattooed left cheek was bleeding. Blood dripped between his fingers.

"Drop your hand, Abran," she demanded.

He shook his head. Kayla, out of patience, pulled it away.

And his tattoo slid off with it. Peeled away from his left cheek, leaving raw, bleeding skin.

Kayla stared at the slick of blood. The complex circuitry that should have been under his tattoo was missing. Tiny bits of crude electronics dotted the raw skin.

As she watched, the skin healed. From Raashida's touch or the punarjanma he'd been using? Taking a cloth an allabain offered her, Kayla swiped away the still wet blood. The bits of electronics came with it, dotting the cloth.

Abran's red-brown cheek was smooth again. Bare. His tattoo stripped away with the last of his lies.

"You're no GEN, are you?" She felt a hundred times more an idiot than him for not seeing it before now. "What are you? Lowborn? No, a lowborn wouldn't be so treacherous. You're a denking, chutting trueborn." She looked him up and down contemptuously. "Minor-status, yeah? No demi would pretend to be a GEN."

"Yes," he said tightly. "Minor-status. But you have to go." He tried for her arm again.

Kayla would have interrogated Abran further, but shouts rang out from across the open space. She caught glimpses of motion as the crowd shifted. Then everyone turned as one away from Raashida. Tekin blocked Kayla's view of what was happening.

Then she heard a familiar zing of energy. Tekin cried out and crumpled at Kayla's feet. She gaped at the shockgun blast that had taken away half the allabain's face.

The Brigade had arrived.

Abran snatched at Kayla's sleeve. "Come with me!"

She smacked him across the chest so hard he went flying. He landed a few meters away, his groan telling Kayla she hadn't killed him.

Kayla looked around her frantically for Raashida, terrified that she would find her dead alongside Tekin. A handful of other worshippers had fallen to the Brigade's shockguns. But the GEN girl had crawled over to Tekin and laid her hands on the allabain man. She sobbed out his name, shook his body. But her healing ability didn't extend beyond Tekin's death. He never stirred.

Kayla knelt beside her. "We have to get out of here."

Raashida resisted, tried to reach for one of the wounded. But Raashida's glow had faded, was nearly gone. If Raashida was like Gemma, trying to heal anyone else now would do her in.

Kayla grabbed Raashida around the middle and pulled her away. The GEN girl was weak enough that she barely struggled. Kayla urged her between the bhaile and into the thicket of sticker bushes. Kayla took a quick look behind them to see if any of the enforcers were in pursuit. But so many of Raashida's worshippers had stood up to the Brigade, in some cases knocking the shockguns from the enforcers' hands, the invaders seemed too occupied to notice Kayla's and Raashida's escape.

Kayla would have to circle around to make her way back to the lorry. The path along the hedge wouldn't be safe—that was where the enforcers had poured into the village.

Raashida slumped against Kayla. "I should have stayed. They need me."

Kayla wrapped Raashida's arm across her shoulders, could feel the heat of fever. "You're sick, Raashida. You won't be able to do them much good like this."

"Not Raashida," the GEN girl muttered. "Dhartri. My duty to heal them."

Raashida collapsed entirely then and Kayla had to drape the nerveless body over her shoulder. Up ahead, the scrub ended. Kayla could see the tops of the buildings and the roadway that ran along the front of the warehouse district. It would be tricky to get past that wide open area carrying Raashida.

As she dithered about stepping from the relative safety of the scrub, she heard the crack of a twig behind her. Sweet Infinite, she'd been followed after all. She whirled to face her pursuer.

Abran. Denking hell.

"I'm sorry, Kayla."

She took a step toward him, ready to finish what her blow in the village had started. But a prickle of energy crawled up her back and the world went fuzzy around the edges.

Raashida slipped from Kayla's shoulder. Kayla slumped beside the GEN girl. As Kayla's vision dimmed, she groped for Abran's ankle, wanting to feel the snap of his bones against her fingers. But he stepped out of reach and everything went black.

25

Kayla woke slowly, sick and dizzy, every muscle aching. She was propped up and swaying from side to side. She must be back in the lorry, her and Risa on their way to their next stop. It had all worked out, then—Risa and Kiyomi had rescued her from the enforcer, or they'd called in the Kinship to extricate her from the Brigade.

Then she opened her eyes. Her vision blurred and swam, but she knew this wasn't the lorry. She was in the rear of a Jahaja multi-lev, leaning against the cool glass of the window. All four rows of seats in front of her were filled, two to a seat. They must all be allabain from Amik. In the dim overhead light, she recognized some of them as Raashida's worshippers.

She couldn't quite see the Brigade man driving the vehicle. But she saw the minor-status enforcer guarding them. He stood up front facing them, his ruddy, pockmarked face set in a scowl, an arm hooked around a pole for balance. He'd drawn his shockgun and had it ready.

They didn't download me, thank the Infinite. Or it wouldn't be me sitting here anymore.

Moonless night flew past the window in a blur. She could see the reflective safety rail of a skyway but nothing but darkness beyond. Her inner clock told her it was well past midnight. Which meant they'd had her locked up here and unconscious for a good long time before heading out. She guessed the allabain weren't easy prey for the Brigade.

Had Risa seen the enforcers coming? She must have since they'd come from the direction of the lorry. Surely Risa knew Kayla had been captured and she'd send help.

Kayla straightened, and pain cut her wrists. She realized her hands were shackled together and locked to the seat in front of her, her ankles locked to the floor with about twenty centimeters of plassteel chain between them. Based on the ones across the aisle that she could see, the allabain were restrained as well.

She pulled against the shackles, but she was still weak, and they didn't budge. She tried again with more force, but the exertion made the world spin and she had to shut her eyes. She thought she might vomit the long ago breakfast she'd eaten with Risa and Kiyomi.

Her brain felt muzzy and her tongue thick from the shockgun. She'd been hit once before with an enforcer weapon, but that had been a high-power, narrow-focus strike. The beam had just clipped her and left a nasty burn.

This had been low-power and wide-spread. It hadn't burned her, but it had jittered all through her body, knocking her out. It had fogged her brain, both annexed and bare.

"Kayla."

She thought at first it was that Infinite-blasted voice calling to her, but then she recognized Abran's voice. She opened her eyes and looked up. He stood over her, a blue bali glittering in his ear, looking somber and sorry. She could see an empty space in the front row. So not every seat had been filled with allabain.

He glanced up toward the ruddy-faced enforcer, then back at her. "I had to do it, Kayla."

"If I could get these shackles off—" She said each word clearly, and with as much menace as she could— "I would put you through a window."

He set back on his heels as if she'd actually landed a blow. Then, moving cautiously, he sat on the corner of the seat, as far away from her as possible. "Baadkar had my family."

Kayla eyed his unmarked left cheek. "Considering the blood when Raashida healed you, that tattoo was more than just decoration."

He swiped at his cheek. "Baadkar had just enough circuitry installed so I could be downloaded. There wasn't much data stored, but enough for a curious enforcer."

And enough to convince her and Risa. Feeling stronger, Kayla tried to rise again, pulling at the bonds around her wrists and ankles. But the plassteel restraints just cut more deeply into her skin.

She sat back. "So Baadkar *had* your family. Not anymore? He let them go after you betrayed us?"

He turned away, his jaw flexing. "He still has my sister."

"But not your mother. So you won something in the deal."

Now his head swung back. "He killed her. When Risa sent me away."

Denk it, she wouldn't feel guilty. Not her fault. Or Risa's.

"You're not a GEN, so Baadkar wasn't your patron. All that nonsense about him beating you—"

"That wasn't nonsense," Abran said. "It was true. He mostly beat his GENs, but when he was angry enough, he'd go after his minor-status workers too. If the numbers didn't add up the way he wanted them, he hurt me. He punched me, broke my finger. And once he did use a shockgun on me."

She desperately wanted out, away from Abran. She strained against her shackles, focusing her rage and sense of betrayal into breaking them. But her strength was no match for the pain of the restraints cutting into her wrists.

She relaxed as blood dripped down her arms. "All that time, I thought you were a devout worshipper with your prayer mirror, but you were mocking the Infinite."

"That wasn't my intention."

"But it comes out the same, doesn't it?" The blood on her arms itched so badly, it burned. Abran might wipe them clean if she asked, but she'd just as soon bite them off at the elbow. "So you told Baadkar where we were and he sent the Brigade?"

"No. Baadkar told me he was done with me. He'd found you and that other GEN girl himself."

"Raashida."

"Yes," Abran said. "I knew your next stop was Amik sector. I stole the councilor's lev-car."

"Where's Raashida?" Kayla made another quick scan of the Jahaja. No sign of the GEN girl.

"They sent her ahead."

"To where?"

"Where you're going," he said, anguish settling in his face. "To Akhilesh's lab."

Another lurch in her stomach. "What are they going to do to Raashida? To me?"

"I don't know."

"Raashida has Scratch. Will they destroy her like they have all the other Scratch-infected GENs?"

"I don't know!"

The enforcer on guard took a step toward the back, his shockgun raised. Abran shook his head and the enforcer retreated.

Abran fell silent. Out the window, Kayla could see the guardrails of the skyway blur past. Below, illumination dotted whatever sector they were passing over.

He was quiet so long, she assumed he was done talking. Finally, he said, "They had me make up some parts of my story, but what I told you about the bhimkay was true. Baadkar owns thousands of acres of adhikar, but between him and his sons, they go through dhans like water. Droms and kel-grain fields don't earn enough so Baadkar brews drugs on the side. Mostly jaf buzz, but sometimes the punarjanma. He sent his youngest son, Ekavir, to a jaf buyer in Shafti, and Ekavir brought me along to carry the load."

"So the bhimkay did kill him."

"Killed him. Ate him. I barely got away." Abran shuddered. "I ran back to Baadkar's compound. He was angry, not because of his son, but because I'd left the jaf buzz behind. By the time another of his sons went to retrieve it, the buyer found it and stole it."

"Then why didn't he just throw you out? A minor-status like you couldn't have been all that important to him."

"Because he could use me," Abran said. "Baadkar and

Akhilesh cooked up this plan to track the lowborn woman's lorry. A tech created the false tattoo and a medic bonded it to my face. They sent along enough punarjanma so I could heal like a GEN."

The Jahaja swung off the skyway, the abrupt motion tugging on the restraints. Kayla sucked in a breath, blinking back tears at the pain.

They pulled up to a building, its exterior illuminators casting a yellow glow on four lev-cars docked out front, three Brigade Daggers and a luxury WindSpear. The letters GAMA were written in small script on the door of the building. A half-dozen enforcers who had been waiting there approached the Jahaja.

The ruddy-faced guard released the shackles from their attachments one row at a time. The guard and driver sent the still-restrained allabain off the Jahaja in pairs where the other enforcers waited.

"Why did they even bring the lowborns?" Kayla asked Abran.

"They were all healed by that GEN girl," Abran said.

In time it was only her, Abran, and the ruddy-faced enforcer. The enforcer came back, his nametag glinting in the dim light. Kinship habit had Kayla storing away his name. Salot.

Salot cocked a thumb toward the GAMA lab. "Boy, you got someone waiting for you."

A short, wide-girthed trueborn stood just outside the lab, younger men on either side of him. They all shared the same cruel faces, cut with shadow from the glare of the exterior illuminators.

"Is that Baadkar?" Kayla asked.

"And two of his sons." His voice shook.

Abran got slowly to his feet and pushed past the enforcer. He glanced back at Kayla one more time before he stepped from the Jahaja. She tried to feel a little sympathy for him, but couldn't summon so much as a gram.

Now Salot leaned close to Kayla, the stink of stale curry and devil leaf wafting off him. "I know your sket, jik. Even with the restraints, I don't trust you not to break free and run. If it was up to me, I'd give you another blast with the shockgun, but Akhilesh says no. He doesn't want your DNA juggled any more than it is. So a download will have to do the trick."

Salot pulled out a datapod. Kayla's whole body went numb as she realized this was how it would end. She'd never find out what Akhilesh had planned.

Salot only wanted her to black out from the download so he could get her safely inside. But once the download started, the Kinship failsafe would trigger. Her annexed brain would erase itself and her bare brain would fry. She would no longer be Kayla. She would be nothing but an empty shell.

As the ruddy-faced Salot placed the datapod against her tattoo, regret filled her, grief and terror on its heels. She wanted to cry out, to beg him to stop.

The extendibles bit her skin. Salot thumbed the datapod. Any moment the download would start and Kayla's life would be over.

26

She could still feel the restraints cutting into her wrists. She could still smell the stale curry on Salot's breath, could still see his pockmarked face.

I'm Kayla 6982, nurture daughter of Tala. She waited for her identification to be wiped away.

Confusion darkened Salot's ruddy face. He pressed the datapod harder on Kayla's cheek as if that would make it work better. "Denking hell?" he muttered.

He thumbed the datapod to deactivate it, then yanked it out before the extendibles had retracted. Plugging the small device into his sekai, he tapped at the hand-held's screen, then released the datapod again. The device's ready light had switched from download to upload. He slapped the device back on her tattoo.

A stream of data should have fed into her annexed brain. But she detected nothing moving along her circuitry. She'd become so adept at tracing the data uploaded into her, she certainly would have been able to track even a few bytes of information.

The datapod deactivated, then dropped from her cheek. Salot snatched it as it fell. "What sector am I from?" he asked.

"I don't know."

"What's my father's name?"

Kayla shook her head. "I don't know."

He swung at her in clear frustration. She tried to dodge, but her restraints made that impossible. She couldn't get her head out of the way and his open gloved hand struck her already-sore tattooed cheek.

Her cheek throbbing, she glared at the enforcer. "You can't knock the information out of me if it isn't there."

He lifted his hand to strike her again, then thought better of it. "Won't download, won't upload. What the denking hell is wrong with you, jik?"

Just then, the dark-skinned driver returned from escorting the allabain inside. Salot snarled at him, "Give me a hand, Nafti. I've got a chutting broken jik."

Salot pressed the barrel of his shockgun against Kayla's head as Nafti released the restraints. Then Salot yanked her to her feet, gripping her arm so hard his drom leather gloves pinched her skin. With the shackles still on her ankles, she barely kept her feet as he all but dragged her up the aisle. At the Jahaja's door, Nafti took her other arm.

They hustled her into the GAMA building. What looked like a guard station in the foyer was unmanned. The long hallway they pulled her into seemed quiet, everything shut down for the day. There were no lights under the doors, except for the one on the left with Akhilesh's name on it. The door farther down on the right, labeled GURU LIANG LING, hung open, but the room was dark inside.

Guru Ling made her think of Junjie, which brought Devak to mind. Was there any way either one of them knew she was here?

They'd muscled her to the end of the hall when she heard shouting from where they'd entered, a familiar rusty voice. Kayla twisted to look over her shoulder and her heart sank as enforcers dragged Risa and Kiyomi along the hall. The enforcers must have swept Risa and Kiyomi up during the raid of the allabain village.

Kayla had an instant to meet Risa's gaze, to see the regret in the lowborn woman's eyes. Then the enforcers pushed Kayla through a doorway and up a flight of stairs.

She heard Risa yelling, the lowborn woman's bitter complaint at her detention. She shouted out that they would answer to Councilor Mohapatra.

Then Kayla heard the sound of a shockgun and her heart seemed to stop. Resisting the pull of the enforcers, she strained her ears, praying to the Infinite that she'd hear Risa's voice again. But she only heard Kiyomi's keening cry.

The impulse to escape spurted through her and she fought against Nafti and Salot, surprising them enough that their grip loosened. But bound as she was, she fell like a rock against the steps. She lay there dazed as Salot and Nafti yanked her to her knees. Her legs hit every hard edge as they toted her up the stairs.

Another long hallway on the second floor. They pulled her into the third door down, and slung her inside. It was large and brightly lit, maybe twenty meters by forty. To the left, banks of scientific equipment—microscopes, surgical lasers, computer arrays—lined the walls. Her tech-crazy nurture brother, Jal, would be dancing with joy to get his hands on those sophisticated devices.

On her right were rows and rows of gen-tanks filled with thick green gen-fluid. A few tanks were unoccupied, but Scratch-marred GENs, stripped to their skivs, floated in the rest of them. Besides the breathing tube down their throats, skinnier tubes had been inserted in their bodies—at the upper arms, neck, and pelvis. The slender tubes joined to a single larger tube that led to a transparent box filled with pale yellow liquid.

The color, the translucence of the fluid filling the box, it reminded her of something . . . was it punarjanma? Were those GENs here to be treated for their Scratch? Would it heal them the way she'd seen Abran healed, do what their circuitry seemingly couldn't do, cure the Scratch infection?

Nafti and Salot pulled her past the gen-tanks toward four metal float tables, three of them occupied by allabain, two men and a girl. Kayla's heart fell when she saw the girl was Lak. Each of the allabains' restraints had been locked to the float table, their arms separated and secured on either side of their hips. A band of plassteel circled their necks, tight enough that they could turn their heads left and right, but not lift them from the table.

Lak and one of the men watched as the enforcers dragged her to the empty float table. The third allabain stared glassy-eyed at the ceiling.

No, he wasn't staring. His chest no longer rose and fell. He was in the hands of his god Iyenkas.

The enforcers heaved her up, then dropped her none too gently on the empty float table. While the dark-skinned enforcer, Nafti, activated the connection between the float table and the ankle restraints, Salot used his datapod to signal the wrist shackles to separate. He attached them on either side of the float table, then shoved her flat and clicked the throat restraint around her neck. She tried to raise her head, but the pressure cut off her breathing.

Salot made one last check of the restraints, then he and Nafti walked off between the rows of gen-tanks and out of the room. Kayla could turn her head just enough to see Lak's blue gaze fixed on her.

The allabain girl asked, "What do you think they're going to do to us?"

"I don't know. Were you able to get a warning out to our friends?" The Kinship, she meant.

Lak just shook her head. Then the Kinship had no idea they were here. Despair washed over Kayla.

She slid her gaze to the left toward the row of four bubbling gen-tanks closest to her. Horror dug its claws in her as she stared at the thick green gen-fluid that filled each tank.

The three nearest tanks were unoccupied, but someone floated in the fourth one. At the angle she lay, she couldn't quite see the occupant. Then the body within rolled, the face pressing closer to the tank wall.

It was Raashida.

Kayla tried to kick, to pull her arms free. The restraints held her down even as her heart raced with a flood of adrenaline. Finally, she surrendered to the pain of the bonds cutting into her and lay still.

She wanted to believe that Raashida was in the tank to be cured, but it didn't make sense. Abran had infused the punarjanma via a vac-seal. Why not do the same with Raashida and the other GENs? Why put them in gen-tanks?

Her wrists and ankles throbbing, despair lapped at her. Risa was at the least injured, possibly even killed. In any case, both Risa and Kiyomi were captives. All because of Abran? Or some other treachery? Certainly Baadkar had played a part.

The door latch clattered. As the high-status trueborn came into her field of view, his face triggered a hopelessness in the pit of her stomach. She didn't know him—why the instant fear? The friendly smile he sent her way did nothing to reassure her.

Then he spoke and her unnamed terror amplified. "I'm Akhilesh. Kayla, isn't it?"

He was close enough she could see the bali in his right ear now. Why was Akhilesh wearing a demi-status emerald bali when he should have been high-status? His perfect skin color and elegant facial structure marked his elevated rank. Something buried deep in her bare brain told her she'd seen this man before and when she had, he'd worn a diamond bali.

He touched her hand, gently and without the least revulsion despite being unprotected by gloves. It should have put her at ease that this trueborn had no qualms about skin-to-skin contact with a GEN. But her fear grew so large, she had to swallow back a whimper.

"There's nothing to be afraid of, Kayla," Akhilesh chided. "I'm not hurting you, am I?"

Unwanted tears burned her eyes. He pulled a float tray closer to the table, then took a lase-knife from it. She followed the path of his hand as he brought the surgical tool closer.

But he only used the lase-knife to carefully cut the length of her sleeve, from wrist to shoulder. He pulled aside the fabric, exposing the mottled skin of her arm that she so despised.

"Hard to run away from this," Akhilesh said softly. "Isn't it, Kayla? Or perhaps . . ." He stroked the tattoo on her right cheek. ". . . I should call you Elana."

Kayla heart stuttered in her chest. Before she'd become a GEN, when she'd been a minor-status trueborn, her name had been Elana Kalu. That Akhilesh knew her trueborn name filled her with dread.

Beside her, Lak struggled against her bonds. "You have no right to take me into custody like this," the girl cried out. "I'm a freeborn allabain. You're violating the Lowborn Welfare Laws."

Akhilesh glanced over at the girl. "You're right," he said pleasantly.

Setting aside the lase-knife, he plucked a square vac-seal from the tray and rounded Kayla's table to Lak's. With one hand, he yanked up the girl's sleeve, with the other he thumbed the activator tab and slapped the vac-seal to the crook of Lak's arm.

Lak gasped and jolted, spasming against her shackles. Her body shook, ugly, guttural sounds forced from her throat. Then she fell back, her body still, her eyes half-lidded like the dead allabain man's.

Kayla stared at Lak's chest, prayed she would see it rise and fall. Sweet Infinite, was she gone? Pain lanced Kayla at the loss.

The second allabain man moaned and fought against his restraints until his wrists bled and he coughed from the pressure of the band around his neck. Akhilesh moved to the man's side to pat his shoulder. "There's nothing to fear. Be at peace, friend."

Then Akhilesh tugged over the float tray and retrieved another square vac-seal. The allabain man shrieked as Akhilesh pulled up his sleeve.

Kayla wanted to look away, shut her eyes and ears, anything but watch a second execution. But someone had to bear witness to the man's death, so she forced herself to look. As the allabain grunted and spasmed toward death, Kayla sent a silent prayer to the Infinite that He would guide the man toward Iyenkas.

When it was quiet again, Akhilesh turned to Kayla. Rage wiped away her terror of him.

"I need to place these three in cold storage to wait for experimentation." He gave her shoulder a gentle pat and her skin crawled. "I'll be back as soon as I can."

He pushed Lak's float table from beside Kayla and headed for the door. Kayla waited for the door to click shut and his footsteps to start down the hall, then she fought her bonds with new energy. No telling how far he had to go with Lak's body or how long he'd be.

A quick scan of the float tray told her it contained the lase-knife, the much larger lase-cutter, what looked like a sekai and several other vac-seals of varying shapes, their contents of various colors. There were more of the square vac-seals that had killed the allabain. She'd use it against Akhilesh if she had to.

She turned her attention back to her struggle as she felt the slightest give at her right wrist. It wasn't the restraint loosening, but its attachment to the float table. If she ignored the pain of the plassteel bands around her wrists, she could break the attachment.

She allowed a little bit of hope to rise in her chest. She pulled and twisted and fought against the bond on her right wrist. She could feel it breaking away, even as she felt blood dripping from her wrist again. Her eyes kept returning to the door where Akhilesh had exited.

Just as the door latch clicked, the restraint snapped from its mooring. Triumph flared inside her even as Akhilesh ran toward her, grabbed something from his float tray. Just as she reached up to twist away the neck band, she felt a chill on the crook of her left arm.

Akhilesh pressed a vac-seal against her arm. Kayla whispered, "No," a sob rising in her throat.

He took his hand away, and she saw the triangular shape of the vac-seal. Not square like the one that killed the allabain.

Akhilesh turned his back on her and tugged over the float tray to drop the emptied vac-seal on it. Kayla reached for him.

But her arm wouldn't move. It lay across her chest, her fingers still curled around the neck band. But no amount of will could force it to lift, to close the space between her and Akhilesh.

He smiled down at her. "Just a temporary paralytic. You can still breathe. I'm afraid you can't speak, but you can still hear. Which is good, because I've waited so long to meet you again."

She tried to speak, but her tongue wouldn't work, her lips wouldn't move. She could moan, the formless sound breathy and useless. A fog dulled her mind as if even her thoughts were paralyzed.

"I'm sure you want to know everything," Akhilesh said. "But first I have a few questions. The enforcer tells me he couldn't download or upload you. Why is that?"

Because I've been made immune to you. To all trueborn intrusion.

Her anger at the unasked for FHE programming gave way to gratitude.

Akhilesh picked up what had looked like a sekai reader from the float tray. But when he held it to her tattoo, it formed itself to her cheek. She felt the bite of extendibles, except they pierced deeper than a datapod. The paralytic did nothing to ease the pain.

Akhilesh studied the device's screen. "The sekai recognizes the tattoo pattern. Knows you're Kayla 6892. But there's no longer any external access to your internal electronics." He peered into her face. "Who did that to you? Who ruined all that lovely circuitry I took so much trouble to install eleven years ago?"

Terror crept through her again. Familiar images flashed in her mind, not exactly memories, more like she was watching them on a sekai screen. She had no arms, and she was being torn away from her mother. Enforcers carried her off and gave her over to a trueborn.

Gave her to Akhilesh.

Now she could see his face, a decade younger, a diamond bali in his ear instead of an emerald. His hands had been so large against her small body. They spanned her waist as he plunged her into the gen-tank.

She remembered the scrape of the breathing tube down her throat, the chill of the gen-fluid, the weight of it. Even with the tube feeding her air, she felt smothered by the fluid for endless moments before she blacked out.

"The memories are still there, aren't they?" Akhilesh said. "Have you figured that out yet?"

They were the same nightmares she'd always had. She'd

been born without arms and had been put into the tank to grow new ones, transformed at the same time into a GEN. Except . . . With her greater ability to track her own circuitry, to see what moved where, revelation hit her like a bhimkay strike. The memories weren't stored in her bare brain. They were in her annexed brain, and were being fed to her bare brain.

He must have seen the realization in her eyes. "It did all happen. But you were wiped afterward, just as all conversions are. We don't want you remembering your trueborn life.

"But I like the converted to know that I made them. Like a signature. So I plant true memories in your annexed brains and use a program to send them to your bare brain."

Now she understood the fear. She might not remember the details without Akhilesh's planted memories, but she knew him at a cell level—his eyes, his smell, the sound of his voice. He was the one who had torn her from her mother and thrust her into slavery.

Except—hadn't her mother given her up? Abandoned the fourth-year child Kayla had once been when she couldn't be made perfect? Akhilesh had changed her, but hadn't it been at her parents' request?

The gen-tank holding Raashida beeped and Akhilesh turned away to attend to it. Pulling on a pair of protective gloves, he picked up a tong-like tool to avoid touching the gen-fluid filling the tank. Kayla had learned in Doctrine School that gen-fluid had to be programmed for the occupant of the tank. The gooey green liquid was set for Raashida's genetic profile, not Akhilesh's. So while it was safe for the GEN girl, it would mutate and deform Akhilesh if it touched his skin.

Using the tongs, he pulled out Raashida's arm. As he bent to examine it, Kayla caught a glimpse and nausea gripped her again.

The GEN girl's beautiful dark skin was gray, her arm sunken around the bones as if part of her had been sucked away. That yellow fluid, what Kayla had guessed was punarjanma, had been pumped *out* of Raashida. Out of the other GENs.

Kayla!

She jolted at the sound of that inner voice. *She could move!* Not much—her fingertips. Her skin. And the paralysis had faded from her mouth and tongue.

But she stayed silent, not wanting to let Akhilesh know the paralytic was wearing off. She let her thoughts run, let the realizations tumble out. Akhilesh wasn't using punarjanma to heal these GENs. He was pumping it out of them. Was it a side-effect of the Scratch? How did Akhilesh know?

The answer came to her an instant before he spoke. Because Akhilesh had created Scratch.

He glanced over his shoulder at her with a smile, clearly proud of his cleverness. "It was a beautiful piece of genetic engineering. Use GENs as factories. Once infected, their own healing system manufactures the punarjanma." He carefully eased Raashida's arm into the tank fluid, then lifted the other. "What better way for GENs to serve trueborns? It not only heals, as it did our friend Abran, it restores youth. Corrects illness, neural damage, no matter how serious, how chronic."

Neural damage. Like Zul's. Devak's great-grandfather been so improved when she'd seen him in the Beqal sector safe house. *A treatment personally derived for me,* he'd said. *By Akhilesh Garud. The head of GAMA.*

Did Zul know his good health came at the expense of Scratch-infected GENs?

Kayla!

Her left arm still remained inert, but strength was returning to her right arm. Akhilesh had left her right wrist unbound, no doubt certain that the paralytic was restraint enough.

He turned his back to her. Her fingers were still wrapped around the neck restraint. She tightened her grip, willed herself to pull.

Kayla!

The voice sounded different. Clearer. More imperative. What did that mean?

She shut her eyes, listening. Held her breath, waiting. Akhilesh's footsteps returned to her side.

"You can close your eyes." He stared down at her. "The paralytic should have lasted longer than that." He reached for another vac-seal.

"No!" Kayla shouted. She tried to grab him, to stop him with her right hand. But she could only lift it a few centimeters. Then he applied the paralytic to her left arm and all strength faded.

He reached for another vac-seal, this one hexagonal and the contents deep red. "I think it's best if I start the process with you. Your genetic makeup is not as ideal as Raashida's and the others I've used. You won't produce as much punarjanma. But it seems like a fitting ending for one of my creations."

She watched, horrified, as he pressed the red vac-seal to the crook of her left arm, squeezed its contents into her system. Scratch was now running through her and her body's healing process was helpless against it.

Anger and desperation warred inside her as Akhilesh

returned to Raashida's tank. No one knew she was here. No telling how long before the Scratch took effect. Her body would produce the punarjanma, paradoxically the same thing that could heal her if administered properly.

Akhilesh was bent over Raashida's tank, trying to lift her right leg for examination. The tongs slipped and her leg dropped, splashing the liquid from the tank. Some of it must have landed on him despite the gloves because he ripped them off and rushed to an emergency spigot on the wall. When he returned from rinsing his left hand, Kayla could see an ugly purple growth on the wrist where the liquid must have touched.

Kayla! Where are you?

The words went through her like a bolt of lightning. She scarcely dared hope that the message meant what she thought it did.

Someone outside her *was* communicating with her. Could she communicate back?

Her eyelids still wouldn't work, so she stared up at the ceiling, doing her best to shut out the beginnings of a fever ache and Akhilesh's busy preparations of the empty gen-tank next to Raashida's. He held his left hand close to his body. She hoped the growth there burned him.

Inside her annexed brain, she traced the path the voice seemed to come from and focused a message. *Can you hear me?*

The long, silent pause filled her with dread. Her skin started to throb, where the restraints cut her wrist and ankles, but also along her forearms, her lower legs.

I hear you, Kayla.

She could have wept. She didn't even care who it was. *I need help.*

Where are you?

GAMA. Send Devak. Send Junjie.

Are you safe? the voice asked.

No! Paralyzed. Scratch-infected. Restrained.

You can fight the paralytic.

Code dumped into her, new programming. She hated that they were invading her annexed brain again, but this wasn't the time to argue the point. She recognized it as an auxiliary to her healing, and she could sense the electrical signals it sent throughout her system to counteract the paralytic.

But she couldn't lie still as the stimulation flooded her body. When Akhilesh turned back to her, she froze in place, hoping he wouldn't notice she'd shifted. But then he took up his lase-knife from the float tray, and narrowed it down to needle focus. He touched it to her skin ever so lightly. She couldn't help it, she jumped.

Akhilesh took another triangular vac-seal and squeezed a little more of the paralytic into her arm. Everything went numb again. Her system would have to start over.

But it might be too late. Akhilesh still had the lase-knife in his hand. He increased the blade size, to the width of her pinky. He studied her left arm, running a finger down its length as if considering where to begin.

"I need to open up this arm," Akhilesh said absently. "Discover whether the circuitry has been dissolved or simply broken."

He lowered the lase-knife. Kayla willed her healing system to work faster against the paralytic. She tried to move away, but her body lay inert and useless.

"It *will* hurt, I'm afraid."

She shrieked at the first touch of searing heat in her upper arm, unable to hold back the cry of pain. Akhilesh set aside the lase-knife and she could feel him parting the wound.

Kayla! What's happening?

"I'm seeing increased healing too," he marveled. "The wound is already closing itself. Something's been restructured here. I believe I'll have to take the whole arm."

Kayla let loose a formless sound of pain and terror. Inwardly, she screamed, *Help me! Help me, now!*

Akhilesh had turned to his float tray and fidgeted with the tools arrayed across it. He lifted the larger lase-cutter, and Kayla knew it would have the power to cut her arm clean off.

Akhilesh fussed with the adjustment, widening, then narrowing the beam. Kayla squeezed her eyes shut.

Which meant her body was fighting off the paralytic. But did she have enough time to restore her strength and break her bonds?

Sloshing started up in Raashida's gen-tank. She was awake, trying to get loose, struggling against the gen-fluid's embrace. Raashida had no chance, had had her very essence pulled from her by Akhilesh, but she was fighting. Kayla had to find a way to fight too.

Akhilesh set down the lase-cutter and walked over to Raashida's tank. It was almost as if the girl knew Kayla needed the distraction. Raashida's arm flailed out of the tank, reaching for Akhilesh. He barely jumped clear of the dangerous splash of fluid.

Kayla let rage build up inside her. Rage at Akhilesh's casual cruelty, at the hundreds of GENs he'd infected, had used for the benefit of trueborns.

Her anger seemed to burn along her circuitry. Electrical impulses stimulated her healing process, burned away the paralytic. At the same time, it fed the Scratch, and she knew using her improved healing would be a devil's bargain. She would fight off the paralytic, but super-charge the Scratch.

Feeling came back to her, toes and fingers first, feet and hands, ankles and wrists, sensation accelerating through her body. Along with sensation came the heat of fever, the pain of Scratch.

Her right hand was still free. She grabbed the throat band and let her rage fuel her, tearing the restraint away from the table. Going up on her left elbow, she used the strength of both hands together to rip her left hand free. Then she tore loose her feet from the table.

Akhilesh tried to get past her to the big lase-cutter. Her feet still bound together, she kicked out at him from the table, sending him stumbling back. He slammed against the empty gen-tank he'd been preparing for her. Gen-fluid splashed his hands and he cried out as the unprogrammed green muck randomly restructured the genetic material it had touched—his wrists and forearms.

Kayla slid from the table, swinging her joined hands at Akhilesh like a club. He tried to block her strikes, but she heard the crunch of bones. His right arm hung at an odd angle.

He staggered, tried to back away. He shouted into his wristlink, "Nafti! Salot!"

The two enforcers came running through the door, fumbling for their shockguns. Before they could get past the first row of gen-tanks, Kayla swept up the lase-cutter, slapped the control to its widest setting. She sent a blast at Salot, and the cannon-like beam punched Salot's chest, sending the enforcer flying. The peripheral hit smashed Nafti into the wall before he could even aim his shockgun. Both enforcers went down.

Akhilesh came for her. She swung the body of the lase-cutter at him, striking his head. He tried to break his fall and bounced against the unprogrammed gen-tank again.

She scuttled backward as the gen-fluid gushed out in a wave and soaked him from shoulder to waist. He screamed as the fluid reached his skin. As Kayla watched, his fingers shriveled, lumps popped on his forearm. He tried to scrape away the gen-fluid, but layers of skin went with it. He hit his knees, then fell face-first onto the floor.

With a twist of her hands, she broke apart the bonds on her feet. She would have to leave the shackles on her wrists and ankles.

She went to Raashida's gen-tank. How would she get Raashida safely out of the gen-fluid? If Kayla just pulled her out, she could do more harm than good to both of them. She'd have to come back for her. She stumbled away from the tank.

Nafti was moaning, but Salot was dead silent. Akhilesh had stopped screaming, but he made little animal sounds, his ruined body curled up on the floor.

With the immediate fight over, Kayla's fever pulsed over her in waves. Her joints ached, she felt light-headed. She feared she didn't have much time left.

Kayla crouched between the enforcers and took their shockguns. When she pushed to her feet, she swayed and had to put a hand on the wall to catch her balance. Then she saw the Scratch marks striping her skin, from wrist to elbow. The fever burned even hotter.

She gripped one shockgun in her trembling right hand, shoved the other into her waistband. She staggered toward the door, praying for enough strength to find Risa and Kiyomi before the Scratch overtook her.

As she stepped through the lab door into the hall, she heard the thunder of footsteps coming up the stairs. Her heart squeezed tight—her victory over Akhilesh had meant nothing. More enforcers were here to take her.

Setting the shockgun on its highest setting, she aimed it for the stairwell. Her arms shook. Her knees gave way and hit the floor. The Scratch seemed to roar through her body, its course increased ten-fold by her enhanced healing process.

Her vision blurred, strength seeped out of her. She couldn't make out the two figures who'd appeared at the end of the hall. Were those Brigade uniforms? She still had the shockgun, but couldn't hold it up as she sagged sideways to the floor.

One of the figures ran toward her. She blinked and struggled to bring her eyes back into focus.

Finally, she saw his face. It was Devak.

He lifted her in his arms, and her world spun. That had to explain what she thought she heard him whisper in her ear.

"I love you, Kayla."

The words melted away as relentless Scratch drove her into unconsciousness.

27

Kayla woke with a start from a long dreamless sleep. She lay in a soft bed in a plain, white room, wearing a long sleep shirt that tangled around her ankles. Daylight spilled through the window above her head and she could hear quiet conversation through the walls. Her internal clock told her nearly three days had passed. She had only the dimmest memory of floating in and out of consciousness since Devak found her at GAMA.

She sucked in a breath as those moments came back. Scratch roaring through her body. Devak rescuing her, whispering in her ear.

I love you.

Was that part even real? She freed her arms from the bedclothes. She could see faint marks where the Scratch welts had been, the only signs that she'd been infected.

The door opened a crack and to her delight, Mishalla poked her head in. Kayla held out her arms to her friend and Mishalla ran to embrace her. Kayla's lifelong friend sat beside her on the bed.

"Where are we?" Kayla asked.

"Zul's house. That's Devak's bed."

Kayla flushed at the thought, remembering those whispered words. Was it his sleep shirt she was wearing? "What about my Scratch? Is it healed? And Raashida—were they able to save her?"

"Yes, you're healing. Raashida and Gemma too, although it's taking them longer." Mishalla said. "After Junjie gave Jemali the formula for Guru Ling's Scratch treatment, Jemali has been working with some of the GAMA gene-splicers to create doses of the cure. You, Raashida, and Gemma got the first vac-seals."

"*GAMA* gene-splicers." Kayla rubbed at her arms, uneasy that her cure had been developed by GAMA.

"They had the facilities, the staff," Mishalla said. "The ones who helped didn't work directly with Akhilesh, and what they knew of the man they didn't like. Jemali has been supervising them. We know the cure is genuine. Your blood has been checked, along with all the other Scratch-infected who have been inoculated so far."

"Is Akhilesh . . . ?"

"Still alive." Mishalla's mouth twisted. "But he had to go in a gen-tank. It'll take a while to fix him. If they even can."

"Those two enforcers?" Kayla asked.

Mishalla squeezed her hand. "Nafti survived."

Then she'd killed Salot. All the times she'd been so angry at trueborns, enforcers especially, had thought about using her strength to end their lives. And now she'd done it.

She felt sick at the thought, not triumphant as she'd sometimes thought she would. Had her actions lost her a place in the Infinite's hands?

Mishalla stroked her arm. "So much of this is my fault. It was me telling Hala where Raashida was. He told Akhilesh and Akhilesh sent the Brigade."

"You shouldn't blame yourself," Kayla said. "Abran—the boy traveling with us—was working with Akhilesh. He could have reported where we were." Abran had said he hadn't but he'd told so many lies.

Kayla remembered the necklace with its tracking device, and how happy Akhilesh had been to get his hands on her. Akhilesh might have wanted Raashida back for the sake of his punarjanma yield, but he'd been keeping tabs on Kayla too.

"Was there any truth to what Hala told you?" Kayla asked. About fixing GENs so they could have children?"

"Akhilesh lied to Hala about that to get Raashida back. Hala felt like a stupid old fool for being taken in. His words." Mishalla gave her another quick hug. "Risa and Kiyomi are here too. I brought you in some clothes from the lorry. There are some sani-wipes on the dresser."

Mishalle left the room as Kayla tugged off the sleep shirt, resisting the urge to hold it to her face to see if it smelled like Devak. She used the sani-wipes to clean off three days of grime and dressed quickly, then went out to the living room.

Mishalla sat with Risa and Kiyomi on the sofa, and Junjie fidgeted on a float chair. Devak stood by the open front door, leaning against the jamb. He wore an embroidered copper-colored korta and chera pants, the pants a little short for him, the korta a little tight in the shoulders.

As she moved to sit on the sofa beside Kiyomi, Devak seemed to drink her in. She wasn't sure she was ready to face whatever might be in his heart. Not when she didn't know what was in hers.

"How do you feel?" he asked.

"Good. Thank you for coming for me." Her gratitude sounded stilted and formal to her ears.

"It was Junjie who knew where you were," Devak said.

Kayla's gaze shifted to Junjie. He tilted his head toward Devak and nodded. Kayla took that to mean that Devak knew about FHE. Knew that the desperate message she'd passed to her had reached Devak through Junjie.

Kayla took Risa's hand. "Are you okay? I heard the shockgun strike."

"Hardest punch I've ever taken." She lifted her shirt and peeled back the corner of the bandage on her midriff. Her blackened skin was edged with angry red. "Feel better with the lorry back. Kinship picked it up in Amik, brought it down to Plator. Yomi drove us here."

"The enforcers didn't take the lorry when they took you?" Kayla asked.

Risa snorted. "Not with it half sunk in Amik mud. Brigade Daggers and Jahajas blocked me, so I tried crossing that mess to the next alley over." She shook her head. "Stupid. Lost two lifters."

Kiyomi threaded her fingers in Risa's. "Then while the Brigade was pulling me and Risa from the cab, Nishi came thundering back. The poor seycat was chest deep in the mud, but she clawed to ribbons the enforcer who tried to get behind the wheel. Then she jumped on top of the lorry and kept moving so they couldn't get a fix on her with their shockguns. But if they tried to climb into the cab, she'd claw their heads to shreds."

"So she's okay?" Kayla asked.

"Singed tail," Risa said. "Yomi doctored it up. Seycat's out hunting by the Chadi."

Risa sighed and Kayla could see the exhaustion in the lowborn woman's face. Kiyomi clearly saw it too. "Let's go, old woman," Kiyomi said. "Leave the young ones to themselves."

Mishalla turned to Kiyomi. "Could you take me to Plator? I'd like to get back to Eoghan."

"We're headed up to Qaf anyway," Kiyomi said. "Plator's on the way."

Kayla got to her feet, but Risa put up a hand to stop her. "Not you, GEN girl. Not yet. Medic's got to clear you."

"I feel fine," Kayla said.

"Jemali's got to check your blood levels," Junjie said. "He'll be here later today."

She wanted to argue, but she wasn't as fine as she'd told them. She felt weaker than she was used to feeling, her head still muzzy from the long sleep.

"I'll help Risa out to the lorry then." Kayla took Risa's hand and pulled her to her feet, hooking the lowborn woman's arm around her shoulders.

As they stepped past Devak at the door, his wristlink beeped. He read the message. "Pitamah needs me to pick him up from Jemali's."

Kayla looked back at Devak. "Zul isn't taking the punarjanma anymore, is he?"

"Lord Creator, no." Devak seemed shocked that she'd even asked the question. "Pitamah had all of Akhilesh's stores of it destroyed. Now Kinship gene-splicers are trying to figure out if they can manufacture the punarjanma artificially. No one's going to use GENs for that anymore."

Devak seemed convinced, but Kayla wasn't so certain. How many clients had Akhilesh had besides Zul? She imagined they wouldn't be happy to know the rejuvenating fluid wouldn't be available anymore.

Despite the lowborn woman's objections, Risa leaned heavily on Kayla and tightly gripped Mishalla's hand as they crossed the street to where Kiyomi had docked the lorry. It seemed to take all of Risa's energy to walk the short distance and for Kayla and Mishalla to get her up into the sleeper.

Kiyomi whistled for Nishi. The seycat must have been nearby because she appeared in an instant. Nishi leapt into the cab, then into the sleeper with Risa.

Kayla took Kiyomi's arm as she was about to swing up into the cab. "Is Risa going to be okay?"

With a glance up at the sleeper, Kiyomi shut the lorry door. "Her heart stopped while Jemali was treating the shockgun strike. He got it going again quickly enough, but Jemali ordered me to make sure she takes it easy."

Kiyomi climbed up behind the wheel. Kayla went around to the passenger side to give Mishalla a last hug goodbye. As she watched Kiyomi drive away, she wondered when she'd see Mishalla again.

As she returned to the house, Devak drove away in Zul's AirCloud. Junjie was still sprawled in the float chair, the motion of his swinging leg rocking the chair.

Junjie's agitation told her he was holding something back. Kayla caught his leg on its forward arc. "What?"

He tugged his leg back and slumped forward. "I'm so sorry. For what the FHE put into your annexed brain. For the block they put on you. For me being involved with those sanaki people in the first place."

Kayla had to think through her response to evade the block. Although it seemed easier to talk to Junjie with no one else around, maybe because her subconscious understood he was safe.

"Not that I wanted any of it forced into me," she said, "but it turns out some of it is what saved me. Helped me fight off the paralytic, call her, whoever the denking hell she is, so she could call you."

He sighed heavily. "Still. I'm sorry. I told her I wasn't going to have anything else to do with them."

"Apology accepted." Kayla dropped to the sofa. "One thing I still haven't figured out—how was it Raashida and Gemma could heal people when the other infected GENs couldn't?"

Junjie relaxed finally in his float chair. "Their particular genetics. Their bodies created double or triple of the duwu—what Akhilesh called punarjanma. So much that they kind of sweated it out and that sweat penetrated the skin of anyone touching them."

Kayla rubbed the fading Scratch scar on her wrist. "So, was it a virus Akhilesh created?"

"It was a virus and uploaded programming both. Similar to the kind of reprogramming FHE did to you." He gave her another apologetic look. "But Akhilesh didn't inject it in just any GEN."

"When he gave it to me, he said my genetics weren't right."

"Only about ten percent of GENs fit the profile," Junjie said. "But as head of GAMA, Akhilesh had access to all the

GEN genetic databases. Once he identified a GEN he could use, he'd find them using the Grid. The enforcers would bring them in."

Kayla could put together the rest. "He'd infect them. But he'd have to let them return to their Assignments. Then at some point the enforcers would gather them up, and Akhilesh would harvest them." She shuddered, remembering Raashida and all those other GENs in Akhilesh's gen-tanks.

"Some of them actually survived harvesting," Junjie said, "once the punarjanma was out of their bodies. Akhilesh would let 'em go back to their Assignments to produce a whole new crop."

"He'd have to reset them, though, right?" Kayla asked. "So they wouldn't remember being harvested. But someone did a denking poor job with Gemma, leaving parts of her old personality intact."

"Yeah, sloppy realignment," Junjie agreed. "And the gen-fluid in her tank must have been contaminated, so Gemma ended up with double DNA."

"Is Gemma her real name?" Kayla asked. "Not Gabrielle?"

Junjie's head bobbed. "Looks that way."

"What about Raashida?" Kayla asked. "Was she someone else before?"

"Nah. She really *did* escape the lab, that much of Akhilesh's story was true. So they never got a chance to reset her. One piece of good news, though," Junjie said. "Akhilesh kept good records of who he infected, where they were Assigned. So if there are any other survivors, we can find them again."

Kayla heard the whine of a lev-car engine and looked out the window just as Zul's AirCloud passed by. Devak was back. Uneasy anticipation pushed her to her feet. Junjie rose too, opening the door that led from the house to the garage.

Devak helped his great-grandfather in. The old trueborn wore white and leaned heavily on Devak.

As he stepped into the living room, Zul saw Kayla. Remorse burned in his dark eyes. "I am so deeply sorry. I would never have let Akhilesh inject me with the punarjanma if I'd known its source."

Kayla tipped back her head, squarely meeting Zul's gaze. "Did you ask him?"

Zul shook his head, shoulders sagging. "I wanted it too much. To my great shame."

Devak nudged Junjie. "Would you help Pitamah to his room?"

Junjie took Devak's place at Zul's side. They headed down the hall.

Devak studied her face as if memorizing every curve and shadow of it. "Come outside with me."

Less than a demand, more than a plea. She nodded, then when he gestured, she preceded him out the door.

On the small front porch, a bench ran the length of the living room window. Devak waited for Kayla to sit before seating himself beside her. He left a half-meter of space between them, at once too close and too far.

Devak leaned forward, elbows on knees. "Councilor Mohapatra got Abran back." He glanced over at her. "I thought you'd want to know."

She shrugged. "I suppose the councilor still wants him to testify against Baadkar."

Devak stared down at his hands. "The Judicial Council

could ignore ill treatment of GENs. But they finally took notice when it was a trueborn."

"In other words, Abran's worth more to the councilor as a trueborn than as a GEN."

Devak grimaced, but he didn't deny it. "They were able to find Abran's sister too. A GEN in Baadkar's household knew where she'd been taken."

"And was his mother . . . ?"

"Dead."

Kayla felt a pang of sympathy for Abran. The murder of his mother had been a sad piece of truth in all his lies.

Devak looked over at her. "Were you and Abran . . . did you . . . ?"

"There was nothing between us." *Except that kiss.* "I never trusted him." *And he wasn't you.* "What happened with your father? Did it turn out he wasn't involved?"

"He had nothing to do with Akhilesh's scheme. Turns out the Brigade found him a few weeks ago. Living in a rundown drom shed in the Northwestern Territory adhikar. A lowborn herder found him and turned him in." His jaw flexed with tension. "They tell me he stank of drom."

Devak stared at the row of houses lining the other side of the street. They were small and modest like Zul's, no holographic projections concealing their plainness.

He gestured across the street. "Demi-status live in most of those. That would have mattered so much once. Now it doesn't mean anything to me." He glanced over at her again. "What does mean something, what is truly important, is what I said to you at GAMA. I love you, Kayla."

She couldn't deny the joy inside, but at the same time,

she realized she didn't know how to answer him. After what she'd been through, the realizations she came to, everything had changed.

The expectation and hope in Devak's eyes dimmed a little. "I spoke with Jemali when I picked up Pitamah. With the Scratch crisis nearly handled, Jemali can have a dose of the restoration treatment ready for you within a few weeks. You can get rid of the GEN circuitry and be a lowborn. And we can be together, no matter what anyone says."

Kayla slowly her head. This was one truth that was crystal clear. "I don't want to be restored, Devak. I want to keep my circuitry, stay a GEN."

He stared at her, stunned into silence. Pain flickered in his eyes, then she saw his struggle to put it aside.

"That doesn't matter," he said. "GEN, lowborn, trueborn, whatever you are, I feel the same about you."

How could she ask anything more of him? Yet she still couldn't give him the answer he wanted.

"But I'm not sure how I feel, Devak. I need time." She rubbed his arm, her touch tentative, although she ached to have him hold her. "You need time. You were right that night in Daki sector. You and me together, high-status trueborn and GEN, would be impossibly hard."

He took her hand. "Not impossible."

"Even so, no matter what I feel for you, I need time."

"Kayla . . ."

He tugged her closer and when she didn't resist, he embraced her. Of their own accord, her arms wrapped around him.

She could have this moment, couldn't she? Share his warmth, let his love inside?

Then he leaned back, his face so beautiful. He pressed his mouth against hers and the world dissolved around her.

For only an instant, then she let reality crash in again. She wrenched from his arms. Jumped to her feet.

"Someone could see us." All those windows across the street, so many trueborn eyes that could be staring out of them. "We can't."

He rose too, and took her hand again. "We can."

She pulled away. "Please. I have to go." She hurried down the stairs.

"Kayla!"

She kept moving down the walk to the street, then turned left toward the trueborn warehouse district. She glanced back once at Devak. He stood at the top of the stairs, watching her walk away.

Then she passed the holographic hedges that screened the warehouses from the residential area and left Devak behind, his kiss still burning her lips. She cut across the plasscrete aprons behind the warehouses, drawn by the sound of the Chadi River just beyond. Homesickness churned inside her, and she felt as unsettled as the familiar brown water of the Chadi.

Maybe she should go home again, to Tala's. Sleep in her nurture mother's flat and regain her strength there. Try to work out what to do about Devak.

But where would her life go after that? She couldn't just stay in Chadi without an Assignment. Could she continue on with Risa and the Kinship? Did she even want to be part of the Kinship? If not, she'd need another Assignment and a patron, someone who would treat her fairly. Would the councilor take her on if she no longer did Kinship work? Would she ever really find a way to be free and to be herself at the same time?

No matter what, she was certain of one thing. She would stay a GEN. And find a way to be as free as she could manage. Whether or not that life included Devak.

Could she bear it if she never saw him again? She touched her mouth, both wishing he'd never kissed her and that she could have let it go on forever.

Kayla.

The voice stopped her in her tracks. Angry at its intrusion, she shut her mind and refused to respond. Yes, the FHE had helped her escape Akhilesh's lab, but their invasion into her life, her self, had to stop.

"Kayla!"

She shook her head, confused. Then she realized it had been Devak's voice. Walking backward, she peered back the way she'd come. The brother suns had both risen, and their brilliance threw his figure into silhouette.

She'd asked for time, yet he'd followed her. Should she let him catch up? Yes! her heart said, but uncertainty still twisted inside her.

As she hesitated, she heard a lev-car engine from the other direction. She turned toward the noise just as a WindSpear pulled up at the far end of the row of warehouses. Not a Brigade vehicle, thank the Infinite.

Still, odd to see a lev-car where ordinarily only lorries traveled. The glare of the brother suns reflecting off the windshield made it hard to see who was inside. Maybe two people.

She was crafting an excuse for her presence there in case the WindSpear's occupants asked, when a new message jolted her.

Kayla, come to me!

The urgency of the summons sent a chill through her. The voice seemed to echo in her inner ear.

And to her utter shock, she realized she *knew* the voice. Recognized it, the same way she'd recognized Akhilesh. And as the familiarity struck her, she felt herself filled with that same unwanted warmth and comfort.

Kayla stood frozen by her discovery, as the driver and passenger climbed out of the WindSpear. A man and woman.

Even from the hundred or so meters separating them, there was something naggingly familiar about the woman. She was small in stature like Kayla, her long hair just as wild around her shoulders.

"Kayla!" the woman shouted.

She wasn't the least surprised that the voice was the same as the one she'd heard inside. Hearing its physical timbre, the sense of familiarity grew stronger.

Behind her, Devak called to her again. Confusion and longing, both toward Devak and the woman, kept her rooted. Kayla turned toward Devak, feeling torn in two.

"Kayla!" The woman screamed her name now, tugging Kayla back around toward her. The woman had come close enough for Kayla to see the fear and alarm in her face. *"Elana! Come to me!"*

Elana. How could this woman know Kayla's trueborn name? Kayla realized there was one way she could, a way that explained the woman's strange familiarity.

"Kayla!" Devak called as he ran toward her.

She needed space. From both of them. Kayla spotted a narrow alley between two warehouses and cut toward it. She heard the woman scream her name again, calling out Kayla and then Elana, her panic clear. But Kayla kept moving toward the relative safety of the alley. She would cut back to Zul's house from the other end. Hopefully, Devak would figure that out and follow her.

In the dimness of the alley, she could barely see the graffiti scribbled just above her head. By the time it registered, she was halfway along the alley and it took vital seconds for her frantic brain to decide whether to run forward or back.

Her gaze fixed on those three scrawled letters, *FHE*, as she started to run. Then the world exploded, flinging her high in the air.

In the next moment, everything turned to black.

adhikar: Tracts of land that only trueborns possess. The more adhikar a trueborn owns, the higher their status. Only trueborns are allowed to own adhikar.

allabain: A nomadic subset of lowborns. They use temporary tent-like homes called bhaile that they carry from place to place.

annexed: A partitioned section of a GEN's brain that the GEN brain circuitry accesses and utilizes as storage and computational space using datapod uploads. When GENs are created in the tank, their brains are partitioned to create the annexed brain and bare brain sections.

Assignment: The "job" to which a GEN is Assigned. According to the Humane Edicts, GENs are to be Assigned to a job to which they are suited, i.e., one that utilizes their genetically designed skill set.

Assignment specialist: A trueborn responsible for uploading the appropriate information for GENs, both for their first Assignment and for subsequent Assignments if their situation changes.

bali: The earring worn by trueborns in their right earlobe that identifies their status. High-status wear diamonds, demi-status wear emeralds, and minor-status wear sapphires. A genuine bali can detect the DNA of the wearer and will be rejected by the body of someone who is wearing it illegally.

bare brain: The section of a GEN's brain where ordinary memories of experiences and study are stored. It's effortless for a GEN to retrieve memories from this section. They must learn to access their annexed brain to retrieve data and programming from it.

bhaile: A tent-home used by the nomadic allabain lowborns. The supports are made of shaped sticker bush branches. Historically, the sides were made of pounded, felted sticker bush root, but with the advent of GEN labor and cheaper production costs, allabain now use plas scine sheets for their tents.

bhimkay: The meter-high spider that is at the top of the arachnid food chain on Loka. A bhimkay can easily bring down even an adult-sized drom. Trueborns use electrified fencing to protect their drom herds from the bhimkay.

Brigade: Loka's police force. At least one Brigade is assigned to each sector within Svarga.

chera pants: Derived from churidar pants, tightly fitting pants worn by men and women in South & Central Asia.

crèche: A daycare center for lowborn children. The cost of the care in the crèche would be deducted from the pay of the lowborns.

datapod: A thumb-sized device used to upload and download information into GENs. It is also used to interface with hard-ware such as computers.

demi-status: A class of trueborn lower than high-status and higher than minor-status. They're affluent, but not as wealthy as a high-status. Demi-status trueborns hold 32 of the 160 seats of the Lokan parliament.

dhan: The currency on Loka.

DNA Mark: The official name for the GEN tattoo. Each tattoo is unique for a given GEN.

drom: A shaggy camel-like six-legged mammal that roams the open scrap grass plains. The native droms are about the size of a pony, and therefore more vulnerable to the bhimkay. The genetically engineered version of the droms are the size of a dromedary camel.

enforcer: A member of the Brigade. Largely comprised of minor-status trueborns who have lost their adhikar and would be demoted from trueborn status to lowborn if not for their service as a Brigade enforcer. Each Brigade includes one or two GEN enforcers for duties such as physically handling GENs and delivery of GEN tack (clothes and equipment) for GEN Assignments.

extendibles: Metal pins that extend from a datapod when it is activated. When the datapod is applied to a GEN's facial tattoo, the extendibles pierce the skin and link with the GEN's internal circuitry.

GAMA: The Genetic Augmentation and Manipulation Agency. GAMA is responsible for creating GENs and all other genetic alterations that take place in gen-tanks.

GEN: A Genetically Engineered Non-human. Using mostly human DNA and some animal DNA, each GEN is created with a specific physical or mental ability. They are gestated in a tank.

gen-tank: A large fish tank-like vessel filled with gen-fluid that's used for both the gestation/alteration of GENs and for healing certain trueborn injuries and diseases.

gen-fluid: A thick green fluid that's used in a gen-tank. Gen-fluid must be programmed for the specific genetic makeup of the occupant of the tank.

gene-splicer: A trueborn genetic engineer (likely minor-status) who designs and creates GENs. Gene-splicers also use the tank to correct trueborn abnormalities, but a gene-splicer with that position would likely be a demi-status trueborn.

Grid: The Monitoring Grid that tracks every GEN on Svarga. It has two modes—active tracking, where the software searches for particular GENs to check that they are where they belong, and passive mode, where the GENs' locations are read and stored in a database for possible later use.

healer: An uneducated GEN medic of sorts. They use mostly folklore and dubious, untested methods to treat their GEN patients.

high-status: The highest level of trueborn. They are lavishly wealthy and hold 120 of the 160 seats of the Lokan parliament.

Humane Treatment Edicts: An agreement reached two decades before the start of Tankborn. The Edicts specify how many hours GENs are to work in a day, give them one rest day a week off, forbid physical abuse, and require a safe and sanitary living space. Trueborns tend to follow the Edicts as it suits them, many ignoring them entirely.

jik: An extremely derogatory term for a GEN. Used largely by trueborns.

Judicial Council: The judiciary on Loka. The JC adjudicates laws passed by the parliament. This includes passing judgment on GENs who break trueborn laws (such as straying outside their radius or disrespecting trueborns). In these cases, they decide if a GEN should be realigned and reset as punishment (if a Brigade enforcer hasn't already done so). Trueborns have many ways to both avoid judgment by the JC and avoid any punishment if they're found guilty.

kelfa: A hot GEN drink made from roasted kel-grain. GENs often compare the skin color of high-status trueborns to the color of kelfa.

Kinship: A secret group of trueborns, lowborns and GENs whose goal is to secure fair treatment for lowborns and equal rights for GENs.

kit: Derogatory term for a young GEN.

korta: Derived from kurta, a tunic-style Indian shirt.

lev-car: A form of transportation that uses a suspension engine. Like a sedan. They are electrically charged. There are also micro-levs (like a sports car) multi-levs (like a small bus) and pub-trans (like a large bus).

Loka: The barely habitable planet where the refugees from earth settled. Loka has four continents, but only Svarga is suitable for humans. The others are polar Virynand, earthquake-ridden Utul, and volcanic Peralor.

lowborn: A class of humans who are born of a mother but do not own adhikar. The poorest among them are somewhat nomadic and live on the outskirts of trueborn-only sectors, often where the sector borders GEN-only sectors. The more prosperous lowborns are merchants or factory supervisors who live in mixed sectors with minor-status trueborns.

medic: A trueborn physician. A high-status medic would treat high or demi-status trueborns. Lower status medics would treat minor-status trueborns or possibly lowborns if they had the funds to pay. A demi-status medic might also be required to work in a GEN sector, but that would be a short-term assignment.

mini-cin: A small, indoor incinerator for burning trash.

minor-status: The lowest class of trueborns. If they're smart, they become technology specialists in some computerized area (such as the Grid) or teachers. If they're not deep thinkers, they work in bureaucratic jobs or serve in the Brigade. Minor-status trueborns hold 8 of the 160 seats of the Lokan parliament.

nurture mother: A nurture mother is a GEN female who has been genetically engineered to nurture young. They might be assigned to nurture GENs in their home sector or another, or possibly nurture lowborns. Trueborns would be cared for by lowborns. A nurturer could be male (nurture-father). GEN siblings within the same home are nurture-brothers or nurture-sisters.

plasscine: A processed form of plassfiber that is used to make cheap furniture and other home items, clothing, jewelry, etc.

plasscrete: A processed form of plassfiber that is mixed with a cement-like mineral native to Loka to create a very strong material used for construction.

plassfiber: A naturally occurring mineral on Loka that is mined from the western side of a mountain range called The Wall. Plass is analogous to a solid form of petroleum and can be processed similarly provide an energy source (it fuels the electrical grid on Svarga). As plasscine, it can be molded into furniture and even fabric for clothing. Plasscrete and steelcrete are used in construction.

rat-snake: A spider creature with a rat-like head and a thorax that is long and flexible like a snake's.

realignment: The first step before resetting a GEN. Realignment erases the GEN's current identity by both wiping the annexed brain and disrupting neural pathways in the bare brain. The bare brain isn't physically damaged by realignment, but all memories are essentially destroyed.

reset: The process of creating a new identity in a GEN after their previous identity has been wiped away with a realignment.

scrap grass: A grass native to Loka that is fodder for both the native droms and the genetically engineered variety.

sector: A portion of a territory. Of the 106 sectors in Svarga, 63 sectors are defined as trueborn only (restricted to high-status and demi-status trueborns), 28 are mixed (minor-status trueborns and lowborns allowed) and 15 are GEN (GENs only).

sekai: A hand-held reader and networking device.

sewer toad: A small toad-like arachnid (it's about the size of a large grapefruit) that prefers wet, dank places. It loves polluted rivers.

seycat: A six-legged feline, about twelve inches at the shoulder, with a striped pelt and large tufted ears. Ratsnakes and sewer toads are seycats' favorite prey. They're very fierce and although they are sometimes kept as pets, they can never truly be domesticated.

shockgun: A weapon carried by non-GEN Brigade members. It disrupts the central nervous system. Depending on the setting, it can simply incapacitate an individual or kill them.

sket: Slang for skill set.

skill set: A GEN's special skill or ability. Using human and animal DNA, the skill set is genetically programmed into a GEN in the tank early in the gestation process.

Social Benevolence: Social Benevolence, or SB, is responsible mainly for lowborn welfare. As a consequence of the lowborn insurrection in 359 (thirteen years prior to the start of Tankborn) the parliament passed laws creating Social Benevolence to placate lowborns.

steelcrete: A processed form of plassfiber that is mixed with iron and other minerals to create an extra-sturdy material used in larger, taller structures and for especially secure places (e.g., prisons).

Svarga: The single habitable continent on the planet Loka. Svarga is divided into five territories and each territory into sectors.

synth-protein: Vegetable-based protein made from a soy-like legume.

tank: The gestation tank that is used to gestate GENs in lieu of a woman's womb. The tank is also sometimes used to correct trueborn abnormalities or injuries.

tankborn: A derogatory term used for GENs. GENs do use this term amongst themselves.

thinsteel: A steel-plass amalgam that can be extruded as thinly as paper yet is as strong as centimeter-thick steel.

trueborn: The ruling class on Loka. They are born of a mother and posses varying amounts of adhikar to establish their status. The three status levels are high, demi, and minor.

warren: The large apartment complexes in which GENs are housed.

ACKNOWLEDGMENTS

Writing is a solitary profession, publishing is not. I'd like to acknowledge the usual suspects, those who have helped me take *Awakening* from an idea to published book.

First, my agents, Matt Bialer and Lindsay Ribar of Sanford J. Greenburger Associates. I appreciate your behind the scenes work on seeing this latest *Tankborn* installment come to fruition.

Many thanks to my editor extraordinaire, Stacy Whitman. With Stacy's help, I transformed my characters from wimpy and confused to strong and determined. She assisted in unraveling knotty story problems and pointed out the Mack truck-sized plot holes I needed to close. I would be lost without a great editor like Stacy.

A big thank you too to Lee and Low's marketing and publicity manager, Hannah Ehrlich. Her support in promoting *Tankborn* has been fantastic.

And much gratitude to Uma Krishnaswami for her generosity in answering my Sanskrit and Hindi language questions as I wrote *Awakening*. You're a gem, Uma.